BRIGHT LINES

TANWI NANDINI ISLAM

PENGUIN BOOKS

PENGUIN BOOKS

An imprint of Penguin Random House LLC
375 Hudson Street
New York, New York 10014
penguin.com

Grateful acknowledgment is made for permission to reprint an excerpt from "Dhaka Nocturne" from *Seam* by Tarfia Faizullah. Copyright © 2014 by Tarfia Faizullah. Reprinted with permission of Southern Illinois University Press.

LIBRARY OF CONGRESS CATALOGING-IN-PUBLICATION DATA
Islam, Tanwi Nandini.
Bright lines : a novel / Tanwi Nandini Islam.
pages cm
ISBN 978-0-14-312313-2
1. Young women—Fiction. 2. Family life—Fiction. 3. Domestic fiction. I. Title.
PS3609.S55B85 2015
813'.6—dc23
2015011851

Printed in the United States of America
1 3 5 7 9 10 8 6 4 2

Set in Guardi with Futura and Hoefler Text
Designed by Sabrina Bowers

BRIGHT LINES

TANWI NANDINI ISLAM is a writer, multimedia artist, and founder of Hi Wildflower Botanica, a handcrafted natural perfume and skincare line. A graduate of Vassar College and Brooklyn College's MFA program, she lives in Brooklyn.

Praise for Tanwi Nandini Islam's

BRIGHT LINES

"*Bright Lines* is the most daring, emotionally dense work I've ever read by a debut novelist. I can't remember the last time a novel kept me breathless, wandering and reconsidering the decisions of my own life. Tanwi Nandini Islam has created a fictive world where race, place, desire, violence, and deception beautifully cling to nearly every page, and really every part of her Brooklyn and Bangladesh. She is completely unafraid of insides and outsides of the characters she's created. I dreamt about Ella and Anwar for weeks long after I finished the book. I'm sure the characters here, and the actual range of Islam's talent, will wonderfully haunt readers for a lifetime. *Bright Lines* is brilliant and absolutely soulful."
—Kiese Laymon, author of *Long Division*

"Whether it's entirely fictional or not (and I really don't care) the New York City of Tanwi Nandini Islam's novel is the one I want to live in! What a radiant, abundant, worldly, sharp, and spirited novel! And what a good and powerful imagination, heart, and soul seems to have produced it. *Bright Lines* is very special."
—Francisco Goldman, author of *Say Her Name*

"Tanwi Nandini Islam is among an emerging generation of American writers giving voice to people, places, and concerns that have escaped the notice of the mainstream. Such is the range of her talent that in her first novel, *Bright Lines*, Islam shows us two locales, Brooklyn and Bangladesh, that are as varied and vibrant as they are restrictive and horrible, no small achievement. Hats off!"
—Jeffery Renard Allen, author of *Song of the Shank*

"Every detail in this rich novel is evocative of transformation. . . . A sensitive and subtle exploration of the experience of gender nonconformity across cultures . . . A transcontinental, transgenerational tale of a family and its secrets."
—*Kirkus Reviews*

For my water, fire, and earth
Ma, Bajan, and Prom

BRIGHT LINES

PART I

GIRLS ON THE MOVE

Brooklyn

Your house shall not hold your secret nor shelter your longing.

—Kahlil Gibran, *The Prophet*

1

Girls, everywhere. Anwar Saleem stared brazenly at the flock that strode down Atlantic Avenue. He wondered if they noticed him sucking in his paunch, as he stroked the last ribbon of lavender paint across the awning of his apothecary. LOTERÍA Y CIGARILLOS Y SE HABLA ESPAÑOL disappeared into the settling twilight, erasing the last traces of the previous owner's bodega. Anwar wiped his brow. A band of paint stiffened on his forehead. He climbed down, light-headed from the fumes.

On that first Saturday of June, everything in Brooklyn, everything except the sun, seemed to rise. Around the corner, on Third Avenue, petrol vapors blazed from cars in standstill, and traffic shimmered as if recalled in a dream. Trails of a street hawker's incense disappeared into the scaffolding of an art deco phallus, where pigeons clamored in its eaves. Anwar's Apothecary, sober and secular, nestled between Ye Olde Liquor Shoppe and A Holy Bookstore. A shout from the apartment upstairs startled Anwar enough that he nearly lost his balance.

"Thas not bad for business, now is it, Anwah?" called out the Guyanese street hawker, Rashaud Persaud, from his table down the block.

"Got a very good feeling about this color, my friend!"

"Naw, man, the fire escape! A girl on da move!" Rashaud laughed and pointed to a young girl climbing out of the window above the apothecary.

The girl hopped down the fire escape, her rump facing the street. Anwar craned his neck to see. She peeled off her hijab, revealing hair cropped as short as Audrey Hepburn's. Mad dash toward the train; the girl did not look back. A fantasy sobered him: Charu the Runaway—slinking outside with her singing hips, those taunting kohl-painted eyes—ready to meet Internet confidants.

He shook this image of his younger daughter from his mind. They'd been having some trouble lately; she was moody, but she was going to NYU—that counted for something, right? Anwar looked once more to admire his brand-new storefront. The color was—*feminine*—but this last bit of paint could liven up their bathroom walls, which had become tinged gray with neglect. His wife, Hashi, would disapprove. She hated *pink-tink,* as she told him every time he wore his beloved polo shirt. She rhymed her displeasure: *skinny-tinny, Spanish-Tanish, sex-tex*. And they always began with the letter *T.*

Rashaud helped Anwar pull down the heavy, screeching gate.

"Needs some grease," said Anwar.

"Try this." Rashaud smacked him a high-five, pressing a Ziploc bag into his palm.

"Trail mix?"

"Majoun. Dates, raisins, walnuts, hash, and honey."

"Thank you," said Anwar, shaking Rashaud's hand good-bye. It was curious how they'd known each other for almost ten years, but how little he knew about his friend. Rashaud had been hawking since he was eighteen, after some problems at home with his mother. But that was as much as he knew. Anwar handed him a *New York Post* from his back pocket. "And you take this. I've gotta quit reading this shit. Gives me nightmares about freak accidents and Mets games."

As Anwar made his way home, he nibbled on the majoun. Sweetness coated his tongue. He unbuttoned one more button of his cotton plaid shirt, to let the evening breeze in. He surrendered to the humdrum of dusk, and listened as the voices, wares, wisdoms, and gods changed.

Coralline tendrils of cloud revealed a gaping hole where the sun had been. As he walked down Hanson Place and crossed onto Fulton Street, eateries changed names as frequently as bandits. Farther down on Fulton, he passed a mosque with all the exterior charm of its neighbors, a 99-cent store and a bodega. Anwar never ventured there, and strode past the hennaed beards.

He did not believe in the god of these men.

Years past mingled with the unknowns of tomorrow on these evening walks home. He had lived atrocity during the 1971 war in Bangladesh, questioned the Supreme for allowing it. Thirty-two years later and still the ugliness of the war stayed with him, a dull ache, for the most part. The life he managed to have unnerved him: Hashi, Charu, his home; and of course, his elder daughter, Ella, who could not be called beautiful, but was on the *inside*. He pictured the perfect end to his day: a cold shower, then sitting in his studio, penning the memoir he never could start, about a pair of vagabonds during the war.

As he left-turned onto Cambridge Place, a maze of dominoes collapsed, each tick synchronized with the blinking eyes of the hustlers who ruled this corner. They nodded at him and he nodded back. There was nothing like this, the brownstone streets of his neighborhood. Children ran through an unleashed fire hydrant, hopscotch chalk erased in the wasteful gush of water. The aroma of grilled burgers brought tears to his eyes; he missed red meat.

As Anwar walked up to his brownstone on the corner of Cambridge Place and Gates Avenue, a hibiscus blossom landed by his feet. He had believed the tree would induce restful sleep in Ella, who struggled with insomnia. Within a year, it was already five feet tall; now, after ten years, it was taller than the house. Ella had slept peacefully, he believed, ever since. *It's good to be high,* he thought, running his tongue on his teeth for remnants of the majoun.

He saw a solitary light in the kitchen. His wife's beauty salon, the eponymous Hashi's, was closed for the day. His third-floor tenant's apartment: lights off. He mouthed her name, *Ra-mo-na Es-pin-al.* She worked the night shift today. No glimpses until morning.

Anwar cleared his throat as if to give a speech, but decided to watch the scene in the kitchen window.

His wife, Hashi, cast a fistful of onions into a pot, then several pinches of spice. She dipped a spoon into another pot and had a taste.

She closed her eyes and took a deep breath, then yelled, "Charu! Charu!" A minute later, their daughter Charu entered, giving Hashi a light hug from behind. Hashi turned to look at her.

Anwar tiptoed into the house, hoping to surprise them. He paused for a moment, in the darkness. *Do not enter,* he thought, suppressing the urge to giggle.

From this angle, Hashi's back was turned. Staccato chopping of carrots filled the room, breaking his reverie. The pot of onions and turmeric hissed in canola oil, splattering grease onto the wall. Charu sat at the table, staring at an array of objects arranged like a daisy on the plaid tablecloth: a pile of empty cigarette packets, some rather compromising photos of Charu at the beach, and the prize, in the center: a condom wrapper, empty of its goods.

"Do—you—want—to—*die*?" he heard Hashi say.

Charu protested, "Ma, I told you! I was at the beach—that's what people wear to the beach! Those are my cigarettes from a long time ago—I quit! The condom was from sex ed—I just wanted to see what it looked like!"

"You—are—*not*—my—daughter—You—are—*nothing*—like—me," Hashi said, her back pumping up and down as she chopped.

"Ma," Charu implored.

"Nothing!"

Anwar decided this was the moment to walk in.

"Er, what is happening, ladies?" he asked. He swiped a carrot from the cutting board. A second later and Hashi would've severed a fingertip.

"Your daughter tells lies and your daughter is doing sex and your daughter is doing smoking and your daughter is not mine," Hashi said. She turned to look at Anwar. She set down the knife and crossed her arms, as if waiting for his response.

Anwar stared at Hashi, and then at their child, back and forth. Hashi's hair was pulled back in a severe bun, her cheeks flushed with anger. She was yellow-skinned, slender, eyes sharp as a hawk's; he still glimpsed traces of that haughty girl he'd been incensed with back when he knew her as his comrade Rezwan's little sister. And Charu, skin tanned by these secret beach excursions, womanish curves she'd inherited from neither him nor Hashi. He imagined Charu's visage as his own mother's. He couldn't remember; she'd died before he'd known her breast. The sole photograph of his mother had been eaten by the elements, marring her face.

Charu's enormous eyes were dead cold. It was a look that often corrupted his daughter's sweet face. Long gone were the days when they rode the subway all the way to Queens for singing lessons.

"Hashi, I am sure Charu's explanation is sufficient," he said.

"No!" Hashi spat.

Guess that's the wrong answer.

"No dinner. Charu will be alone tonight, and I won't hear another word."

"*Arré*, Hashi, it's not fair—she is a growing girl. She must eat."

"Fine by me!" yelled Charu. "I'm going out, anyway."

"It's almost nine at night. You aren't going anywhere," said Hashi.

"I'm eighteen. It's Saturday night and I can do—"

"Shut. Your. Mouth. You're not eighteen yet. You don't even have a summer job. That would keep you in line." A fleck of spit from Hashi's mouth landed on her chin. Anwar thought better than to dab it away.

"I *told* you, I'm working. On my clothing line."

"With what money? What fabric?"

Charu inhaled—Anwar knew this was the momentary calm before the storm. If he remembered correctly, Hashi had promised her leftover dresses and textiles from wedding parties.

"I'll be gone soon enough. And I'm *never* eating this shit again!"

Charu shoved the dining table. Photos flew through the air like a dandelion clock. She ran into her father, and let go a wretched banshee shrill when he didn't move out of her way. She forced her way past, stomped to her bedroom, and slammed the door. A minute later, the sound of objects being thrown against a wall—a stiletto, a dumbbell, anything within her reach. Then, a furious clanging of a Tibetan meditation bell, found at a German exchange student's *schnickschnacks* sale.

Fathering a teenage girl, rough stuff, thought Anwar, as he picked up a photo that had landed by his foot. In the photo, Charu's lips kissed a dreadlocked boy's ear: Malik. He felt a strange pang seeing the picture, jealousy tinged with admiration. He had suspected his younger daughter was dating Malik. The boy was his intern at the apothecary, and *did* seem to be around the house often these past few months. The kids had grown up together in the neighborhood. Both were seniors at Brooklyn Tech; graduation was in two weeks. Charu would be headed to NYU, while Malik would be going to the New School. Anwar wondered if this meant they would continue their relations; it *was* pretty convenient. Malik was a soft-spoken, handsome Black boy. A solid, sensitive young man, better than what any stern, absentminded father could ask for. Anwar could stand him and that meant a lot.

Anwar wondered how Charu knew this feeling of love. It was further proof of their distance. Had the movies taught her?

Hashi bent over and picked up the photographs.

"I cleaned her room today and came upon this," said Hashi. "She's not growing up a good person. Look at this." She pointed to another photo: bikini-clad Charu, eating a corn dog at Coney Island, pursing her lips around the thing rather—suggestively.

He missed Ella. She was a sophomore at Cornell's agricultural school—a choice she'd made given her knack for tending their gardens. Ella remained remote, but within his grasp. She never intruded upon Anwar's sensibility and listened to him about most matters. Her left eye had a tendency to turn this way and that behind her spectacles, and he wondered what she was looking at. If she were here, thought Anwar, her calm would keep Hashi's nerves intact; she would find some way to make Charu laugh.

His two children were as different as their fathers had been.

"What on *earth* is on your face?" Hashi scratched his forehead with her thumbnail. Paint shavings tickled his nose. He'd forgotten about it.

"What is this? Paint? You walked home looking like some madman?"

"I decided to paint the shop today. Such a beautiful day outside—"

"So you decide on this color?" Hashi shook her head. With a damp corner of her apron she tried to wipe the stuff off, but it had crusted over. "Take a seat." She clumped mashed scoops of rice, lentils, potatoes, and broccoli onto his plate, and sat across from him. "It's summer. Three months of this and I'll be an old woman." She chewed on an unripe tomato as if it were an apple.

"Dinner is very good," said Anwar, licking the smorgasbord from his fingers. He remembered the enticing smell of grilled burgers on his walk home. "Let's have some beef next time?"

"It's a miracle I have energy to cook at all. I'm on my feet all day at the salon," she snapped, slumping back in her chair. "It is summertime, which means weddings until death does me part."

"Just suggesting a bit of protein," said Anwar.

"If you want steak, you cook it." Hashi took another hard bite of tomato, squirting the table with juice.

Anwar wiped the slimy seeds with his finger and licked them off.

"Disgusting, Anwar," said Hashi, grimacing. "Aman Bhai called earlier. He asked if he could stay with us for a week or so. I guess the divorce is final?"

"I can't understand why he doesn't stay at a hotel or something, not like he doesn't have the money."

"Or he should try to work things out with Nidi." Hashi started clearing the table. It took Anwar a minute to realize she was fixing a plate for Charu.

"Point is, he should find another place to stay," said Anwar.

"He's your brother. He let us stay with him for all those years—"

"We lived in his *basement*, and I paid him rent, yet never had heat."

"Well, he may have money but you have me, Charu, Ella. He needs your support. Your love."

"My love," repeated Anwar. Bah! His brother did not need his *love*. Aman owned a triad of pharmacies around Brooklyn, and was indecently self-sufficient for a family member. His wife, Nidi, had fled after years of neglect. And as much as Anwar believed in support and love and other filial bonds, he and his brother did not share them.

"We don't need another lunatic in this house."

"Are you calling me a lunatic?" asked Hashi.

Anwar put his hand up to end the conversation before it started. "I need to do some work in my studio."

"It's always you in the studio-tudio," said Hashi.

"Yes, dear."

"She gets her wild ideas from you, you know."

"We all flounder before we flourish."

"You enable the worst in people."

"I still live with you, don't I?"

Anwar left Hashi in the kitchen. Above him the patterns of flowers and vines cast in the white molding calmed him, and he felt the evening's argument subside. He recalled the days before Charu and Ella became women—their first bleeding had changed everything—on walks to P.S. 20; they were tiny girls trundling the street in their snowsuits, looking like miniature cosmonauts. Anwar was the wittiest character they knew, and he captivated them with obscurities: The seeds in one apple produced eight different trees; potato fruit was poisonous; New Delhi had the oldest alluvial soils in the world; cicada larvae took seventeen years to mature. He was their magician, their scientist, their Baba, and they adored him without much effort on his part. Nowadays, it was ever more evident that his girls had grown into adults. He grew flustered by everyday accidentals: Charu walking naked from the bathroom to her bedroom, or Ella sobbing while planting rosemary in the herb garden.

He touched his painted forehead. A raw scrubbing and hot water would get it off. He worried for a second—maybe the stuff was so impenetrable he'd need a toxic paint thinner to remove it.

No, I will leave it be, he thought, smiling sleepily.

Anwar made his way upstairs to their bedroom, climbing with heavy feet. The floorboards creaked, harmonizing with his knees. He had built his home in the spring of 1988, along with a band of men now known as the legendary construction company Brownstoner Brothers. They were the first renovators in Bedford-Stuyvesant, years before it was sliced into neighborhoods with fancy names ending in Hills or Heights. He'd met the head contractor, a bespectacled Saudi named Omar, his first weeks in the city. Anwar had grown tired of suburban somnolence on Long Island, where he worked in a pharmacy and lived with Hashi and the girls in Aman and Nidi's basement. Each day assaulted his pride, and when he'd saved enough money, he left at once for Brooklyn and drove a black gypsy taxi, vowing never again to shell pills in a pharmacy. Omar was one of his first passengers. He asked Anwar to drop him off at an abandoned property on a tree-lined block. The brownstone stood empty and gutted, windows boarded up with rotting planks of wood, the unforgettable phrase CALL ME DIG BADDY spray-painted over the rusty wrought iron door. Sneakers dangled off the phone lines in front of the house, commemorating the dead. *City'll give ya this crack house for a dollah*, Omar told him. There'd been a DEA raid on the brownstone, making it available in one of the first housing sweepstakes in the city. It was the first time he'd signed up for anything since the war, besides those Publishers Clearing House sweepstakes.

Anwar won the decrepit 111 Cambridge Place for one dollar, as there were no other bidders interested in such arduous renovations in a notorious neighborhood. The inside of the home lay rotten with water damage, broken stairs, vermin droppings, and a general ill aura. As beautiful and settled as the houses and generations of families surrounding them appeared, their new neighborhood was renowned as a war zone, impoverished and violent and isolated, something Anwar had never imagined existing in America.

It suited him perfectly.

He orchestrated the renovation of the squatter house using his inheritance of his father's lithic Buddhist statues and gold coins from Bangladesh's Pala period. Seeing no use for his father's artifacts, Anwar sold them to Sotheby's for a tidy sum. (His father, an archaeologist trained in the UK, died a second time around for his son's insolence.) He hired Omar and his men at Brownstoner Brothers. Many of them were undocumented young men living underground, surviving on part-time construction and painting work. Hashi begrudgingly cooked the rice, lentils, meat, and vegetables for the workers. Years later, her succulent meals were lauded by the men who had transformed the drug den into a sunlit warren.

They started with a shared staircase between all of the floors in the house. Anwar's chronic indecision between modernity and tradition led him to build two of everything. Two master bedrooms: one for lovemaking, which he and Hashi shared, and one for solitude, which was now his studio. He built two smaller bedrooms for his daughters, with Ella on the first floor, looking outward onto the gardens she so loved, and Charu's room on the second floor, directly above Ella's. As a child, Charu was prone to illness and Hashi wanted her close. Two kitchens: one with a tandoori oven and copperware, the other composed of state-of-the-art appliances. (When they built out the third-floor apartment for a tenant, he relented and permitted the installation of modern appliances; the tandoori sat unused in his studio.) He built two expansive bathrooms. The one in their master bathroom had a slate-tiled archaic stone bath with crevices in the walls for candles.

Anwar debated whether or not to have a Turkish toilet, but Hashi put her foot down, saying, *What is the point of America if you still squat like a dog?* He built a veranda just outside their master bedroom, which overlooked the backyard. The veranda was a quintessential feature of any respectable flat, a place to smoke and think. Sure, this wasn't a flat. But having lived in Aman's basement for so many years meant Anwar would not live in a house without immediate access to escape.

Hashi had two requests. One, he would pay for her to get a BA in psychology at Brooklyn College, because she'd cut off her studies to marry him and had never gotten over the embarrassment of not finishing school. Two, as a way to even the score of having to cook for the horde of builders, she wanted Anwar to build her a beauty parlor in the garden apartment, the most dilapidated part of the house. He praised her independence, and was happy that it absolved him of the responsibility of adjusting her to city life. She was lonely in the neighborhood and wanted the company of other women. At first, few neighbors would venture into their half-built home, once notorious for its illegal transactions.

When the final touches were complete and Omar's crew had departed, Anwar planted three hibiscus trees. The scent and beauty of his garden spread an air of nostalgia and clarity on Cambridge Place, and the neighbors praised Anwar for his contribution. Last month, fifteen years after he'd planted the trees, the block association awarded him the coveted Neighbor of the Year award.

Anwar paused for a moment in front of Charu's bedroom door. He heard muffled whispering, a girlish laugh. Three clangs of a bell and a flat drone saturated the hallway. The sound filled Anwar with an unnamed dread—*stop, you are being paranoid.* He shook his head at the feeling of dread. There lingered the invisible dust of some old horror, for who knew what had happened in this house before their time here. He imagined the desolation of addiction, women stuffed with bags of rock, beaten in murderous rages. He did not believe in ghosts. But if there were any, he wished them on their way.

Another giggle from Charu's room. *And then, there was peace,* he thought, making his way to his bedroom.

All of the ceilings at 111 Cambridge Place had the same beautiful white floral molding. However, in the master bedroom, a door handle was embedded in one of the leaves in the pattern. Once opened, the door revealed a fold-up ladder, which led upstairs to the third floor, to Anwar's studio. To reach the door handle, Anwar stood on a chair and pulled down the ladder. He hoisted himself into the room and sat for moment to steady his trembling knees.

Heaven. He inhaled the wisps of baked blueberry in the air. A refrigerator preserved fresh fruit extracts, yogurts, and soy and oatmeal scrubs for Anwar's Apothecary goods that he concocted in this kitchen. Wicker furniture scored from weekend stoop sales. Leather-bound journals and old magazines created a skyline of paper towers on the floor. Hashi never came upstairs, preferring the make-Anwar-do-it system. She would holler, "I need cleanser!" Then Anwar would send the products down in a bucket attached to a rope.

He unbuttoned his daytime shirt and pants and changed into his night gear, a plaid lungi and a plaid shirt.

Time for a toke, Anwar thought. On the floor was a border of nineteen empty pint-size mason jars, courtesy of none other than Rashaud Persaud, who grew a potent crop out in an abandoned house in the Rockaways. Anwar had never been there. He squatted down and unscrewed the lid. The pungent leafy aroma floated into his nostrils. He plucked a dark green bud laced with purple hues, packed a nugget in a wooden pipe, lit it with a match. One luxurious drag let the evening's quarrel subside.

"Unnh," he heard, as he inhaled. *Did I make this sound?* Anwar thought. He inhaled and then exhaled again out the tiny arched window. What was this sound? He kept the space vermin-free. He heard drumming, then another long, melodious sigh.

"Unhhhh."

"Hashi?" he asked.

No answer.

Hashi had not come upstairs. The drumming sound beckoned him to investigate the wall he shared with their tenant, Ramona Espinal. A thin wall and a locked door separated them. Only Anwar had the key. He rolled toward the wall, his elbow hitting it with a thud. Drumming ceased. He took another toke. Laughter. He chuckled along. Was Ramona Espinal with a lover? He pictured a sweaty, stubbly mariachi, riding the spur of his boots down her tight, voluptuous hips. *I must have seen this on TV,* he thought. Ramona was a Mexican nurse-midwife at Brooklyn Hospital, and nearly half his age. He checked his watch. It was a quarter to midnight. She shouldn't be home at this hour.

Drumming commenced. A man laughed. *It is the headboard,* Anwar realized.

"Anwar!" he heard Hashi shout from below.

"Yes, darling!" As soon as he said it, he clasped his hand over his mouth. Abruptly, the drumming stopped.

"Bedtime, *na*?" called Hashi. "And the shampoo!"

"Yes, darling."

He rolled away from the wall and opened his eyes. *Ah, my old friend.* Rezwan's severed head floated around Anwar. He blinked several times and Rezwan's head did the same. Ghastly bits of spinal cord and purple-black windpipe trailed from Rezwan's neck. A machete scar sliced open cheek into mouth, yellow half-moon smile. *How many times can I answer for your death? I am sorry for abandoning you.*

As if hearing Anwar's thoughts, Rezwan's head nodded yes. Anwar nodded back. He had loved Rezwan, his brother-in-law and comrade, more than any man before or since. Years after the war, in 1985, Rezwan and his wife, Laila, were both shot to death by an unknown gunman. They had planned to settle near Laila's hillside family home in Rangamati, away from the decaying city Dhaka had become.

They were killed mere days before the move.

Rezwan's anti-government views about President Ershad were

well known in Dhaka. But Anwar did not believe the gunman was an unknown assassin or a government operative.

He suspected it was an act of revenge.

Yet Anwar was too far away to investigate. There were weightier matters involved. Ella had been spared, having slept over at her grandparents' flat that evening. Upon hearing the news, Anwar and Hashi begged to bring Ella to New York, to live as their daughter. It took two years for Hashi's parents to agree to let them take her.

Today would have been Rezwan's thirtieth wedding anniversary, Anwar remembered. Married on a pristine beach in Cox's Bazar, barefoot upon the striated black-and-white sands. Save for Anwar, Hashi, and their immediate family, all the other guests were villagers whom Rezwan and Laila had met while installing tube wells in the surrounding villages. That day, one of Anwar's happiest—rice wine, song and dance aplenty—was etched in his mind forever. He realized that besides the bride and groom, many of those in attendance had suffered for years afterward, poisoned by arsenic-laced well water.

"We die. Memory is fragmentary. I believe in nothing," said Anwar to his friend. "But there are times when scripture relieves a sense of flailing."

They moved their lips in recitation, Arabic into Bangla into Arabic again, scraps of *Surah al-Noor (The Light).*

> *See how Al—h created the Seven Heavens and Earth*
> *Made the Earth, a niche*
> *Made the moon, a lamp*
> *Made the sun, a glass, a brilliant star*
> *Lit from a blessed tree neither of the east nor west*
> *Its oil luminous though no fire touched it*
> *Light upon light*
> *Speak to us in parables, knower of All—*

I must be with your sister now, thought Anwar. Rezwan stuck out his tongue and disappeared into an air vent. Anwar wanted to hold the closest thing to his dead friend, his daughter, Ella. But she had not yet come home.

2

A quiet backpack-clad figure walked to 111 Cambridge Place. Ragged from a bus ride, Ella considered turning back to the steep hills and collegiate abandon of Ithaca, where night skies held the ancient grand stars like Alphard the Solitary, in the constellation Hydra. Down here in Brooklyn, stars lay stitched under a veil of gray-black clouds and light pollution, lost to city dwellers.

The wrought-iron front gate was unlatched. Ella paused for a minute. It didn't seem like anyone was awake. She made her way around the side of the house to the backyard. She did a quick walk-through—the garden looked healthy; it was something she worried about at college. She circled back to the hibiscus tree that led into her cousin's room. She stepped onto the tree's lowest branch and climbed up to Charu's second-floor window. Through the sheer curtains, Ella could see the selection of mood enhancers: a Virgin de Guadalupe pillar candle, burning sticks of Nag Champa, white Christmas lights framing the bed. And there was Charu, strutting around in a pair of lacy black panties and bra. Ella flushed, shamed by her spying. She blinked her eyes a few times to make sure what she was seeing. Her eyes weren't so—reliable.

It was hard coming home. Ella was drawn to her uncle's rambling anecdotes and flower gardens, but she loathed her aunt's curling iron and frills. She never quite felt she was in her aunt's favor. She switched between calling Anwar "Uncle" or "Anwar," and he didn't seem to mind either way, understanding that if her mood permitted intimacy, she'd allow it. She never called Hashi "Ma." But for Charu, words failed her. The word *sister*—in any language—missed the mark, though she knew Charu felt that they were sisters. Charu was the one person for whom Ella would do anything. She had been a bright-eyed bouncy toddler with an infectious laugh, and Ella, scrawny and nearsighted, had claimed the role of protector.

As they grew up, Ella loved everything about Charu, even her contradictions: The same girl who despised capitalist materialism owned enough fine threads to open a used-clothing store; the same girl who scoffed at other girls for idiotic flirting was a clever coquette. She demanded an end to anorexic beauty ideals, but lamented her "third world body": protruding belly, scrawny arms and legs. Charu, the unapologetic fashion chameleon—on certain days she dressed in plaid shirts and baggy khakis; other days, monochromatically. And once, when she was a sophomore and Ella was a senior, Charu channeled pop culture celebrity with short shorts and stilettos made to stab a man in the chest. She changed right back into jeans and a T-shirt when chided by the dour-faced Principal Jenkins.

At Brooklyn Tech, Ella fell in line with the smart and lonely characters whose sights were set on the Ivy League. Her senior year she was known as the "hot Indian chick's sister." Charu's entry into the school gave Ella an ounce of attention (and, she suspected, pity) for inheriting the short end of the genetic stick. She remembered once when walking home from school, a boy on the street said, *Dang, you ugly,* and Charu shouted, *Shut the fuck up, mushroom dick!* The boy let it slide the second his eyes made contact with Charu's. Ella mumbled they should keep moving—he didn't go to their school and they'd never see him again. Charu seethed the entire walk home. Ella knew that if she herself had said such a thing, the kid would harass her more. But he hadn't done anything but laugh, for he, like Ella, was not immune to Charu's charm. Charu aligned herself with outsiders, with fringe dwellers. She accepted the weird, the freakish, the perverse, the gothic, and the queer. She loved people different from her; Ella was a perfect complement. As Charu grew curvy, Ella's muscles became long and limber. Ella refused the pains of contacts and was damned to thick glasses with plastic frames.

During Ella's senior year, two springs ago, while planting rosemary in the herb garden, she realized she was in love with Charu Saleem. From that day, Ella lived in constant suppression. She'd grinned at Charu in the hallway, and it was easy to avoid her in the twelve-floor behemoth of a school, since she had her schedule memorized. Charu never fathomed Ella's infatuation, and remained free and uncomplicated with her cousin. Charu changed in and out of her clothes all the time without a thought to decency.

Ella never let her mind wander to Charu's body at nighttime, committed to being chaste. She pondered why, over and over. The word *lesbian* felt as foreign to her as the word *sister.* There were other kids in school who were more comfortable with being queer, and formed clubs and events that she seemed to get invited to. The idea of belonging to a group because a crush on Charu would "qualify" her as a member—that just wasn't okay. It wasn't like anyone else had ever caught her attention at school, and during those sleepless nights, Ella wondered if anyone ever would.

Once during a game of Taboo, Charu's clue was *like you,* and upon learning the word was *adopted,* Ella stormed off, not speaking to Charu until the next afternoon. She walked around with fists clenched, and developed a teeth-grinding habit that would last for years. Anwar attributed this behavior to a sedentary adolescent lifestyle and asked her to help him build the fence for the vegetable garden. This worked for a while; she was too exhausted at night to desire. But after the fence was built, the old insomnia persisted. It was Hashi who cured her, with lovers rock. The Guyanese hawker Rashaud Persaud had brought the reggae CD as a gift to Hashi during a salon visit. Finding no use for "such slow" music, Hashi passed it on to Ella, who listened to it every night till she left for college. She stopped seeing images in her dreams—she dreamt as though born blind.

And now, seeing her cousin in her bedroom, Ella hesitated for a second before rapping on the window. Even though Ella had wrapped up her sophomore year at Cornell, met some good folks, she flushed with that same embarrassment.

Charu's face switched from seductress to sister. "Ella!" She hugged her cousin through the window.

"Charu," said Ella, lightly returning her hug. Charu hugged back tighter, and pulled Ella through the window into her bedroom.

"Shit, I wasn't expecting *you*!"

"Who were you expecting?"

"You'll never guess who I'm dating."

"Who?" *This takes the cake for shitty guessing games.*

"Malik. Can you believe it? After all these years?"

Ella scanned her memory—Malik? Ah, Anwar's intern. Same year in school as Charu. Skateboarder extraordinaire. Stupid bastard. "How'd that happen?"

"He just offered to teach me how to skateboard. See?" Charu pointed to a scab on her knee. "Isn't that awesome?"

"Yeah, awesome."

"Should I wait in the nude? Should I wear this?" Charu grinned, holding up a lace teddy. "I made it."

"God, Charu, I don't know about that stuff." Ella grimaced at the lingerie. "Did you two . . ." She let the sentence fade. "Wait, you made that?"

"No, we haven't had sex yet. Maybe tonight's the night. And yes, I've been hittin' the sewing machine like crazy."

"It does look a little crazy in here," said Ella, looking at the mess everywhere. Charu's sewing machine was covered with lace and fabric swatches, paper patterns, pins, and spools of thread.

"Well if they'd let me go to FIT, like I wanted, I wouldn't be hoarding all this shit."

"I'm sure if you made more of a case—" *Bullshit,* thought Ella. While the Fashion Institute of Technology was Charu's first-choice public school, Ella knew Charu blaming Anwar and Hashi was a load of crap. When it came down to it, Charu had chosen NYU and a pretty decent financial aid package because of the slightly higher probability that she would meet a straight guy.

The unmistakable sound of a shaking tree interrupted Ella.

"Shit, he's here!"

At the same moment, they heard Hashi's militant footsteps approaching Charu's room. Charu fumbled to turn on the overhead-light switch, her signal to Malik that it was not safe to enter. The rustling of the branches stopped. Just as Charu yanked on a terry cloth bathrobe, Hashi turned the doorknob without bothering to knock. Ella saw the heat of resentment rise in her cousin's face and could not help but laugh.

Hashi pushed her way through the door, carrying a plate of food. "Charu—it is late! Have your dinner."

"I'm not eating this late, Ma."

"Then go to bed, *now*." Hashi sounded tired, with a hint of sadness. She took the plate back. The shawl arranged around her head slipped to her shoulders, exposing a fringe of gray hair along her temple.

Hashi pointed to Charu's bed and her eyes narrowed. "What's this, some Hindu puja? You'll burn yourself alive. Stop the fire!"

"Ma, aren't you going to say something?"

"What—" started Hashi, then she noticed Ella. "*Arré,* Ella? You're home!" She leaned in to give Ella a kiss on the cheek; then she took a step back. "How on earth did you get in? I didn't hear the front door."

"You know Ella's burglar quiet, Ma," said Charu.

Ella stared at the floor, deciding it was the smartest thing to do.

Hashi's gaze wandered to the window, as if she sensed something awry but could not locate it. She walked over to the closet and opened it. After finding nothing, she gave Charu one last killer look. She patted Ella's shoulder.

"Maybe you can bring some sense into your sister," said Hashi. "It is good to have you home." She left them without saying good night to Charu.

"Goddamn, the woman's an evil psychic," Charu said, exhaling.

"She knows you," Ella said, starting to leave. "Have a good—"

"No, El, stay a bit. She'll get suspicious if you leave right away. It's better if she thinks I'm awake talking to you."

"You've got it twisted, but—all right."

Charu turned off the light, and once again, Malik could be heard climbing the hibiscus tree.

The tree shook with the expectation and longing of an eighteen-year-old. Malik tapped the window. Charu slid it open. His feet were on a branch; his hands gripped the sill. His short legs, back, and arms were taut and straight—he resembled a small bridge. He reached for Charu's arm, but she lacked the strength to pull him in. She gestured for Ella to help her.

"Thanks, guys," Malik said, as they struggled to hoist him into the room, trying to be quiet. He looked around, sniffed with pleasure at the scent of incense trailing. He was bathed in cologne, and his black plastic-frame glasses slipped down his nose. Ella couldn't stop herself from appreciating the nerd in him. He wore cutoff shorts and a black tank top with a screen-printed red fish skeleton, FISHBONE scrawled across. He presented Charu with a gift: a pink rose, with two Valium pills taped to the stem. "It's good to see you, Ella, how you been?" Malik offered her his hand. Ella shook it, firmly.

"You got *two* pills?" Charu joked. "Guess there's limited perks to you working in my uncle's pharmacy," she said. She dropped the flower on the bed and pulled him closer.

"Hey, your dad's gonna kill me if he finds out I'm giving his daughter drugs," said Malik. "I'm a lucky dude for getting this gig, but I gotta say, I miss ol' Anwar. I might still help him out a couple days a week."

"He won't even know you're getting them from Aman's pharmacy," said Charu. "Should we take 'em now?"

"Naw, let's hold off for a minute, sugar."

"Too late!" Charu popped a pill into her mouth.

"Well, shoot," said Malik. "You want this one, Ella? I didn't realize you'd be here."

"No. I'm good."

"A'ight. Well, fuck it. Here goes," said Malik. "Got water?"

Charu fished a water bottle from under a pile of fabric. "It's not old. Promise."

Malik took a swig and swallowed.

"My uncle's got the personality of a prison warden, huh?" said Charu.

"Dude's getting a divorce. I got sad today, hearing him talk about his wife." He looked around, as if Hashi might appear behind him. "Your mom asleep?"

"She's been killing me softly, but yes, the wicked witch sleeps." Charu gave him a few tiny pecks. He let Charu kiss his ears and looked at Ella. She looked back at him with undisguised loathing.

"I—uh, brought this film I thought we could watch," he said.

"Oooooh, that's sweeeeeet, Maliiiik," Charu said.

Why do girls add so many vowels when they're into someone? Ella wondered. "I've got to sleep," she said. "That bus ride did me in."

"It's—it's good for inducing sleep," Malik stuttered, excited. "It's a French film set to this incredible music and y-you-you-just watch this bit of forest grow from nothing into, well, a forest."

"C'mon, Ella, I haven't seen you in months! I'll be studying and taking Regents all next week!"

"Yeah, right," Malik said, and they laughed.

Ella frowned, but sat down on the bed. The longer she stayed, the longer she would be able to keep an eye on Charu.

Charu put the DVD into her computer, and sat between Ella and Malik, spreading a thin kantha blanket over their legs. Ella was practically pushed off the side of the bed, like a pineapple-flavored Life Saver, unwanted, at the end of the pack. She kept glancing to see if Malik was petting Charu, but he kept his hands by his sides, eyes on the screen as if he wasn't using the film as a ploy to bed her cousin.

After a while, Ella relaxed. The film's music wafted over her. She took off her glasses to rest her eyes. Her vision was in the negative nines, and most things were fuzzy outlines until she put her glasses on. Around the time of her parents' death, something else had started happening, usually set off by a headache or stress. From twilight until she slept, she would see bright lines and shapes, plants, or people. And now, the time-lapse frames of the documentary became a riotous, psychedelic hallucination of blossoms, fauna, the curling, spreading, mixing within a microcosm.

Ella's visions ranged from meditative to wacky. A waning moon over a placid lake, a bevy of Egyptian blue monarchs, a television set bouncing up and down around the room. For much of her childhood, she assumed her eyes were making up things for her to see; she'd wondered if she were going insane. And she worried that telling Anwar and Hashi might then involve seeing a shrink. Or being sent back to Bangladesh.

She'd even taken a couple of classes to make sense of her visions. Her Neurological Disorders seminar mapped the fearsome world of disorders and delusions, from migraines to schizophrenia. In the Hallucinations class, Ella devoured any literature she could get her hands on to figure out the cause. Getting an MRI at the medical center was easy enough, but she always found excuses to not make a doctor's appointment. Poring through study after study led her to two conclusions: It was either a tumor or trauma that caused her phantasms. Each case bore a resemblance to Ella's. Lilliputian beings or kaleidoscopic visions at dusk. Perpetual insomnia. Yet it didn't happen every single evening; rather, something would set it off, if she was stressed or dehydrated or had a migraine. Ella wondered if years of depression, another possible cause, had done her in. She'd tried therapy in fourth and fifth grade, upon her teachers' suggestion, but she didn't ever find comfort in talking about herself.

She couldn't figure out a way to tell Anwar and Hashi that she hallucinated without worrying that her aunt would fall into hysteria. So Ella picked up a prescription for antidepressants, after telling one of the student health center counselors her story. She hadn't yet taken the pills the shrink so readily prescribed.

Coming home stirred up thoughts of the parents Ella had barely known. Anwar spoke about Rezwan and Laila like they were characters in an epic. Freedom fighters. They survived a war, only to be murdered just before her third birthday. There was one black-and-white photograph of them, perched against a graffiti wall marked with sickles and hammers. Rezwan Anwar, undeniably regal, in aviator sunglasses, standing next to Laila, nearly six feet tall, her arms holding baby Ella. She stood with her head cocked to the side, daring the camera to capture her. A teenage boy stood beside Rezwan, almost hiding behind his enormous bell-bottomed pant leg—Ella vaguely remembered the boy hugging her good-bye when she left Dhaka. Her only lucid memory of her homeland was leaning into her grandfather Azim's chest in the car en route to the airport. He hummed a fisherman's tune, smelled of sweat and cloves.

There was wriggling on the bed. Charu was kissing Malik wildly;

he flopped and gasped like a fish struggling in the open air. Ella was rigid. She had drifted off but was now witness to the spectacle. She was anxious to leave, anxious to watch. Charu squinted with the cunning of a girl who believed she knew how to pleasure a man, but then she started giggling; she must have felt the release of the Valium. Malik shushed her, to no avail.

Ella Anwar, orphaned, adopted, with her wayward visions, her frizzy hair, her large hands and feet, a bass voice. She longed to nestle in the burning that filled the air. She edged herself off the bed, leaving them to each other.

Crisscrossed parquet floors creaked under Ella's step. Gold leaf wallpaper, beloved of the old Brooklyn bourgeoisie, gleamed in the dimness. On either side of the stairs were two archways: To her left were the living room and kitchen; to her right was her bedroom, and a bathroom behind the stairs. Hashi called this the "guest bathroom," a bad habit from the renovation days, though Ella was the only one who ever used it.

She saw something looming in the living room—a headless naked figure. She went inside and touched the form. *Just one of Hashi's mannequins, idiot.* She hurried back to her side of the house, to go to the bathroom. She scrubbed her hands raw and splashed water on her face. She looked up at the mirror. Mirrors were never a part of Ella's day. Long arms and legs and coarse hairs everywhere. She was rough as a prehistoric man. She wore an oversize T-shirt with relaxed-fit Levi's. She'd had these clothes since her freshman year of high school. Ella pressed her nose against the mirror for a closer facial evaluation. Her pores—at least what she thought might be pores—were enormous. She scraped her nose with a nail, loosening tiny, hardened yellow flecks. *Damn, you ugly.*

Ella took in her old room—one wall with three rows of framed pen-and-ink botanical drawings, freshman biology textbooks on a bookshelf, a poster of Simone de Beauvoir. The windowed wall was painted verdigris, with the bed pushed up against it for the best view of the garden. Everything was just as she'd left it when she was home over Christmas break, except—she blinked her eyes several times to be sure—there was a person sleeping in her bed.

This was a girl; Ella could tell from the slope of the body under the sheets and the scent of floral shampoo. Ella got on her hands and knees and stared at the girl. She was lithe, hair shorn in a pixie; a small diamond studded her nose. She shivered in her sleep. Somehow, she was familiar, but Ella did not know how she knew her. She found herself matching the sleeping girl's breathing. She wasn't about to climb into the twin bed with a stranger. For an evening without hallucinations, this was the weirdest (and maybe worst) night Ella had experienced in a long time.

The summer air was warm and crisp. The sky had not yet brightened. She moved past the headless mannequin, the overwhelming smell of onions in the kitchen, out the sliding back door. She would sleep outside.

3

The songs of sparrows stirred Charu awake at dawn. Soft computer glow beamed on the high ceiling, eerie as an alien confessional. Ella's glasses sat in the mess, an artifact left behind in a raid. In her high, Charu had lost track of her sister, who had managed to slip out of the room.

After four months of chaste skateboarding and two-slices-and-a-soda specials at Luv 'N Oven, things between Charu and Malik had changed in the past week. Each day after school, a new lesson, the unfurling of their desire. Monday, riding the G train back and forth between Queens and Gowanus, kissing. Tuesday, humping jeans over jeans in his empty apartment in Bed-Stuy. His mother worked interminable shifts at JFK airport at the British Airways counter. Malik missed her, but freedom (and free trips to the West Indies) was a fair trade. Wednesday, he rolled Charu a joint (*the most potent shit, courtesy of Uncle Bic*); they ate Luv 'N Oven and watched *Total Request Live,* which killed the vibe. Thursday, he churned her insides with strong bassist fingers. *Playing chords in your pussy,* he had chuckled. It hurt terribly. But it was the first time she could ever remember something that hurt terribly but felt good all at once. Maybe Chinatown massages or tattoos or gym class, but she didn't know much about those things either.

Charu closed her laptop and watched Malik sleep. Her mouth watered, wanting to nosh and suckle flesh like a newborn. She raked him with her teeth, tasted hard salty shoulder, vein ridges along his sinewy arm, a slim wrist and musky fingers. He whistled air from his nose. She straddled the morning tent that sprouted from his underwear and bent down to kiss his snoring mouth. His locks lay gnarled on his chest like a prized fleece. She sucked his breath and kissed him harder. He heaved and gasped as if drowning and pushed her aside.

"Whaaat?"

"I—I—couldn't breathe," said Malik. "Stop."

She flinched at his tone. "Maybe you should leave," she told him, peeling herself off his body.

He took a few more deep breaths. "Relax. No need for salt, sugar," he said, chuckling. He spread his fingers over her belly. She stiffened, but let him suck on her breast, eyes still half-asleep. She pressed against him to imprint a raspberry star, one more in a galaxy of bruises.

He pulled her closer, swiped a condom from her bedside table.

"Wish we could listen to music," he said. "Maybe we should just wait to do it in my house."

She ripped the wrapper with her teeth. "We can't wait." She handed him the condom, uncertain.

He slipped it on and rubbed himself on her thigh. She took a few deep breaths and closed her eyes.

Malik grinned and she grinned back. She looked up at him as a drop of his sweat fell onto her cheek. The silver cross on his neck brushed her mouth, and she opened to swallow it. She clasped the charm under her tongue like a thermometer. Rays of morning sun filtered inside her eyelids. Somewhere, far away, she heard the crackle of thunder.

She opened her eyes to find Malik's face stricken with fear.

"Oh *shit*," he wheezed. He jumped out of bed and froze, then brought a finger to his lips.

"What's wrong? What's *wrong*?"

Her locked door rattled furiously.

"Charu!" yelled her mother. "How many times must I tell you not to lock the door? You took my thread! I have fifteen bridesmaids' eyebrows waiting!"

"One sec, Ma!" said Charu. "I-I'm getting dressed."

"You are already awake? You must be hungry," said Hashi. "Hurry up, child!"

Go go go! Charu mouthed to Malik, pushing him inside the closet. She grabbed the spools of thread and opened the door a sliver to drop them into Hashi's extended hand.

"What is the matter, are you getting sick?" asked Hashi. "Let me make you breakfast now. Come. Ella will join us."

"No!" yelped Charu.

"No?"

"I'll do it. I'll make brunch for all of us."

"You sound like me," said Hashi, laughing. She pinched Charu's cheek. "It's still early, child. Get some sleep."

As soon as Hashi's footsteps faded, Malik broke out of the closet. He headed toward the window. "Fuck this," he mumbled, looking down at the drop from the tree.

"I need to get downstairs. I forgot Maya is sleeping in Ella's room."

"Looks like it," said Malik, pointing out the window. There lay Ella, snoozing on the patio tiles.

"Ah, that's her usual weird," said Charu.

"I'm out, sugar." He leaned out to set his foot on a branch and then grabbed another to steady his hand. Feeble and slick with dew, the smaller branch snapped. Sparrows shot out of the tree and he lost his balance and plummeted down, somehow managing not to scream. She heard a thud against the wet mulch Baba had set under the tree. Malik sprung up without turning up to look at her, his cutoffs falling to his knees.

He shuffled around the side of the house onto Cambridge Place.

Charu heard the B52 bus whoosh by, and she crossed her fingers that Malik would hail it in time before her mother caught him. From her bedroom window, she looked again at her sister snoozing in the backyard.

"Shit."

Charu ran down the stairs, past the living room and kitchen, through the sliding glass door. Ella snoozed against a vine-covered cucumber trellis. In sleep, she shed her grumpy awkwardness. She was strangely handsome lying there. Charu bemoaned her curves. Why had she not inherited the lanky build of the Anwar line like

Ella and her mother? Charu put on her sister's glasses, and held her face close to Ella's ear.

"You know, you look good without those glasses," Charu said, in a nerdy voice.

Ella's eyes popped open. "You scared me!"

"Second time I've done that today."

"I'm . . . tired," said Ella, squinting up at the sky. She rubbed her eyes and sat up. "I need my glasses. I need water."

"You *are* blind," Charu laughed, peeling off the glasses. She dangled them in front of Ella. "Not giving you these unless you get your ass up and help me cook brunch."

"Come on, Charu, just give me the damn glasses," said Ella, swiping them back.

"What time did you get to bed? I passed out."

"Do you . . . remember anything?" Ella asked.

"Valium isn't for kids?"

"Not funny, you addict. Where's your boyfriend? And who the fuck is the chick in my room? You know I like to keep my shit private."

"First of all—chill the fuck out."

"Chill the fuck out? You ask me to hang with you and Malik. Then I get to sit there watching you two freaks act like it's normal to start fucking when someone's *right there*. And when I try to get sleep like I wanted to all along, there's a stranger sleeping in my bed. You know I can't sleep, bitch; I'm not going to chill the fuck out."

"Bitch? You're a bitch!" Charu smacked Ella's chest in surprise. She and Ella had never once had a true tussle, and it was odd to begin so late in life. Ella didn't even curse much. She looked at her sister's face, all dirt streaked and wet. Pitiful. Charu took a breath. People told her that one of her best qualities was that she never stayed mad. This was some grudge-worthy shit, but she didn't want to lose the title.

"I came down here to check and see if you were all right. You slept outside. Come on."

"There was a girl in my bed."

"Come. Meet her."

Charu led Ella inside to meet Maya. The girl lay on her belly, legs crossed upward, black nail-polished toes curled, at home in Ella's bed. In her hands: Ella's copy of German biologist Ernst Haeckel's 1904 volume, *Kunstformen der Natur,* a book of biological lithographs.

"To see the world like this you've got to be a genius," she said, closing the book on *Cyanea annasethe,* the tentacled jellyfish. "I'm Maya." She extended her hand to Ella, but didn't get out of her bed.

"Jellyfish reminded Haeckel of his dead wife's hair," said Ella.

"And here's my infamously morbid sister, Ella," said Charu. "Maya's going to stay with us for a few weeks."

"Hi," said Maya, waving.

"And you were going to tell me this *when*?"

"Don't—" warned Charu, but Ella didn't seem to hear her.

"There's a *stranger* in *my* bed and you're telling me she's staying with 'us' for a few weeks? You mean with *me*. You mean, 'Ella, handle this shit while I'm busy fucking around,' literally fucking an asshole who can't climb a goddamn tree—"

"So, Ella, I'm figuring things out," interrupted Maya. Her voice was hoarse, as if she'd smoked a pack of cigarettes. "My father doesn't . . . want me to go to college."

"Not just college—she got into Berkeley, and he wants her to stay home!" cried Charu. "It's a fucking travesty."

"I deferred a year to figure shit out. My father wants me to stay home because Mema's got lupus and my twin brothers are devils, so you can imagine—oh goodness!" Maya caught sight of something outside the window.

"What?" asked Charu, hopping onto the bed for a better look.

"Seems your boy left part of himself behind," Maya said.

The three of them leaned into the window. Sitting in the mulch, translucent and forgotten, Malik's rubber.

"Disgusting." Ella left the room, slamming the door behind her.

"At least it wasn't used," Charu called after her.

4

Ella sat outside on the stoop watching their block. There was a curious chain of seven matching pink racer bikes locked in front of the downstairs garden apartment, which housed Hashi's salon. Streamers and baskets adorned the bikes, and on all but one, a single cardboard placard hung from the handlebars, spelling C-A-R-M-E-N. In front of the apartment building across the street, neighbors were barbecuing hamburgers on the sidewalk with a portable grill, blaring "Saturday Love" from a Caprice Classic. Dr. Duray, the retired dentist, rested on a lawn chair and sang lyrics from his original ditty, "The Girls on Cambridge Place Are Oh So Pretty." He waved at Ella, and she waved back.

"Want some barbecue, girl?" he called over to her.

"No thank you, sir," she said.

He nodded his head side-to-side the way the elderly trailed their words, but stopped singing his song. She wondered if he'd lost his muse upon seeing her. *Barbecue.* The word made her want to hurl. Uncontrollable trembling and nauseating heat had eaten away most of her morning. She couldn't shed the image of Malik and Charu's contorted bodies from her mind. Ella heard Charu's glossy words—*You look really good without those glasses*—echoing inside her. Noonday sun emblazoned their block, and the brownstone steps singed Ella's bare feet. A pack of teenage girls pranced through the bursting arc of water from a hydrant broken open, sundresses plastered against their supple bodies. Ella felt a burning shame return and turned her gaze to her neighbor's scarlet oak tree. All parts of the tree were completely green—the shiny leaves, bushy tail-like catkins, the immature acorns—with no hint of the rich autumnal red the leaves would turn in just a few months. She squinted for a closer inspection—the female flowers grew on much shorter spikes than the male catkins; all at once, the monoecious *Quercus coccinea* bore male and female parts. She'd worried about leaving Ithaca, she realized. She felt much more at home in nature, hiking in the woods, alone, listening to Debussy on headphones. She volunteered at the student-run farm. She had even considered staying over the summer, to serve as a manager in the Market Garden project. Along with other students and volunteers, Ella could plant and harvest a two-acre vegetable plot and herb garden, and then market the produce at local farm stands.

But she couldn't bear the idea of not coming home.

Staying in Ithaca meant no Anwar and Hashi, and no Charu. After the whole family dropped her off on campus for freshman orientation, Ella had refrained from inviting Charu again. She knew that her cousin would undoubtedly provoke the oversexed undergrads, the frat boys, dorks, and potheads in her dorm, and that would make Ella—sad.

Her glasses slipped down her sweaty nose, and everything became blurry. All the parts of the scarlet oak morphed into one large, green mass. A thick, smoky breeze shook the tree, and it appeared to expand immensely, then contract. It did this many times, and Ella saw each phase of the tree's metamorphosis. With one cycle of expansion and contraction, the tree bore foliage; a second time, there were flowers. The final expansion sprouted acorns, followed by a final tightening that produced the seed. All the parts of this oak sprouted from one archetypal plant, which took on multiple forms. But in essence, it was all one being. Ella pushed her glasses back up. The tree was just as still as it had been before.

There was a loud popping sound coming from the garden apartment—a champagne cork shot upward—and Ella found herself walking down to her aunt's salon.

Peeping through the vestibule door, Ella saw the mélange of thread, hair spray, and toasted bridesmaids painted and waiting. The bride, a young girl of twenty, stood in front of a mirror, gazing at the hive of hair frozen in place.

"Beautiful, no?" said Hashi, nudging the girl.

"Carmen's getting married!" whooped one of the bridesmaids. The laughing women rushed toward the door, billows of satin and taffeta nearly knocking Ella over.

"Excuse me." The party of seven paid no mind to her as they made their way to their matching bicycles. They hitched their dresses above their bottoms, revealing old-fashioned bloomers. They hopped on and pedaled to the Presbyterian church around the corner, hollering as they rode.

Hashi grimaced. "Please do not sweat off the makeup!" she called after them. She bumped into Ella as she turned back toward the house. "Ella!" she exclaimed, as if she were the one person who could have surprised her.

"I'm sorry, I was just . . ." Ella began.

"What is it, dear?"

"I—I don't know."

Hashi squinted at her, calculating, tapping her chin with her forefinger. "Come," she said. She flipped the Open sign to Closed, and locked the salon entrance.

"Sit down, my dear," she said, gesturing to the chair at the sink. "Take off your glasses. Close your eyes."

Without her glasses the hair dryer chairs appeared as globe-headed robots; bottles of shampoo and hair spray became an army of pawns. It dawned on Ella that in her whole life with the Saleem family, she could count the number of times she'd come into her aunt's salon on one hand. She closed her eyes. She felt the chair pump backward so that her head lay on the cool ceramic sink, Hashi's tea-tree-flavored breath on her face, her slight and saggy bosom pressed against her shoulders. It sounded like Hashi was rubbing her hands together; a moment later she felt warm olive oil on her head. Hashi rubbed it in, softening the frizz, then ran water through her hair and massaged in a musky shampoo. The water sent a chill down her back. Hashi lifted her head to roughly towel her dry. She brought Ella to one of the salon's high chairs and spun her around. Hashi selected a pair of scissors and began snipping away dead hair; in minutes the back of Ella's neck pricked at the air of the fan. She ran her hand over her hair—it was short, like a boy's. An odd feeling, not unpleasant, and rather uncertain, tickled her. She heard a faucet run—it sounded like the bathtub—Hashi had gone into the bathroom.

Ella heard Hashi coming back into the room. Hashi grabbed her hand and said, "Follow me." She led Ella into the bathroom and then Ella, eyes still closed, heard what sounded like stirring ice in water. Then, the sound of a knife chopping—no one chopped like Hashi—and the air became infused with the scent of cucumber and mint. More stirring.

"Ella, take my hand, and when I say step, you step," said Hashi. "Step!"

She took one step and her right foot was submerged in freezing water. "Aaah, shit!"

"Step!"

She put her other foot in.

"Do not move. Do not open eyes," Hashi commanded.

Ella heard the snipping before she felt her clothes being shorn off.

"Uh . . ." she managed to say, stripped naked and mortified. Hashi pressed her hands into Ella's arms. With one swift motion, she dunked Ella in the water.

"Raaaah!" Ella shuddered violently.

She remembered her route to New York from Dhaka with Anwar and Hashi. She had never met them before, but distinguished them by smell: Fried Onion Uncle and Talcum Powder Auntie. *Want the window seat, child?* Talcum Powder Auntie offered, and Ella had nodded yes. On the plane, she'd leaned against Talcum Powder Auntie's gardenia-scented underarms. After many hours had passed, out the small rounded window, she watched clouds shape-shift into Hans Christian Andersen characters. Somewhere over Arabia, cumulus clouds turned into a wedge of migrating swans.

In Berlin, they switched planes. Skin pale, eyes blue and hard. She spoke not a word, not even as her ears popped on the descent and the burning orange-yellow runway lights welcomed her. Talcum Powder Auntie offered her a cotton swab dabbed in attar of roses, a clean and crisp scent—deafening sound of wheel scraping asphalt.

Outside, it was December, and unbearably cold.

Hashi drew Ella's head up and out of the ice water, then back in again. Every aperture constricted. Underwater, the floating cucumber slices resembled Frisbees in a gray sky. Mint swam around like seaweed. She blew bubbles and spat water out.

"This lets the heat out. You have done very, very well." Hashi enveloped her in a towel that felt like it had been baking in an oven. Ella collapsed against her.

There was a light in the darkness—it appeared red and blue at once, and dissolved into a million flashes. The hot towel worked its magic.

Hashi handed her a bundle. "Wear this."

Ella felt her way through the articles. A shirt made of linen. The other piece was of a stiffer material—a pair of trousers. The new clothes were laundered fresh, but gave her the same sensation as pulling old vinyl out of the sleeve.

"And here," said Hashi, handing her a pair of tinted aviator glasses.

Ella put them on. The glasses were more stylish than her old pair. She caught herself in the mirror. She looked like her father in the photograph, but softer and marked with her mother's lashes and full lips. Her hair: a short, masculine Caesar cut that brought out her chiseled features. *Would Charu like it?*

"An utter incarnation of my brother. *Mashallah!* These are your father's old clothes. I have been saving them for you."

Ella took off her father's glasses—she'd started to get a headache—and held her aunt's hand. She saw Hashi's face, stern and lovely, and felt a comfort with her aunt for the first time since that plane ride. Without thinking, she squeezed Hashi's hand.

"What is it, Ella?"

"I don't know what to say," Ella replied, looking down. She fingered a tortoiseshell button.

Hashi cleared her throat. "Your father often fell into long silences, sometimes for days on end. I never could penetrate this quiet, as much as I would tug his hair, try to make him laugh. This changed during the war. Training with the freedom fighters in the Mukti Bahini, meeting Anwar, and of course your ma, Laila, pumped this fire into him. Afterward, when little had improved for the poorest in our country, he fell into a dark depression. But when you were born, Ella, something took over him, like wood kindling on a stove, where it's warmest deep within. You know, he called us just to let us listen to the new baby, the first one in our family. 'Listen, listen to this little giggler,' he told us. And you laughed into the receiver. Oh, I don't have words for what we've lost. All I do know is that something will change. Something great will happen to you, Ella. Someone great. This will fill you up."

Ella patted down a wrinkle in the shirt. She did not yet have the words. All her life, she had never felt pretty. Now, the person in front of her was perhaps the truest she had ever felt to her insides. If they were alive . . . It was a refrain she avoided as resolutely as she avoided Charu. She wondered if they would see themselves in her, if she would be this way if they were here. She probably would never have left Bangladesh. She doubted she would feel anything for Charu if they were alive. Right? Ella doubted she could be sure about that.

She recalled vague memories of her mother lining her eyes with kohl to stave off the evil eye; standing on her father's feet while he ran like a madman through the house. She had a fleeting sensation—being enveloped in her mother's arms, lost in her dry hennaed tresses.

As quickly as it came, it was gone.

5

Weekends are no fun anymore, thought Anwar. He wandered from the bedroom and hesitated to knock on Charu's door to see if she wanted some breakfast, even though it was noon. He wasn't much of a cook, but he could poach an egg. Hashi had stopped making breakfast on weekends and holidays, since these were her busiest days. Today she was at work in the salon tending to a gaggle of bridesmaids. She'd been rather quiet in the morning, but Anwar didn't probe her for the source of her discontent. Weekends were precious; he had the time to enjoy a home-cooked meal. He was hungry, angry, lonely, and tired—also known as HALT, something he'd picked up from a self-help book lingering in the bathroom a while back.

He preferred Hashi's heavy sighs to conversation. Those sighs were indicators that required shamanic intuition to decipher. Sometimes they were related to slow business or joint pain; other times it was a forgotten Mother's Day present or anniversary (they'd said "I do" on a telephone call, so the day didn't quite stick in Anwar's mind). He knew that she worried about Charu's indiscretions, whether she'd done her duties as a mother and a Muslim. It affected their sex life. Even in sleep Hashi cocooned far away on the bed, and Anwar could hardly get a good cuddle. Sex was not something Anwar had ever fathomed talking about with their daughter, and he trusted that Charu had a strong will and plenty of smarts to be on the right side of trouble.

Anwar went to the bathroom to splash some water on his face, plus a spritz of his special rosewater tonic. Further discouraging was that in a couple of hours his brother, Aman, would arrive. His elder brother was the successful owner of three pharmacies, childhood tormentor of Anwar, and now, most recently, a divorcé. Anwar noticed a pile of hibiscus petals in the bathroom wastebasket. He removed the petals and set them into a small bowl he found under the sink. Dried hibiscus wasn't the best choice for potpourri; it smelled musty, with a dash of tomato. His obsession with olfaction masked the smell of mud and shit from the garden. While he was oblivious to his own fishy odor, he used a surgical mask when setting mulch and manure for his plants. He spaced out in a squatting position, sniffing the petals.

"Baba, what are you doing?" Charu interrupted his meditation, pinched her bath towel tight across her chest. She wore that damned Tibetan bell around her neck. He cleared his throat, embarrassed. He wished that this middle stage in their relationship would hurry up and pass. He longed to be white-haired and holding a grandchild already.

"Charu, you look like a holy cow. I am thinking," Anwar said. "What are you doing up oh so early? I worry about you making it to classes on time."

"Aw, Baba, c'mon. I went to bed without dinner."

"That was your choice."

"Well, hurry up; Maya needs to use the bathroom, and I've got to shower," said Charu.

"Maya?" Anwar hadn't seen the girl behind Charu.

"Thank you, sir," said the girl.

"Remember I said she'd stay over last night?" asked Charu. "Remember?"

Anwar suspected that anytime Charu said, *Remember . . . I told you,* most often he did not remember because she had never said a thing. He raised an eyebrow. "I pretend you are singing when you are lying. It is nice to meet you, Maya. A short, sweet, and powerful name."

"My father's a weirdo," said Charu.

"I am not a weirdo." Anwar gestured up to the ceiling. "Gods and demons conjure the world's illusions with Maya—"

"I thought you don't believe in gods or demons."

"Good point. Shouldn't you two be outside? Isn't it summertime or something?"

"Where's Ella?" Charu asked, winking at her friend. "Did she go into the room last night?"

"I was knocked out. I didn't hear anything," said Maya.

"Ella is home?" Anwar hopped up out of his squat, wincing at his strained knees. "Fantastic news!"

"Yeah, yeah, we know you're all smiles now," said Charu. "Bye!"

"Yes, bye. Now, hurry and shower so you can make us lunch." He stood up and stroked Charu's hair; a hibiscus petal crumbled in his hand. "Petals are everywhere today!"

He shooed the girls away. "Ella is home," he said, smiling. There were two places she might be—her room, or the gardens. Like her uncle, she was a creature of habit.

Anwar walked downstairs and peeked into Ella's bedroom—the bed was neatly made, sheets tucked under the mattress, pillow fluffed. He shook his head with admiration—if there was any proof she was an Anwar, not a Saleem, it was that neat streak. He turned in to the living room. The floor bumped with the sounds of music from Hashi's salon. He continued on to the kitchen, which smelled like last night's onions. His stomach growled.

Someone really needed to do something about lunch.

He took a quick peek through the kitchen's sliding glass door. No sign of Ella. He decided to go upstairs to sulk in his studio.

On his way upstairs, he heard the vestibule door wiggling. Did Aman somehow have keys to the apartment? Anwar opened the door to let the struggling fool inside.

"Ah! Ramona Espinal," he said. His tenant wore dandelion yellow scrubs, her face bright and symmetrical as a honeycomb.

"Hello, Anwar," said Ramona, smiling. "How's your Sunday?"

"Wife is busy, kids are nowhere to be found—typical. And yours?"

"Had an overnight birth at the hospital."

"Wonderful color," said Anwar. "All colors are good colors—I don't have a favorite—but yellow suits—"

"Ha. Yes. This is my *Comadrona* Ramona jumpsuit. Need to do laundry."

"Coma-what?"

"Midwife. Another word to add to your Spanish."

"I will, La Enfermera," said Anwar.

"Very good. I'm a nurse-midwife, so you will be even more precise."

He'd learned the word for *nurse,* but here she was, throwing wrenches into his lessons. "Any plans for today?"

"I should do laundry at some point. I don't want to disturb Hashi," said Ramona, nodding toward the salon, where the washing machine and dryer were housed. "Sounds like a busy day. I'll do a load later in the evening. I'm so tired. It's time for a long bath."

"Very good idea. I am right behind you," he said, gesturing for her to go first up the stairs. "I mean, not for the bath; I just meant, for you it's good, and I, too, am going upstairs—*arré,* never mind me, please."

"I wrote a note to myself," said Ramona, raising her palm to Anwar. PAY RENT, it read, in blue ballpoint pen. "If you don't mind, I can write you a check now, before I pass out."

Her apartment was a replica of the first floor, without access to the backyard. Walls painted in marigold and tourmaline evoked picturesque adobe haunts. Everything was messy, complicated, indulgent. A vintage Schwinn Le Tour, much like his first bicycle in America, leaned against the wall. *It is the same weight as a third-grader; how does she carry this upstairs by herself?* Some things never went out of style: a cartoonish plastic Polaroid 600 camera and a scattering of self-portraits shot one-handed, with rather uncreative titles scribbled with black Sharpie pen: Ramona at the park, Ramona in her scrubs, Ramona eating a hamburger. Anwar noticed the dictionary refrigerator magnets, and went over for a closer look. He mouthed the nonsensical strings of words:

rugged-mariner-betrothed-never

corrupt-curmudgeon-lover-escape

"No need to stand, Anwar," said Ramona. "Please sit at the table."

He sat at the little table for two. Ms. Espinal wasn't hosting a dinner party anytime soon—the table was littered with Mexican pesos; postcards from San Juan and Lagos; a tiny red, black, and green flag; coffee rings and a half-drunk bottle of red wine.

"Mal-bec," he mouthed. He wanted to have a taste. He was a smoker these days, and hadn't had a sip of wine since Charu was a young child.

Ramona pulled out a checkbook from the clutter and wrote, *Eight hundred and fifty dollars and no cents*. They could have easily charged a thousand or more for the location and condition of the apartment in their neighborhood, but he suspected the quality of the person went down as the rent went up.

"Here you are," she said, tearing along the perforated line.

At that moment, the downstairs doorbell rang. Two seconds later, a loud pounding on the front door.

"Shit, it's my brother," said Anwar.

"Not the most patient dude, huh?"

"Definitely not."

Anwar opened the front door. "You've got just one bag, bhai?"

"Well, I don't plan on staying here forever," said Aman. He stood wearing a long-sleeve button-down shirt and slacks—his uniform—though it was ninety degrees outside. Their features were distinguishable—Aman's rounder and cherubic, Anwar's wiry and mischievous. Only their mustaches made them look like brothers.

"You'll be downstairs, here in the living room. It's not much privacy, but that's what we have," said Anwar. "Besides, Ella lives on this floor, and she's quiet as a librarian."

"In my day, a younger brother would offer his own bed," said Aman.

"We are three years apart."

"Smells in here, man."

"It does?"

"Perhaps it's just the mess."

"Brother, this is a living room, a room for *living*. You have all the amenities a man could ask for. This is an indecently comfortable corduroy sofa and reclining chair—directly staring at a big-screen television box affixed with surround sound. This carpet, woven by Turks, is lush enough to fill the spaces between your toes. Not in the mood for TV? Read anything on this coffee table: books, cloth-bound and colorful—Rand McNally's 1979 edition of *An Atlas of the*

World; *A Beginner's Book of Knots*; and the last seven issues of *Newsweek*. Goodness, man, smell the fresh flower arrangements from our garden—"

Anwar paused. He wondered how his brother could condemn slovenliness when Aman *himself* was so remarkably offensive! He reeked of an indecipherable unpleasant odor. Anwar ascribed this to a criticizing nature tinged with the misery of irritable bowels.

"How are you feeling, bhai?"

"Like I've been struck by a train car. This is very hard." Aman looked grayer, and softer, than Anwar had ever seen him. In fact, the man looked damned vulnerable. "I tell her that my business is what keeps our family together, alive. But Nidi is a stubborn woman."

"She was so serene," said Anwar. Aman had married a songstress, a woman of great classical training. He'd plucked her out of a crowd of young first-year girls at Eden College, back in Dhaka, pursuing her like mad, writing love letters and leaving roses in front of her dorm room. Instead of running from his obsession, Nidi ran headfirst into it, and now she'd had enough.

"Bah! Serene. The woman's driven me mad over the years. Just as well."

They heard a furious clanging bell from the kitchen.

"What the hell is that?" said Aman.

"Charu is announcing lunchtime."

They found Charu and Maya setting the old elm wood dining table. Anwar marveled at the spread of plates: cinnamon and sugar French toast adorned with berries, scrambled eggs with greens straight from the garden. His mouth quivered. When had this happened? His daughter appeared thoroughly demure and Anwar loved this temporary shift in her character. Watching her quelled his annoyance at his brother's *negativo* vibe.

As Charu garnished the French toast with powdered sugar, she reminded Anwar of his childhood maid Hawa. She had served him lunch with a tacit smile—she was young enough to be his sister, and their father raised her as lovingly as one would raise a servant, without trespassing the bounds of class—she was performing her duty; her performance gave her pleasure. With their mother dead after

Anwar's birth, they'd had a few girls take care of Aman and Anwar as babies. Hawa lasted longer than any others he could remember. But one day, she ran away and never returned. A few years later, Anwar had heard that Hawa was still alive, living in a different border town, Jaflong, in Sylhet. Their father had died soon after the girl's departure, perhaps of a broken heart.

Anwar noticed his brother straighten a folded napkin fallen on its side, appraising the girls' work, as if they were servers in a restaurant. He shook his head at Aman's perpetual obsession with order. It struck Anwar how little a person changed in half a century. He imagined Nidi had grown tired of Aman, a mean-spirited curmudgeon at best. After twenty-plus years together, it was his unhealthy want for control. As a boy, Aman had been skinny, jaundiced, and bitter as a stalk of young sugarcane. He'd been a miniature adult as young as ten, adept at farming and raising chickens and goats, but also excelling in sports and studies. The person he cared to impress was their father, a self-absorbed anthropologist who was oblivious to the violent changes happening in their country. Aman assisted their father with small tasks, filing and chronologically labeling the artifacts. The elder Saleem encouraged his son to pursue studies in archaeology, but Aman dreamt of wealth. When it was evident the old man would die, Aman left Jessore forever to attend Dhaka University, and Anwar followed him to university in 1969, the year he first met Rezwan. While Aman became a pharmacist, Anwar found himself more and more entangled in the country's politics. Aman kept his distance from Anwar, Rezwan, and their rabble-rousing comrades, keeping to his books and nursing his obsessive desire for Nidi.

As they neared middle age—Aman had turned fifty-five in early April; Anwar celebrated his fifty-second birthday in late April—Anwar realized that his brother's troubled nature had not found peace with age. Those old rages lay dormant inside the unreachable parts of his heart.

"Anwar, you don't care that she dresses like that?" said Aman, glancing at Charu.

"I think she looks quite nice," said Anwar. He looked over Charu's dress. She revealed just her shoulders and slim calves. Everything else worth covering seemed to be covered.

"My darling, you should not dress this way at home," said Aman, wagging a finger at Charu. "It's not very—modest."

"Well, I'm sure as hell not wearing this *outside* of my home," said Charu.

"Be careful, brother. Girls are not easy," Aman said. He smiled at Maya, who had not said a word, as she filled glasses of water.

"Now, now—Aman, it's harmless. Besides, I don't bite the hand that feeds me," Anwar joked. Dealing with Aman required different levels of patience, ranging from the empathy of a masseur to the scorn of a correction officer. Anwar stood up and twirled Charu around, as if they were waltzing. As they twirled about, he noticed Charu's friend Maya staring at them. Something genuine, something lost, about this girl. Her look touched him. Her eyes darted between Charu and Anwar, then away from Aman.

Anwar reached his arm to her and said, "May I have your hand, dear Maya?"

The girl looked at Charu, who sashayed aside and nudged her friend toward him. Maya swallowed a deep breath. Her fingers were cool and trembling—perhaps from cutting vegetables, or maybe it was her natural condition; Anwar didn't know—but he steadied the child with his own warm hands. She veiled herself in hijab. She was plain at first, but was fresh-faced and unmarred, a graceful bend in her nose, eyes brown as coffee grounds—

Maya flinched as he swung her once around.

"Don't be afraid, child. My brother has a pagan's heart." Aman shook his head.

"I'm not afraid," said Maya.

Anwar felt dizzy and certain he'd lightened the young girl's mood—he so missed the days when happiness was effortless.

"Arré! I remember you from the masjid, a few Fridays ago," said Aman, snapping his fingers. "You . . . you are the daughter of Sallah S., no?"

The girl clenched Anwar's fingers, and then let them go. Sallah S.? The owner of A Holy Bookstore?

Maya did not answer Aman. She glanced at Charu.

"Where the *fuck* is Ma and Ella?"

"Charu!" Anwar scolded her along with his brother, and stopped himself, surprised at their unison more than Charu's vulgarity.

"What a household you run here, Anwar," said Aman. He sighed and sat down at the table, leaning back as if waiting to be served. "Learn a thing from your friend, Charu."

Anwar cleared his throat to admonish Charu further. Before he could say a word, he heard footsteps in the living room. Hashi's strut was aggressive, but then he heard another. Anwar stopped to listen. There was something extraordinary about Ella's gait, a distinctive poise and purpose.

"My god," Anwar whispered. He did not hear Charu's expletives of disbelief.

Ella, at six feet, was a couple of inches taller than her parents, who had been gargantuan by Bangladeshi standards. Her messy hair was gone—instead, she had a short hairdo, manly yet much more suited to her. She emanated the same reckless sensuality and cleverness that her father had possessed. Anwar was beside himself with a strange pride. It was in that moment he decided that one day, everything he had would belong to her. She was not a son, but she was the closest thing he had to one. Ella could preserve this prosperous and fertile house he had built.

Anwar smiled. As usual, Ella did not seem to be expecting anything from him and said nothing.

"Shall we eat?" he finally said, patting her shoulder.

Ella appeared at ease. She half-smiled at Anwar. "Yes," she said.

They savored Charu's lunch in silence. Anwar watched everyone at his table. Hashi looked at their daughters with pride, and he felt the old marvelous suffocation of being in love. He even appreciated his brother, who ate with the rapidity of the very poor or imprisoned and shot disgusted looks all around, except at Maya, who chewed her food as if she wanted to savor every bite. Anwar took everything in: *We are quite a perfect flower, constructed of both male and female parts—I must write this down.* He grabbed a pen from his pocket and scribbled his musings on a paper napkin, looking up to see Charu and Ella sharing a grin, Hashi staring at him with a sweet look, Aman plagued by his eternal seclusion. Maya nodded at Anwar, as if sensing his feelings. He wiped the corners of his eyes with the tissue. The ink bled, blurring his notes.

6

Some said the backyard in 111 Cambridge Place had been a makeshift graveyard for the souls who overdosed on its grounds. The most popular tale was about a young boarder back in the seventies, born and raised minutes away, who grew up to be a jaded revolutionary, losing his way after his friends were imprisoned or started using. He belonged to the latter lot, but did not die during his binges. Instead, after a brilliant recovery from cocaine-induced cardiac arrest, the young man awoke in the hospital, feeling alive and refreshed. His brain had swelled up to twice its size and then shrunk back down. A miracle, said the doctors. But the young man had inherited a new affliction of the brain. You could show him a flashlight, a pencil, or crack rock, and he could tell you what inanimate objects were. But he could no longer tell the difference between a rose or a radish or a puppy. He'd lost his sense of the living world.

When Ella first heard the story back in fifth grade, she'd been sure the young man had gone mad with confusion, unable to decipher whether to smell or eat or love something. Sometimes she thought that if the man had lost the ability to tell living things apart, his old relationships (to his dealer, his lovers, his friends) would have faded.

Then he would have no longer been haunted by his desires. It could be considered a blessing.

Ella broke soil with her shovel, scared of uncovering bones, though she knew everything had been upturned years ago during the renovations. It was three in the morning, three weeks after she'd arrived home for the summer. Insomnia worsened with the constant nightly presence of the sleeping girl, Maya, who had politely offered to sleep on the floor. Ella told Maya she didn't mind sleeping outdoors, and slept on the hammock unless it rained. She hardly saw the girl anyway. Maya spent her days working and returned very late at night, only to sleep. Ella let her in through the sliding door in the kitchen. If her aunt and uncle were aware of the girl's presence, they did not say anything to her or Charu.

Since returning home, Ella noticed just how preoccupied Hashi and Anwar always seemed to be. Her aunt lived in her salon, busy with summer weddings and beauty regimens; her uncle spent the brunt of the day in the apothecary and his nights upstairs in his studio, busy cooking up products and smoking pot, the smell of which wafted outside the attic window, straight into the backyard. He'd asked her if she wanted to spend some days working at the apothecary, but she declined.

As the rest of her family made their way to bed, Ella lay outside on the jute rope hammock tied between the hibiscus trees. First, Hashi and Anwar's light went off, around midnight, and then Charu's, an hour later. There had been no visits after Malik's spill out of the tree, and Ella suspected the kid had been scared out of his wits. It all made for a very moody and short-tempered Charu, who had graduated from Brooklyn Tech and was now busy meeting up with school friends Ella didn't know. At night, Charu kept to herself in her room, sewing her "independent" clothing line and blasting music until Hashi yelled at her to quiet down.

Around two thirty, Aman's late-night television marathons dwindled, and Ella found some peace. Their uncle's night-owlish ways would make it hard for Malik to enter undetected, as Aman took frequent smoke breaks in the garden. Malik wouldn't risk it now, since he was Aman's employee.

Just as everyone's lights turned off, their tenant Ramona Espinal's blinked on, enough for Ella to make out her silhouette in the window.

Ella dug a compost hole deep enough to fill with scraps from dinner and peat moss. Their garden was built in a circle. Anwar had first envisioned the garden as a compass. He'd built a wooden shed on the eastern side of the circular garden. Jutting out of this shed were birdhouses, drawing a menagerie of kestrels, meadowlarks, sparrows, bluebirds, and scarlet tanagers (a rare treat) for water and seed. He believed his compass became a vital hub in the birds' migrations. Like an old-world astronomer, he placed a tiny magnetic needle in each water tray.

Inside the shed was a walk-in refrigerated vault lined with drawers holding hundreds of seed packets, resembling the card catalog in a library. Her uncle's preoccupation with conspiracies had taken on a life of their own after her parents' murder. It was a miserable period in his life, when he believed apocalyptic demise loomed around the corner. Depressed and mourning, Anwar stocked up on seeds, preparing for the end of days, fancying himself a builder of a botanical ark. By the time Ella arrived in the States, Anwar had already collected two hundred heirloom seeds.

Before Ella had left for her sophomore year, she and Anwar devised a plan to build a Linnaean flower clock. You could tell time according to blooming patterns, as different flowers opened and closed at different hours of the day. Sunflowers towered happily in the center, constant and uninformative as far as telling time was concerned. Anwar had planted morning glories, field milk thistle, white water lilies, and garden lettuce. All of these would bloom between five and seven in the morning. That's about as far as he had gotten with the clock. Aphids collected on the cerulean morning glory blooms. The tiny pests oozed clear pellets of shit all along the petals and stems. Luckily, Ella was prepared to fight the buggers, a common summertime pest in their garden. She'd ordered a batch of butterfly larvae from her university entomology department. *Madeleinea lolita*, a natural enemy of aphids. The species' blue hue matched that of morning glories, its name drawn from its discoverer, Nabokov. Ella had reread *Lolita* a dozen times last year. It was assigned in her sophomore literature elective, Monomania in Modern Literature.

Ella slipped on a pair of latex gloves and removed the larvae from a brown paper bag. She planted the tiny sleeping nuggets into the ground, as a small prayer. One day, they would metamorphose, escape into the world as something altogether different. They would eat away at the pests that plagued the nascent blossoms. Ella covered the larvae with topsoil, and mixed in some green clover manure. It seemed fitting: The garden clock was a disheartening example of letting an idea turn to shit. Ella packed the earth with her hands. Night gardening made her feel light and heavy, all at once. She was sick of sleeping when everyone worked, lived, loved.

The full moon struck whitish flowers with an eerie beauty. Night blooms—that's what Ella would plant. She fetched seeds from the vault and set them down in dirt, wondering if they resembled the packet pictures. She planted evening primrose, night phlox, and the papery white moonflowers: night-blooming cereus, flowering tobacco, *Datura inoxia*. Jasmine, Anwar's favorite, lined their fence, far enough away to not compete. On each packet was a file tab sticker tagged with Anwar's loopy handwriting, notes on each variety:

> Datura inoxia. Sacred to the Aztecs (toloatzin),
>
> Smoke leaves and flowers for asthma (Ayurveda).
>
> Chosen hallucinogen of thuggees.
>
> All parts are poison.

The mash of lentils and soil and cucumber peel flooded her nostrils, and she removed the gloves to feel the earthy mixture ooze between her fingers. She gave the seedlings a gentle hosing and flushed her hands clean of muck. In her sweaty white T-shirt, Ella lay on the hammock and swung from side to side to make a breeze. Her brain refused to turn off, afraid that the stillness would encourage forbidden thoughts.

She pulled her father's glasses from her jeans pocket. It was silly, wearing these. She'd bought new copycat frames—tinted gray aviators—with her prescription, since his overcorrected her vision. But she soon realized that wearing Rezwan's frames provoked her hallucinations. This had happened half a dozen times since Ella's makeover. She thought about how Charu had embraced her, teary-eyed, with an ecstatic "Now we *have* to go shopping, El!" And true to her word, Charu bought her tailored slacks and shirts from Fulton Mall, and even made her a shirt based on one of their purchases. Ella hadn't even gone with her, but all the clothes fit perfectly.

Ella looked at the garden, everything heightened by her father's glasses. Four Benadryls, or sleeping candy, as Charu called it, didn't work. She yearned for company, for someone to talk to, but there was no one she could think to call.

A beeping sound came from her bedroom window. She switched back to her own glasses and went inside to investigate.

She slid open the door and tiptoed through the kitchen and living room, trying not to creak the floorboards. She went into her bedroom. The alarm clock read quarter past six. The beeping had stopped. She cracked her bedroom door open and saw Maya whispering her prayers, knelt in prostration. Remarkable, how Maya set her alarm for so early. As Ella took a step backward, she heard:

"Ella?"

"Don't let me interrupt you."

"No, wait. I'm almost done. This is the part you ask for stuff."

Ella waited for her to finish. After a few more whispery requests, Maya turned her head to the left, then the right, then clasped her hands once more. As she rose up her knees popped like bubble wrap, and she laughed.

"Eighteen going on eighty," said Maya.

"I'm going back outside."

"Can I come?"

"Uh . . ."

"I'll take that as a yes."

"So this is what you spend your nights doing?" Maya shook her head at the mess of soil, flowers, empty packets of seed, and puddles of hose water on the patio tiles.

"I've got something of a sleeping problem."

"A summer job might help with that," said Maya. "I still can't believe Charu and you aren't working."

"I should be helping out Anwar, but I haven't been . . . in the mood. Is that what you do during the day?"

"Yeah, I work over by Fulton Mall, at Finish Line, the sneaker store. Now I've got an outrageous collection of kicks." She lifted up a foot—they were polka-dot Nike Air Force 1s, but that was about as much as Ella knew about sneakers.

"Shouldn't you be asleep if you have work?"

"Today, your sister and I are taking a beach day. Haven't been once this summer. You should come."

"I'm not a beach person. Not a water person at all, in fact," said Ella.

"Then just sit on the sand."

Long, wispy leaves budding with tiny purple flowers burst out of a crack in the tiles. Ella looked closer. It was a mugwort infestation. "Since you're awake, grab a shovel and shears," she said, kneeling on the ground in front of the weedy overgrowth. "Loosen the base with the shovel, then pull, pull, pull." She demonstrated but the mugwort stem broke in her hand. "Sometimes . . . it takes more . . . effort," she grunted, yanking harder and falling back on her rear. "Then, just shear it as close to the root as possible."

"What is it?"

"It's called mugwort. These little purple yellow flowers are pretty, but too much of it isn't. You'd be surprised; if you press oil out of mugwort, you get a pretty good herbal remedy for anxiety, cramps. If you let it simmer in ninety-proof vodka, it makes a tonic. It's got thujone in it, same chemical compound as absinthe," said Ella. "It's good toxic, psychotropic toxic."

"You get drunk?"

"Not really. Sometimes."

Maya grabbed the shovel from Ella and thrust it into the ground, loosening the mugwort from the tile. She did this a few more times, squatting as she did so. "It's not as easy as it looks, but it's all in the legs," she said, snipping the mugwort free. She glanced at Ella. "You could do this all day, huh?"

"Yes, I think so."

Above them the sky lightened to a more luminous gray and they resembled gravediggers, undiscovered in the morning, uprooting weeds that collected at their bare feet. Neighborhood sounds broke the silence between them—the halt and screech of sanitation trucks and whistling workers, dogs shuffling with their walkers, bodega gates grinding upward and open to commuters, who, with morning coffee in hand, disappeared underground onto the rumbling trains. Maya wiped her brow and peeled her veil, using it to wipe sweat from her neck. One minute pious, the next a regular girl—Ella caught herself staring.

"Your eyes have glazed over," said Maya, noticing that Ella had stopped digging alongside her. "Time for you to get some rest."

"What about you?"

"You've got all those books in your room. I'll keep myself busy."

Ella nodded and folded her glasses, tucking them into her shirt.

She went to lie on her hammock and didn't wake up until noon, when she heard Charu's voice:

"Yes, the *beach*! I've been, like, *twice* this summer. Let's go to Brighton Beach! Sexy Russian dudes who might be gay or just Russian. Pierogies and sour cream!"

Ella could make out Charu and Maya sitting on canvas lawn chairs across the backyard, and from the splash of color on bare skin, it looked like they were wearing bathing suits.

"More like Russian mafia," said Maya.

"We could ride down Bedford," called out Ella.

"She shows a rare display of spontaneity!" yelled Charu. "Good!"

"Let's go to Riis beach," suggested Maya. "It's less crowded and less Russian."

"What's your issue with Russians?" asked Charu. "What'd they ever do to you?"

"Rather than get undressed with someone's eyes, don't you like the idea of being naked on the beach?" said Maya. "Nice and private and naked?"

"No," Ella said, just as Charu said, "Hell *yes*!"

To get provisions for their trip, they made a pit stop at the corner bodega, the famously misspelled 24 Ours and Co. The yellow, weather-torn awning was a familiar landmark in the neighborhood. They walked past a group of boys straddling bikes, leaning against the wall. Two of them muttered, "Damn, girl," in unison at Charu. She'd waited to turn the corner from their house to slip off her jeans, and now she sported a miniskirt. Inside the bodega, two cats lazed near the cold drinks, a motherly calico and a cross-eyed albino kitten. They were the feline watchkeepers of the obese shopkeeper, who was arguing with a teenage girl holding a bag of plantain chips and a peach iced tea.

"Mister, I told you I wanted a brown bag, not one of them black plastic joints!" The girl shook her head; the plastic beads tied to the end of her cornrows rattled.

"No!" the man yelled from behind a plexiglass counter. He noticed Maya and lifted a tobacco-yellowed finger, wagging it like a schoolteacher. "One dollar," he said.

"Give her a brown bag, first," said Maya.

"Fine, fine," said the man.

"Thank *you*, miss," said the girl, as she walked out.

Maya picked up a large bag of spicy corn chips, a couple of rolls, and sliced ham.

"You eat ham?" asked Ella.

"My first babysitter was a Puerto Rican girl. I begged her to let me eat ham and cheese sandwiches and one day, she finally did," said Maya, chuckling.

"I just started eating pepperoni last year and now I'm addicted," said Charu.

"You gonna eat this? Ain't you a Muslim?" asked the man.

"Yup," said Maya, pulling out a twenty.

A bike ride from 111 Cambridge Place to Riis beach was a thirteen mile adventure. Ella wasn't one for beaches; she was never sure of what to wear. Bikinis, never. One-piece bathing suits were unforgiving and uncomfortable. She could have finished the ride in forty minutes, but between Charu's bicycle (a Wicked Witch of the West–style cruiser; there was no speeding on that thing), and the monster camping backpack Charu had her carrying, Ella found herself at the end of their cycling line. The backpack was stuffed with a sheet Charu had patched together from old T-shirts, the ham and chips and soda, Ella's boom box and soccer ball, sunscreen, and a change of clothing for when they came home that night. They rode behind Maya, who had made trips to this beach before. Her hijab sailed behind her like a kite, as if she might levitate. The three of them coasted down Ocean Avenue, then turned onto Flatbush Avenue, until they crossed the rickety bridge into the state park. On the boardwalk they hopped off their bikes, and walked down to the beach. Maya stopped a few feet away from the wet sand. "Here's good," she said, spreading Charu's patchwork sheet.

Ella hurled the backpack onto one corner of the sheet and used her soccer ball and boom box to hold down opposite corners. She took a seat by the boom box. The sound of waves crashing matched Ella's mood and she took off her glasses to see the world enveloped in streaks of black and white. She stretched her legs and tipped the ball toward the water.

Charu yelled, "I'll get it!" She caught the ball from a wave and threw it back to the shore. She jumped into the water and whooped with delight.

Maya gestured to the sheet. "Call me crazy, but I don't mind staying right where we are." She broke open the bag of chips, and they crunched together, watching the silver waves, as Charu's bikini top slipped off.

Charu stood up in the water, searching for her top.

"She thinks it's okay to be topless?" said Ella, smirking.

"Yeah. It's the gay beach. No one cares at the gay beach."

Ella looked around for more naked people—there was a group of men kicking a soccer ball. Four of them wore Speedos, and one renegade was completely naked. His dick looked like a shriveled hot dog. All of them were lean, muscular, and brown. Their bare chests glistened with sunscreen and sweat. Ella watched their thick calves as they kicked around the soccer ball. Their backs were as wide as the expanse of a harp. These men roused her. She wasn't attracted to them, exactly. But she was drawn to the way they moved, their bodies.

Ella wished she could join them.

"Yo—you guys! The water isn't even cold!" shouted Charu.

"Liar!" said Ella.

"As gorgeous as you are, we're fine over here," said Maya.

"C'mon!"

Maya stood up. She removed the dressmaker pins that kept her hijab in place. She spread the fabric open on the beach blanket. She took off her clothes, revealing a sports bra and boy shorts. "Shall we?"

"I don't know," said Ella. "I told you I'm not a water person. I can't swim. I didn't bring clothes either."

"So you're earthbound. But I'll bet after carrying that backpack, you gave yourself heatstroke. So get over it and let's go."

Maya started running toward the waves, as Charu ventured deeper to swim. Ella remembered her swimming class failure at the Metropolitan pool in Williamsburg back in fourth grade. Little Charu had learned with no inhibitions or fears in the water, but Ella had felt shy in front of the swimming instructor, a pretty high school student named Beatrice. Anytime Beatrice tried to encourage her to transform her dog paddle into a freestyle stroke, Ella froze from embarrassment. She was still afraid of the water. Maya waited for her, the water up to their shins.

"Come closer to me, guys; the waves are incredible!" called Charu.

"I think we're good here!" Maya replied, cupping her hands around her mouth. Charu shrugged and dove under a wave.

"Let's just sit here," said Maya.

"In the waves?"

"Right at the edge of them."

Maya lay belly down on the crashing point. Her fingers raked the sand, holding her in place. Ella copied her and felt a large wave crash on her backside. She tried to sit but was taken down by another crashing wave. After a few more attempts, she propped herself up. Maya rolled onto her back. Ella watched Maya's skin tinged golden in the sunlight. Her top was covered in sand, nipples hardened and getting browner as her top soaked through. She had an Arabic tattoo etched on her left rib.

"What's your tattoo say?"

"'The hour has come near / the moon is split in two / they see a miracle / they turn away and say / it is passing magic.' Lines from *Surah al-Qamar*."

"I thought Muslims weren't allowed to get tattoos."

"Can't think of anything more godly than tattooing God's words on myself," said Maya. "But you're right. Too late."

"Then why cover your hair?"

"To distract my father's attention, at first. Now it's habit. What about you? Charu told me you came to New York when you were just a kid?"

"Yeah. So I never developed the hydrophilia of my river and ocean people. Left Bangladesh too early," said Ella. "I was five. A couple years after my parents died."

"I'm sorry."

"I remember a bit here and there. It's hard to miss them. I want to."

"Sometimes your folks are gone when they're right there," said Maya. "My folks are Moroccan and Egyptian. My mom's folks didn't want her marrying a Moroccan. They worried he would be too secular. Sure as hell didn't have to worry about that."

"Have you always lived upstairs from Anwar's store?"

"We used to live out by Coney Island when I was real small. Moved to Atlantic around first grade. My father got a job as a line cook at Chez Marcel, until he decided he'd had enough of the booze and sluts. His words, not mine. He generally thinks he's better than everyone else. And that's when A Holy Bookstore was born," said Maya. "My mema has been sick forever. She just got diagnosed with lupus last month."

"But she's there, with you, alive. Do you have to take care of her?"

"Not really." Maya sat up. A large wave crashed on their backs. "The water's not so bad now, is it? Blanket time?"

Ella made sandwiches, while Maya pulled *Kunstformen der Natur*, a stick of charcoal, and a sketch pad out of her backpack. "I hope you don't mind," she said, "but I'm still borrowing your book for some drawings I'm working on."

"I don't mind," Ella said. She had a similar relationship with the book. She'd kept it until it was several months overdue. The library fine had gone up to ninety dollars, the maximum amount before they made students buy the book. She ended up paying twenty-five to keep it. One hundred art nouveau lithographs, designed by biologist and artist Ernst Haeckel, intricately rendered new species handpicked for feature in his book. Ella was drawn to the strange illustrations of medusae. Each jellyfish took on the likeness of hair or fine jewelry; the trilobites appeared as masked knights fitted for battle. It was a matter of arrangement, yes, in that each plate was assembled in such a way that you were drawn to the symmetry. There was no reference to the environment where these creatures lived. Their innate form spoke for itself. Whether it was in the pattern, grooves, tentacles, needles, leaves, or antlers—there was an undeniable beauty, no matter how grotesque.

Maya stopped drawing and set down her sketch pad, lying back on the sheet. She gestured for Ella to join her. A couple of rogue gulls zoomed down toward them, and Maya yelped. They missed her head by a foot, busy scavenging other vacationers' leftovers.

Ella saw the orange sunset through her closed eyelids. She opened her eyes and watched the sun turn blood orange, then neon green. As dusk crept in, the ocean shifted between a violent inkwell and a bubble bath, back and forth, back and forth. When Maya stepped aside for maghrib namaz, using a beach towel as a prayer rug, Ella put her glasses back on. She held her breath during Maya's prostrations, thankful for this respite from her solitude.

Charu sauntered back to them. She pulled aside her bikini strap and pointed to her marked tan. "Shit, I got crispy!"

Maya laughed. "Think your mom will notice?"

"She gets paid to notice. Guys, I'm sta-a-arving."

"Let's—get a slice or something?" asked Ella.

That day marked the beginning of their cycling excursions all over the city. The three of them spent the heart of the summer together. On days Maya had off from work: teatime and concerts in Prospect Park, watching the sunset along the East River in Williamsburg, eating dim sum at Jing Fong in Chinatown, wandering through exhibits at Brooklyn Museum. They were outsiders, the three of them, uniquely aware of themselves against the world.

7

Mid-July rains made for many a quiet afternoon on Atlantic Avenue. It was a Friday, and many of the shops closed early for prayers. Anwar had not yet had a single customer at the apothecary. Outside, a car skidded to a halt. The squeal of its tires broke the steady melancholy of rainfall, and he heard the wind chime tinkling on the door. He looked up. Nobody was there. He was expecting an after-hours customer, his friend Bic Gnarls, owner of the barbershop Bic's Razor, on Fulton Street. Whenever Bic came by the shop, he stayed for a spell. Anwar could never guess his age—he could be anywhere between thirty-five and fifty-five, though he suspected Bic was closer to the latter, for the gravel in his voice revealed years of smoke. His hair resembled a high hedge, squared on top, and he sported a single hoop in his ear. He had a fondness for windbreakers. Bic was a loyal customer to Rashaud Persaud, the Guyanese hawker who had a table down the block from the apothecary but made most of his cash by dealing weed. Bic swore by Rashaud, claiming a lack of potency in other dealers' strains.

Anwar fiddled around on the computer while he waited for Bic. The Internet connection was so slow. He cranked up the radio to fill the empty space. Everything in life was so—slow. He barely saw the girls. Was this the onset of an empty nest? They were always out and about on their bicycles—a healthy pastime, sure, but he worried about accidents. When they weren't outside, Charu stayed in her room. He heard intermittent sounds of sewing or crying. Both concerned him. And Ella's return had been unspectacular and disappointing. College days should be the most carefree of days, though war had marred his own time at university. He did not know how to reach Ella, how to communicate his love to her. She was lost in the garden, up at all hours of the night. Perhaps Anwar should join her. After all, they had built it together. And Hashi—she had thrown herself into the innumerable summer weddings. His wife's first words to him this morning: *Aman Bhai has to leave as soon as possible.* His brother's subtle complaints, late-night television addiction, picky eating habits, and general carping wore Hashi's nerves, and she wanted him out.

Anwar understood her aggravation. But to tell his brother to leave would be a hassle best avoided. So he did the next best thing:

I am a thief, he thought, gazing at the stolen credit card that lay on the counter.

On the back of the card, in unsightly chicken scratch, he'd written: Aman Saleem. His brother's mail, rerouted to their home, consisted of credit card applications and divorce matters. Anwar had scribbled his brother's signature, mailed in the application, and begun his online perusing of his Web favorites: Café THC and Mary Jane's Joint and Topless in Tokyo. Bless this method of discovery, one type-click, which was changing everything; in the online stores countless varieties existed.

Anwar ordered northern lights seeds from Mary Jane's Joint. They would deliver to his new P.O. box in discreet packaging—bubba kush, purple haze, bubba haze, purple kush, blueberry bud, god bud, northern lights, Durban poison, skunk red hair, turtle power, island lady, snow white, wonder woman, white widow, happy outdoors, early sativa, early indica, early girl, early bird special . . .

He paid for his purchase using his new credit card.

Money had been on his mind, and so had space. Personal space. Sure, he had the studio, but he wanted some real privacy. Purchasing the occasional pornographic film (perhaps *film* was a stretch) was too tricky in his girl-ridden home. He had also toyed with growing his own crop of marijuana. There were so many varieties he'd never accessed. *Those lucky Californians,* thought Anwar. Charu's upcoming NYU tuition was a gut-wrenching thirty thousand, even with financial aid; Ella had gotten lucky with Ivy League cred at a state school's public price.

The door chimed, and Bic Gnarls entered. "Hey, man."

"Hi, Bic," said Anwar, hastily pocketing Aman's credit card.

"You got the stuff, brother?" asked Bic.

"Yes, of course." Anwar locked the front door and pulled down the blinds. He gestured for Bic to sit on one of the small wicker stools that matched his set at home. Anwar kept these stools for such moments. From an empty shampoo bottle, he pulled out a Ziploc bag packed with a quarter of Rashaud's freshly harvested kush. Its aroma flooded their nostrils.

"I meant the coconut body soufflé, but hey now," said Bic, laughing. He produced a magnifying glass from his pocket and pulled a nugget of kush from the bag. "This some potent shit. Where's Rashaud at?"

"Good shit," said Anwar. "I don't know, but he should be here any moment."

There was a tinkling of the door chime, someone trying to get in. Anwar stuffed the Ziploc bag back into the shampoo bottle and peeked through the blinds. Rashaud Persaud stood soaking in the rain, smoking a cigarette. He wore a black plastic trash bag as a makeshift rain parka, with a hole cut out for his head to slip through.

"Anwah, I thought I'd try and catch ya before ya left," said Rashaud, stomping his sneakers on the doormat. He sucked his cigarette down to the filter and flicked it onto the sidewalk, before stepping inside. "Been mighty slow out there today." He nodded at Bic. "Hey now, Bic, nice seein' ya."

"Nice raincoat," said Anwar.

Rashaud nodded and looked down, embarrassed. "Mine got stolen."

"At your table in the rain?" asked Anwar, incredulous. "What petty person—"

"Naw, naw. Over the weekend. At a . . . party," said Rashaud. He sat next to Bic on the other little stool. They looked like grown men throwing a tea party.

"Sorry about the coat," said Bic.

"Remember what you call this, Anwah?" Rashaud asked mischievously, pulling out a plastic-wrapped cigar.

"What've you got there, son?" asked Bic.

"Ah, yes, a blunt," said Anwar. "I still do not know how to wrap one."

Rashaud said, "Mr. Anwah, may I?"

"Gentlemen, we are now officially closed," said Anwar.

As Rashaud stripped the tobacco from the skin onto the countertop, Bic and Anwar watched, like children waiting for the first slice of a birthday cake. He crumbled the nugget of kush with his fingers and mixed the purple-green leaves with a sprinkle of tobacco, then ran his tongue on the reassembled cigar to seal the contents. He licked the casing lovingly.

"That's right," murmured Bic.

"You first," said Rashaud to Anwar.

"No, no, please," said Anwar, gesturing to Bic.

Bic slipped a lighter out of his pocket and sparked a flame, running it over the body of the cigar. He held the fire over the tip. He chuckled and said, "Funny enough, though, this ain't a Bic. I upgraded to Zippo."

"Bic's your real name?" asked Rashaud.

"No, it's Earl. I got Bic for running an operation selling lighters, razors, and pens at a dollar apiece. Shame, but I used to buy them wholesale by the carton from this Korean guy in Flushing. The name stuck because of my skills with a razor. I'd never use a Bic on a man's face, though." He laughed and took a long drag. "Got some business that might help you out some, Anwar. Told an actor about your little shop. He should be coming by tomorrow."

"Oh my goodness. Who?" asked Anwar.

Bic pulled out a Polaroid. "You know this guy?"

Anwar recognized the actor, shorter than Bic, with dashing Hollywood looks. But he couldn't place the name.

Rashaud leaned in closer, and blurted, "Blair Underwood?"

"Heard I got the best shave in Brooklyn."

"Nice job, Bic," said Anwar.

"So I recommended your jojoba shampoo," said Bic. "He's got an oily-ass scalp."

"So you standin' next to Mister Underwood . . ." said Rashaud, tapping his fingers along the glass counter. His nails made a rapping sound, like a secretary's on a keyboard. Anwar noticed that his pinky fingers were painted in shiny red polish, and curiously long. "Blair Underwood was in *Deep Impact* with Mister Morgan Freeman who was in that movie *Seven*—oh tha' shit was scary as hell, you know, 'specially the part when the wife's head is in the box—he was in that with Mister Brad Pitt," said Rashaud, ticking off the actors on his fingers, "who was the lawyer in *Sleepers* with Mister Kevin Bacon."

Said Bic, "Maybe being taped on my surveillance camera footage with Underwood—"

"Proves that we are all connected to Mister Bacon?" suggested Anwar.

They laughed, and Bic laughed deep from his belly, so hard he began coughing.

Just then, there was a knock on the door, and Rashaud froze, mid-pass.

"Who is it?" called Anwar.

"It's Malik, sir."

Anwar's mouth was cottony and dry. What did the boy want at this hour? Wasn't he supposed to be at work?

"I told my nephew to meet me here," said Bic.

"Malik is your nephew?" asked Anwar.

"His mom is my girlfriend from high school. Well, she was in high school," said Bic.

Anwar felt his tongue heavy in his mouth, struck by a strange sensation, reminiscent of his first days in the infantry, when he'd not had any friends until he met Rezwan. Friendships lacking the basic exchange of intimacies were commonplace until some tragedy struck—the death of a comrade, a miscarriage, a divorce—then men opened up. He was disturbed by his total ignorance of the connection between his daughter's boyfriend and his most loyal customer.

"He knows about . . . about this?" said Anwar, holding up the last nub of brown paper, which burned his fingers.

"Malik's cool," said Rashaud. "He gets his stuff from me."

"He's a kid," said Anwar. "Why would you—"

He was interrupted by another knock on the door. "Mr. Anwar? Is my uncle there?"

"Yes, yes, my boy, one moment." Anwar unlocked the door. Malik stood leaning on his skateboard. His glasses had little droplets of rain on them.

"It's nice to see you, sir."

"Come in, son. I suppose the secret is no longer."

"I w-w-won't say anything to Charu, sir." Malik crossed his fingers on his chest. He shook Bic's hand, and Bic pulled him into a tight embrace. Malik turned to Rashaud and shook his hand, then another embrace.

"Ah, it's all right," said Anwar. "How is it being a respectable employee?"

"You and your brother sure are different," said Malik.

"Everyone says as much," replied Anwar. "Anytime you would like, come for dinner, my boy. I am sure Charu would like to see you."

Malik looked down at the floor. "Sure."

"Or, whatever, please visit, anytime. *Su casa es mi casa.*"

"Other way around," said Bic.

"Oh, yes, of course."

Malik turned to Rashaud and said, "So, how's business, Rashaud?"

"Same shit—sell a record here, a trinket there. Shall we spark another?" Rashaud held another Dutch cigar, teetering on his fingers like a seesaw, this way and that, waiting for Anwar's response.

"Yes, let's." Anwar sighed, glancing at Malik, who kept his gaze on the shelves and away from him.

As Rashaud rolled another smoke, Anwar grew quiet. Malik told Bic about a band he had just formed. Anwar couldn't quite hear them. The boy's arrival had broken the synergy and flooded him with a hazy paranoia. Would the boy tell Charu? Or worse yet, had Malik invited Charu to partake? Anwar rocked himself with guilt, his daughter's innocence lost. Medicating oneself against life's troubles birthed a new bundle of troubles. He kept business strictly word-of-mouth and Bic had opened his mouth, unbeknownst to Anwar, to a boy he trusted his daughter with. The radio broke his thoughts and he cocked his head to the side, listening closer. "What is this song?"

"'Mo Money Mo Problems,'" said Malik. "It's an old Biggie Smalls track."

"By 'old' he means more than five years ago," said Bic.

"Should be *no* money, mo' problems," said Anwar, giggling. "Or no honey, no problems."

"That's right," said Bic, taking a toke, then passing it to Anwar. Bic coughed long and hard, beating at his chest, and Anwar felt his own chest constrict watching him hacking and wheezing like an old man. Bic spat into his handkerchief.

Anwar heard a loud crash coming from the apartment upstairs. It was Sallah S., the girl Maya's father, having one of his tantrums. "Sorry, my friends. It's my neighbor. He has some . . . anger management issues."

"Damn." Bic shook his head. "Too many fools with a loose fuse like that. He needs to chill the fuck out."

"Tell me 'bout it," said Rashaud. "Just lef' my house, matter of fact. Mama's gone mad. She scream just like dat man, if not worse."

"Where will you be staying now?" asked Anwar, concerned for his friend. Rashaud made decent money with his street side hustles, but was it enough to support his own apartment?

"I'll live in my grow house, I guess. Don't know yet."

"You Trini? You sound it," said Malik, blowing a thick sheet of smoke from his nose like a dragon. It was remarkable how naturally it came to the boy.

"Mama come from the Indies, born in Essequibo Guyana; Venezuelans been pilferin' the lands since God knows. My father, he Muslim and Indian, got himself two wives, and one day Mama found this out getting her nails done in a Georgetown beauty parlor. Miracle of miracles, the other woman, Irma, was getting an acrylic set, while Mama kept hers natural. Thas just how she is. I was a boy of six. Never to this day do I forget her face, all consumed with hatred for my father, for foolin' her in front of all those women in the parlor. She had a brother livin' in Flatbush, and he brought us to live with him. But Mama, she never been the same after all that; she been sinkin' and she been drinkin'. And when she drink she beat the one man she know who love her with his whole heart. Can't hit her back—she more wiry than me, and she my mother, so I wouldn't do that. Suppose I'm just another man she can't ever have," said Rashaud. "In Guyana, they say: One people, one nation, one destiny. But everything I know is split . . . in two. . . ."

"Take a puff, son, please." Anwar patted Rashaud's shoulder.

Rashaud chuckled, sounding as hollow as a laugh track. Anwar handed him the cigar.

"I hardly see mine," said Malik. "She works all the time."

"Money and women steal men's thoughts the world over," said Bic, shaking his head. "My memory's spent. All these years thinkin' on the same girl."

Anwar coughed up smoke. "My god, man, it is a common ailment, it seems."

"It's why I can't come by your house, Anwar; you know that," said Bic.

"This is why you never make our Fourth of July barbecue?"

"It is. Thank you, son," Bic said to Rashaud as he took the smoke into his lips, whistling a note outward like a faraway train. "Back in '64, I used to play in that house when I was a boy of ten, with a girl named Tasha, the only daughter of a police officer named Abraham Bright." He paused to take another toke, and looked at his ring finger, which swelled around a gold band. "Mr. Bright was a known man in the neighborhood, one of a dozen Black patrol officers in Brooklyn. He was a good man, in those days. Happy. Well-read and well liked. No easy thing, patrolling the neighborhood, streets hot, ready to ignite. Whenever a boy was killed by a policeman's hand, Abraham Bright's house suffered. Rocks and milk bottle bombs thrown, and once, an old lady's rocking chair, right through them bay windows, right when the first riot broke. Boy'd been shot up in Harlem and we all felt this remarkable indignation, even me, a kid, a gap-toothed toothpick, before I was Bic. And man, did I have a crush.

"Tasha Bright had a curl in her bangs and in her pretty lips, when she grew mad at me for discovering her in hide 'n' seek. She preferred pants to skirts against her mother's wishes. Her mother was a lady named Omalia, and she was just that, a *lady*, who met Mr. Bright when he visited his grandmother in Montgomery before he joined the police academy. They married right over at Emmanuel Church on Lafayette."

"There's more churches here than any other city in the world," said Anwar. "Everywhere you look there's a chapel of some kind."

"True. Within a block you might find a Lutheran or AME chapel, a Masonic temple, or a Rastafarian Nyabinghi. If you want to know barbecue, Anwar, Mrs. Bright's was the best I've ever had. She was slender with lips drawn and full; her last name was Sunny. Tasha had this joke that the reason her parents had married was to say it was a marriage of Bright and Sunny. But Mrs. Bright was miserable in Brooklyn. Summertime madness set her on edge. Winter crushed her spirit. The cycle of seasons to us natives ain't new; we used to it. But for Mrs. Bright it was cause for dread.

"By '67, Tasha and I had become more than playmates—we were teenagers, after all; we went from playing chase to stealing kisses in the park. Thirteen years old and *a mack*. It was the year before I started selling pens, four for a dollar. But I was foolish to think it'd last. No one knows how Mrs. Bright died. Heard she killed herself drinking an overdose of a poppy tea from flowers she grew in her garden. But when she died, Abraham Bright became distraught, disturbed. Now, in that house on Cambridge Place, light comes from all sides, and it is hotter than hell in summer."

Anwar nodded. It was true about his house. The light was wondrous.

"She died on a June morning, just days after we'd finished seventh grade. And he decided to set her up on a cot in their backyard so that he and Tasha and their neighbors could say good-bye. I remember . . . I remember seeing them flies frenzy on her. Buzzing over her eyes and mouth. I swear I smelt her skin burning.

"He didn't have her buried. Not at the Weeksville cemetery; no, he left her *outside*, for a good week, day and night, rocking in that chair, courtesy of '64's riot. Watching her ravaged by heat and maggots and butterflies."

Bic paused, noticing the embers had turned to ash in his fingers. He looked around, embarrassed for having held the cigar so long that it burned out. He shook the ash and lit the cigar once more. He dropped his voice so low that the rest of the men had to lean in to hear him.

"I saw Tasha for the last time on the day Mr. Bright was caught by his own officers. The smell of death had grown so bad that the neighbors called him in. He signed his daughter over to her aunt in Montgomery. Never saw him again. Might have gone back up to Harlem, where his brother was a policeman. Or maybe out to the

West Coast, to work in defense. Nobody knows. There was a looting of the place during the 1967 riots and all the fine old mahogany furniture, ceramic plates, Omalia's wedding jewelry and silk kerchiefs, dry beans and flour and rice, the doorknobs, the light fixtures, anything and everything was gutted from that house. And then the house slept, for a long minute. Nobody wanted to live there. No one but hustlers and whores searching for a place to hide. As folks say: *'Twas a good place to freebase*. I didn't go back there again until sometime in '75, in need of a fix, not sure what I was looking for. Got a fucking concussion tripping on a full-length mirror. I fell on the floor. Stared right into a shank shaped like the Empire State Building, covered in white residue. I was a man eye-to-eye with his own depraved soul. It was the night I met my wife."

"You married a whore?" asked Rashaud.

"Naw, man. I married the nurse who picked out the glass shrapnel from my face."

Anwar pulled out a bag of spicy corn chips and passed it around. The men grew hushed, crunching their chips.

Anwar daydreamed about the history of his home. Images flashed in his mind like skipping across channels on the television. He saw woman's corpse blackening under a hot sun. Fires and mobs justified in their anger. Abraham Bright in his policeman's uniform. Tasha, living in Atlanta with her kids, a husband, maybe. A 1970s pimp fitted in a fox-fur coat, holding a rose, a revolver, a dead girl's hand.

Anwar stared up at the paper lanterns overhead, wondering how such a simple thing, paper bent into a sphere, could be so beautiful.

"This morning I got attacked by my tenant's lover," said Anwar, breaking the silence.

Bic raised a brow. "How's that?"

"Oh, god."

"She's gorgeous," said Rashaud. "I seen her doin' laundry at Miss Hashi's, just today."

"You saw Miss Hashi today?" asked Anwar. "And Ramona?"

"This morning," said Rashaud. He traced his thin eyebrows with his fingers. "She shapes me up. I also seen that woman Ramona before at the hospital."

"You have?" It had not occurred to Anwar before to visit her at the hospital under the pretense of ailment—a brilliant idea. "Why were you there?"

"Oh you know, she work at the free sexual health clinic."

"I think I know who you talkin' about. That pretty nurse—man, I was embarrassed. That godforsaken prick in the prick," said Bic, wincing at the memory. "She's fine as they come. Why bother renting without the perks?"

"You all know Ramona?" asked Anwar. "And you are all getting tests for VD?" Going to get a VD test from her was not the way to impress her.

"Can't have that VD," said Bic. He cleared his throat and looked at Malik, who looked shyly down at his sneakers.

"Your wife?" asked Anwar. "But you took the test—?" He stopped himself and raised a hand. "Understood."

"Games change," said Bic, laughing. "Good ones, at least."

"I suppose you are right on." Anwar continued, "Anyway, Ramona likes to argue with this man, a shouting man, who I presume is her lover. This morning was the usual fight and like a terror he bolted downstairs from her apartment, jabbing me hard in the elbow, as I was locking my door, so hard that I almost fell over. From the back side the man had the figure of a wrestler, stacked and burly, and a strange long braided strip of hair down his neck." He let the last embers of ganja die in his fingers.

"Motherfucker had a rattail?" asked Bic. He looked over at Malik and shook his head. "I feel high as fuck, gentlemen, but now I must get home and cook my wife some dinner. Here you are." He handed Rashaud a wad of twenty-dollar bills.

"Gentlemen, it's been fantastic," said Anwar. He sighed with pleasure. He was content to be with these men. There was no other company he'd rather smoke ganja with (well, perhaps he could do without Malik). He felt a faint glimmer of paranoia—Bic's story about the Brights—did he live in a haunted house of some kind? He shook his head. No use thinking about it now. "Gentlemen," he said, "next time, I will make bhang."

"Sounds real *dutty*." Rashaud giggled.

"It's quite clean. It's a drink of hash, water, millet, and cinnamon and honey. The trouble is that there is no telling when the high begins and when it will stop."

They all laughed. Anwar turned off the lights in his shop and they walked outside.

Rainfall had subsided to a languorous sprinkle. Steam wafted up from Atlantic Avenue's sewers. Silhouettes of shopkeepers heaving closed their store gates. A yellow taxicab skidded across the slick road and braked hard at the traffic light. They heard the traffic signal click from orange halting hand to white running man. Ye Olde Liquor Shoppe's neon sign hissed. Without the fire between their lips, the summer evening chilled their bones. Bic hailed the taxi and the driver pulled over.

"Will you join me, Malik?" he asked, getting into the cab.

"Yes, sir," said the boy. He propped his skateboard in the backseat, getting in first. He waved good-bye to Rashaud and Anwar. "Thanks, sir. Bye, Rashaud. See you soon."

"Good night, friends, and be careful," said Bic. He got into the car, which sped off following a chain of ticking green lights, changing one after another.

"Where are you off to, Rashaud?" asked Anwar.

"Just meetin' some guys in the city."

"Will you take the train? May I walk with you?"

"Sure thing."

Anwar wanted to tell Rashaud something to hearten him, but he couldn't find his words. They walked toward Flatbush Avenue, and no one was about. Anwar felt like they were the last men on earth. *A strange idea, being stranded with another man.*

"It is always good to see you, Rashaud."

"The pleasure is mine, Mr. Anwah."

"Please, Rashaud, no more Mr. Anwar business. I have known you for years!"

"Habits don't die," said Rashaud. He leaned over and gave Anwar a hug.

Anwar hugged him back, surprised. Though hugs and hand-holding were common between men back home, he felt himself stiffen. He patted Rashaud's back one more time and said, "Home safe."

He watched his friend walk in through the glass doors of the Atlantic Avenue station, waiting until Rashaud was no longer visible. Anwar worried for his skinny friend, worried if he was taken care of. Some jackals out there were keen on hurting an innocent fellow.

It was eight o'clock. Hashi would be waiting, sitting at the dinner table, unwilling to eat without Anwar. He took a different route home that evening, longer and roundabout. He walked down Atlantic Avenue, toward the bright lights of the mall, past the auto body shop and monstrous storage facility, where the world became darker and quieter. As he crossed over to Fulton Street, partygoers emerged from the subway. A legless man zipped around in his wheelchair, in the middle of the street, paying compliments to women. Despite the new culinary developments the busiest establishment was Happy Heavens Chinese restaurant. A new Trinidadian roti shop, which made boneless fluffy chicken roti slathered in yogurt, had become a neighborhood favorite—Anwar had yet to try it. The B26 bus dropped off a few nurses who were about to begin the night shift at Woodhull. They shook their hands to fan their faces, assaulted by the muggy air after their thirty-minute air-conditioned ride. It amazed Anwar how in a few minutes you could be in a different world. South of his shop, reggae blasted from a minivan stereo and somehow the horde of women leaning on it talked fast and slow at the same time, because of the lilt in their voices. Yet, on this side of Atlantic Avenue, the store signs had none of the Caribbean neon or Arabic scrawl; instead there were Black-owned hair salons (more churches perhaps meant more barbers per capita, too) with alliterative names like Cool Kutz and Burkina Beauté, and, of course, one that strayed from conventions of naming: Bic's Razor.

Their own neighborhood, between Fort Greene and Bedford-Stuyvesant, was now considered Clinton Hill. Newcomers remained blissfully oblivious of the longtime residents who lived in prewar buildings and brownstones and housing projects nestled amid tall brick churches and storefronts.

Anwar turned left onto his block, half-expecting to see his home haunted by the Brights. But it loomed the same as it always did, alongside sister row houses, each a slight mutation of the other. On his brownstone were simple rose engravings; on his neighbor's, the head of a lion; wrought iron fences twisted into fleur-de-lis spears. Anwar sat on his stoop. The summer shower had heightened the scent of the trees on his block, and on humid nights like this, there was no place he'd rather be.

8

They celebrated Maya's golden birthday, her eighteenth, on the eighteenth of July, with a small picnic at Fort Greene Park. Despite having to witness Charu and Malik making out on a blanket for much of the afternoon, Ella was impressed at the small, devoted group who came out to celebrate with Maya. They came from wholly different parts of her life—her friends from Bushwick High School, friends from her volunteer stint at the local daycare, friends from Arabic school (where she and Charu had originally met, during Charu's failed two months of Quranic study), and Maya's ex-boyfriend, who was now gay. They'd known each other since they were in fifth grade; their mothers had been friends back in Egypt. Halim's hair was a crown of black ringlets doused in peppermint hair gel. He wore a tight black tank with an even tighter pair of acid-washed jeans. He was lying on the blanket, propped up on his elbows. His boyfriend, a silent young man in retro sunglasses named Marque, was resting his head on Halim's hip. The boy gave a faint smile, and went back to playing his Game Boy.

"We were fast friends, yeah, until I broke down during *My Own Private Idaho*, and was like, I am *so* gay," Halim told Ella, laughing. "But now, she's my wife for life." He swatted Maya's knee. "I don't see you anymore."

"Ay, I've been working. Hanging with these girls," said Maya. "Besides, you've all but disappeared with this new boy in your life."

"Sure. But things are good? I feel like I haven't talked to you since—" Halim faltered. "Sorry."

"Let's just cut this cake." Maya gave his hand a squeeze.

"Cut the cake, guys!" said Charu, coming up for air.

"Red velvet cake with cream cheese frosting?" asked Malik, following suit, lips stained hot pink.

Everyone laughed, but still Halim looked at Maya. "Just tell me you're okay."

"I'm okay," she said.

When the girls arrived at home that evening, Anwar and Hashi were still out at a dinner party on Long Island. Charu went upstairs to work on her clothing line, leaving Maya and Ella to themselves. They sat on lawn chairs in the backyard, speaking little. Speckled violet and salmon clouds filled the evening sky, and dissonant playlists escaped from backyards on Cambridge Place. While daytime had been dank and muggy, the evening air felt less thick. Ella took off her glasses, blinked a few times. Perhaps it was the shift in humidity, or the neighborhood's babble—her visions had commenced for the evening. She tried to make it stop by blinking, then shutting her eyes tight. No use.

"Are you all right?" asked Maya. "Do you have a headache or something?"

"No. I'm just having an—episode."

"What kind of episode?"

"It's weird."

"Well, if you couldn't tell by my friends today, I like weird. So try me."

"Ha. Well . . . I'm hallucinating, as we speak."

Maya smiled, and the gap in her front teeth opened wide into a river mouth, with pebbles spilling out onto the ground. "What are you seeing?"

"Shit that's nonsense. Right now there's tiny elfin creatures building a pyramid of rhododendron flowers, and the seed bank looks like it's stitched out of silk dragon kites. The sky is this portal brewing like a witch's cauldron, and shiny specks are bubbling in it."

"Wow. That's insane. How long does this last? How long has this been happening? Do you need a doctor?"

"It's been happening forever, since I came to the States."

"After your parents died."

"Yes. But I can't remember if I was dropped on my head or something. Might be lesions on my brain."

"That sounds serious as fuck. You need to see a doctor!"

"I haven't gotten an MRI yet." Even saying it out loud sounded a bit ridiculous, Ella realized. "You know, I think I'm going to do that when I get back to school."

"Maybe you should get one now?"

"I don't know, I can't explain it, but I don't want my aunt and uncle to freak—"

"You don't want to get rid of them," said Maya.

"Maybe you're right."

"Maybe there's comfort in it, seeing things no one sees. That's special, Ella Anwar. I would love to be able to see the world like you do."

"I wouldn't wish this on you. Now I won't be able to sleep all night."

"Try Benadryl?"

"Charu teach you that?"

"Ha. You know, I think she did!"

"Melatonin, sheep counting, and Benadryl all make me jittery. Back at school, I usually stay up studying, but I'm lucky just to make it on time for an afternoon class. But at least everyone in college is an insomniac. Here, all of you like to sleep and shit."

"Some of us have *jobs*."

"Sucks you have to work on Saturdays."

"Where am I going? I already got them to give me Friday off."

"How'd you manage that?"

"Religious observance. They're scared of discrimination claims, after a girl threatened one of the managers for sending her sexual e-mails and whatnot."

"That'll do it," said Ella.

"What are you seeing now?"

"Your face turned into a river mouth a few minutes ago. Now you've got neon fish jumping from one shoulder to the other."

All around them, the moon garden's blossoms had opened for the evening. They released an intoxicating brew of aromas into the backyard. Hypnotic flowering tobacco recalled packed pipes on continental voyages. Jasmine's strong notes hit their noses, punctuated by the sweetness of the yellow evening primrose.

"This one's beautiful. It's like a fallen bell," said Maya, cupping a flower in her hand. She leaned in to inhale it. "Smells like peanut butter and smoke."

Ella leaned in closer, unsure if she was seeing properly; the silvery white and violet petals turned like moonlit pinwheels. "That's an angel's trumpet. *Datura inoxia.* Maybe we should get rid of it. I don't want a stray cat or bird to eat it. It's poisonous."

"Dang," said Maya. "They look so—gentle. You know, you know a shitload about drugs."

"I'm a wizard without bad habits, I swear. It's a nightshade, like potatoes, tomatoes, and petunias. They grow anywhere—the seeds lay dormant for years in abandoned lots, timber yards, docks. It's the alkaloids that'll kill you. You stop wanting to eat, but get real thirsty. You can't pee. Your heart races out of your chest. But the Aztecs, Indians, the Oracle at Delphi, shamans and witches the world over drank its tea and smoked its leaves to see visions. Crazy-ass visions."

"Things you see all the time *and* you get to pee." Maya laughed.

"I've never thought of it that way."

Ella handed Maya a bottle of neem oil to spray the morning glory blossoms, while Ella watered the plants. *Aphids must be dead,* she thought, imagining her butterfly larvae sleeping, wrapped in their cocoons, bellies full of the pests.

"I hope this is a fun way to end your birthday," said Ella.

"This was the best. It *is* the best. It was so good to see everyone."

"Halim's sweet."

"He is. He's done a lot for me."

"Like what?"

"Things no one should have to do."

Ella nodded, but did not want to pry. This happened often. Maya would offer a bit of information, then end the conversation, matter-of-fact, with a note of finality. Ella would be unable to pry further or think of something clever to throw back at her, so she would say nothing, until Maya spoke again.

Evening became night, and eventually, Maya dozed off in the lawn chair. Ella covered her with an old Mexican wool blanket, a Christmas gift from Ramona Espinal.

"Want to come inside?" asked Ella.

"Nmmhm."

Ella took that as a no, and went to lie in her hammock. She stared at the sky turning colors like a disco ball, listened to the unquiet that belonged to the city. That first tickle of fear—*summer is almost over*—occurred to her. All of them would move forward. Ella would return to Cornell, as a junior, and start applying for programs abroad in Latin America; Charu would start at NYU, and she would forget about Ella. Would Maya follow through on that half-formed plan of staying in Charu's dorm room? Why had Halim been so concerned for her? Ella realized that she didn't know very much about Maya, but she felt like she'd known her for years. Maybe she could come to Ithaca.

"Don't be stupid," said Ella aloud.

Maya had gone and come back from work by the time Ella awoke in the afternoon. She grabbed Ella by the hands and pulled her off the hammock. "You started snoring so hard I had to go inside."

"Crap. I should lie on my side. Sorry."

"I was just glad you fell asleep. Let's go find Charu."

The steady drone of the sewing machine led them up the stairs to Charu's room. Maya knocked a rhythm on the door.

"Who is it?"

"Guess."

Charu opened the door and gasped. "You are a fucking psychic! Get in here!"

Charu's room was as disastrous as it had ever been. There were hundreds of fabrics slung about anywhere there was space: old saris, cuts of West African kente, Thai silk dupioni—random leftovers from weddings that drove Hashi crazy when they piled up at the salon.

"So this is what you've been up to all day?" asked Maya.

"I've been busy with this project, girls. Maybe you can wear something for when we go check out Malik's band tonight! What do you think of my dress?" Charu struck a pop star pose in a dress that was brown, buttoned, and sacklike.

"Out of all the beautiful things you got in your closet, you want to wear that?" asked Maya.

"It's simple. I like simple."

"You sure you aren't trying to blot yourself out of the scene?"

"This is what I want. Now, I must get you dressed, Maya, my dear."

"Oh, I don't want to go. I've been working all day—"

"It's Saturday night." Charu pulled out three scarves from the mound of textiles on the floor. "Model for me? You can wear one out tonight. I call this collection of head scarves—haute hijabi. It's either that or jihadi hotties."

"The latter probably won't sell," said Ella.

Charu chose a bright red fleur-de-lis print. Gently, she unpinned Maya's hijab, careful to stick the pins into a tomato cushion. Once she dressed Maya in her creation, she squealed, "You look divine in it!"

It was hard to look away. The bright color of the head scarf accentuated Maya's skin, framing her aquiline nose. Maya caught Ella staring and smiled.

"The show is in Williamsburg. I'll pay for the car back. Let's go," said Charu.

"With what money?" asked Ella.

"Baba gave me a hundred and fifty bucks for business expenses. He likes my sense of entrepreneurship."

"Lucky girl," said Maya. "You know, I think you're onto something."

"Is Malik's band even good?" asked Ella.

"You're coming, too, El," said Charu. "I'm not gonna take no for—"

"Aw shit, Charu, I'm not interested."

"Okay, fine. But later tonight we'll need you to distract the parentals while we sneak out," said Charu.

"Use your tree," said Ella.

"You know I'm afraid of heights," snapped Charu. "Stop being so fucking righteous for once."

Ella quivered, thinking of the night's promises: Cigarettes. Alcohol. Infrequent late-night trains.

"How are you going to get in? You don't have ID. I guess you've got Malik," said Ella.

"Malik got me these," said Charu, holding two laminated cards. "And I *don't* want to talk about it." She turned to the mirror and pouted at her reflection.

"So it looks like my birthday party jump-started you two again," said Maya.

"Yes. Well, something like that. He's been busy working. Maybe tonight we can—connect."

"Give him time. He'll come around." Maya looked down at the laminated ID that Charu had handed to her and said, "Hey, Charu, I don't think we can both go in with the same name and be from South Carolina."

Ella glanced at the name on the card. "*Salma Hiyuk?* You must be joking."

"We're both pretty and brown and motherfuckers can't tell the difference."

"Ella, it's the spirit of the evening, no?" Maya said. "Will you come? It's not like I do this all the time myself."

"I'm just not into this sort of thing."

Charu sneered, "You're never into *anything*."

"I'll be back," Ella said. She left the two of them deciding which one of Charu's haute hijabi samples Maya should represent for the evening.

The last thing she wanted to do was zap the night's fun. She made her way downstairs to her bedroom. Hashi was still in the salon; Anwar had not yet come home from work. She'd been looking forward to another night with Maya, and seeing Charu and Maya together was making Ella's head pound. Charu's anger would dissolve as soon as she got what she wanted. Ella just had to let them out the door, maybe stop by her aunt and uncle's bedroom. It would never occur to them that Ella would tell a lie.

Maya stayed upstairs in Charu's room during dinner. She mentioned not wanting to risk Aman seeing her. After being gone for a month and a half, Maya worried he might tell her father at the masjid. Charu chatted about her hijabs, Aman looked dour and complained about his divorce proceedings, and Hashi and Anwar listened to everyone. Anwar asked Ella if she'd want to come by the apothecary. She had been avoiding the shop. Something about being stuck with Anwar without knowing what to say to him for hours was too awkward, even for her. She said, sure, yeah, why not, but gave no specifics. After dinner, Hashi went to her bedroom to read the Bangla paper, while Aman watched his favorite TV programs, and Anwar went to his study to concoct batches of jojoba shampoo for some famous actor.

Around ten p.m., Charu texted Ella:

> Can you chk on parents?

Ella did her due diligence and knocked on Hashi's door.

"Open!" Hashi lay in bed, reading the Bangla newspaper. "Everything okay?"

"Yeah. I'm uh—going to sleep."

"Good. Maybe you can wake up earlier, then!"

"Right. Good night."

"Good night. Good night? Turn off the stupid TV, Aman!" Hashi hissed. "And if my stupid husband would join me in bed. *Jaihok*, Ella, see you tomorrow. In the morning, okay?"

Ella bid her good night and shut the door. She heard Aman chortle at something—it sounded like *Queer Eye for the Straight Guy*—and tapped her fingers on Charu's door. Charu opened the door, and let Maya out. She had painted Maya's mouth a suggestive red and dressed her in a skintight black jumpsuit that made her look like a Muslim version of Spider-Woman.

They took off their high heels to tiptoe downstairs and out through the sliding glass door.

Once they were outside, Charu cried, "You're the best, El!" and hugged her.

"You're sure you won't come? Please?" asked Maya.

"I'm sure."

Ella watched them disappear around the corner of the house. She crumpled onto her hammock. Moonflowers had started to bloom. A hibiscus flower landed on her face. She plucked one of its petals. She slipped off her glasses and the petal took on shapes: a lazy-eyed halibut lumbering along the ocean floor, an ungraspable mermaid, a severed head.

She closed her eyes. She didn't want to see any more.

Overwhelmed, she decided to cool off in the seed vault. She opened the door to the vault, and found Anwar sitting there, his hands resting on his belly. His head lay slumped on his chest.

9

Ella shook Anwar hard by the shoulders. He was breathing, but his skin felt dangerously cold. "What the hell are you doing in here?" asked Ella.

Anwar jerked his head up. "Hmmph?"

"Anwar, it's freezing—it's not safe to pass out here—what the hell were you thinking?" Ella bent down beside him to help him up.

"Same as you. Getting away from all *that*." He fluttered his eyes wide awake. He waved his hand toward the house. "I can't take it in there anymore. You know, your father was much more of a brother to me than my own brother."

"I didn't see you come outside. Do you want to be alone?"

"Do you want to be alone?" asked Anwar.

"No."

"Same as you. Come. Sit down."

Ella joined him. He patted her knee. "It's your father's birthday tomorrow, did you know that?" he said.

"I—I forgot."

Anwar shook his head. "It's a terrible thing I've let you forget. We should be having a party. We should be lighting those sparkler things. We should—"

"It's okay."

"Hmph. What can I say? The older we get, the dimmer these memories become. I know that Hashi will remember out of the blue that it's her brother's birthday. And then Charu will do something crazy or some hairy woman will come in for a treatment, and

Rezwan goes out of her mind. It's hard to hold on to sadness." Anwar gestured to the drawers of seed. "I call this 'permanent winter.' In this perpetual cold state we can preserve these little seeds, for hundreds of years. Heirlooms that no one else has. This is all yours, kid," said Anwar.

"Really?"

"It's not much. I have not much to give you, Ella, besides this house, and these seeds."

"That's a lot."

"I like to think so."

She felt her throat clump and squeezed her uncle's shoulder.

Anwar squeezed her hand.

Ella wanted to feel a swelling in her chest, of longing, for her father and his memory, but she didn't. *Maybe it's too fucking cold in here,* she thought. *Too cold to think.*

"I would like to get some herbstuffs from the garden. It is also freezing in here," said Anwar.

"Yeah, seriously." Ella stood up and propped the door open. Anwar followed her out, seeming as disoriented as a miner released from a cave. "Ah, wait, one minute," he said, going back inside. He came out again, holding a handful of Ziploc bags. He squinted, as if deep in concentration, and counted off a list of inaudible ingredients. Ella locked the seed vault.

"Ahem." Anwar cleared his throat. "I need to pull some herbs, some bark, some flowers. Here, hold these." He handed her the Ziplocs and grabbed a shovel from beside the shed.

They stood in the center of the circle, appraising the garden, unsure of where to begin.

"Let's start with herbs," said Anwar.

They walked over to a hodgepodge of scented plants in the sunniest corner of the garden. Anwar got on his knees and brushed his fingers through the tangle of herbs. He ripped the tiny white petals of chamomile and sniffed them.

"*Manzanilla,* in Spanish, or, earth apple. I call it 'the plant doctor.' It helps increase the production of oils in our mints—spearmint, sage, oregano—stronger in scent and flavor. Bag, please." Ella held open a Ziploc, and Anwar stuffed it with the fistful of the daisy-like chamomile flowers. He yanked the sweet pink-flowered valerian by the base of its stem. He used the shovel to loosen it from the soil, then pulled the entire plant, roots and all. He gestured for her to help him up, and she felt her uncle heavy on her shoulder as she pulled him out of his squat.

"You know, I just got rid of an aphid infestation," said Ella. "Used the neem oil."

"Aphids are not a good sign."

"They were on the morning glories; I think the pink roses, too. But they're gone now."

"It's the first time, I think, that we've had pestilence in our garden."

"It's common, Anwar, especially after years of having a garden that's been pest-free. They find a way to break that seal of luck."

"Of course, you're right, my Ella. And you've done a fantastic job. These midnight flowers have bloomed perfectly. All praises to jasmine."

Ella rolled her eyes and followed him back into the house, through the sliding door, into the kitchen. He filled a kettle with water and placed it on the stove. He pulled out a pint-size mason jar from the cabinet under the sink. He opened the jar and crinkled his nose at the aroma. "The stuff smells like French onion soup, but it is a very effective fungicide, m'dear. It's a thick oil, and becomes pasty when it's not hot enough."

"How do you know all this stuff?" asked Ella. "Didn't you study geography in college?"

"Yes, I was a phytogeographer; my love of botany and history drew me to the subject. To understand nature, I wanted to study our beginnings. Buddhists Palas, Hindu Senas, conquered subjects of the Delhi sultanate. Were we shit collectors, gravediggers, and temple minions, cast under India like a putrid armpit? Our balmy monsoon and one hundred inches of rain was tantamount to exile for Brahmin priests. So, as I studied, I came to love geography and its great shifts. Since Sultan Muhammad Bakhtiyar's invasion of the flooded delta plains in the thirteenth century, the Ganga's diversion into the Padma-Meghna tributaries had not yet happened. With the arrival of the next band of Turkic emperors in the sixteen hundreds, the great Ganga rose higher, unable to sieve the silt in her waters. Eastward expansion dried up the old western banks. Once sites of pilgrimage and holy Brahmin rites, the Adi Ganga's vestiges became stagnant, diseased.

"In my westward hometown, Jessore, we grew up hearing about Mehr Ali, a Sufi mystic who taught the people to cut through dense sal forest and cultivate rice in the wet plains. Mehr Ali and other Sufis' metaphysical, supernatural powers, coupled with an ability to feed us—that's when we took their faith. Before long, Brahma, Vishnu, Adam, and Muhammad were a continual succession of holy prophets.

"But the hilly parts of our country—Sylhet and Chittagong—remained undiscovered territories for centuries, where pirates, pirs, and outcasts disappeared. Of course, some resisted. The Jumma tribes wanted no part of it, and continued to slash and burn from way up in the hills. Resin, betel leaves, honey, and oil were abundant and plentiful. For those matrilineal peoples, the Islamic practice of feminine confinement held no charm or purpose. Why should men work outside in the sun, reaping and transplanting the rice seedlings, while women remain chained to the domicile, winnowing, soaking, and parboiling the spoils?

"To them, the jungle—home, God, family—shouldn't be flattened into a sacrilegious rice bowl."

Anwar shut his eyes tight, as if trying to wince away a memory. He cleared his throat. "Your father was not caught up in the romance of bees and trees. Nor did he question his faith. He was a chemist who believed Allah had created atoms. But he did not see the world as a simple accumulation of atoms. You can draw elements out of a plant—oxygen, carbon—but nothing you do will create a plant out of these elements, the dead dust of life forms. He would freak out to know that scientists are devising ways to clone humans." The kettle started to boil. Anwar lifted a finger and said, "I have an idea—I will make us some tea with the chamomile and valerian. It will help you sleep."

He opened the Ziploc bag of chamomile flowers and took a luxurious sniff. Ella pulled out the tea strainer and two mugs: one from NYU that Charu had bought after her acceptance, and another in the style of the quintessential blue and white Grecian paper cup, inscribed with the message *We Are Happy to Serve You*. As soon as the kettle started to whistle, Anwar shut off the stove. He didn't want to wake Hashi or Charu. He opened the lid of the pot and stirred in the chamomile, then shaved a few pieces of valerian root into the kettle. He grabbed a tangerine from the fruit bowl and peeled it, offering Ella half, and eating the other in one bite. After throwing the peels into the mixture, he squirted plastic-bear honey liberally. "Let's let this steep for a few minutes. Now, where was I?"

"Everywhere. My father, Sufis, atoms—" said Ella.

"Ah, right, of course." Anwar scratched his chin and leaned against the kitchen counter. "Two people in particular, besides Mehr Ali, influenced me to follow my course of study. The renowned polymath Jogodish Chondro Boshu. As for Dr. Boshu, every person in Bangladesh grew up learning about him. While the West credits the Italian, Marconi, for transmitting the first electrical signal, Boshu beat him to it at a Kolkata town hall in 1895. Boshu's wave fired off a faraway pistol and exploded a small mine.

"His book, *Plant Autographs and Their Revelations*, detailed his experimentations with his invention, the crescograph. The minutest motion of a plant could be recorded and drawn with this instrument. I became inspired by his tenets, that the invisible lines between all things, living and nonliving, were just that—invisible. He conducted marvelous experiments! Plants swayed like drunks when injected with whiskey. Spray it with chloroform, and you can transplant a giant oak tree, one that usually would die if uprooted. At death, plants spasm, much like a dying man."

"We haven't learned about him in anything I've studied," admitted Ella.

"That's America for you. I don't know how you commit yourself to studying all those excruciatingly boring Latin names."

"I like taxonomy. I like figuring out who named it, or what myth or character inspired the name."

"I suppose. But be too busy learning that, and it becomes . . . unsexy, if I may say so. Now, I'm not sure where you stand on this . . . love business. . . ." He peered at her.

Ella avoided a response, and turned her gaze to the kettle. She busied herself with straining the tea into their mugs.

"Well?"

"What do you mean, where do I stand?"

"Have you ever—been in love?"

She handed him the NYU mug, trying to keep her hand steady. "I . . . I don't know."

"Then you haven't."

Ella took a sip of the chamomile tea. It was supposed to calm nerves. She wanted him to stop looking at her. She stared into the petal bits that had escaped into her tea. "I guess not."

"It will happen; you are an intelligent, compassionate girl. My first love, in the purely innocent, pre-Hashi sense, was Hawa, daughter of a village herbalist in the Northeast, near the India border. She lived in my hometown, Jessore, with some of her cousins. She worked for us as a housemaid for five years, just to send some money, until . . . unfortunate circumstances stole her away. But I fell in love again, just five years after that."

"You never saw her again?"

"No."

"And then you found Hashi."

"Er . . . yes. Something like that," said Anwar. "Anyway. The point is, I grew up with a modest farm, decent a yield as any: rice, dal, potatoes, tomatoes. Hawa was very young, but a consummate tiller of earth. As am I. As are you." Anwar cleared his throat. "I have never forgotten those little moments—Hawa collecting pulses in her apron and storing them away for another year. Each seed tells this story: Everything that happens is already written."

10

Charu and Maya rode the G train to a converted factory in Williamsburg. The behemoth in the middle of an empty dead-end street didn't look illustrious to Charu, but no one appeared to mind the wasteland. She noticed the plethora of prints—animal, plaid, floral, West African—and took internal haute hijabi notes. She pulled out her reserve (and stale) pack of cigarettes that she'd stolen from one of her father's tweed fall coats. (Anwar had a habit of forgetting things in his pockets; over the years Charu had collected packs of gum, dollar bills, and cigarettes.) She offered Maya a cigarette, but she refused. Maya pulled the front zipper of her jumpsuit higher. Charu wished she'd dressed up a little more. She leaned on the brick wall, inhaling. There was so little summer left. She'd even gone to visit Malik at work, but Aman Uncle sent her home, saying it was a place for business, not pleasure. It had been awesome to see Malik at Maya's birthday party yesterday. She hadn't heard from him much because Aman Uncle lived with them now, he told her. Being Aman's employee, sneaking up the tree was exponentially more risky.

She stuck her finger in her back pocket, where she'd stuffed her school schedule, to remind her of the freedom that waited for her around the corner. Her classes were interesting enough:

1. The Postcolonial Metropolis (third world city, life is gritty)
2. Introduction to Feminism and Gender Studies (Intro FAGS)

3. Introduction to Psychology (for understanding the effects of religious guilt)
4. Islamic Religious Traditions (in response to Ma's "What in hell are we paying for?")

Then she saw him. But Malik did not see her. He stood with the radiant, blond-dreadlocked Aisha Ali-Marchand, lead singer of their renegade, avant-garde (according to the band's Web site) jazz outfit Yesterday's Future. Her chest clenched. Where'd he get the suit and skinny tie? Had he changed his nose ring?

"Let's go inside," hissed Charu. "Before he sees me."

"Isn't the point for him to see you?" said Maya.

"Not when he's with her."

The stairs leading up to the main venue were precarious, made of wrought iron, with wide gaps between each step. They found a spot next to a huge amp, hidden from the stage.

The crowd whistled and whooped as Aisha Ali-Marchand and her black-suited band made their way up to the stage. Last in line, Malik spotted Charu, and stopped. "Glad you could make it," he said, planting a kiss on her cheek. He turned to Maya. "Nice to see you again. Happy birthday weekend." He nodded once more at Charu, then joined his band onstage. He tuned his bass, unaware of the crowd. Charu caught sight of a girl standing next to her. She had hair so long it grazed her bottom. The girl raised her hand and waved like a mock pageant girl. Charu looked back onstage, and saw Malik mimicking the same idiotic gesture, both of them grinning.

"I need air!" Charu yelled to Maya. They pushed their way out of the mass of people, back onto the sidewalk with the smokers.

Maya took Charu's hands in her own and said, "You're better than this."

"Who was she?"

"Who was who?"

"This bitch," sneered Charu, waving her hand just as the girl had.

"It could be anyone—she could just be a friend."

"I want to wait here. To talk."

"I think that's a terrible idea."

"What the hell do you know?

"I know that waiting around for someone who makes you feel like you can't breathe gets old real quick."

"I want to stay."

"I'm going to get on the train. It's full of lunatics at this hour, which is way more interesting than this." Maya hugged Charu good-bye. "Be safe."

Charu smoked her pack of cigarettes outside for the duration of the show. She spoke to strangers, mirroring their drunkenness when they asked her for a smoke, and she wondered if this was what college was like. She felt desperate and immobile. She was trying to picture the moment when Malik would come outside, and regretted with each passing minute missing the show.

"Who are you, bitch?" As soon as she said it, a rush of people exited the warehouse entrance. She saw Malik. His bass was strapped to his back and his tie was unraveled. Horsehair Pageant Queen wasn't next to him. No one was. She watched him scan the crowd until their eyes met.

"Where were you?" he called out, striding toward her.

"I started to overheat in there. But I heard you. You were great."

"Thanks, girl."

"What are you . . . thinking of getting into?"

"The guys want to smoke at Aisha's house, but I don't feel like being around people. Rashaud Persaud told me about this thing out in Flatbush, some fried chicken and waffles party, but that sounds messy."

"Oh." *Do I count as people?* Charu wondered. "Rashaud Persaud from Atlantic Avenue?"

"That's the one."

"Didn't know you guys kicked it like that."

"We do. He's cool. What are you up to? Where's your friend?"

"Wasn't her scene. She went home. Where's *your* friend?"

"What friend?"

"This chick—" Charu did the pageant wave, once again.

"Ah . . . She's Aisha's friend from college. Cool chick."

Charu nodded, as if she knew the girl was a cool chick.

"You want to drop off equipment with me?"

They drove to Malik's rehearsal space in a musty black van reminiscent of a TV crime show kidnapping vehicle. In the back, instruments and amps rattled. She rested her palm on his leg, and when he looked over at her, she pulled out of her seat belt to kiss his neck.

"Careful," said Malik, but he didn't stop her as she unzipped his pants. "I'm driving."

She pressed her fingers against the stiffened inseam of his pants. It felt warm and sweaty.

"Pull over."

He didn't refuse, as she expected. He parked at the waterfront park on Grand Street, where she and Maya and Ella had often watched the sunset before Maya went MIA. The back sides of buildings looked like an illuminated checkerboard. In all of those tiny squares, Charu imagined some people slept, some people lay awake. The Williamsburg Bridge resembled an illuminated playground slide. There was another car parked in the lot, a red sports car. But the riders surprised her. They were a group of Hasidic men. The eldest looked old enough to be everyone's father; the youngest, like a freshman in high school. They stared for a moment, but lost interest. The van had tinted windows.

Malik leaned over her to release her seat backward so that she was lying down. He pushed the seat back as far as it would go until it toppled a set of cymbals. The crash sent goose bumps down her bare legs. He squatted down in the space between the glove compartment and her legs.

"You look ridiculously comfortable."

"Aw, shut up," he said, grinning. "Let's try this." He climbed on top of her and she felt the cotton of his suit pants rub against her legs and arms.

"Shouldn't we get naked or something?" she asked.

"Do you see a dressing room in here?"

Charu tried to push the seat back farther, but it didn't budge. She unbuttoned his shirt and he pulled it off.

"Pants, really? You want to have sex with me with your pants on?"

"All right, all right. Help me, please," said Malik, groaning.

She yanked his pants and briefs off and let them slip to the floor.

"You ready?"

"I've been ready." She pulled out a condom from her bra, where she also kept her fake ID and a wad of bills.

"Good. The ones I got are stuck in the glove compartment."

She felt something cool on her bottom and reached to pull it out—a quarter.

"So I'm not gonna even lose it in the backseat?"

"Front seat keeps my lady neat," he said. He tore the condom wrapper with his teeth and slipped it on, one-handed. He tried to pull down her panties with his free hand, but his knuckles burrowed hard into her thigh, and he couldn't pull his hand out from under her.

"Let me." She wriggled her underwear down to her calves. *So much for wearing my nine-dollar Victoria's Secrets,* she thought. They inhaled a deep breath together and she looked at him, wanting to *connect,* but he had his eyes closed and his mouth pursed into an O.

She clenched herself tight when he started to break into her skin. She reached over to tilt the air-conditioner vent downward. She let loose a bit more and, finally, Malik was all in her. His eyes popped open and they started to laugh. At the same time her eyes burned from the blast of cool air.

"Are you okay? Are you okay?"

"It's the AC. I'm not crying. I'm okay."

He thrust up and then down, and then again a little harder, just as she'd pictured it, and each time he pressed against her, she felt a little more skin tear away. It hurt, but not unbearably so. She realized that Malik's penis might not be as large as penises could be. She giggled again. But this time, he didn't join her. He scowled.

"What?"

"Oh, nothing."

Minutes later, when he finished, he triple-checked to make sure the condom was intact. He climbed over to the driver's seat, and released it back so he was lying next to her. He turned off the car's ignition and rolled down his window. A tepid breeze from the waterfront filtered into the van.

"I think coming is easier for guys. We're just doing what we need to do for the inevitable."

"Mm."

"It was good, though."

"It's so weird that I'm starting school in less than a month."

"You'll still be in Brooklyn, girl."

"Will you come see me? You barely did this summer."

"Your mom had me stressed. And your uncle. Dude has this weird gripe about you, but also talks about how gorgeous you turned out. He couldn't stop grillin' me about dating you."

"You serious?"

"I'm here now."

"You want to sit outside by the water?"

He yawned. "Sugar, I'm tired as twilight."

"Why are you talking like an old man?"

"Happens when I get sleepy. I think I need to take a lil' nap so I can drive you home." He closed his eyes and smiled once more before passing out.

She waited five minutes before letting herself out the passenger's side.

Charu walked over to a large rock and sat down. She watched the water crash below her feet. The bridge's lights made the ripples appear like streaks of lightning. Each ephemeral pattern in the tide gave way to a new one and then another new one; she wondered if this was how Ella saw the world. Being over here made Charu realize how landlocked her own neighborhood was. Something about being next to the water, even if it *was* the dirtiest water in the U.S., made shit seem—*bigger.* Malik slept in the van, while here she was bursting with energy, ready to try again, or go back to the warehouse and dance with hip kids who thought she was drunk. She skipped a stone in the black water and imagined it made a thousand ripples. So good ol' Aman had scared Malik from coming near her. Bastard.

Warmth spread through her crotch, and she stood up, her bottom numb from the rock.

"Fuck," she said.

Blood was running down her thighs.

"Hey, sweetheart, need a ride somewhere?" yelled the youngest Hasid boy, suddenly, as if by doing so he'd earn points with his posse. It worked. They were all staring at Charu. The boy took a step closer, and she shook her head and walked over to the car. She opened the door and found Malik sleeping still. She fiddled with the glove compartment for a tissue to blot the blood, and sure enough, there was no tissue, but a school nurse's yearly allotment of condoms. She looked around to see if anything else could be of use. Musical instruments and road maps and little scented tree fresheners. Malik's clothes were crumpled on the floor of the passenger's seat.

Take the pants or the jacket, she thought. The jacket was fitted and he wasn't much bigger than she. It wouldn't even cover her ass.

She took the pants.

She knew it was safer to walk up to Bedford and hail a yellow cab, but she wanted to walk along the waterfront for as long as possible. She decided to risk the hour's walk.

Ella heard a single pair of tapping heels before she could make out the figure walking toward the stoop. She checked her watch; it was two a.m.

Under the orange glow of the streetlamp, Maya's silhouette had the ominous aura of a mugger. As she came closer, Ella saw that she wasn't wearing a hijab.

"You're back alone?"

"She wanted to stay. And wait," said Maya.

"You came back without her?"

"She insisted on staying."

"So she's with Malik?"

"Yes, of course she is. She's grown."

"He doesn't give a shit about her."

"Does anyone give a shit about anybody but themselves?"

"I see you're not wearing the scarf," said Ella. It was better to change the subject, for there was no way Maya would understand.

"If I'm going to break one rule—then why not all of them? Charu was just so intent on me wearing it, so—"

"She has a way of getting what she wants. Are you tired?"

"I am," said Maya. "But I know you aren't. So . . . 'Salma Hiyuk' bought a little something on her way home." She pulled out a travel-size bottle of Malibu rum. "A taste of the islands, maybe?"

They sat on the stoop and took minuscule sips. Ella took the last drop and passed the bottle to Maya.

"It's empty," giggled Maya. "Lightweight, I am. I am that I am." She leaned in toward Ella, until they were nose-to-nose. "Ella

Anwar, you beautiful girl." She pressed her lips against Ella's, then let her tongue through. Ella gasped in Maya's breath, a mix of rum and bubble gum.

She pushed Maya away. "I—I can't do that."

"Why not?"

"I don't know."

"What is it, Ella?"

Ella said nothing. She just shook her head. *If she knew, she'd run the other way.*

"Let's go inside."

"You can sleep on the bed." *A consolation.*

"The floor is fine."

111 Cambridge Place was dark and silent by the time Charu came home. She crept through the sliding glass door, unaware of her uncle awake in the living room.

11

The next morning, Anwar decided to help Hashi with laundry (both professional and personal). Inspired by Bic Gnarls's cavalier husbanding, he diligently separated the white towels from the rest of the load. In the pile of clothes was a windbreaker that she'd given to him more than twenty years ago as a thirtieth birthday gift. *As many complaints as she has about me*, thought Anwar, *stretching the value of things is not one of them*. As Hashi measured softener, he nuzzled her and pulled her against his burgeoning hard-on. Something about doing the laundry was—sexy.

"You often wish for a husband to whisper *petit riens* in your ears, *na*?" He felt the urge to slurp her ear.

"My god, Anwar!" Hashi lifted her shoulder to her ear to wipe away the wetness.

"I was a merely giving you a kiss."

"That is not a kiss! It is a shame!"

"Oh, forget it."

"*Arré*, Anwar. Don't be upset now. I'm just surprised you're helping at all. I've been surprised. Last week, the girls came to help me with laundry at the end of a long day. It's been a while since a sensible child like Maya has come to our home, *na*?"

"She is here often, it seems."

"The girl offered to help me fold the pile of towels. I refused her offer, of course. What good it does to have faith in the home. Aman mentioned her father is Sallah S., the alternate imam at the Fulton Street masjid—do you know him?"

"I don't know him personally. But his home is right above our shop."

"Well, he should be proud of his girl. Our own—they are a different matter. Charu appeared ill, but said she was just tired and hot."

"Perhaps we should get an air conditioner."

"I thought you did not believe in air-conditioning."

"I do not. We have to be careful about the electricity bill."

The wrinkles that corresponded to any mention of Charu's name appeared on Hashi's forehead. "Could she be pregnant?" She shook her head into her knees.

"I do not think she and Malik are an item anymore."

"Oh?"

"Yes. I saw the boy a while back—"

"I thought he worked for Aman now—"

"He does. He is a nice boy and stopped by to say hello."

"Why do you suspect they are no longer together? He has decided *he's* too good for *her*?"

"At first you say you would rather die than see them together and now you are offended?"

"Do I burn for my daughter's sins, her missteps? For my lack as a mother?"

"These are the questions, my love, thieves in the night, which steal our sleep," said Anwar. He kissed her fingertips, nails torn from running them through sudsy hair. "Now, tell me something to make me smile. I have heard enough misery to last me a while."

"Well, you may find this quite interesting." Hashi laughed.

"Before you begin, I want to tell you, your smile is the loveliest smile of all," Anwar said, giggling. "Tonight, I will help you with dinner."

"Oh? What is the special occasion? Laundry and dinner?"

"I am inspired by Mr. Bic Gnarls."

"Bic Gnarls? The barber?"

"Yes. He's a very helpful husband."

"So I hear. We must have him and Mauve over for dinner soon. Save your helpfulness for another day. I ordered a pizza."

"From the Three Luigis?"

"Yes."

"Did you know that two are Italian Luigis? The third is Alvaro, a Mexican."

"Do you want to hear my story or not?" asked Hashi.

"Yes, of course."

"Then please, no more interruptions. It is annoying."

"Chup chup," said Anwar, miming a zipper across his lips.

"So, your friend Rashaud Persaud came to see me a few weeks ago wearing those baggy pants, stinking up the place with his fake designer cologne, like all these boys nowadays. But today, he came in and said, 'Miss Hashi, I wan' you to do your magic!'" Hashi mimicked Rashaud's voice.

Anwar laughed and clapped his hands. Her imitation was perfect.

"I closed my eyes and let the visions come. And I tell you—I never know what I will see. Rashaud has these very diminutive features—high cheekbones, bow-shaped lips—and I saw him as a girl, a blond girl, in my mind. I said to him—I didn't want anyone to hear, in case he became embarrassed—'Rashaud, I am seeing a girl. Is this what you see?' Rashaud stared at me, solemnly, and took my hand into his own manicured one. And then he said, 'Yes, Hashi, that's wha' I want. Wha' I see every day.'"

"What are you saying? Rashaud Persaud is a *cross-dresser*?" Anwar asked, incredulous.

"Well . . . yes," Hashi said.

"He asked to look like a woman? He is a very sweet fellow," Anwar said. "But I admit the ways of the young are lost to me. Yes, I suppose without a mother, you mother yourself. . . ." Anwar paused. It was amazing, how she had understood exactly what Rashaud needed in that moment. Her whole business was built around manifesting people's desire to be their best, most attractive selves. It was interesting to him that he never thought of his wife as a scientist. But now he felt he understood something. Hashi's chosen discipline, psychology, and her chosen path, beauty and cosmetics, were experimentations in uncovering a person's true nature. He couldn't deny that. Anwar was impressed with her openness, her skill at coaxing Rashad's hidden self outward. While Anwar fancied himself a liberal, once upon a time—a radical—with issues of sex, he was rather sensitive.

"Anwar, he is his own person. I give people what they wish. And he was looking beautiful."

"As are you." He tickled her chin.

"Come, let's go. Pee-jah will be here any minute."

They made their way upstairs after folding the laundry, holding hands. From the vestibule they heard laughter in the living room. Aman's guffaw resonated loudest of all.

"Seems that man can't watch enough television," said Hashi.

"He finds comfort in reruns."

"You know, last night, I asked him to turn the volume down, and I swear that as I went back to the bedroom, he turned the volume all the way up, before turning it down."

"He doesn't like women's authority."

"He comes by the salon on days he doesn't have work."

"What?" Anwar was incredulous; this was not something that he or the girls ever did.

"He's . . . critical. And to think how much I complain about you, but you never say anything like him. He finds the roundabout way to say everything: 'Is this in need of some salt? I think so!' Or—'I just love my soda flat and sweet!'"

As they stepped into the living room, Anwar heard his brother:

"Pluck these gray hairs from my chin, Charu *Ma*."

His brother lay sprawled on the couch; the girls and Maya sat on the carpet, arranged about him like temple devotees. He lazily twirled a ringlet of Charu's hair around his finger. She swatted his hand away, as she hated any sort of affectionate petting of her hair.

"Don't do that. We're trying to watch this," said Charu, shushing her uncle with a finger to her lips.

"Where exactly did you go last night, Charu?" asked Aman.

"What are you talking about?" She scowled and looked to Ella, widening her eyes.

"What is going on?" asked Anwar.

"Just watching this idiot program on television," said Aman. "How's the day?" When Aman, Anwar, and Hashi spoke, often they switched between English and Bangla, depending on how much they wanted the girls tuned in.

Hashi seemed unsure how to address his unseemly request of Charu. Aman had said it in a tone so banal, as if it were an ordinary request, and Anwar supposed it was not *that l*ewd—he was their uncle, after all, and it was the simple request of a saddened man; Anwar could imagine asking the same of his daughter. *Well, not in that voice. And, she's not his daughter.* Why had Aman asked Charu where she'd been? An odd thing to say. Quite odd. They'd had dinner and the girls had just been in their rooms. *Right?* His brother's presence in their home was whittling away at him. Aman appeared normal, and on the outside he was, undoubtedly, a beautiful man. Full-lipped and round-cheeked, like the black-and-white Bengali cinema actors of their youth—Uttam Kumar and the like. But no one knew his brother quite as he did.

And now, Anwar wanted him to leave.

"Women are a mystery. I'll never understand," said Aman, pointing to the television. "Stupid shows will make you lose focus, girls. Now, let's have some lunch."

"So you must be real disoriented," muttered Ella.

"We ordered pizza," said Hashi. She had a baffled expression on her face, trying to understand what was going on.

"Perfect," Aman said. He snapped his fingers, as if something had just occurred to him. He turned to Maya. "I saw your father, child, at Friday afternoon prayer."

"Don't call us 'child,'" said Charu. "It's obnoxious."

"Well, if you behave like that, then how can you blame me?"

"Now, Aman, please," said Anwar, holding up his hand. "No need for that. Charu, don't talk to your uncle like that."

"My father?" asked Maya.

"Yes, he is very concerned for you," continue Aman. "Says you haven't been home in weeks."

"How is that any of your business?" demanded Charu.

"Her father made it my business when he mentioned it."

"Exactly, brother, what do you mean?" asked Anwar, surprised by Charu's reaction.

"Do not talk to me that way, child," said Aman to Charu. "I am not your father."

"Don't. Call. Me. Child."

"Well, excuse me, she cannot speak that way to me either," said Anwar.

"I told Sallah S. today at Friday prayer that his daughter has taken to sleeping in our home, which is to explain to him that she is not lost, she is here," said Aman, smiling, as if he were talking to a group of children. "Your father misses you very much, Maya. I told him I would walk you home this evening."

"I . . ." started Maya. She turned to Hashi, then Anwar. "My father won't let me work, or go to college. So, Ella and Charu have let me stay here." She said the words plainly, staring at her hands, realizing the conversation had to do with her. Anwar tried to imagine Charu at home past high school. Would all the growing she had to do be away from home? This was the case for all teens, as it had been for him, and for Hashi. He felt somehow he should not let Maya go. But this was a family matter, a family other than theirs—was it improper to let the girl stay?

"Maya, you are welcome in our home, but do you think you should see your father?" said Hashi.

"No, Mrs. Saleem, I don't," said Maya. Still she did not look up.

"Ma, please," said Charu. "She's eighteen. It's just a month until school starts. She's saving up money every day. She's good at saving money; she's not like me."

Hashi looked at Anwar, who hesitated for a moment.

"Imagine how we'd miss you, darling," said Anwar, wagging his finger.

"It's not the same."

Maya said, "Charu, please, no worries. Your parents have been generous. I should leave."

"How did you know she was here, Aman?" asked Ella. Anwar noticed her tone, cold and pointed. "Did you come into my room?"

Aman dismissed her with a wave of his hand. "In family, all business is an open matter."

"My room is not."

"Well, I'll walk you over there—" said Aman.

"No!" Maya said. She covered her mouth, as if to apologize.

"She's not leaving," said Charu. "We—we can't let her lose all her money. He'll take her money."

"You girls are absurd." Aman shook his head.

"Maya, is there any way I can talk to your father? Vouch for you?" asked Hashi, seeing the girl's distress.

"No."

"Hashi, I don't understand how a mother could allow another woman's child—" started Aman.

"You do not have children. And Maya is eighteen. She's not a child."

"Her father is concerned for her—have you no concern for that? I told him I would attend to this matter. I'll walk her home after we eat."

"We *are* going to eat, and we're going to relax. It's Sunday, my one damn day off!" Hashi spat. "I will pack two slices for you before you leave, Aman Bhai."

"Before I leave? Excuse me?"

"Now, you listen to me. These girls have grown up here all their lives, before this house was anything, when it was no better than trash, when people loitered on the streets with nothing good to do. Let the girls be without a sad old man looking over their shoulder—is that *too much to ask*? And if that is such a *mystery*, and you can't understand it, then perhaps you can understand why you have failed as a husband. And you should not stay here! Anwar is too nice to say this, but I cannot do it a night more."

Just then, the doorbell rang.

"It's the pizza," said Anwar.

No one moved to answer the door, transfixed by Hashi's outburst.

"Charu, please," said Hashi. "All of you, go."

"No . . ." started Charu, but she stopped as her father handed her a twenty-dollar bill.

"Keep the change," joked Anwar. "Now, shoo! This is adult talk."

Charu, Ella, and Maya left the room, feet lagging to answer the door.

"After what I have been through," said Aman, his voice cracking. His eyes became watery, then narrowed.

"Maybe once was not enough for you to learn," said Hashi.

"It is my birthday in two days. Never did I think you would throw me out."

Hashi looked struck at that instant, by a thought that had just occurred to her. "Y-you are welcome to have a party and invite us," she stuttered. "Excuse me." She rushed past Anwar, upstairs.

"Ha. Well, I have very few articles." Aman gestured to his suitcase, packed as if never opened, a small travel bag perched on top. "Call me a cab service, Anwar."

Aman left without the promised slices. Anwar carried the pizza box upstairs to their bedroom.

"We can eat in bed?" asked Anwar, from the doorway. Hashi lay curled in bed, reading a passage from her Quran.

"Today we can."

He lay with her on their multitude of pillows and nibbled at a slice of pizza. She closed her book and joined him. But their appetites had waned.

"Are you all right?"

"I . . . I realized that it's Rezwan Bhai's birthday," said Hashi. "I had forgotten. Our brothers couldn't have been more different. But their birthdays are so close. He would be fifty-two."

Anwar shook his head. "I remembered late last night, and then forgot again. I forget that technically I was older than him. He always seemed so much older. He wasn't a man for silly celebrations. I never remembered even back then."

"This is true." Hashi nuzzled Anwar's shoulder with her cheek. He pulled away from her and sat up.

"Are you—upset with me?" asked Hashi.

"No, my love, no. You did what I couldn't do."

"Should I have sent Maya home?"

"You're right; the girl is eighteen. It seems like she could use a place to get things in order." Anwar paused. "You know there's something to what you say."

"What's that?"

"That maybe I've had an inferiority complex."

"That is because he has so much money. Which doesn't matter."

"Doesn't it?"

"It doesn't."

"You know, when we were younger, growing up in Jessore, I looked up to him."

"I looked up to my brother as well—"

"I did that, too," said Anwar. He fell quiet.

"Please talk to me."

"We were two rail-thin boys with big mustaches. My father was a self-absorbed anthropologist, and a widower, oblivious to the world around him. Aman was Baba's precocious assistant. But when Baba died, Aman left Jessore forever, and moved to Dhaka University. When he got to Dhaka he never wanted to know a damn thing about me, or Rezwan."

"Rezwan Bhai never liked Aman."

"Who could blame him? Before long, Aman was obsessed with Nidi, a lovely songbird. Aman sulked if another man so much as complimented her singing. I pity her for spending the best years of her life with a man like my brother."

"Poor Nidi."

"Aman has done terrible things," whispered Anwar.

"What things?"

He looked down at his half-eaten pizza.

"Let the origins of her seams keep her steady," he said.

"I don't get you," said Hashi.

"I have mentioned, of course, the servant girl, who lived with us as children, a girl named Hawa, yes?"

"She was your servant? I thought she went to school with you."

"We were in school together until class five. My father hired her when her family could no longer afford the books to send her."

"What does this have to do with Hawa?"

Anwar started to get off the bed. "Never mind, dear. I'll be in my studio."

"No. You will talk, Anwar."

He removed the pizza box and rested it on the side table. He crept back into bed, this time under the covers, and held her body close to him. Her chest rose and fell, and in his own chest he felt a tightening. For so long he could not bear to trespass the walls he had built for her sake. "Much of my adulthood I have hated my brother. We two, born of the same mother and father, me being the reason my mother died. I've yearned to join my adopted brother, Rezwan my comrade, in the afterlife. I scan my memory for a glimpse of good in my brother."

"It is hard to find."

"Hawa hailed from the hills of Sylhet—"

"Near where we stayed? In Jaflong?"

"Yes. Thereabouts. In the Khasi village just beside the Piyain

River. She stayed in her small room, fitted with a woven mat upon which she slept, prayed, dreamt."

"A child with that name carries the burden of the world on her shoulders, *na*? The world's first woman?"

"Something like that, yes."

"What did she look like?"

"Not brown like me, or yellow brown like you, but honey skinned, cut from the Pahari fabric. Unfortunate thing for natives the world over: They appear as strangers, when in fact, they are the originals. Moonfaced-almond-eyed-narrow-hipped-Hawa from Sylhet."

"How old were you?"

"Fifteen, like her.

"But Khasis in Jessore? I've never heard of such thing."

"Her family had mixed origins. Her great-grandmother had married a Bengali from Jessore. The fellow worked in the Shillong government under the British, at the turn of the nineteenth century. He ran a few large plant nurseries in Jessore, and I'm sure some of the descendants still do."

"You've always loved this sort of thing."

"I do. But my brother's a cold, saturnine fellow, with a heart of rock. I've never been like that. Our father had converted to Buddhism, a great source of shame for my brother. I rather loved it. Before he left for a trip to Pala to research idols on Moheshkhali Isle, he wanted me to build him a structure. A safekeeping place for his antique collection of lithic statues, ornaments, and coins from the Pala period. This structure resembled an igloo made of dirt and grass. I was outside, planting a small betel tree inside of it, a tree of life. This had practical use, since my father chewed paan like mad. I promised to make a home for the artifacts. When I had finished, I wanted to share my masterpiece with the one person who mattered—

"Hawa."

"Yes. I tried to open her door, just a little room off to the side of our kitchen, but it was locked. When she came out to prepare our evening meal, she would not look at me, but her lip had swollen, and she did not speak. I saw Aman, laying inside the room, tying up his lungi, smoking a cigarette."

"He—he *took* her?"

"To rape a girl after Friday jummah prayer is an unimaginable horror. It is hardly as simple as taking something." Anwar paused and closed his eyes. "She ran away before dawn's prayer, as we slept. The next morning, over the breakfast she had left on the table, Aman told me, never trust a tribal broad."

"You didn't say anything to him? Or me? What if he would've tried something with Charu? Or Ella?"

"No, I didn't say anything. And yes, I should've said something."

"You are younger than him. At that age the difference is pronounced. But I wish I'd known. I'd have kept him far from us. I never would have lived with him."

"At the time, perhaps I thought he might kill me. Did I know this evil was the first of dozens I would witness during the war? Was I any better at stopping those evils from happening?"

"Where did Hawa go? Did you ever try to find her?"

"Some said she traveled farther north than Sylhet, to India, disappeared into the mountains. To live on her own, in her ancestral forests, back to the origin of her seams."

"Did you look for her when we lived in Sylhet?"

"I found you there. My wife of great talents and whims, my beloved brother Rezu's little sister, parabola drawer, maker of smiles and frowns. You have blessed me with a darling daughter. I cannot have asked for a better outcome. But I am a man of simple desires with complex memories. I have never said any of these things aloud, nor will I, again. But I pray—"

Anwar paused. He had told Hashi the story as truthfully as possible. But it had exhausted him.

"Let the origin of her seams keep her steady."

He realized that perhaps she understood him better than he knew.

Charu excused herself from Ella's room, leaving her sister and Maya to the pizza. She'd lost her appetite. Aman had somehow seen her sneak out last night. But her parents hadn't believed him. Would they pry further? Her mom had run out so suddenly, without acknowledging them as she flew up the stairs. What the fuck was happening?

All morning, Charu had been rocked with a sensation of dread. Last night she'd lost her virginity. *In a motherfucking van.* If her mother or father knew, it would sicken them. She hadn't told Ella, sure that her sister would respond with something snide, judgmental; she didn't seem to like Malik. Charu just wanted a hug for her latest move toward womanhood.

The constant lying took its toll on her. She caught herself in the vanity mirror on her desk, which stood right next to her sewing machine. Sometimes, while sewing, she just looked at the mirror, so as to not feel lonely. Did it look like she'd had sex? Had her face changed? Ma once mentioned that girls who were sexually active broke out in pimples from the hormones; indeed, Charu had a constellation of zits on her cheek, probably from putting her face on Malik's chest. Maybe this was some Dorian Gray–type shit—the more she dived into the forbidden the more marked her face would become. Did other people tell their mothers about having sex? Heart-to-hearts and whatnot? Charu was still bleeding, and was pretty sure this was what happened after your first time. She hadn't yet turned eighteen, and didn't want to go to Planned Parenthood, in case she was ordered to tell her parents. People talked about how great Planned Parenthood was, but the prospect of going alone freaked Charu out. It was impossible to find the words with her parents to communicate her feelings with precision and honesty. She'd tried to explain this dilemma to Maya once, but Maya dismissed this as a common affliction for all teenagers. Muslim teenagers got a score of zero on a one-to-ten scale of being able to talk about sex with their folks. But Charu felt it had to do with language. She never could express her love or her sorrow in Bangla, the language of her parents. She had English for that. If she tried to say, "I want to explore a number of relationships before I'm ready to commit myself to one person entirely," it was like screaming into a ravine.

Charu turned on her sewing machine and started working on a sundress pattern she'd found online. Zippers were a challenge. She preferred invisible zippers—if she messed up the stitching, who would know? She was so distracted, her sewing machine jammed. Malik hadn't called her yet. Should she call him? She dialed his number and was met with his voice mail:

Hey yo. Leave a beautiful message.

Mustering up her best soft and husky tone, she said: "Malik. It's Charu. Last night was the jam. Want to see you, soon. Lunch at Mike's Diner, soon?"

The jam? What the hell is wrong with me? That was as smooth as my bumpy-ass face. She resisted the urge to immediately call him again.

"Charu! Ay, Charu!" She heard her father's voice, sounding old and far away, as if he were calling her like she was a child.

"I'm coming," she called back, her voice hoarse.

She found Anwar and Hashi, snuggled next to each other like two black-haired paintbrushes, side by side, a pizza box full of uneaten crusts beside them.

"Come here, baba," said her father. "We just wanted to see you." He patted the bed next to him.

Charu sat down, gingerly, but Anwar pulled her into his arms. Hashi rubbed her back. Charu buried her face into her father's underarm.

"Baba, you stink!"

"Why are you crying? Hugs and stink are supposed to make you smile."

"I—I guess . . . I'll miss you guys," she cried.

Charu remembered this curious feeling as a child around five or six. Ella would have therapy appointments, and for that hour, Charu, Anwar, and Hashi would go eat at Wendy's, or she'd get a gift from one of the stores at Fulton Mall. On those days, she felt that she was their *real* daughter, that they three were a unit. Just Ma, Baba, and Charu, without the worry of whether or not Ella was okay. And, as she had back then, Charu quickly shook the thought out of her mind.

"You guess? I suppose that's the best we can ask for!" joked Anwar.

12

July turned into August and the neighborhood grew hot with petty lootings and street brawls in the dead of morning. One such argument, regarding a stolen ten dollars, woke Anwar in the middle of the night. The scuffle was over as soon as it had begun—maybe the ten dollars had been sorted out, or maybe he'd dreamt the whole thing. He put an arm around Hashi, feeling a sudden chill take over him. He hadn't had a good night's sleep all month, not since his brother had left the house, and when he'd admitted the secret of Hawa. He had assumed that this would relieve a terrible burden, which had clung to him for more than thirty years. By speaking the memory, he no longer had to feel a sense of duty to his brother, and even Hashi disavowed Aman. *Have I wronged my brother?* Anwar wondered. He had not heard a word from him.

Bic's tale about the House of Bright had also unsettled him, and now, Anwar thought he heard a skittering in the vents. Spooked, he clutched Hashi even tighter. A sliver of moonlight cut across her face. The clock read five a.m. He felt like writing or smoking something. He opened the drawer of his nightstand for his quick-fix one hitter—just a drop of ganja would relax him—but he'd left the little pipe at the shop. He didn't have the energy to climb up to his studio. He decided to write letters on the veranda instead.

The letters were for his children, to be read after his death. He realized that perhaps this meant they would lie unread for many years, but there were stories he wanted to tell his children, stories that he felt too embarrassed to utter aloud. The stories themselves were not embarrassing. But the act of telling them about the past, when he'd been in the company of his best friend, the handsome, rebellious Rezwan Anwar, this made him feel like a fool. Where had he ended up? A shopkeeper in Brooklyn, far away from the country he'd have once died for, just to see it born.

On the veranda, he lay back on one of the canvas lawn chairs. Hashi had purchased matching pairs for both the garden and the veranda, but the ones up here were rarely used; he preferred the privacy of the attic. Price tags—SUPER DUPER BLOWOUT SALE $15.99—still dangled off the armrests. He fiddled with the tag on his chair, but the plastic tie refused to be ripped off. He gave up, his fingers raw from pulling. He hovered over the paper, afraid of penning anything less than brilliant.

> 1971—In the Sylheti forest, Rezwan and I travel by night to ensure our safety. I have neither the stomach for killing nor the propensity for destruction as my dearest friend, but I watch, praying what I witness will not make me lose my mind.

He stopped writing. He didn't have the stomach to write the story and he let the pen linger too long on the word *mind*. The inky mark bore a hole in the paper. He set the papers and pen aside and decided to enjoy his lawn chairs. The air was sticky and it would be a hot day, the hottest yet. The sun still had not peeked out. He looked up, as the sky often held an answer to the moment. He watched the electric blue sky between the branches of the hibiscus trees. Then, he noticed Ella down below, swinging like a pendulum on the hammock, heavy with terrible loneliness. He had not had a decent conversation with her since the evening Aman Bhai left the house. She spoke little, kept busy in the garden. She'd be leaving for Cornell in a matter of weeks, and he wouldn't see her again until Thanksgiving at the earliest. From where he stood, he saw the wonder of her green thumb upon his garden. White blossoms of different shapes and sizes glowed still in the dawn.

He wanted to comfort her now. He was tired of being so considerate of her solitude.

"Come with me to the apothecary today, child," said Anwar, poking Ella's shoulder. "Let your old uncle make you a special cup of coffee."

"Well—"

"C'mon. We've hardly had a chance to talk properly since you've been home."

"All right, Anwar. I'll come."

They walked back into the house through the sliding door. Ella sat down at the dining table, and Anwar began making his "special coffee." He heated up a cup of skim milk (this *skim-tim* was Charu's idea; everyone else liked 2 percent). Meanwhile, into mugs he measured one teaspoon of Folgers instant coffee and two teaspoons of sugar, with a splash of water. He stirred this mixture fast to make a paste, and then poured the warm milk into it.

"Here you are, dear."

"Thanks." Ella took a sip, and pursed her lips.

"Too hot?"

"It's real sweet."

"Well, you liked it as a child—"

"Charu did. I like it black."

"Ah, well," said Anwar, at a loss for what he should say. He swiped a couple of eggs from the refrigerator and poached them with a dash of salt and pepper. Ella ate her egg so hungrily that Anwar let her have his. He settled for a slice of toast. She raised an eyebrow at his liberal use of butter.

"Come along with me to the shop today. I've got a box of lavender soaps I must bring and it would be fantastic if we could cycle them over."

"Sure."

Ella got up and went to her room. She came back out in a worn navy polo shirt of Anwar's and jeans with grass stains on the knees. He considered suggesting she might change into a cleaner pair, but thought better of it.

They split the lavender soaps into two burlap satchels, which they carried in their bicycle baskets. They wheeled their bicycles outside, where Ramona Espinal sat on the stoop, drinking a cup of tea and reading the *New York Times*. She wore her scrubs, light yellow cotton printed with daisies. Beside her was a pint-size mason jar of honey.

"Buenos días!"

"Hola, Anwar," said Ramona. She nodded hello to Ella.

"Going to work?" asked Anwar.

"I am. I'm switching shifts since one of the nurses has a terrible case of morning sickness."

"So, no more rowdy nights for you?"

"Pardon me?"

"I—I mean—y-you won't be coming home so late—since you've swapped shifts and all?"

"Well, I . . . I guess not."

"You know, those honey bears are quite efficient, and weigh hardly anything!" Anwar gestured to the glass jar.

"Those things get clogged up."

"Sí, señora, sí."

"Qué bonita el dia, no? Tengo que ir al hospital, te veo!"

Anwar nodded, as if he understood.

"You know, we've got to run and open up the shop. Stop by anytime," said Ella.

Anwar hopped onto his bicycle. Never one to forget his helmet, he had forgotten it this morning. He said a quick dua, for the asphalt to spare his brains, and rode away from Ramona Espinal. He swore he felt her eyes burning holes into him.

The world had not quite awakened on their block, but as they made their way onto Fulton Street, morning buses and commuter traffic sped by, and a couple of cars honked at Anwar to let them pass. He felt his knees creaky with each revolution of pedals, but Ella effortlessly weaved through the morning traffic until he could no longer see her ahead.

Anwar's Apothecary looked—*gay and so incredibly lavender,* thought Ella, as she locked her bicycle to the parking sign on Third Avenue.

She hoisted the matching bars of soap on her shoulder and waited for her uncle. She hadn't wanted to leave him in the dust, but it was impossible to ride that slow. She couldn't remember sleeping, and she didn't remember being awake when Anwar tapped her shoulder.

Ella saw her uncle wheeling toward her.

"You're fast, child," wheezed Anwar, his foot skidding on the road.

"Sorry about that, Anwar."

"For what? Your youth?"

It was still dim inside the apothecary, as the sun had not yet hit their street. The walls of glass bottles gave the room an old-world flavor and Ella suddenly felt glad she'd come. She sniffed the air the undeniable stale smell of cannabis—and she smiled at her uncle's brazen potheadedness. She'd only smoked a handful of times up at Cornell—drinking was more her sport—but she didn't feel prone to addictions. She hated being high, the slipping away of her thoughts into discombobulated scenes from a bad sitcom. Hallucinations were quite enough.

On a separate table, Anwar showcased his prized copper alembic. He used the apparatus to distill flower waters, essential oils, and spirituous elixirs. It was composed of a long copper minaret-like pot connected by tube to a large coffee can. Oxidation had turned the alembic a deep red. Nowadays Anwar preferred to make his oils and flower waters in the privacy of his home studio. He no longer used this alembic, for years of oil and vapors impregnated the copper pores, so he displayed it as a work of art. Translations of the *Book of Crates*, a master catalog of ninth-century Arab spirit-makers and alchemists, inspired him to use a medieval technique that had been long refined by more sophisticated industrial stills. But as they knew then, copper conducted heat most efficiently, reduced bacterial contamination, and produced the prime scent and flavors, as brewers of scotch and whiskey were well aware.

As a child, Ella had watched him distill oil from seeds and flowers countless times. He would stuff a batch of lemon verbena leaves and boiling water into the pot. He'd heat it on the stove, attaching a tube from the pot to a condenser bucket. He would commission Ella to make a paste of rye flour and water to seal any part of the pot leaking steam. She'd hold a test tube to collect the essential oil and flower water trickling out of the condenser bucket. It amazed her as a child, this transmutation of any old garden-variety shrub into a new, potent substance.

"What do you want me to do?" asked Ella.

Anwar motioned for them to dump the satchels of lavender soap onto the counter. He grabbed a stack of brown paper and hemp tie. "We're going to package these, and it will take a while."

Ella wrapped each bar of soap in the brown paper, each crease hard and resolute, reminding her of those old origami books she'd order from Scholastic as a kid. She tied the hemp strings into even bows, and felt all her wayward thoughts focus on this meaningless task.

When her fingers cramped up she checked to see how far her uncle had gotten. He hadn't been packing the soap at all. She'd seen his fingers moving from the corner of her eye, and she assumed he'd been wrapping and tying.

He was writing on a large piece of brown paper.

"What are you doing, Anwar?"

"I am composing a letter."

"For who?"

"For you."

"Why not just tell me?"

"Well, child, it doesn't seem as though you want to talk."

"I guess you're right. Why don't you tell me now?"

"There're some things . . . that are too terrible to tell when a man is in his right mind. I believe I'd have to be on my deathbed, or in some dire condition, to be able to utter certain things. But to write them is to have an astronomer's distance."

"It's hard to imagine what you're talking about."

"When I write these things that happened so long ago, it's as if I am orbiting the past, safely away from Earth, from the moon. If I should speak the past aloud, then my words belong to me, but also to the listener, to you."

"But isn't it the same thing if I read the words?"

"I won't be around to see the reactions."

Ella looked at the paper, but Anwar's loopy scrawl was a mess. She could make out the title, "Black Forest," which was three times the size of the rest of the words.

"Is this about my father?"

"Yes."

"And you won't say more?"

"When trying to explain one thing, the history of a particular event, say how Rezwan and I joined the Mukti Bahini, it becomes this infinite history lesson. I'm sorry for that; I felt that same way when I asked my father a simple question about his Pala artifacts, and he'd start recounting the grand battle between Alexander the Great and the Gangaridai forces on the mouth of the Ganga, as if he'd been there. I want to tell you—yes, there was a war. And it cannot be isolated from the cyclone that preceded it, or the language movement in which students were murdered for wanting to speak Bangla instead of Urdu. You know, when I hear Charu begin to complain, 'I am alone, no one gets me,' or '*that's racist,*' or 'Hashi bitches and moans,' I feel like shouting, and you, my dear, you know I'm not one to shout. 'You are not a single person. You are not a minority, child. You belong to a billion people, goddammit. You can't sit in this house and complain about nothing, because you haven't experienced a drop of what I've experienced, what sort of hunger and ordinary evil there is in this world.' But of course, she doesn't want to hear that. So I don't say it."

Anwar paused. He walked around the counter to the back room, and Ella heard a faucet running. She heard her uncle gulping a glass of water. He blew his nose loudly—*into the sink,* thought Ella. He came back into the room, his hair slicked back with water. His face was wet.

"Today I've gotten the itch to write this out. I dunno why; maybe since your uncle Aman left, I got to thinking a lot about brothers. I mean, I've never had that sense of brotherhood with any man before or since your father. But I've never been more afraid of a man before either."

"You were afraid of him?"

"Not in the way I feared Aman as a young boy. Your father was a force of nature, an elegant brute."

"Where did he meet my mother?"

"They met twice at an Alliance Française film screening."

"That's it?"

"Well, that and one long, epic night before their wedding day. War has a way of making you want to get married and have babies. Rezwan and Laila's fathers had gone to medical school together. Your parents were both tall and spirited. They both agreed to get married." Anwar paused. "I must tell you more another day."

Ella felt a warm ache in her throat. There was no more paper to fold, but there were a few more bars of soap left. "No. I want to . . . I want to hear about what you're writing."

"I'm not sure that you want to hear about your father in this phase of his life."

"I want to know everything."

"Then we must talk about where we were during the final front of the war. In less than two weeks, along with the Indians, we crushed the enemy." Anwar gestured to his letter. In the center, Ella noticed a mass of scribbles that looked like a tree. "It is a place called the Black Forest," he said.

Just as he said this, they heard a loud shout come from upstairs. They heard a muffled roar, "WOMAN, REMEMBER WHAT I SAID!"

The apothecary's bottles rattled, and they heard a child's cry.

"Shit," whispered Ella. "Is that . . . Maya's father?"

"I am afraid so. Sallah S.'s temper has no bounds. These damn buildings are made of filler and particleboard. All manner of horribleness may pass through." Anwar stepped back, knocking into a bottle of shampoo, which fell to the floor. "How about some lunch, Ella? I feel my blood sugar is so low I must tend to my nerves."

"Kebabs?"

"You read my mind."

Outside, the high noon sun transitioned Ella's glasses into sunglasses. Anwar smiled at this neat trick of technology. He locked the front door and taped a sign, BE BACK IN 20. PROMISE.

"As-salaam-wa-alaikum, Brother Saleem!" called a voice, loud and familiar.

Anwar turned around. It was Sallah S. He was dragging a rolling suitcase. He wore a navy blue suit and wire-rimmed spectacles, and sported a neatly shaven beard. *He is quite handsome,* admitted Anwar. Three young men, one bearded, one goateed, and one balding, stood alongside him.

"Wa-alaikum salaam, Sallah," said Anwar. He nodded hello to the other men, who nodded but said nothing.

Sallah S. lit a cigarette. "Want one?"

"No thank you," Anwar said. "I am trying to quit. How's the day?"

"The usual. My wife's been very sick, and I've got another meeting up in Albany for a brother's deportation hearing. He's being held in Wasatchie."

"Wa-satch-ie," repeated Anwar. *Names of old Indians used to lock up new ones.* "Will it work out for him?"

"No. It's a disgrace what they've done to Brother Karim. Decent man—owned a grocery in Kensington, children born here. Nothing his lawyers can do for him. He is being shipped back to Tunisia in a week." He flicked his cigarette onto the sidewalk, where it bounced off Ella's shoe. "And you, young brother? Saleem's son?" asked Sallah S., turning to Ella.

"Eh, this is my niece, Ella."

"Yes, yes." Sallah S. glanced sideways at his trio. They stifled laughter.

"Wa-alaikum salaam, sister," said the bearded fellow.

"You know, you and your brother are as brotherly as Bush and Clinton," said Sallah S., chuckling at his own joke. He coughed and spat up a gob of phlegm.

"That is to say, we're not different at all?" Anwar joked.

Sallah S. didn't laugh. "Not a bad point. Anyway, how is your business? How is your family?"

"All is . . . well, as can be expected in a house full of women. Your daughter is quite lovely—"

"What?"

Anwar noticed Ella wince. "Is there something the matter?"

"Aman mentioned you knew of her whereabouts," said Sallah S., holding up his hand. "I suppose . . . a girl needs company. We just hope it is good company." He smiled.

"We must go; the pleasure was all mine." Anwar skipped over Sallah's spittle on the ground.

"Anwar, I remembered—I need to go do something. I'll see you back at the house," said Ella. She felt a slow constriction in her throat, feeling guilty just talking to Maya's father with such civility. His yelling had penetrated the walls of the apothecary, and Ella could imagine him in his full might and terror. As for Anwar's story, she knew that she wouldn't hear the story of the Black Forest until much later, maybe even years later. That's how things seemed to go when it came to stories about her father. She unlocked her bike, and rode into traffic. Noon heat burned her skin. There was the smell of a distant barbecue, and Ella's stomach panged. As she rode along Atlantic Avenue, she rummaged through the old images that flashed in her mind, and she felt uncertain that these were true memories. Had her father run around the house with her standing on his feet? Had her mother bathed her in the kitchen sink, and taught her to kiss with her nose? Her mother had long black hair, which she'd worn in a loose braid. Ella remembered chewing on her mother's hair. It had been crunchy and dry. She knew that their murder had been related to the war, that somehow the people who had taken their lives had been pro-Pakistani Bangladeshis. But the obsession to know the details had been diluted by time and distance. As a small child, she had been transported to a new homeland. She did not speak those first few months. She was mute, and now, remembering, she realized that she had made the decision not to talk. No amount of talking would bring them back to her. She felt that she had never quite fit in, and even after she started to speak, she never quite did.

She rode onto Joralemon Street, weaving around the hunkering buses and lackadaisical crowds of summertime shoppers, high school kids with summer jobs, along the strip of sneaker, electronics, and discount clothing stores.

Finish Line.

Ella caught the name of the store from the corner of her eye. She hit her brakes so hard to look in the store window that she almost rode into a shopping cart packed with a mountain of glass bottles.

"Watch the road, kid!" shouted the man who was pushing the cart. He wore a soda jerk cap constructed of newspaper; he looked like a mad waiter on the run.

She pulled over to the sidewalk, and the man stood still, as if waiting for a more adequate response. Ella busied herself with pretending to lock her bike on a rack, while sneaking a glance through the storefront window of Finish Line. The man lost interest and continued to push his cart down the street.

Ella fumbled with the bike lock, and looked again into the store.

There she was. Maya. She was not wearing her hijab on her head, but Ella saw it draped on her shoulders as a scarf. Her pixie haircut had grown longer onto the nape of her neck, into the start of a mullet. Ella could not see her face. Maya was kneeling on the ground as Ella had seen her do so many times, but this time, she did so in front of a girl her own age, helping her try on a pair of bright colored kicks. The girl checked out her feet in the floor mirror.

They spent almost every night together in the garden. But the past couple of nights, Maya had been exhausted after work, going straight into Ella's bedroom to pass out.

"Look here, come on," whispered Ella, standing in the middle of the sidewalk, transfixed, hearing nothing but: *Then you haven't.*

Anwar's summation of her love life.

Maya smiled at the girl, who nodded that she wanted the pair of sneakers. Maya beckoned a boy to take the girl to the cash register. As soon as the boy whisked the girl away, Maya leaned against a mirrored pole, staring up at the ceiling. She did not see Ella. Maybe it was the glare from the fluorescent store lights. Maybe it was some unseen magic in the ceiling, or a leak. Maybe Maya did not feel Ella burning a hole through the glass.

Whatever it was—

"Yes, I have."

A minute later, Maya caught Ella's stare, and stared back. Maya shook her head, slowly, but Ella couldn't read the gesture. All Ella felt was the massive tightening in her chest, a brilliant sensation of lightness and heaviness all at once. She waved. Maya lifted her hand up.

Just as Maya's attention was taken to a toddler picking out her first pair of sneakers, Ella was gone.

13

After Ella had left, Anwar started walking in the direction of Rashaud Persaud's table. But Rashaud and his table were not there. *Strange,* thought Anwar, *Rashaud is not one to take days off.* His friend was already inhibited by weather patterns. *Perhaps he's fallen ill.* Anwar found himself wanting to eat at Prospect Park. He could not remember the last time he'd lain on a blanket to take in passersby. But it was too far a walk to make in the middle of the day. He debated whether or not to go back into his shop for a quick smoke. He settled for his favorite halal truck on Atlantic, and sat with a kebab in the plaza of Atlantic Terminal Mall, in the middle of the blazing afternoon bustle. He wiped his brow with the cotton handkerchief he kept in his pocket.

He had almost told Ella the story of the Black Forest, and he was grateful, as appalling as it was, for Sallah's interruption. Anwar closed his eyes, recalling the first night that he and Rezwan had taken over a command post by themselves, without any of their other comrades. Their orders were to stake out a farmhouse in Kadipur. A farmer and his family had been burned alive by Rajakar twins, who had taken a killing tour of the hillside towns around Sylhet. Rajakars were like local travel guides for the Pakistani forces, traitors to the cause. After the killing, the twins allegedly occupied the farmhouse and surrounding land, turning it into a morbid clubhouse to rape women and rest on their laurels.

Anwar and Rezwan's training—swimming through leech-infested muddy swamps—was unnecessary for tonight: They rode to the farmland on their new black Royal Enfield motorcycle, which they'd claimed during their first guerrilla attack. They parked the motorcycle in a field of spinach and watermelon crop. The plants thrived despite their owner's absence.

After surveying the farmhouse for the enemy—no one was there—they stopped at a trickling khal, a tributary of the Piyain that irrigated the land. In the night water, the full moon's reflection appeared. Anwar turned up to see the real moon, but it had disappeared. He looked back down at the river, which now seemed invisible. The entire sky had gone pitch-black. He felt a shudder in his heart, and glanced at Rezwan, who was busy with ablutions for his night prayer. Something as silly as the moon in a puddle did not interest him.

"What is it, man?" asked Rezwan.

"The moon."

"What about the moon?"

"I saw its reflection in the water. But now I cannot see it. It's disappeared."

"It's the passing of clouds, the rotation of the earth, which veils your precious moon. She'll be back," said Rezwan, chuckling. "It's the nature of Maya."

"You sound like my father."

Anwar wondered if he had offended his friend by comparing him to a conservative archaeologist. He clutched his bayonet, trying to relax. His father often spoke of Maya, man's illusion, which kept him separated from the truth. The moon existed in the puddle, but not when he had looked up to behold it. And still, he knew the truth—the moon existed, even if he didn't see it with his own eyes.

"Look, Anwar, there is your moon."

They sat at the foot of the tree for a while, without speaking, staring at the moon as it rose higher in the sky.

"Do you fear anything?" asked Anwar.

"I fear God," Rezwan replied without hesitation.

"I cannot believe that."

"Not in the way you think."

"Eternal punishment?"

"Of how possibly meaningless this all is. How he laughs at our stupidity. I was also thinking, if I'd had a brother like yours, I'd cut his balls off."

"I can't do that to my brother. Besides, I don't want to touch his balls."

"Point is—men like that are preprogrammed. They're perfect for war, but too indifferent to others to fight."

Anwar wondered what would happen if he and Rezwan came upon these brothers. Killed them. What made their killing right and the brothers' killing wrong? Anwar knew the answer he hoped was true: Mukti Bahini did not rape, raid, or kill innocents. But there were disturbing rumors: Mukti Bahini had raped Bihari girls as revenge. Anwar did not want to believe this, but the way he'd seen a couple of his comrades stroking their rifles, lusty and mad-eyed, sometimes a grave doubt about independence flared in him—Anwar admitted this once—that the wisest move would be to remain with India. "Remain with India?" Rezwan thundered. "And resign ourselves to being India's armpit? Fuck your mother, man!" As soon as he said this favorite catchphrase, Rezwan grew remorseful and apologetic.

"I've got no mother to fuck," Anwar replied. On the hardest nights, he found himself whispering for his mother, whom he had never known.

Before sunrise, they decided to head back to the Black Forest, which lay on the border between Tamabil and Dawki, dividing East Pakistan and India. Once they reached the river, a boatman took them across to Dawki, to the India side. They wheeled their motorcycle through a clearing, just west of the BSF jawan's post—it was a long "shortcut" to avoid dealing with a checkpoint. They came up to a bridge composed entirely of gnarled rubber tree roots, which ran over a stream. The road from the bridge tapered into a barren moor. A single stone obelisk stood on a hill, erected by ancient Khasis. As they entered the sacred land, the trees at the helm of the grove were sparse, flute-thin supari and betel leaf. Deeper into the forest, everything multiplied, and the air was thick with dew and the scent of burning teakwood. Rezwan brought a finger to his lips. For a well-built man, he was graceful. Anwar followed him toward a woman's cry, and a baby's wail. The harder they tried to be quiet, the more sounds he imagined: a smattering of laughter, exploded mortars. Anwar shook his head. Out here, in the Black Forest, they were safe from the war.

They followed the ominous timbre to a circular house in the center of the woods. Once they arrived, Rezwan relaxed. He knelt beside the woman, nursing her child on the porch. He kissed her forehead.

"Hello, my love."

And now, on a bench in Brooklyn, Anwar chewed overcooked halal beef kebab of questionable origin, like a cannibalistic cow smacking her lips. He spat the meat into a napkin. The sun had drained his energy to eat, to move, to think anymore. He was glad he had made this time for Ella, whose remarkable likeness to Rezwan saddened him. Not because it was a bad thing to be like one's father, but that he had spent the past sixteen years playing at it. She was nearly twenty-one, an adult in her own right, but still, Anwar wondered if he'd made any impression. He felt he had failed to teach Ella who her parents had been, where she came from. He hadn't wanted to haunt her childhood, he supposed, just as he found himself haunted. Rezwan's head trailed his highs like a broken memory. *I have to type up the mess on that paper,* Anwar told himself, remembering the brown parchment he'd titled "Black Forest." He closed his eyes and fell asleep for some time. When he awoke, Atlantic Mall was still as crowded as when he'd sat down. He touched his face, which felt painfully raw.

All this dreaming of the moon and I've been burned by the sun.

Anwar walked back to the shop, ready to close.

Anwar walked up to his storefront and blinked his eyes several times to be sure of what he was seeing. The window of the apothecary was shattered in a cracked spiderweb of glass, with shards scattered inside the shop. His tower of Magic Jojoba shampoo had toppled over. He leaned into the gaping hole of his storefront window. Bricks. Anwar counted four, and on one of them, someone had written "Pig" with a white paint marker pen. Anwar paused to catch his breath and leaned against the wall between the apothecary and A Holy Bookstore. His bones hurt; never had he felt so run-down. He remembered a book from Charu's childhood, and thought: Anwar and the Terrible, Horrible, No Good, Very Bad Day. *Kids are smart,* he thought, *especially those three boys with Sallah S. No older than eighteen, alive and trigger-happy, comfortable in packs. But they are unlike wolves and more like feral dogs.* Each boy held allegiance to himself, first and foremost, united when it was time to play. For a moment, Anwar considered that maybe this was a message from Sallah S., a blatant warning about his daughter's chosen company. Unlikely, he decided. This was a wanton act. Summer's usual mayhem.

By eight o'clock in the evening, the world basked in the setting sun's amber glow. Ella had biked around the park, and through their neighborhood for hours, working off her elation at seeing Maya. She turned onto the quaint ride up Willoughby Avenue. On Willoughby, things were quieter, dotted with a car or two, a dog walker, a lady sitting on her stoop. She felt she was riding in a foreign land, saturated with color and secrets. *I've never left the country since I got here,* she realized. She wanted to whisk Maya out of those fluorescent lights, into all that was out here. They could ride their bicycles cross-country, maybe even into Mexico. She pictured them trekking through a desert, into the night, counting constellations, building a fire.

When Ella arrived back at 111 Cambridge Place, she heard nothing but the drumming of Charu's sewing machine. There was no smell of dinner. No sign of Anwar, or Hashi. Maybe they were on one of their evening walks, though she couldn't remember the last time they'd done that.

Ella wondered if she should tell Charu, or even Anwar, that she loved Maya.

No, Ella thought. *This is mine.*

Later that night, Maya invited Ella and Charu to a warehouse party along the border of Bed-Stuy and Bushwick. This time, Ella agreed to go.

The party was at an old garment factory, a behemoth concrete structure that had survived mass arsons in the seventies, workers' strikes, and squatting artists. Young people strutted at all corners of the spot, leaning against walls, waiting in line for the bathroom, vogue-dancing in the center of the room. Ella realized she'd never been to one of these legend-in-the-making, underground-type parties before. She let Maya take her hand and lead her into the barrage of action: chain-smoking, rum-punch sipping from flasks masked with paper bags. Two girls in different shades of lipstick, lip-locked. They parted and smiled at Maya.

"Maya! You made it!" said the pink-lipped girl.

"I did. It's a fabulous party."

"Get a drink—who're your fly-as-hell friends?"

"Heyyy, daddy," said the other girl, grinning a red-smeared smile at Ella.

"She's not *your* daddy, sweetheart."

"She yours!" the girl howled. "Have a beautiful night, ladies, as-salaam-alaikum!" sounding more like *a salami lake 'em*!

"I should've worn my heels," complained Charu.

"Not smart if you want to dance," said Maya. "Come this way."

Ella was conscious of people looking at her. Did they find her attractive? Queers everywhere, every which way she looked. Girls, women, boys, men, and some she couldn't be sure. She contemplated removing her glasses to let all these kids take bizarre shapes and hues, but she didn't want them to catch her looking.

"Let's walk to the fire escape. I told Halim I'd meet him there." Maya pointed toward the massive wrought iron staircase zigzagging three stories.

"I can't do that," mumbled Charu.

"Why not?" asked Maya.

"She's afraid of heights," said Ella.

"With that tree outside your window? What a shame, girl!" Maya laughed.

"Yeah. I don't really do rooftop parties, fire escapes, or roller coasters," said Charu. "I try to stay grounded."

"I like that," said a girl, who appeared out of nowhere by Charu's side. "Wanna dance, ma?" She had a freshly shaved head and sported cologne straight from a magazine insert.

"Sure, why not?" said Charu. "See y'all in a few."

On the fire escape, a few couples smoked and chatted, away from the clamor of the dance floor. Ella sat on the landing between the second and third floor, and Maya moved with a tightrope walker's poise forward and backward to her own rhythm. A breeze crept into her hijab and the multicolored fabric flew around her head.

"You look like a hot air balloon," said Ella. She grabbed Maya's ankles, so that she fell neatly on her bottom next to her.

Maya yelped, "My poor ass!" She pulled off Ella's glasses and took out a small silver flask from her purse. "Take a sip."

Ella took a hearty swig and then another. She checked her watch—it was midnight. Black, yellow, and brown kids rocked wondrous hairstyles. Braided, dyed, feathered, twisted, cornrowed, flat-topped, matched with mesmerizing fashions—stirrup pants, Adidas tracksuits, tattoos, piercings, spray-painted sneakers. She envied their freedom.

There was a shot of rum left. The alcohol made it hard to focus her eyes. She saw Maya engulfed in scarlet waves, then cloaked in white foam. She shook her head but the image remained.

"You take a sip," said Ella, handing Maya back the flask. She swiped her glasses, which were perched on Maya's head.

"No, not for me. I can't right now."

"Why's that?"

"I can't right now."

"Guess I might as well," said Ella, swishing the last drop in her mouth like it was Listerine.

A loud couple ran onto the fire escape with the same abandon she feared would cause someone to fall.

"Stop, Halim! Give it back!" yelled his boyfriend, the formerly mouse-quiet Marque, whom Ella remembered from Maya's birthday picnic in July.

Halim held Marque's backpack a foot above his head. "Not until you kiss me," said Halim, holding the bag higher.

"Hell no—not till you give it back!"

"Now, now, Halim," said Maya, laughing. "That's a very bad idea."

Halim dropped the backpack into Marque's hands. "Sweethearts!"

"You've got me worried. What if you'd fallen?" Maya shook her head. "When are you leaving for Rutgers?"

"Not until Labor Day. And you? What's your plan? Come with me. You can crash at my dorm when I start school."

"I've got offers all over the tristate area," joked Maya. "That's the pipe dream of a stupid girl."

"Why are you giving up now?" asked Halim, sitting down next to her, the same worried expression on his face as on her birthday.

"You won't understand."

"I won't? I know your mother's worried as hell that you haven't called."

"Why hasn't she called the police, if she's so fucking worried?"

"Well . . . she got a lung infection; I just heard about it today."

"Poor Mema." Maya sighed.

"I know, baby, you don't want to see him. But your mema, think about your mema," said Halim. "As you can tell, Ella, my mom loves gossip."

"I saw your father today, too," said Ella.

"What? Why didn't you tell me? Is that why you came by work? To tell me? Did you love him like everyone else does?"

"He thought I was a boy."

Maya half-smiled. "He brokers deals on behalf of our community. He's a respected guy. Everyone loves him."

"I understand," said Halim, shaking Maya's shoulders. "You were gonna rot in that house the way he's got you locked up. You had to leave when he started getting on you—"

"Shut the fuck up!" screamed Maya.

Halim looked stricken; never had Maya raised her voice to him—or to anyone, for that matter. "I just want to help you."

"Then get the fuck away from me."

"You don't mean that."

"Yes. I do."

Halim stood up, taking Marque's hand into his. He raised his chin and pursed his lips. "C'mon, Marque, let's go."

"What's going on here, guys?" asked Charu from the window, without her dance partner.

"Hold my hand, baby. I'm drunk!"

The voice was angry, the unmistakable voice of the street hawker

Rashaud Persaud. He climbed through the window of the floor above, onto the fire escape. His long, stiletto-clad legs clanked down the stairs. Behind him crouched Malik, who balanced his hand on Rashaud's shoulder.

"Rashaud's legs are quite nice," Maya commented to Ella.

As they came downstairs, Malik saw Charu in the window. His eyes widened with fear. He dropped Rashaud's hand.

"Hi, guys," he mumbled. "Hi, Charu."

"What are you doing here? Why didn't you . . . call me back?"

"I've been busy, sugar. Rehearsal, work . . ."

"You're at a party—"

"I'm just"—Malik leaned in closer—"looking out for Rashaud. She—he's drunk. I need to get her home before my shift starts. I'll call you. Tomorrow."

"Tomorrow. Right," Charu said. She moved aside as Malik squatted to enter the building. He helped Rashaud inside.

"See y'all later, dearies," slurred Rashaud as they walked away.

"Is he fucking Rashaud Persaud? I want to go home."

"Charu, he's a teenage boy. They're practically, like, ninety percent erections," said Maya. "Come out here."

"I want to go home."

"He's not fucking anybody. They're just friends. Try not to think about him," said Ella.

"I had sex with him, and then he went dark. I haven't heard from him, and he's just gallivanting around here like an asshole," Charu said, choking on a sob. "I'm an asshole."

Ella stiffened at the mention of them having sex. "We all do stupid shit."

Maya smacked her arm, as if to say, *Don't be a jerk*. "Look here, Charu, my love. You'll get to college, you'll find someone new, and forget Malik in no time."

Leave it to Maya to say something kind and true while stirring up Ella's unwieldy imagination.

14

At 111 Cambridge Place, Anwar lay awake next to his sleeping wife, after an hour of being unable to perform. Brushing his teeth beforehand had ruined everything. The imbalance in his mouth, the pervasion of mint toothpaste—it was gross. He'd even applied deodorant on her request. But when he came to her, there were more complaints.

They'd kissed for many minutes until she winced and pushed him off. "Shave your beard."

"Shave yours," he said, clamping his hand on her crotch. He let her go. His libido waned like a deflated balloon, and he rolled onto his back to stare up at the ceiling.

She poked him in the jaw. "What are you looking at?"

"You ever notice these ceilings?"

"It's the same old ceilings, Anwar. They could use some paint." She jabbed his forehead with a cold finger.

"They are beautiful. The builders who molded them kept in mind the wives on their backs."

"You're mad."

He said nothing. She nuzzled under his underarm, and sniffed. "You'd do well to find a shower."

"Don't be a negative parabola, girl," he said, tugging the sides of Hashi's mouth upward. "What else is wrong?"

She looked at him blankly.

"Nineteen seventy?" he asked, trying to jog her memory.

"I don't remember yesterday."

"The big test."

"Aha-ha," she said, snapping her fingers. "You told me *your paper is smiling*—and—"

"And you said, 'It's a *parabola*!' Anwar mimicked a schoolgirl. "You were so easy."

"Easy?"

"Easier. Come," he said, pulling her on top of him.

Hashi perched on him like a young bride, but then became very still, and cocked her head to the side. "Did you hear that? I felt the ground shake." Just as soon as she had straddled him, she rolled off.

"Don't be crazy. This is Brooklyn. No fault lines. Not even a breeze on this muggy night."

"An intruder, then?"

"The earth's rotation would make you jumpy these days, woman."

"All right, all right. It's nothing."

He felt a swelling of energy and climbed on top of her, letting himself sag onto her. Hashi waited underneath him, gripping his hip-bones, whispering, "Unh, Allah," until he'd given up. The moment had come; the moment had gone. He fell away from her, and stroked his flaccid cock on his side of the bed.

Now he lay beside Hashi, arm going numb from the weight of her snoring head. He admired the strong cheekbones she'd inherited from her father. Anwar couldn't imagine her life before he'd been a part of it; she'd been so young. He was the one man she'd ever had, and unbelievably enough, she was his first and last. He had loved Hawa before her, but that was innocent, imaginary, as Hawa regarded him as a boy, privileged and helpless. He remembered being smitten by Hashi—she was a beauty on university grounds, and Rezwan Anwar's little sister. Rezwan would never let just *anyone* get near her. He'd chosen Anwar.

He wiggled his arm out from under her. He fiddled in the night-stand drawer to take out his one-hitter, which he'd remembered to bring back from the apothecary. He'd take one puff and that was it, and by the time Hashi woke up in the morning she wouldn't smell it anyway. He sparked the tip, and took a deep breath, waving the smoke away from Hashi's nose. He puffed a couple of times more, then threw the pipe back into the drawer.

He closed his eyes and squeezed his penis, trying to work up the heady lust he'd had for her when they'd first been married, but he couldn't muster much more than a warm, enveloping feeling. He suspected people spent their entire lives to find this feeling of total surrender, but that he belonged to a whole other lot of selfish bastards who spent their lives trying to find the feeling he'd had this morning, the jolt straight from his heart to his loins when he'd seen Ramona Espinal. He closed his eyes and imagined her rump on the stoop, stroking himself until he was rigid.

Ra-mo-na, he mouthed. To not say her name was almost as terrifying as saying it, and he let the rhythm of holding back rock him, back and forth. He wanted to sputter his juice all over those glorious breasts, just one more stroke—

He felt a stirring next to him, and his eyes popped open, just as he felt himself about to come. He felt a pang of fear, pure and perfect, of being caught, of lusting after another woman, and the tide reversed itself, buried deep inside him, once again.

He slid open the drawer of his side table. There was a little stash, something to nibble on. He found a Ziploc of majoun, a new batch, in which Rashaud had mixed up the recipe. His secret this time: Craisins and brown sugar. Anwar nibbled, a child tasting his first bit of sugar. Still, Hashi slept. He felt the dull ache in his balls subside, as the majoun settled into him.

Rezwan's head appeared as a shadow on the wall.

"Rezu, hello."

Together, they recited a fragment of *Surah al-A'raf,* for the juncture between the garden and earth.

We inspired Musa
His thirsty people asked for water
We said: "Strike the rock with thy staff"
Water gushed from the springs.
We offered them the shade of clouds
Sent down to them manna and quails
We said: Eat the good and plenty
They rebelled / They did not harm us / They harmed their own souls.

Rezwan's expression was harsh. *You've not tended your garden. You left Ella to it, and it is ridden with pests; it is infested with aphids. You've received manna from the gods, aphid shit—honeydew, manna, miracle food of those travel-weary Israelites. No, my friend, you've not dealt with any of your problems. You are a thief, a drug addict, coveting women other than my sister—what is my child to learn from you?*

"You aren't here," said Anwar, shaking his head. "I must spend time with your sister now."

He shook Hashi and she swatted his hand away.

"My love, get up, get up, let's go outside."

"Whaaaat is outside?" Hashi moaned.

"The world, fresh air, people, everything," said Anwar. "It *is* Saturday night."

"In the thirty years I've known you, have you ever felt deprived of Saturday night?"

"No. But tonight I do. Let's go to the veranda."

He slid the door open and the quiet of their home met the never-truly-still neighborhood. There were no stars. Hashi shivered next him, kept her eyes closed. No matter; he appreciated her warmth. He'd long ago discovered that she'd never be a true partner of his thoughts, his romanticism, these moments of being one with whatever was out there. Anwar opened his ears to the marvels of dawn. He heard a faint crunching, a desperate rustling of something very small—it sounded like someone was unwrapping a lozenge. Were the aphids eating away at his plants right under his nose? He listened closer and the continuing hollow sound tickled a rage—a curious feeling—inside him. The gall, the absolute gall of these devils! "I'll kill you all!" he feebly shouted into the air, raising his fist. The rustling continued, stopped, continued.

"Anwar, are you mad?" Hashi said, lifting her head off his shoulder. "You'll wake the neighbors!"

"*Arré*, Hashi, shhh, *shoono*."

Hashi widened her eyes, as if to say, *Yes, you loon, what in the hell do you want me to hear?*

Rezwan's head rushed through their embrace. Anwar flinched, but Hashi did not see her brother. Rezwan's grayed skin and hair appeared silver in moonlight, giving him a spritely mien. He dipped down low, down to the garden, no longer visible. With an upward whoosh, his head appeared again, this time a blue creature sitting perched on his nose.

"Anwar, dekho, dekho, projapoti!" Hashi exclaimed, pointing at the butterfly sailing in front of them.

"Arré, Hashi," Anwar croaked. Rezwan swept back downward, up and down, and up again, until Anwar's head was spinning, too.

Rezwan mouthed:

We sent plagues, signs / a people steeped in arrogance

A people steeped in sin.

"Stop, *ya,*" Anwar whispered. "Please stop."

"Ay, Khoda," Hashi yelled. "Anwar, dekho!"

Rezwan brought back another blue butterfly, then a cerulean bevy of butterflies hovered in the sky. Anwar gripped the deck railing and looked down at the garden. An indiscernible figure crept through the garden. Had Rezwan been reunited with his body?

—A wailing from down below—

Hashi tore herself away from him and ran back inside. She'd gone mad with fear, Anwar worried, trying to rush after her, clanking down the stairwell, attempting to catch her before she hurt herself. Speedy for her years, she hurtled out the back door and tackled the figure into the ground. Anwar doubled over, cupping his knees. *Ah, it is Charu,* he thought, chest heaving, relieved, *and Ella and Maya.* Too out of breath to stop Hashi from bringing down the garden hose—the only object she could find—onto Charu's face.

"Take Maya home. She cannot be here."

Hashi spat the words, as Anwar and Ella pulled her off of Charu. Maya ran into Ella's bedroom, collected her things in minutes.

"Just wait, wait. You can leave tomorrow morning," Ella pleaded.

"No, I'm going to leave now."

"You're going back to your parents' house?"

"Not yet. I need to think."

Ella followed Maya onto Cambridge Place, and they walked in silence on the sidewalk. The slabs of slate had been weathered over the decades, smooth enough to walk barefoot all the way to Fulton Street. Streetlamps guided them, as did the occasional taxi whizzing by.

"Turn right," Maya said.

When they arrived at the masjid, Ella realized that it must be time for morning prayer, Maya's prayer. There was a short, squat man wearing a fez and long kurta top, his beard white as Santa's, gossiping with a trio of young men. Ella couldn't quite recognize them in the predawn light. *Are they the same boys from this afternoon at the apothecary?* Maya nodded salaam, and led Ella to a small prayer room. The place was covered with plush Turkish carpets and a stickered wall of a hundred hologram Allahs.

"This is it," said Maya. "Head covers." She pointed to a cardboard box brimming with multicolored fabrics. She took a plain black hijab, and tied it around Ella's head.

"I don't actually know what to do. . . ."

"Just follow my motions. Think about whatever you want," said Maya. "You can't talk out loud. Men can, though." She started on her feet, bent over her knees with a flat back, then sat down on her rug.

Ella had never been inside a prayer house before. Anytime Hashi had tried to get them to go as a family, Anwar had, for as long as she could remember, refused to attend. He would stay home or cite work duties, and Ella stayed behind with him. Charu, on the other hand, went along with her mother, even attended Arabic school, which was where she'd met Maya.

Ella had a terrible headache. Perhaps it was the rum. She hadn't had any water all night. She peeled her glasses off, and the glittering wall of Allah decals twinkled under fluorescent lighting, waxing and waning rainbow shapes. Some of the words appeared to be swimming. There were two other women—both older than Hashi—praying in the room with them. *Women their age were shielded from the lustful eyes of young men,* thought Ella. The man and three boys who lingered outside now stood at the head of the room, muttering aloud, permitted by scripture.

Ella tried to copy Maya's position and movements: arms folded across chest, flat back, bend over and squat. Rest. Repeat. Maya's demeanor had shifted since they arrived at the masjid. She was different from the ham-eating, bike-riding spider-woman-jumpsuit-wearing girl Ella had come to know this summer. She remembered Maya's father's sly, scary presence. He was a person who could get anyone to do what he wanted—sort of like Charu, but for the purposes of obtaining more power.

Pray. For the souls of my mother and father. For my aunt and uncle. For my garden. For Charu. For Maya. I will do anything. Ella finished a good ten minutes before Maya, even after repeating her short litany.

Maya said, "Sorry I took so long. That's the part—"

"You ask for stuff."

They chuckled. There seemed to be no space for laughter in here. "What will you do at home?"

"Take care of Mema. The boys. Figure out how to go to school."

"What about your father?"

"My father's busy these days. Too busy to get into my business. Don't worry. Anyway, maybe now you'll sleep." Maya pulled Ella into her arms, pressing every bit of her body against her. "I'll talk to you so soon, Ella Anwar."

"I leave for school so soon. In three weeks," said Ella. Her voice felt tight, her mouth dry. She'd never heard herself so—desperate. "Never mind."

"Maybe I'll get a dorm room invite? Maybe *you'll* get one."

Somehow, Ella knew that she wouldn't.

15

Anwar's Apothecary was closed on Sundays. But this Sunday, Anwar wanted to run from the tremendous tension that had taken over his home. Since her indiscretions last night, Charu was under house arrest until she left for college. Though Ella had offended Hashi, she was an adult, and so, beyond her scope. Hashi had cried herself to sleep and somehow willed herself awake at seven o'clock in the morning for the day's wedding party. Anwar agreed to buy her maxi pads, just for an excuse to leave the house.

The church crowd was out and about on the streets. Anwar admired their accoutrements and commitment to the higher power on Sundays, his favorite day to sleep. He had not spoken to his brother in a month. Aman ignored Hashi's peace-offering phone calls. Anwar knew his brother, an extraordinary grudge holder, would never again respond to Hashi as he had before, and would not call her back unless he needed something.

Anwar was going to make the peace today. He would walk to his brother's establishment, called Kings Pharmacy, which Aman claimed was for the borough, but Anwar knew it was a matter of ego. It was a place he hated; he had worked in one on Long Island for a decade. Dredging up the old memories in that nasty basement did nothing to assuage today's stress, so Anwar pushed his own grudges out of his mind. Yes, he would go to Kings. Another bonus: not having to pay for maxi pads.

He passed a new store on Atlantic Avenue, On the Silk Road, which housed a collection of renowned silks: charmeuse, dupioni, shantung, crepe de chine. He paused in front of the large glass storefront to take in the bolts of fabric that lined the shelves like brilliantly colored Japanese scrolls. It would be nice to get Charu some of this stuff. Poor thing would lock herself in her room with her sewing machine for company. Inside the shop, a pair of elderly women negotiated the price of a royal purple swath of cloth. As he turned around, a jaunty West African fellow in matching lime green linen shirt and pants knocked Anwar down with a gigantic baton of fabric.

"I'm sorry, man, I didn't see you," said the man, offering Anwar his hand.

Anwar stood up and said, "I will take the entire roll, please." He reached into his pocket for his wallet—no cash. The sole credit card in the damned thing was under Aman's name. Anwar cursed his habit of stuffing credit cards into his pants pocket rather than his wallet. He was given a ten-dollar liability discount. Using the bolt as a makeshift cane, Anwar went on his way.

Atlantic Avenue's steady rush of cars accompanied him as he neared his brother's pharmacy. Anwar let out a breath he hadn't realized he'd been holding. This place sickened him. Gratuitous air-conditioning. Advertisements galore: L'Oréal! Plan B! Rogaine! SpongeBob pencil kits! Radio: the nauseating buzz of today's generation! In the back of store, the pharmacy reeked of that oppressive Aman smell, the lingering smell of a flushed toilet. *For god's sake, man. Burn some Nag Champa and do us all a favor.*

"What brings you around?" Aman said, without bothering to look up from his *New York Times* crossword. He sat at the pharmacy counter, while a young Indian woman pharmacist filled a prescription beside him.

"Oh, I need to pick up some antiseptic cream and perhaps a shaving razor, and, eh—some womanly items for Hashi," said Anwar.

"Hashi's little errand boy, huh? Go get your things and Rinku will ring you up. That's funny, isn't it? Rinku ring you up? Ha!" Aman turned up the radio and turned back to his crossword.

The woman named Rinku nodded. She widened her eyes, so that only Anwar could see. It was a look that people who'd spent enough time with Aman could understand.

Aisle 5 had Advil and other analgesics. Last night had done him in; he was paying for running down the stairs to the backyard. He admitted perhaps he was used to being a slender man who was terribly out of shape. He headed over to the bacterial ointments and creams aisle. He made an Anwar's Apothecary Cocoa Butter Scar Away, which lightened scars. Yet when it came to healing his daughter's face, he wanted that Neosporin.

Right after she had hit Charu, Anwar saw Hashi's face grimace with immediate regret.

From out of nowhere, Ella tore Hashi off before any real damage had been done. Besides the bruise on her jowl, Charu had minor scratches on her cheeks, some self-inflicted from clawing her way out of the swarm of butterflies. She'd survive, but Anwar was sure she was just as shocked as he. They'd never raised a hand to their children—once or twice a bottom had been smacked when they were toddlers, sure, but nothing as far as using an object. A garden hose, at that! What shocked him was Hashi's full control of herself in the garden. There was no manic, crazed beatdown. Hashi had been resolute and aware. She held the hose across Charu's throat and snarled, "Never lie to me again." Charu gagged under the pressure. Anwar heard Hashi's thought: *Fuck with me, child, and I will beat the life out of you.* Anwar stood there, paralyzed and a little high.

He was surprised to see that Ella and the girl Maya fled right after Hashi's outburst. Hashi's look was similar to the one Sallah S. had given him and Ella yesterday. Her disgust for their children was palpable.

In Aisle 6, land of diapers for infants, women, and the elderly, Anwar saw his tenant, Ramona Espinal.

He tapped her shoulder and said, "Boo."

"Oh!" she yelped. "Anwar, you scared me!"

"I am in this aisle to buy . . . sundries for Hashi."

Ramona chuckled. "You're a good husband."

"I hope we did not disturb you this morning."

"I wasn't home. Late shift at the hospital." She tapped a box against the palm of her hand. "Well, I've got what I was looking for. I should get some sleep. I have to be at work at ten o'clock tonight."

"Come with me. Perhaps I can get you some kind of discount. I am on the free-for-family plan."

"Sure. I could use the extra four dollars."

They walked over to Aman's register.

"Let's see what you've got here," said Aman, scanning Anwar's purchases. "That'll be twenty-three forty-nine."

"Wait, what are you doing?" asked Anwar.

"Counting up what you're taking, so you know how much you owe," he replied, as if Anwar were a simpleton.

Anwar set the bolt of silk down and searched his pockets, pretending to look for his wallet. "I—I did not bring any cash. In the past you've—" Anwar sniffed. "Very well, brother."

"I have enough," offered Ramona. "It's not a big deal."

Aman held up a hand to silence them. "This is a corporation, not some black market shampoo shop. I don't do any favors for those who don't do me any."

Ramona glared at Aman and slipped him her credit card.

"I'll pay you back as soon as we return to the house," said Anwar, as they made their way through the automatic doors into the already sweltering morning.

"What a pinche piece of shit," muttered Ramona. "Sorry, I know he's your brother."

"Whatever you said sounds about right," said Anwar. "I'm so sorry. I will pay you back when we get back to our house. When I get back to my house, I mean, whenever you get back to your house—"

Ramona laughed. "Why don't we shave this off my next rent check?"

"Then I'd have to explain to Hashi why and—oh, never mind."

"I understand," said Ramona.

"I'm walking home. Are you walking home? Do you want to walk home?"

"Yes, let's walk home."

As Anwar and Ramona arrived at 111 Cambridge Place, he could hear the radio blaring from Hashi's salon. There were two weddings this weekend. The last thing Hashi would want was for him to drop by with a bag of maxi pads. He didn't feel like saying hello, or making small talk with the wedding party: "No-way-you-met-at-the-food-co-op?" "He's-Jewish-*and*-Buddhist?"

Anwar tied the plastic bag on the vestibule doorknob and leaned the bolt of fabric against the bannister. Hashi would find them eventually.

Ramona zipped up the stairs in front of him. Step after step, he was captivated by her sashaying rear. He wanted to lay his head on it like a pillow.

They reached the third floor.

"I'll come back to repay you for the items," said Anwar.

"I said no worries—"

"I'm not letting you pay for my wife's maxi pads. Will you be home for a while?"

"Until my shift at ten, yes. Bye now."

Anwar rushed downstairs to his bedroom. He needed a smoke. He shook from the rush of electricity between his heart and crotch. He stepped on the chair and unlocked the attic door. His bare feet were sweaty on the rungs of the ladder. Once upstairs, he pulled the ladder back in and locked the door. He packed his pipe with a nugget of herb and took a long toke. He felt like he'd just run a mile. If he *were* indeed having a heart attack, smoking was a stupid idea. Ah, well. He puffed and paced. He bumped his head a few times against the wall he shared with Ramona Espinal.

"Hello?" he heard Ramona say.

Should I say anything?

"Hello?"

"Oh! It's nothing! Hello!"

"Anwar?"

He tapped a faux Morse code against the wall.

She tapped something back.

He pressed his cheek against the cool drywall, and pictured a cross-section view of her doing the same.

"Anwar?"

"I want to—" he started to say, but stopped. He hurried himself over to his table to sit down. Where did he keep the key, the key that would open the partition? He went over to the wall and tapped his knuckles on it once more. She tapped an identical rhythm back to him.

They did this a number of times.

"Where are you?" she said, sounding as if she were speaking underwater.

He found the key taped to the side of his refrigerator. Given his tendency to forget items in pockets and crevices, he'd taped it there a couple of years ago, before they'd even had a tenant. He removed the key and slipped it into the doorknob, praying for it to work, for it not to work.

Ramona pulled the door open.

She stood there wearing nothing but a pair of rather large underwear and a utilitarian-looking bra. Not what he'd pictured. Her body dripped with sweat—she did not have air-conditioning in her bedroom. His kind of woman.

Anwar took a step forward and tripped on the matrix of extension cords on the floor. Every appliance she owned—iron, hair dryer, lamp, CD player—was plugged into a flimsy power strip. "Fire hazard, you know."

"Yes, Señor Propietario, thanks for your warning," she said. They laughed and sat next to each other on her bed.

Anwar felt her eyes on him, waiting for him to do something. But he'd already done the unthinkable: He'd walked through a wall.

"It's strange to have you over here like this," said Ramona.

"It's strange to be here."

She sniffed the air. "I wondered if I were imagining marijuana."

"You are not imagining things. Do you want some? I can go get it—"

"No. How about a drink? How about a shot of tequila?"

"Tequila, I've not had since 1982!" he exclaimed. "No drinks, for that matter."

"Well, then, let's drink some tequila."

She hopped off the bed and disappeared.

In his fantasies, they never spoke. They never shared anything. They were just fucking. He looked around her room. She had built a bookshelf into the wall above her bed—a nice touch. He stared at some of the titles. *The Bell Jar, This Bridge Called My Back, Ulysses, NCLEX-RN Examination, Davis's Drug Guide for Nurses*. She kept things pretty neat in her bedroom, besides the extension cords. Late afternoon light filtered through the blinds in stripes along the floor.

Plants in plastic vessels dotted the windowsill. They needed watering.

Ramona reappeared with a bottle of clear tequila marked TRES GENERACIONES, and two shot glasses—one held in her lips, the other balanced on her forefinger.

"You have a lot of books."

"Yes." She dropped the shot glass into Anwar's palm.

"You know the layout of your floor is like ours," said Anwar. "I wanted to build two of everything, so that maybe I could have my own place within a place."

"No tengo limas. You'll get the full taste." Ramona poured the clear liquor into his tiny glass, and then into hers. She sat down next to him, and said, "On three . . ."

"Let me try—" said Anwar.

"Uno, dos, tres," they counted together, laughing.

Anwar felt his mouth explode. "Fire," he sputtered.

Ramona shook her head, feigning exasperation, and slid even closer to him. Her breast grazed his arm.

"You know, I thought you had a boyfriend," said Anwar.

"I just broke up with my husband of seven years."

"Husband? The stocky man with a"—Anwar flicked an imaginary ponytail—"a rattail?"

"Ha. Yes, that's him."

"Your husband?"

"Well, once upon a time we did it for the papers, but we were in love. Now I've got the papers, but there's no love."

"Who is this guy?"

"Hugo. He's a biology professor at NYU."

"Biology professors have changed since my day. How did you meet him?"

"We've known each other since we were in college in Mexico City, but we fell in love here."

She stopped speaking and poured another shot of tequila, and Anwar pushed his glass forward. Again they counted to three, but this time they said *ek, dui, teen*. The shot burned less this time around. He leaned forward and met Ramona's lips. Each rapturous tickle of her tongue, each whiff of her breath that tasted like salt, breath mint, and tequila, engorged every cell in his body with desire.

"What madman would ever let you go?" he found himself asking.

"That's the funny thing. He's already let me go once before. But this time, he's sure. He never wanted to be married."

"Not worth a second more of your time," said Anwar.

"It's hard to just stop loving someone, no?"

"You never will stop. But seven years, it's not so long. Try twenty-five."

"I wish." Ramona said the words with a touch of sadness.

Anwar wanted to get her back to a kissing mood. Sometimes, talking it out did just the trick. "How did you two meet?"

"We met in 1992. He'd just published his landmark publication, *Coleópteros Británico* (*The Beetles*). Others in the Biology Department were jealous of his success. His attitude was just like any other brilliant man. Ego, humongous. Dick to match. Always unchallenged. So when New York University offered him a tenured position, he accepted, and the night he told me this, he said he couldn't get me a visa. I asked him to marry me."

"You asked him to marry you?" Anwar said, incredulous.

"If I didn't, he never would."

"He said yes?"

"He didn't answer me and we spent hours fucking, until we were too dehydrated to keep on. He snuck out while I slept, no good-bye, nothing. From that morning, I had massive headaches. Nothing could help me. *La migraña*, said the doctor, *es por causo del estrés.* No shit, I told him, of course I'm stressed. The doctor wrote me a prescription for painkillers and told me to think positive. I lay in bed, nibbling codeine, dousing it with tequila. Needless to say, I didn't get better. This went on for four months; by the end of the term, I had failed every class. Dead broke, couldn't afford our place, refused to move back to my parents' house in Zacatecas, so I rode a bus north to Cuautitlán, to live with my cousin Leticia. She'd never been one for school like me, the family nerd, so she toiled at a Kimberly-Clark paper mill. Kotex pads, tampons, diapers—for babies and for old folks when they laugh or sneeze—it was that type of place, where all the girls felt plugged up in others' shit, piss, and blood, just like nurses. A foreman called Pepe messed with Leticia. He favored his girls short, soft, and brown like caramels."

"Did you start working there?" asked Anwar.

"Please, of course not. I was not about to start working in a maquiladora for shit money and perverted bastards. I kept trying to convince her to leave that awful place. One evening she agreed, after a treacherous day at the mill. We figured the highway toward Mexico City was a straight shot; all we needed to do was hitch a ride. We set out around four a.m., and scored our lucky break."

"Isn't hitchhiking deadly business in Mexico?"

"Not more than any other place. It was safer back then. We found a ride with two boys in a truck—brothers or lovers; we couldn't tell at first."

"So, you hitched a ride with these fellows."

"Yes. So, the platinum blond, called Art, was born and raised in Phoenix, Arizona. He was studying moles in Oaxaca, where he seduced Paco, a Spanish national and fellow student at their cooking school. They skipped out of that town to play house in Mexico City, renting an apartment in Zona Rosa, but they decided to return to Phoenix to open a restaurant."

"The Spaniard was an illegal, too?"

"Yes. And they just took a liking to us, I guess. They thought we were lesbians."

"Oh?"

"My hairdo was short in those days."

"But how can you ride a car across the border? Don't the police check everyone's papers? I took a plane so I've no idea."

"Art, the solo American, drove us a mile south of the Arizona border checkpoint at Nogales. It was around eight o'clock in the evening. Deadly hot if you go any earlier in the day. You risk getting caught. Paco, Leticia, and I walked for three miles in the desert, armed with bottles of water, Paco's flashlight, and each other's company. I think we stopped once, when Leticia stepped in some prickly pear and we had to pull out the thorns. I don't remember being afraid, but it's easy to die of thirst. I don't remember much except about the desert itself, for I was too captivated by the millions of stars guiding our way. El Carro guided us, all the way to the access road on Interstate 19, where Art was waiting in his pickup truck. We drove the next couple of hours to Phoenix. Leticia and I waitressed at their new restaurant, Los Amantes. We crashed upstairs, in a one-bedroom with three other waiters, well-bred men who offered us a curtained-off square, the size of a playground sandbox. Leticia married one of them, Victor, and they moved to Las Cruces, New Mexico, to start their own Los Amantes. I waited until Leticia left to telephone Hugo in New York. It was December twenty-fourth. I hoped that maybe the season, his birthday, and maybe, my voice, would soften him enough to score a plane ticket to New York."

"And he married you?"

"Yeah. We loved each other. And I could get my degree."

"And now, you are no longer married."

"For now, we're apart."

Anwar wanted to feel her as he'd fantasized about her. Without words. He pushed her back onto her bed and straddled her hips. He took a moment to look at her lying beneath him, sprawled open. She put her hands to his cheeks. He scratched her nails along his stubble as if it were an emery board. Her eyes twinkled—was it her story or the tequila? She leaned upward, until they were nose-to-nose. She wasn't wearing a drop of makeup. There was nothing artificial about her.

"You are beautiful, Ra-mo-na."

"That's the tequila talking."

"No. It isn't."

"We shouldn't be doing this, Anwar."

"Do you want me to leave?"

"No."

The glass honey jar he saw her use every morning was on the nightstand. He grabbed it and struggled to unscrew the lid.

"This would be *no problem* if it were a plastic bear!" he grunted. "One moment—ah!" He rolled off Ramona, onto his back, and she propped up on her elbow, frowning. Trying with all his might, *ek . . . dui . . . teen . . .* finally, he popped open the jar. Debonair and determined, he dipped his finger into the honey, and stroked her collarbone with it. He licked it off her skin. Euphoria.

She shuddered. He pressed his forefinger against her lips to tell her to be quiet. She fell backward onto the bed. He straddled her, feeling himself swell up against her pussy. With his finger, he painted her lips with honey, and bent down to kiss it off. They did this for what seemed like an hour.

He pressed his hand against her crotch, but she shook her head no.

"I guess diapers are the theme of the day," said Anwar.

He wanted to fuck her for hours and leave her there, begging him for more. He slid his rigid hard-on between her breasts, just as he had pictured—

Ek, dui, teen, he counted his thrusts.

Two minutes.

A shudder of ecstasy.

"Been a while?" Ramona asked.

"You've no idea."

"I think I do."

"I—I must go back home."

"Of course."

Anwar crept out of her room. "See you—"

"Soon," she said.

And once more, he walked through the wall, back to his side.

After a couple of puffs of the old pipe, Anwar passed out on the floor of his studio. A loud pounding beneath stirred him awake. He looked at the wall clock—it was eight p.m.

He opened the door and nearly got hit in the head with a broomstick.

"*Arré!* Watch it, Hashi!"

"You'll suffocate up there! What if you have a heart attack? We'd never know!"

He checked his body for marks or stains—everything was intact. But just thinking of Ramona stirred his pants. He shook his head to clear his thoughts. "Coming, coming."

Hashi stood at the foot of the ladder, watching him miss the last rung. She wore a long robe over a silky mint green nightie. It clung limply to her breasts.

He pulled her toward him, and rammed his tongue deep into her mouth. Hashi didn't resist. He was surprised when she jutted her tongue against his.

"You taste salty," Hashi whispered.

They collapsed onto the bed. Anwar pinned her down. She raised her backside without any cajoling on his part. He brought her bottom up and down, picturing Ramona until he finished.

Hashi lay naked on the bed, legs splayed open, like when they were first married. "Check the door, please. The girls walk in without knocking."

Anwar obliged and then rejoined her on the bed. Hashi wrapped her legs around his.

Anwar looked up at the ceiling. "I wonder where all the bits of dust and matter go. Maybe we breathe it in." He paused. He couldn't make sense of this: He was able to fuck Hashi, for the first time in a long time.

"Everything becomes dust, I suppose," said Hashi, leaning her body in harder against him.

Anwar wanted to go back upstairs, take a toke, steal his way into Ramona's bed.

16

I hate Mondays, was Anwar's first thought as he awoke to Hashi looming over him. He opened his eyes a sliver—she was whispering a quick protection dua and leaned over to kiss him on the forehead. She shook him. "Anwar? It's already eight thirty. Aren't you going to the office today? Do you want anything for breakfast?"

He had never understood why the woman persisted in calling his store an office. "Unnnnh," he moaned. "No, no breakfast. I am not hungry yet."

Hashi sat next to his head and started stroking his chin. "I heard your stomach rumbling; I can fix you something—"

"No breakfast."

"All right, then. I am going downstairs. Bye."

He waited for another ten minutes, in case Hashi forgot a spool of thread or a face cream. She did not return.

Anwar sprung out of bed to shower. Hot water stripped away last night's musty scent. He dressed himself in his favorite periwinkle blue polo, khaki pants, and always, his leather Batas. Where was the key? He rummaged through his pockets, conscious that he'd worn the same pants yesterday. No key.

He jumped up to reach the handle of the ceiling door. He pictured himself a basketball player and jumped to pull it open. No use; he was five feet ten (on a good day). He propped up the usual chair to get into his studio. He knocked on the wall he shared with Ramona.

No answer.

Anwar knocked again. Still, no answer.

He heard a rapping on the wall. "Come!" said Ramona.

Anwar turned the knob to Ramona's bedroom, but it was locked. "Unlock the door, Ramona."

She couldn't hear him.

"Open the door, woman! Unlock!"

"What?"

This could go on forever, he thought. The key wasn't next to the refrigerator. Where had he put it after they had made love? He retraced his steps from the door to the chair, where he'd fallen asleep. He knelt down to inspect the ground. Nothing.

"The key, I cannot find the key," said Anwar. He fumbled in his desk drawer for his Spanish dictionary to find the word for key. Those damned two-*L* words intimidated him. *How on earth do you pronounce* llave*?*

He checked his watch—they were wasting precious time. It was already nine thirty. Hashi wouldn't be so busy today, after a weekend of weddings. She'd come upstairs to check why he hadn't stopped by for breakfast. He felt his erection would cut a hole in his pants. He began sweating profusely and didn't want to stink before seeing Ramona. The key was nowhere to be found, not even in the pocket of the pants he'd worn for ten consecutive days.

"Fuck me," he said. He climbed back down the ladder to search his bedroom for the key, knowing it was not there. Hashi could enter at any moment. He tried to calm his brain. Where could it be? He looked up at the ceiling, to his studio, to a god, a god of love—

He made the bed, which he never did, before he decided to knock on Ramona's front door.

Ramona opened the door wearing a NY YANKEES jersey, bare legs, hair mussed, horrified expression. "Why are you coming in through *here*?"

Anwar stepped inside and tried to kiss her neck.

She swatted him off. "No, you can't come in this way. This is the stupidest thing you could do."

"I can't find the key. I can't leave without fucking you." He kicked the door closed behind him.

He rocked her onto the bed and pushed himself upon her. He wanted her to suck his fingers clean. "I want to feel you," he said, quivering.

"You do feel me," she said.

He drove himself into her wet, bloody, yawning pussy. *Stop*, he told himself. *This is dangerous, you are stupid, a stupid old man—*

"We shouldn't, we shouldn't," moaned Ramona. Each time she said it, she pushed herself harder against him.

My woman, my house, he thought, unfurling her fingers. In that moment, he shed all of his troubles inside her.

"You could use a shower, Anwar."

"That's the word on the streets."

"Let me make you some tea," said Ramona, jumping out of bed. "Use the shower if you want."

"I'll take a shower at my place. You have mediocre water pressure, correct?"

"Not funny." She left him and went into the kitchen.

Anwar felt rejuvenated and ready to get to work. It was now eleven o'clock. He had to get out of the house before Hashi took her lunch, which would be at half past one.

"I should get going!" he called to Ramona.

She returned carrying a tray topped with a pink ceramic teapot and two steaming cups. "Do you want milk and sugar? Or honey?"

"I'll take it as you have it."

She grabbed the honey jar from the nightstand. She squinted, seeing something in it. "It's the key!" she exclaimed. She held the jar up to the sunlight. The key was suspended like a fossilized bee in amber. She handed it to Anwar.

"Quite sticky. I'll wash off the honey. I need to get out of here before Hashi realizes I've never left," he said, sitting up. He grabbed his shirt and started buttoning before realizing the juices on his navel had soiled his clothes. "Shit, this was a fresh shirt!"

"I'll wash it. Now go!" Ramona opened their shared door. "Hasta luego."

He looked at her and nodded.

Anwar sighed relief as the door shut behind him.

He showered and rinsed off the key and erased traces of Ramona. He felt giddy and dirty, all at once. He was starving. Would pretending to have come home for lunch as a surprise be wrong?

Yes, you old bastard, Anwar scolded himself in the mirror.

He tiptoed downstairs, until he made it outside. He hurried away from the sound of Hashi's laughter and her clients' gossip.

At the apothecary, Anwar set up a flimsy plywood board to cover the unsightly broken window. He'd have to get Ella to help him fix it, or call a guy, as Bic always said. Bic had dozens of these guys, for accounting, buying property, plumbing—and Anwar couldn't think of anyone except Ella. He passed the day mindlessly. A customer or two came, but no one bought anything, nor did he try to convince them to. *I've crossed an invisible line.* He felt abandoned by his old friend. There was no conjuring Rezwan, even when he smoked. He spoke the beginning of *Surah al-Noor,* a fearsome prologue to the verses on light:

> ***Adulteress and the adulterer—***
> ***punish each one of them with a hundred lashes;***
> ***and may you not have pity on them.***

When Anwar arrived at home around eight, a dim nightlight was plugged into the kitchen wall. The table was set for one person. A plate of cold rice, lentils, mustard oil mashed potatoes, and beef curry lay under a piece of tinfoil. Where was Hashi? The girls? He heard no radio from Hashi's downstairs, no stuttering from Charu's sewing machine, no sign of Ella. Anwar ate his meal alone, chewing the rice, which tasted like paper, and the beef, which tasted like rubber. Not for the lack of flavor in Hashi's food, but for the lack of flavor in his mouth. He wanted to see Ramona. She'd be leaving for her shift soon. He had the key. She was just on the other side of the wall.

He wondered what to do, until he fell asleep sitting up.

An hour later, he felt a tap on his arm, the sort of tap to see if he was warm and alive, and he tried to will himself awake in the dream he was already forgetting.

"Arré!" Anwar shouted.

"Uncle? Sorry to wake you."

"Rezu—forgive me, forgive, I am bad, very bad," slurred Anwar.

"It's Ella."

Anwar's eyes widened. "Ellaaa? Ella! I was worried. I know you don't need my worries, but I offer them to you."

She stood close to him and wiped his nose off with her sleeve. "Why don't you get some sleep?"

"Don't worry about me, child. I'll be on my way upstairs."

Ella squinted at him. She appeared unconvinced. Anwar patted her arm and motioned for her to go out to the backyard.

Upstairs, Hashi was not yet in bed. Anwar found himself climbing up to his studio, beckoned by the promise of Ramona on the other side. He said a prayer in front of their door, and kissed the key. Aware that this was a brazen act, he let adrenaline chart his course. He turned the key and walked through the wall.

A candle flickered. He caught two shadows first. Short, yet elegant fingers caressed Ramona's hair, parting the coffee brown waves in the middle, just along her spine. Each vertebra poked through her back as little stones molded in clay. This man, who must be the brilliant and stout Hugo, smelled as though he'd been soaking in lemony dishwater.

Anwar felt his fist punch her spine before he could stop himself.

"Agh!" yelled Ramona, turning around. "Anwar, what the fuck are you doing? You can't just come in here—"

Hugo, or who Anwar assumed was Hugo, leapt over Ramona with unpredictable dexterity, and slammed him back toward the door of his annex. Anwar fell to the ground. He crawled to escape the hulking man advancing.

"I—I didn't mean to hurt you—who are you?" stuttered Anwar.

The man picked him up by his shirt collar and growled, "I'm her husband, you goddamn piece of shit. How dare you put your fucking hands on her? I'll kill you." He punched Anwar's face. Anwar winced at the splitting of skin. He tasted his own blood, for the first time in twenty years. He tried to scratch at Hugo's face, but felt his own rage consumed by the man who straddled him, as Anwar had straddled Ramona.

Hugo began squeezing his fingers against Anwar's throat. His fingers were sticky.

Anwar stuck his tongue out to taste. "Honey?"

"You fucking faggot Indian son of a bitch. How dare you touch my wife?" Hugo struck Anwar's cheek with the back of his hand a couple of times, and then banged his head up and down against the floor. From far away, Anwar heard, *Stop!*

But he couldn't follow the voice.

"Anwar."

His eye was already swelling shut. Through the bloody slit, he saw Hashi.

In and out of consciousness, Anwar heard his worst nightmare come to life, as if he were underwater:

"I—I—I think that it is time for you to find another situation, Ramona. All that has happened is something beyond our control. It is not good for me. Or my children," said Hashi.

"I'm sorry, Hashi."

"You have two weeks."

Anwar tried to stir himself up, but couldn't bear to open his eyes.

"As you wish."

He didn't hear anything else.

At midnight, Anwar woke up on the floor of his studio. He'd soaked the dhurrie rug beneath him with blood. "Hashi!" he shouted. He willed himself to roll onto his side. He felt as though he'd broken a rib or two. He propped himself up. Smashed bits of glass were everywhere. The entire kitchen was trashed—bottles of oil broken on the floor. Anwar realized that for the first time in all these years, Hashi had seen his studio, his home away from her.

Anwar summoned the courage to descend to his bedroom, to face Hashi. He took one rung at a time.

Hashi had left the chair for him to land on.

But there was no Hashi. He heard the sound of water from a

faucet. The bathroom door was tipped open, and he let himself inside.

Hashi had lit candles on the four corners of the slate-tiled tub. Her breasts, smallish and deflated, floated over the surface of the water. She leaned against the rim of the tub, her eyes closed. She had a white mask on her face, giving her the countenance of a mummy. He saw himself in the mirror: battered, black-eyed, and ugly.

She didn't move, didn't speak. He wet his fingers in the water and dabbed her cheeks in a circular motion. The mask became mud on his fingers. She slipped underwater.

Anwar tried to pull her up, but she resisted. Particles of poppy seed whittled away and floated on the surface. She pulled herself up and out of the bath, splashing him wet. She stepped past him, and walked over to the sink. She rushed through the motion of ablutions; it was time for the last prayer of the night. *Rinse the mouth, thrice. Clean the hands and feet, thrice. Don't forget behind your ears.*

He took in her nakedness, her body slender as a girl's, at ease.

Anwar hated the wetness of wuzu. Watery pools lay stagnant, breeding mosquitos and disease that killed believers the world over. He followed Hashi out of the bathroom, into their bedroom.

She did not speak or acknowledge him. He took a seat on the bed. Everywhere there were photographs of them throughout the years, from when they'd first arrived to Charu's last birthday. He didn't notice these artifacts of their life together anymore. But now, seeing a picture of the four of them posing in front of the home they'd built—it jarred him. He clasped his hands together, as if praying with her.

He watched as she laid her prayer rug on the floor. She pulled out a nightie from the closet, a worn embroidered thing that brought more comfort than he ever could. She stood on the rug and began her prostrations. Each time she knelt, her knees popped. She bent all the way down, touching her forehead to the rug. The soles of her feet were callused and dry. Anwar wished to rub them for her. He was ashamed by his arousal at her surrender. He pinched the tip of his interloper cock to chill out.

Hashi prayed into clasped palms, whispering fervently, until

Anwar realized she was weeping. She collapsed on one side, almost in slow motion. She folded into a fetus position. Anwar knelt to stroke her back, but she became rigid and pulled her body away.

"Let's go to bed, my darling."

She shook her head no.

He found a shred of strength, using all the muscle in his legs, to lift her up to the bed. Her body became light and she didn't try to stop him. He laid her down on her back and hovered over her, though it pained him to sit up. She stared past him at the ceiling.

"I'm sorry." Anwar wrinkled his forehead in pain. "Please, say . . . anything."

"All the dust from the ceiling," whispered Hashi. "We breathe it in. Everything turns to dust." She pulled something out from under his pillow. "I found this."

It was the checkered shirt he'd been wearing this morning.

I should've just washed the damned thing in the shower.

"I remember I bought this at Macy's, with my first paycheck from that terrible Manhattan salon. You have taken pretty good care of it, even though this button you've sewn on is white; the others are tortoiseshell. You know, these days, I go out for lunch. Not in restaurants. But I'll pack some food, then sit in the park, or stop by and talk to old Dr. Duray. On my way out of the house, Ramona came down to the salon with a load of laundry. I was on my way out to visit one of my favorite clients, Gladys. She's a minister over at Emmanuel Baptist Church on Lafayette. She is my age but broke her hip when she missed a step walking out of her house. Bedridden. Can you imagine? So, I paid her a house visit. I washed and blow-dried her hair, waxed her arms and legs, did her brows. I kept her company for about an hour, until her goddaughter came home after school.

"When I came back to the salon, Ramona was folding her laundry, chatting on her cell phone. And there was your shirt, just folded into neat rectangle, stacked on top of all her undergarments," cried Hashi. "The bitch heard me come in and threw her laundry into the basket—mussing all the folded pieces along with the unfolded ones. She said something into the phone, in Spanish, and rushed past me with barely a hello. I looked up the word in your Spanish-English dictionary. *Esposa del propietario*. Landlord's wife."

Anwar did not know what to say. He'd been caught, by a moment of stupidity. Why had Ramona left the shirt out for the world to see? Why did he have that damn dictionary, knowing he'd never learn Spanish?

He wished that he'd never gone through the damned wall.

"I have loved you since you first met me. I thought of you as the handsomest friend Rezwan Bhai had ever brought to our house. I wanted you to be in our family." She knew that any mention of Rezwan would work its magic on him, for he had the resolve of a noodle.

"Forgive me. I am a terrible man. A terrible husband. I swear to you—it was the shortest affair in the world."

"I do not keep secrets from you. But, from here on, you can keep yours."

They stared at each other for a long time. For how long, neither of them knew. They read the lines written on each other's faces—lines carved out of sharing a life together for twenty-five years.

They read each other's minds:

You are tired of me. You hate me. I love you. I hate you.

Hashi looked at him, until she could no longer keep her eyes open, tired from a day of working, cleaning, crying, discovering and confirming the worst. Her eyes fluttered closed, then open again, until Anwar shut her eyes with the palm of his hand. He kept his hand on her forehead until she started snoring.

He hugged the cotton kantha quilt over his body. Hashi had stitched it years ago, when she was in twelfth standard. Yellow and red threads stitched together thin layers of worn old saris, which had belonged to generations of women. Each separate layer was so fine he could pull it through his wedding band. The stitches on the quilt were perfect and small. He missed that longing, thinking of her as a teenage quilter. He buried his face into the kantha. Each stitch was a small part of a long dotted line. The multitude of lines secured all the layers. So they could never fall apart.

Three days and one man with a van later, Ramona and Hugo packed up her life into six cardboard boxes. They left the place spotless and empty, save for an envelope with a set of keys. Anwar would not realize they had left until days later.

17

By the thirteenth of August, Ella wondered if she should rack up the nerve and go up to Maya's apartment. Once, she'd gone to A Holy Bookstore, but Sallah S. hadn't been in. But what if it made things worse for Maya in the end? Her father might lose his shit. Anwar claimed he hadn't seen Maya since the night Charu got caught. With only two weeks until summer's end, Ella had taken to spending more time at Anwar's Apothecary. He'd asked for her help replacing the storefront window and creating another batch of the destroyed Magic Jojoba shampoo. Poor guy. Ella felt a pang of sadness thinking of Anwar's innocence—he believed the whole business a random attack, a few "brick-happy" teens. But Anwar had never had problems in the neighborhood. Ella had a strange feeling about this unusual vandalism. She kept his team-signed Brooklyn Dodgers baseball bat under the counter in case anyone came around to mess with them.

Anwar had found the collector's item during one of his rummage sale binges. She was unsure why he hadn't sold the thing for a small killing, but Anwar had not yet met a worthy owner.

That afternoon, Ella decided to pay Anwar a visit. Just as she was walking in, a customer entered behind her. She was a Black woman in her twenties, with thin brows shaped like crescent moons, the long eyelashes of an old Hollywood starlet. Her head was wrapped up in a batik beehive, and she carried a small baby on her breast in a sling of the same cloth. The baby slept and gurgled in his dreams. Anwar tickled the baby's drool-covered chin. The woman gave Anwar a bemused half smile, and stepped back to move her baby's chin away from his finger.

"How may I help you?" asked Anwar.

The woman gestured for Ella to go first. "I'm just visiting my uncle; please go ahead," said Ella.

"I'm looking for an alopecia ointment," said the woman. "I've been looking for something herbal. Don't want any injections or chemicals."

"Of course not, of course not."

The woman pulled out a stuffed corner of fabric and unraveled the wrap on her head. Her head was as smooth and brown as an egg.

"You've got alopecia totalis," said Anwar, peering in closer, but careful not to touch.

"Universalis. I don't have hair on my entire body."

"My wife would be out of business if this were an epidemic," said Anwar, but he waved his hand when the woman returned a confused look. "Never mind." He turned to scan the shelf of ointments. "Amla oil stimulates scalp growth," he said, grabbing a small bottle marked AMLA (INDIAN GOOSEBERRY). He unscrewed one of them, infusing the air with the scent of Indian gooseberry.

"Please hold out your hand," said Anwar.

The woman did as instructed, and he squeezed two drops onto her palm.

"Rub your palms together; let the friction create heat. Massage the oil into your scalp."

The woman raised her arms to her bald scalp and closed her eyes, inhaling the scent. "This cures alopecia?" She raised a skeptical, pencil-drawn brow.

"I believe it can help."

"I guess that's good enough," she said, laughing. Her baby awoke and started crying. "I think the smell of this stuff made him either hungry or upset," she said.

"Him and me both," said Anwar. "You know, you look quite attractive bald, which is not easy for most women. Why wear such a huge cloth in this heat, unless of course you are doing it for faith's sake?"

"It's not for faith or fashion. I just stopped feeling like a woman when my hair started to disappear. I've spent so many years processing it, and then, when I got pregnant, I decided to go natural. But as the months passed, all of my hair fell away. How stupid, right?" She retied her batik back on her head; this time it took on a turban formation.

"Try the amla; perhaps it will work for you," said Anwar.

"You know, I'm not sure if I care. I'll use them like a magic bottle of intention, not for hair to grow back, but to remember it's all an illusion," said the woman. "Having something or not having it. Can't do anything about it either way."

"Excuse me," said Ella. She grabbed her backpack and left her uncle and the bald lady inside the shop. She sat on the curb and slipped off her glasses. Cars whizzed past like mechanical fish. *Why am I acting like I'm here to hang with Anwar?* For the past couple of weeks, Ella had managed to spend hours in the apothecary without running into Maya. A few stolen glances at the window upstairs revealed nothing; the curtains were always drawn.

An archipelago of droplets wetted the back of Ella's shirt. She heard the flapping of a wet fabric, then felt a splash on her head.

"Hey!" exclaimed Ella. She put on her glasses to see who was up there.

"Did I get you wet?" said a girl's voice. Maya hopped from the last rung onto the pavement, right in front of the bald woman, who had just stepped out of the shop.

"You've got to be careful. These rickety old fire escapes aren't safe." The woman nodded at Ella and Maya before disappearing around the corner with her giggling baby.

"How have you been?" Maya clamped a hand on Ella's shoulder and gave it a squeeze.

"Why haven't you call—" began Ella, but she stopped, catching Anwar staring at them through the store window.

"Follow me," Maya said, walking over to a rack with six bikes arranged in a modernist sculpture. Her bike rested on top, hitched upward as if ready to escape.

Ella helped Maya bring her bike down from its perch, and then walked over to unlock her own bike from a parking sign.

They rode down the midday madness on Atlantic, all the way to Bedford Avenue, where they cut a right onto Eastern Parkway.

At a red light, Ella asked, "How'd you manage to leave the house? And not before?"

"You're mad at me."

"I just want to know how you've been."

"I'm fine. I'm alive."

"Are you going to get in trouble now? For leaving?"

"My father left town for a couple of days. My mom is sick in bed and sleeps most of the day. She doesn't know what I do half the time!" Maya sped away, racing the green lights.

They rode to the Prospect Park entrance on Ocean Avenue. They stopped at Maya's favorite spot, near the Boathouse, under her favorite tree, a *Pinus densiflora*, or Japanese red pine. Ella recalled when they had come to this tree once before, when they'd gone to see Erykah Badu's tribute concert. While they waited for the show to start, Charu taught them yoga postures for relaxation. Maya had given Charu a disciple's attentiveness, but as soon as Charu lay on the ground with her eyes closed, Maya had stolen a glance at Ella, silently giggling.

The tree was coppiced into multiple trunks, like a giant polydactyl hand giving them a high six. Rough-hewn bark peeled into reddish orange sheets. Ella and Maya sat on a blanket of its dried needles. Passing clouds cast shadows on the lake's surface. A young couple was making out under another tree. A svelte West Indian nanny chattering into a headset strolled blue-eyed twins around. An ice cream truck was surrounded by a horde of other nannies with their sugar-high charges.

"So, to answer your question. I won't get in trouble," said Maya. "My father's upstate. He's at a detention center, providing spiritual counsel to a man about to get deported for selling fake Chanel. Imagine the insult—you make a few bucks on some knockoffs, then spend two years in jail waiting to go back to Guinea. Spiritual counselor. Fuck you."

"We . . . we don't have to talk about it," said Ella.

"Close your eyes."

Maya spider-crawled her fingers across Ella's temples, neck, and back. Ella shuddered with a chill. Maya stopped, and swiped Ella's glasses off. Ella felt her eyes waver. She tried to hold them steady, to look at her friend, but couldn't.

They stayed in the park for many hours, finding different nooks and corners away from people. Ella pointed out the different wild edible plants that grew all over the park. Cattails grew beside the lake, corn-dog-shaped and full of calcium. They nibbled on pink clover flowers, wild grapes, and treacle berries.

"I'm finding you when the world ends. We'll have all the food." Maya laughed. "You ready to ride back?"

In the distance they heard the evening concert begin. Thunderous applause faded into a drumbeat. Ella could hardly imagine returning to the cold and beautiful Ithaca. In just two weeks, she'd be away from all of this life.

They locked their bikes down the street from 111 Cambridge Place. Ella and Maya snuck their way to the garden along the side of the house. The humid air was thick with the scent of night phlox, moonflower, and evening primrose. And the vestiges of a cigarette, Ella realized.

"You're back." Charu was sprawled out by the flower clock, and didn't bother to sit up.

"Hey, sweetie," said Maya. "How are you?"

"In motherfuckin' house arrest. What do you care?"

"Easy, now," muttered Ella.

"Shut up," said Charu.

"Do you want to talk?" asked Maya.

Charu jumped to her feet, but lost her balance and fell down.

Ella and Maya rushed to kneel beside her. "Ella, she looks like she's going to pass out," said Maya.

"Have you eaten anything today?"

"I can't," cried Charu. She dry-heaved a few times and swooned backward into Maya's arms.

"Get her some water," said Maya.

Ella slid the back door open and fetched a glass of water. She checked for Advil and lavender oil to help Charu relax. She stepped back outside, remedies in hand. Ella held the glass as Charu drank it in one long gulp.

"All she's had today is this," said Maya, holding up a bag of low-fat Reese's peanut butter cups and a pack of American Spirit cigarettes.

"I don't want to be a fatty in college," mumbled Charu. "My chest hurts; it hurts real bad."

"Do you want me to call Anwar or Hashi?" asked Ella. "Where are they, anyway? Have you been smoking out here?"

"Fuck those fools, fuck no. I don't know where they are. I think they went for a walk or something. I couldn't hear what Baba said through the door."

"What does it hurt like?"

Charu gestured up and down her sternum. "It feels like a man wearing Timberlands is stomping on my chest."

Ella gave Charu the Advil and sprinkled a drop of lavender oil on her wrist. "Sniff this."

"Let's go upstairs," said Maya.

"Disaster zone" was an understatement for Charu's room. Stifling and hot, it was covered in shreds of fabric, loose threads, and 150 hijabs.

"Let's get this window open," said Maya. She grabbed the box fan from the floor and placed it in the window. She adjusted the speed to the highest setting, which sent fabrics flying around. "I think you should just strip and lie down in front of the fan. You will feel better, I promise."

Ella had never seen Charu like this. Her cousin's skin glistened, sweaty and unwashed. Her hair was matted on her forehead. As Maya helped Charu out of her clothes, seeing Charu naked was without thrills for Ella. Charu's face quivered, as if she would cry. "Everyone hates me."

"We don't," muttered Ella. She peered closer at her cousin. Tiny Charus were running up and down Charu's shoulder down her abdomen. Ella pinched Charu's shoulder, to grasp one of the Lilliputian beings.

"Ow!" Charu yelped.

"I'm sorry. I thought you had something on your shoulder."

"Ella, why don't we get some air and let Charu rest?" Maya said.

Outside, Ella saw moths and fireflies multiply into millions, skating up and down the trunks of the hibiscus tree. Blossoms twirled like cocktail umbrellas. Leaves flitted as wings, trying to whisk their flowers upward.

"You seeing your visions?" asked Maya, as they sat down on the lawn chairs.

"Yeah."

"You ever been to a doctor for it?"

"I think it's getting better."

"I wish I could see like you. Wild and twisted and beautiful shit."

"No, you don't."

A phrase—*maya lage*—came to Ella's mind. Anwar said it all the time. It was fitting whether someone's house foreclosed or an earthquake claimed thousands of lives. "Maya lage," Ella said.

"What?"

"It's like feeling empathy and sympathy and love and hurt—all in one."

"That's cool. I always felt like Maya was about as interesting a name as Sarah."

Maya stood up from her chair to join Ella. Ella tried to let Maya relax into her arms. They watched the sky darken and the night critters claim their flowers.

Hours later, Ella woke up and realized that Maya was not in her arms. She recalled the distinct sensation of Maya's hair bristling her chin. But where was she? Fireflies, tiny Charus, flower cocktail umbrellas, and winged leaves—Ella recited all of her visions. Maya had been with her.

"Maya," Ella said into the garden. She couldn't remember falling asleep, nor did she remember being awake.

No answer. No Maya.

Ella tiptoed inside the house, through the living room, upstairs to Charu's bedroom. She twisted the door open. For once, it was unlocked. Charu lay with her mouth hanging open, whistling through her nose.

Ella shook her cousin awake.

"What the fuck! Are you fucking crazy?" Charu snarled, snapping to attention.

"Where's Maya?"

"There." Charu pointed to a person-shaped pile of hijabs.

"That's just your mess. Where the fuck is she?"

Charu switched on her bedside lamp, and reoriented herself. "We were talking, and then . . . I don't know. You think she went back home?"

"I don't."

"Let me try calling her." Charu fumbled for her cell phone. "Shit. Straight to voice mail."

"I think I know where she is," said Ella.

"Let me come with you."

"No, you'll be too slow."

"Fuck you, I'm coming—"

Ella was already out the door.

Ella biked as fast as she could, zipping down Vanderbilt Avenue, swerving to avoid potholes. She swerved left to the Prospect Park West entrance to the park and slowed down in case she saw Maya.

"Good morning," said a passing jogger.

Ella didn't answer him. As she neared the Boathouse, she hopped off her bike and dropped it there. There was their pine tree.

Maya wasn't there.

A splash. Someone was in the lake.

"Maya!" she shouted. She ran toward the sound and jumped in. Maya was at the water's edge, slurring, "It's been a real good year, baby girl."

Ella tried to propel her arms to get closer. She gripped Maya—*she's really here,* thought Ella. In her fear, Ella pulled Maya down into the water. Maya sputtered and resisted Ella's arm. Ella tried to forget she didn't know how to swim. *I can still stand in the water.* Ella hoisted Maya onto her back, and trudged back to the grass.

"Gimme that cigarette, bitch, gimme," murmured Maya.

"There's . . . no . . . cigarettes," Ella said, heaving. She dropped Maya to the ground to catch her breath, and fell beside her. Maya swiped off Ella's glasses and spun them round and round, like a child. She started sucking on a stem as if it were a cigarette. Maya's pulse throbbed against Ella's shoulder. It was erratic, forceful, inhuman.

As daylight broke, the trees started to lose their ominous shadows. Ella yelled for help, and was spotted by another jogger, who raced over and called an ambulance.

Ella rode in the ambulance with Maya to Brooklyn Hospital. Maya started convulsing in a seizure. The paramedics attempted to stabilize her.

"Is she an epileptic?"

"Not that I know of."

At the ER, triage nurses informed Ella that no one was allowed in the room, but she was welcome to wait. Ella called Halim, who picked up on the first ring. He had just gotten dressed for his morning yoga class. Together they waited like soldiers awaiting orders. Five hours later, a young Indian doctor, Dr. Kumar, came to talk to them. She reeked of cigarettes and Ella almost asked her for one. She extended her hand, and Halim clasped her slender fingers.

"What is it, Doctor, tell us? Can we see her?" Halim's anguish softened Dr. Kumar's exhausted deadpan. "This young woman—Maya Sharif—ingested datura seeds. We found a bag of jimsonweed seeds in her pocket. Regular, garden-variety seeds. There's a weird jimsonweed trend among teenagers." Dr. Kumar squinted in pity, and said, "Don't know if you all know about it."

"I know it," said Ella, her mouth dry.

"Why on earth would she do that? What does it do?" asked Halim.

"Well. Perhaps she wanted to experience their hallucinogenic effects, or maybe this was an attempt to—" Dr. Kumar paused. "As little as one-half teaspoon, about a milligram of the alkaloid atropine per seed, can cause cardiopulmonary arrest. She's lucky, though. We pumped her with activated charcoal. She'll be okay in a couple of days."

"I want to see her!" Halim cried.

"She's resting at the moment. Do you have a number for family?"

"She—she doesn't have any," said Halim.

"We'll wait here. Until she's ready to see us," said Ella.

Dr. Kumar looked at them, sensing something amiss. "You sure you don't have a number for her folks?"

"No, we don't."

Maya was allowed to have visitors after a few days, as Dr. Kumar had promised. Ella and Halim had held vigil in the waiting room, leaving for a quick meal or a shower and change at home. Charu joined them, as soon as Ella told her Maya had landed in the hospital. Ella wasn't sure if Charu's look had been accusatory—Maya had learned about the seeds from Ella, after all. *Let me get some stuff together,* Charu had told her, assembling a basket. She included Reese's peanut butter cups, a floral hijab, black eyeliner, a sketch pad and pencils. There she was, always ready with the right gifts or sentiments, when Ella had stayed up for forty-eight hours waiting. Empty-handed.

"You're all here," said Maya. She lay propped up on an array of uncomfortable-looking pillows, an IV connected to her arm. Dark circles rimmed her eyes, and her usual raspy voice sounded even more parched.

"We're here, baby," murmured Halim. "Until you get out of here."

"I brought you some stuff," said Charu.

"A why-the-fuck-did-you-OD present?" Maya laughed.

"Stuff to keep you occupied."

"You're the best," said Maya. She turned to Ella. "And you. You found me."

"She saved your life, kid," said Halim.

"And you can't swim, Ella. I know that must have been scary."

"I told you how dangerous it was," said Ella, her voice cracking.

"That made her want to do it," Charu snapped. "Anyway, Baba said he's going to do a thorough inventory check of all the seeds in the bank. He's throwing out anything poisonous."

"You told Anwar?" asked Ella.

"Yeah. We shouldn't have shit that can kill people around the house." Charu seemed defiant, but Ella could tell she was troubled by the worry in Maya's face. "Don't worry."

"I'm not," said Maya. "I'm just tired."

"We should let her rest," said Halim.

Just as soon as he said it, Maya let out a gasp. They all turned to see what distracted her. Through the window, Anwar stood with Maya's father and a woman with a cane who looked old enough to be Maya's grandmother, but Ella realized that she must be her mother.

After speaking with Charu, Anwar checked the seed bank to see if his *Datura inoxia* was missing. It was gone. Thorn apple was a common weapon of choice for thieves and Kali-worshipping thuggees, assassins who murdered in the goddess's name. One of the forbidden flowers that Anwar would not have suggested planting. He hadn't, in fact, because he had young children. Poisonings were the stuff of Socrates or Turing's cyanide apple, not his garden in Brooklyn.

Heavyhearted, Anwar waited until after lunch to inform Sallah S. about his daughter's whereabouts. Lunch made a man sluggish and less hot-tempered, or so he hoped. For the first time in years, Anwar set foot in A Holy Bookstore. The sole impression he'd made on the place in all this time was his rosewater and sandalwood oil diffuser, which, mixed with the scent of books old and new, was tantalizing. He inhaled the ancient blend, hoping to imbue himself with courage.

"Looking for anything in particular?" asked Sallah S.

Anwar hesitated. Sallah S. was delightful at times—and this could be the last time Anwar felt his charm.

"It's Maya," said Anwar. "She is in the hospital."

"What did you do?" Sallah S. grabbed Anwar by the collar, and pulled him close.

"Nothing—nothing—I've been informed of this matter by my daughter. It seems that Maya got ahold of some seeds, and swallowed them. I'm sure it was an accident, but they . . . they are poisonous. Naturally, of course. See, I've got a seed bank to ward off any apocalyptic—"

"Shut. Up. Where is my daughter?" Sallah S. remained as level and unflappable as ever.

Murderous glint in his eyes, yet such charisma. Anwar felt his heartbeat collapse into his stomach.

"I warned her against false love and godless idiots. She believed your house was salvation. Full of life and learning. Now I hope she's learned the consequence of plucking fruit from an ill-borne tree." Anwar saw the man's chest heaving, as if every breath kept Sallah S. from punching him in the face.

But he couldn't understand such didactics in this moment of distress. If Anwar knew Charu had tried taking her own life, he would most certainly not blame *her*.

They took a very silent cab ride, along with Maya's mother, Maryam, to the hospital. Anwar's daughters and a young fellow stood around Maya's bedside.

"My wife and I want time with my girl," said Sallah S, raising his voice. He rushed to Maya's side and took her hands into his. He kissed her fingers gently, and she yanked them away. Anwar noticed that even he felt discomfort at the tender gesture, as the girl seemed so put out by her parents' arrival.

The young man glared at Sallah S. and gave Maryam a welcoming kiss on the cheek. He helped Maryam sit down, setting her cane against Maya's bed.

"Mema," whispered Maya, her voice cracked lower than usual.

"I'm sorry," said Mema. She buried her face in Maya's underarm.

"I said, leave," said Sallah S. There was no mistaking that he would lose his wits if they didn't go.

Mema said something softly in Arabic, but Sallah shook his head and responded angrily back.

Anwar had never really had the patience with the language to learn all of the nuances. But there was no need to understand anything complicated—Sallah wanted them out. He beckoned the kids to follow him.

Ella did not move.

"Come along, Ella," said Anwar, and together they left the room.

The door slammed behind them.

18

Ella rode her bike back to the hospital the next day at noon. She ran into Dr. Kumar smoking at the entrance.

"You're a good friend, kid," Dr. Kumar said as she took another pull before flicking the butt into the overflowing cigarette dispenser. Ella wondered if it was customary for doctors to do the opposite of what they told their patients.

They took the elevator up to the third floor. As they were getting off, Ella noticed Ramona Espinal getting on. "Hey, Ramona, sorry to bother you—but have you had a chance to check on the patient in 303?" asked Dr. Kumar.

"Hi, Ramona," said Ella.

"Ella, hey," said Ramona, looking flushed. The elevator started to close and she stepped in front of it to bounce it back open. "Last I checked was around five a.m. She was asleep. I've been helping Dr. Bixby with a birth all morning."

"I thought today was your last day. Aren't you moving to Mexico?"

"It is. But Dr. Bixby doesn't like change," said Ramona.

"I didn't realized you'd moved," said Ella.

"What? Oh, yeah. My—my husband and I found a place together. Sorry, but I gotta run!"

"You two know each other? This neighborhood is way too small. Anyway, get out of here! Get some sleep," said Dr. Kumar, shooing Ramona into the elevator.

"Bye," said Ella, waving, but the elevator was already on its way down. "Ramona used to be my aunt and uncle's tenant."

"We'll miss her loads. But when something good comes up, you just gotta go for it," said Dr. Kumar.

Dr. Kumar and Ella walked over to Maya's room. Everything was dark, with narrow shafts of light peeking through the blinds.

The bed was empty.

"Strange," muttered Dr. Kumar. "She's not here. Not in the bathroom, either. Hold on a second." The doctor stepped out to speak to a nurse at the front desk. The nurse shook her head, confused, and seemed to be irritated at whatever the doctor was saying.

Ella's chest pounded. Halim's bouquet and Charu's gifts weren't here. Had her parents taken her out of the hospital? Ramona had just said that she'd last seen Maya asleep. Did Sallah S. somehow kidnap her in the middle of the night—?

"She's gone," said Dr. Kumar. "We just tried calling the number she gave—apparently her folks don't know where she is, either. They're threatening to sue the hospital. Fuck."

Surveillance camera footage showed Maya leaving her room—wearing Charu's hijab and a change of clothes. She held the bouquet of roses, as if she were going to visit someone. No nurses were at the station while Maya escaped. Ella realized that the nurses' station was visible from the window in Maya's room. She'd waited until the nurse had gone to the bathroom. The elevator camera showed Maya get off on the second floor, greeted by Ramona Espinal, who led her down the hallway, then into a room. No camera footage of them together. Minutes later, Maya reentered the elevator, the flower bouquet gone. The last shot of Maya showed her walking out of the hospital lobby, until she broke into a run.

As Ella rode back to 111 Cambridge Place, she understood that Maya didn't want to be found. She'd found her avenue of escape—Ramona. No telling where they'd be now. After seeing Sallah S. at the hospital, Ella didn't blame her.

She entered the house through the front door, something she rarely did. *Where the fuck is Charu?* The drone of her sewing machine led Ella upstairs. Her door was open. Charu was hunched over, tapping her foot to an odd rhythm. Sensing a foreign presence, she turned around. Her face was puffy and smeared with mascara, tears, lipstick.

"It's over between me and Malik. Like, for real."

"When are you going to get over that shit? He's not into you."

Charu flinched and wiped her face with a scrap of cloth. "He thinks we should break up, like, not see each other this first semester."

Each tap of her foot on the machine sent a surge of resentment through Ella. "You know what you did?"

"What?" Charu asked.

"You fucking told Anwar, you fucking idiot. Then Maya's parents got involved because he doesn't know enough shit about how crazy her father is. Maya's gone."

"What do you mean she's gone?"

"She left the hospital without a word. Slipped right under the night nurse's nose. When it's time to keep a secret for someone else, you're a fucking snitch!" Ella shouted, her face an inch away from Charu's.

Charu pushed Ella back with both hands, using the momentum to stand up. "What do you want me to say? That I'm stupid, I shouldn't have said anything?"

"You are an immature, stupid, fat little girl." Ella twisted Charu's wrist.

"Ow, stop. You're hurting me!"

"Shut up."

"Get off me. If you loved her so much then why did she leave?"

"You delusional bitch!" Ella pushed Charu down to the floor. Charu's head hit the corner of the headboard, and she howled in pain. Ella tore the machine off Charu's sewing table and threw it against the floor, breaking off levers and the needle plate, but Hashi's old Singer was sturdy enough to handle the attack.

"Ella, stop! You're fucking crazy!" Charu charged at Ella headfirst, but Ella knocked her back onto the bed. She ripped two months of Charu's labor, the stacks of folded, finished hijabs—the lone neat pile in the room—in a matter of minutes.

"Stop it, Ella! Stop it!"

The door swung open. It was Hashi. "What in hell are you girls doing? Like animals!"

"What is the problem, girls?" said Anwar, from behind her. "What is the commotion?"

Charu rushed up at Ella and slapped her across the face.

"Stop this, Charu, this instant!" Anwar yelled. He held an arm to divide the girls from each other.

"I want to know what this is about," Hashi demanded.

"Ask her," they both replied.

Neither Ella nor Charu would say anything. Ella marched out of the room, just as Charu began screaming, *"Get the fuck out of my room, all of you!"* Anwar and Hashi looked at each other, dumbfounded.

Wailing women are unbearable unless there is good cause, thought Anwar, watching Hashi bang on Charu's door.

"She's ruining everything before she leaves," whispered Hashi. Her voice was quiet, rounded out by a deep exhale.

"It's futile to keep trying." Anwar shrugged, but as soon as he said the words, Hashi's eyes narrowed. She swept her shawl around her and left him in front of Charu's door. A second later, he heard their bedroom door slam.

Anwar sighed. The last thing he wanted to do was follow her, sure of some retribution or angst that he wanted nothing to do with. Yet guilt trumped self-preservation every time. He knew that even greater than his want for escape was the feeling that he deserved Hashi's rage. She never gave it to him.

He stepped into their bedroom and saw her curled into herself on the veranda, her face buried in her knees. She made no sound, but he saw her shudder, as if it were thirty degrees out instead of ninety.

"Darling, are you all right?" Anwar squatted next to her, ignoring the sensation that his knees might snap.

"Why are you here? Why aren't you at the store?"

"Honestly, I don't want to risk running into Sallah S. I can't blame him if he blames me for this mess; though that would be unfair, I still—never mind. Please. Talk to me."

She held herself tight and would not unfurl herself. He gently took her in his arms, as if she were an overgrown child. He made a meager attempt to lift himself up, but those days of valor were long gone. So, they sat.

"I cannot do this, Anwar," said Hashi. She lifted her head up to speak, but stared at a point on the ground in front of her. "I've given you my girlhood, my womanhood. What do I get? Two daughters who won't talk to me. A husband who doesn't have the decency to conduct affairs in hotels. You didn't spare me the humiliation—you didn't even think of me. I made the fool's mistake of shitting where I eat. My business, my passions—all stuck in this house. This old house I built with a liar. A bad liar, at that."

"You cannot do what?" asked Anwar, stuck on her first sentence. He listened but didn't truly hear what she was saying.

"I don't know if we can work. I've been thinking a lot about Baba—he's so old and I haven't seen him in years. Maybe I'll go live in Bangladesh for a while. Take care of him. Charu and Ella will be in college. You'll find a new—tenant . . . in no time."

She let out the sob that had been lodged in her throat. "And now this mess with Sallah S. Even at the masjid I felt that devil's face burning mine. I went to the masjid last night. You know, it's been a while. Sallah S. spat nonsense about evil straight from Eden's belly and sisters guarding the company they keep. He looked at me the whole time. Chilling, I tell you. I can't even find peace where I pray. Why on earth would I live out my days here?"

"I've always loved your dramatic flair, my dear," murmured Anwar, stroking a wayward tendril from Hashi's forehead. "But I can't be without you. And Sallah S. will cool down, eventually. His daughter is eighteen, an age when any young person must venture out into the world on her own. Look at us—we left the family fort at sixteen; it is the proper order of things. A child must chart her own path, no creed or paternalism to obstruct the way. His delusions should have no bearing on our lives." Anwar felt himself growing loquacious, impassioned—but he'd experienced the same evil eye from the man yesterday evening at the pharmacy. Sallah S. had convened a small group of talibes at A Holy Bookstore for a study group to discuss deterring temptation. Anwar had felt a rattle against the wall of tinctures, until a few bottles of rosewater crashed to the ground. When he rushed outside to see if anyone else had felt this earthquake, he saw the group of Sallah's students banging fists against the wall between them and the apothecary. Was it some religious method acting? Were they trying to intimidate Anwar? No one besides Sallah S. heard him rapping at the window. Sallah had just stared and shook his head. It had chilled Anwar. Sallah might as well have gestured slashing his neck.

"How can we blame the man, though?" asked Hashi. She flinched as Anwar tried to wipe her tears. She held his hand to stop him, but didn't let it go. "I've been too wrapped up in my work. Even though I'm home all day—a choice I made to keep an eye on you, the girls—I've missed everything. I've been too consumed with how things appear, and not how things actually are. And now I'm stuck. Stuck with you."

They felt a violent slam of the sliding door downstairs. They peered over the edge of the balcony. Ella was cursing them for raising a brat.

Every corpuscle pulsed, furiously. Ella spent several minutes ripping up the garden. Soon, the ground at her feet was littered with severed blossoms and headless stems.

"Just sit, child. Don't let her get to you," she heard. She spun around. It was Hashi, sitting in one of the lawn chairs. Ella realized she'd never seen Hashi sitting in one of those chairs, let alone lounging outside. *Has she been sitting there creepily watching me lose my shit?* Her aunt cut slices of cucumber, letting them fall onto her apron. "Have some?" Hashi offered. "Do you want to tell me what is going on?"

Ella shook her head. "I don't want any—it's—it's nothing."

"Well, from what I gather, it's Maya, isn't it? He doesn't tell me much, but Anwar mentioned she had taken something from our garden, something *bishakto*."

Poisonous. Ella nodded. "Yes, but she's alive."

"I never took the girl to be into such—risky business. But, I also know that her father's a very strict man."

"Sorry, I've made a mess."

"It's all right, Ella. They don't live very long anyway, these big showy flowers," Hashi said, chewing a cucumber slice. "I've always liked wildflowers better, anyway. They're small and can grow anywhere. And they dry beautifully. Not like peonies-teonies that last for a day or two and make a huge mess."

Ella started to collect the debris in her hands, but realized she'd probably need a broom.

"Don't worry. It will just help the next batch grow, *na*?"

Anwar knocked on the sliding glass door, as if asking permission to come outside. Hashi seemed perturbed but beckoned him to come. "Fool," she muttered.

"When do you go back to school?" asked Anwar. He snatched a handful of slices from Hashi's cucumber, and she smacked his hand away.

"Get your own, *na*?" snapped Hashi.

"Next week," replied Ella.

"Can I give you a ride?"

"I'm good with the bus."

"Anwar, we were having a good time out here—" started Hashi.

Anwar held up a hand. "I have rights to my kid, too, *ya*?"

"Fine!" Hashi leapt up, spilling the cucumber and knife to the ground.

"I can't deal with any more dramas," snapped Anwar. "You've wasted the cucumber I would've eaten."

"Take the shit cucumber!" Hashi flung it into the pile of dead flowers, before going into the house.

"You left your weapons, woman," Anwar said, pointing to the knife Hashi had left on the ground. He dug into his pocket and found half of a joint. He tried and failed thrice to spark it. "Sorry, my hands are sweating. Could you please help?"

Ella lit and inhaled the joint to get it going. "What's her problem?"

"I couldn't tell you."

"What are you doing with that thing?"

"I am smoking ganja. Would you like to puff?"

"You don't care if she smells it?" Ella gestured to the house.

"This is the least bad of bad things I have done. You want?"

"Yes, sure." Ella took three long drags.

"This is my dilemma."

"Pardon?"

"I smoke ganja. I am planning to grow my own, but it is very stinky business. I also steal."

"You steal?"

"I am naughty in many ways."

"I guess I see your point," said Ella, suddenly feeling the urge to giggle.

"Please, always take care of Charu."

"She's a grown woman."

"Oof, this is even more reason." He laughed and punched Ella on the back. She snorted, making them laugh harder.

Ella heard what sounded like a muffled scream.

"Shhh, shhh." Anwar's eyes widened. He brought a finger to his lips. "Hashi's going to eat us—Shhh!"

"No, Anwar, look!" Ella pointed to the sliding glass door.

Hashi was running toward them.

As soon as everyone had left her room, Charu began stitching the leftover scraps of Ella's violent mess into an escape ladder. Fuck them all. They wanted to keep her locked in the house? She was almost eighteen fucking years old and in college. In less than a week she'd be free. She was sure that wherever Maya was, she was better off away from her parents and this damned house. Charu pushed her bed's headboard up to the window. She was confident that her impenetrable lockstitch would support her weight. She tied twenty-pound dumbbells to the limp legs of her fabric ladder, and then slung the weighted end outside her bedroom window. Just a few more yards of fabric and the ladder would be long enough.

Suddenly, her sewing machine groaned to a halt. Her window fan's full blast wound down to a slow rotation, until it stopped. The Christmas lights blinked off and her digital clock was out.

"What the fuck?" Charu shouted.

19

This is a blackout, Ella realized. She left Anwar to squabble with Hashi, who yelled at him for fiddling around with the circuit breaker. He held up his hands, pleading innocence, stoned and giggling.

Ella rode her bike onto the street. Many of their neighbors were outside, confused. Dr. Duray sat in his wheelchair, looking upward as if the end of days had arrived. Ella turned onto Greene Avenue to the traffic light on Grand to confirm her suspicions. Two cars waited on either side of the intersection, waiting for the other driver to move.

The traffic light was out.

Holy shit. Where would Maya go now? No traffic lights, no way out of the city. Had Ramona taken her somewhere? Ella's mind raced, high and paranoid about all the things that could go wrong. She had no idea where Ramona lived now, but she suspected Maya was with her. Why else would Maya stop by the second floor? They didn't even know each other. *Why hasn't she called me?* There was nothing the hospital could do about Ramona—she hadn't answered the phone when Dr. Kumar called. They didn't have a new address on file, either. She was still listed as a resident at 111 Cambridge Place.

And, so, Ella began searching. There was only one thing she could think to do—ride to Prospect Park. Perhaps she'd be lucky again.

On Fulton Street, subway riders emerged aboveground, looking frazzled and spooked. Without traffic lights, Ella weaved easily between the deadlocked cars headed toward the Manhattan Bridge. Hordes of employees in Atlantic Mall stood in the plaza looking confused as to what they should do. Their shops were closed early, since no electricity meant no business.

Ella rode a lap around the bike path. Maya was not by the tree, nor the lake. Ella started to feel delirious, her knuckles sore from clenching the grips. She looped twice more around the path, until she felt sick with dehydration. She couldn't ride any longer. The park was alive with joggers, families, lovers. Everything sickened her. She pulled over and vomited on the bike path.

"Gross!" yelled a kid who rode past her.

"Ugh!"

"Gnarly!"

Ella started dry heaving, unable to move out of the bike path, where disgusted bikers yelled at her.

"Time for you to get up, son," said a baby-faced cop driving up in a go-cart. "There's been a blackout. Things are about to get real crazy."

Ella stood up. The cop drove away, stroking his gun. She watched him until he was out of her sight.

The first thing that everybody should do is to understand that there is no evidence of any terrorism whatsoever. Anwar was glad that the mayor had spelled it out. He felt jittery, remembering what the city had survived two years ago. Thankful for his radio, he had spent the afternoon in the garden, listening for updates, watering the plants, and smoking his ganja pipe. He was enjoying the unexpected loss of current. Electricity outages were commonplace back home. In Brooklyn, he remembered only once or twice having lost power during a thunderstorm. As evening fell, they would light candles. Though he knew he lacked in many ways, Anwar excelled at emergency preparedness and a tendency to hoard in case of disaster. They were fully stocked with water, flashlights, batteries, canned food, and candles, enough for at least a year.

He heard footsteps and a spinning bicycle chain.

"Ella? Where did you go?"

Ella dropped her bike to the ground and sat down in the lawn chair beside him. "To the park. Streets are packed with stranded commuters. People are hitching rides. Power's out all over the city."

"Yes, it will be madness out there tonight. We are lucky we're home."

Ella nodded. "I think I need a nap."

He offered her a toke, but she shook her head. "Naps are always a smart idea. You know, I quite like this world without television and bright lights. It's nice to think." Just as he said it, he heard the sound of shattering glass.

"Did you hear that, Uncle?"

"What the hell?"

Ella leapt to her feet first, and Anwar got up, confused. Two figures had run along the side of the house to the backyard. By their sinewy limbs Anwar guessed they were no older than eighteen. Despite the heat, they wore 99-cent store ski masks and clownish black gloves. One of them threw a Molotov cocktail into the garden. A loud explosion resounded like thunder, and its echo sent a flock of brooding pigeons into the evening sky. Anwar watched Ella pick up Hashi's cucumber-slicing knife, the garden hose in another.

She lifted both high in the air. Anwar stared at her, mesmerized.

Ella slashed the air with the knife and charged forward to stab one of the boys. "Fuck. You," she growled, as she blasted the boys with hose water.

The arsonists shouted and started to run.

Ella turned to her garden. Flames curled and flower petals disintegrated to ash. Each of them grew tiny eyes and mouths, begging to be saved. But there was no saving them. She hosed down the burning petals to put the fire out. The humid night air was dense with the scent of blackened flowers, hibiscus bark, and petrol.

She gripped Anwar's hand. They ran to the front of the house toward Hashi's screams. Her aunt stood on the sidewalk, looking as if she might swoon. Ella pulled her onto the street, away from all of the flammable sprays exploding in the salon.

"T-t-they destroyed my salon." Hashi gasped to catch her breath. Ella stroked her aunt's back, trying to calm her.

"Why on earth would these hooligans do this?" cried Anwar.

"These psychos were sent by Sallah," said Ella.

A crowd had collected on the block. A small circle of neighbors had pinned down two of the young men, who thrashed about in a futile attempt to flee. A few teenagers yelled profanities after the one boy who had gotten away. Faraway siren wails trailed behind her. All summer the hydrants had been broken open for children's pleasure.

Maybe there's no water left.

"Where is Charu? Where is my daughter?" Hashi broke away from Anwar's grip and ran barefoot over the splinters of blasted glass strewn about the stoop and sidewalk.

"She's going inside," whispered Anwar, immobile.

Ella ran after Hashi. She ignored her neighbors yelling behind her to wait for the firemen.

Hashi had flung open the front door, but fumbled with the vestibule lock. With a forceful kick, Ella busted open the rickety old door. The main floor of the house was thick with black smoke rising from the salon. The scorched air pricked Ella's arms, giving her goose bumps.

"Charu!" Hashi yelled.

They didn't have to go far. Charu sat at the bottom of the stairwell.

"I thought no one would notice."

"You're all I've made that matters in this world." Hashi gathered her into her arms. She stroked the light scar near Charu's eye, the only reminder of her beating. They started coughing. Hashi covered Charu's face with her shawl. Ella blinked as the black smoke took on forms, black demon faces and silhouettes. She was heady from the assault of fumes.

A fireman shouted, "Over there! Get 'em!"

The two firemen, one tall and built like a basketball player, the other stocky and short, grabbed each of them. The stocky one grabbed Ella. He tried to lift her up, but she accidentally kicked him in the crotch. He dropped her and keeled over in pain. He rejected their attempts at assistance and instead picked Hashi up and slung her over his shoulder. Behind him, his more dashing partner carried

Charu outside. Ella waved at the cheering crowd that greeted them as they exited the house.

Poisonous fumes and smoke damage from the fire in the salon made 111 Cambridge Place uninhabitable for at least a week. Bic and Mauve Gnarls had passed by the commotion during their evening stroll and offered to take them in. Bic's townhouse was a stone's throw from Anwar's, near Emmanuel Baptist Church on Lafayette, right before Saint James Place turned into Hall Street.

Bic's wife, Mauve, one of Hashi's longtime clients, was half her husband's size, with double his energy. "Come on in, y'all," said Mauve, leading them into their house. "We'll get a candlelight dinner set up. I've made some of my famous coq au vin for dinner. Thank goodness for gas stoves! And don't you worry about the wine in the chicken—all the sinful stuff evaporates. Except for the flavor, of course. Girls, let me take you into Nia's old bedroom."

Charu and Ella followed Mauve upstairs, while Hashi took a seat in a luxurious armchair, a Queen Anne style that was a stoop sale classic. She looked like a bedraggled queen. Standing in their living room, Anwar felt himself transported to Havana, Tokyo, Marseille, and Lagos, given the artwork and varieties of furniture that Bic and Mauve had acquired over the years. It was harmonious. Anwar had always known Bic to be the truest of syncretics. Anwar smelled a chicken roast, the trail of incense. He felt the strangest guilt. Standing here, while his own home stood burnt, Hashi's salon disintegrated. All these years of work tarnished by the whims of a madman. Anwar realized he was slow at connecting dots. The broken shop window. The hammering of hands against the walls of A Holy Bookstore. And now, a fire.

Was this his punishment for sleeping with Ramona? He shook his head. *There's no such thing as divine ordinance. It is the will of a man out to get me. Sallah S.*

"Mauve and I are happy to have you as long as you need, brother," said Bic, grabbing Anwar in a bear hug. "We're thanking the universe you're alive."

"We can never thank you enough," said Hashi.

Anwar wept in his friend's arms.

Mauve led the girls to Nia Gnarls's old room, which was adorned with floral wallpaper and bedcovers. Ella opted for an air mattress on the floor beside the bed, where Charu would sleep. Without electricity, Ella would have to inflate the mattress manually with a bike pump.

"Back in the seventies, fires were everyday occurrences," said Mauve, resting two glass candle jars on the shelf. She shook her head. "I certainly hope we aren't returning to those days of destruction. The city is no place for fires. No place for fires except in the forest. See you downstairs in ten minutes, ladies, okay? Bring the candles with you." She gently closed the door.

"What does she mean no place for fires except in the forest? I have the distinct memory of that bear telling me only I can prevent forest fires," Charu said.

Ella started pumping the mattress—this was going to take a while. "Ha. Those days of Smokey the Bear are over. She's right. Trees need natural fires. Those giant coastal redwoods will spontaneously fucking combust. Because those fires let their seedlings and other plants grow in the forest floor. Fires clear the clutter, the junk. It's rejuvenation. It's necessary. Without the fires, all the debris and waste would build up, and eventually there'd be a much greater, much more destructive fire."

Charu rested her hand on Ella's shoulder. "We haven't had an easy summer, El, but I'm glad you're here. Of course, I had to damn near die in a fire to realize it, but it's true."

"Me, too."

"I wonder who would try to hurt us. I know blackouts mean people go crazy with the looting and whatnot. But you'd think it would happen to Baba's store or some shit. No, scratch that. Who needs body cream when they don't have food?"

"I'm almost positive that I've met the three guys that started the fire. I've seen them twice. They're with Sallah. I think they're the same ones that threw bricks at Anwar's storefront."

"Shit. Well, they caught two of the assholes. I'm sure they'll connect it back to Sallah S. Unless the cops are too dumb to figure it out. All this drama is making college look pretty sweet right about now."

Ella nodded. "In a weird way, though, this was the best and shittiest summer I've ever had."

"You know, I have no idea where Maya is. But I know wherever she is, whatever she's doing—it's necessary."

After dinner, Hashi and Mauve made a pot of tea and replayed Hashi's dramatic exit with the firemen.

"Girl, he was *cute*!" said Mauve, and Hashi hooted with laughter.

"Quite cute. Smelled like a barbershop and burnt wood at the same time." They all howled with laughter again.

"Let's have a smoke, man," said Anwar. "I actually think I deserve it."

Biç led Anwar through the house to the backyard. Unlike the mess the arsonists had left behind, Bic and Mauve's garden felt like an oasis, with voluptuous red and pink blossoms. Hollyhock, rose of Sharon, and English roses spiked the air with their bold notes—an eternal Valentine's Day. Anwar closed his eyes to breathe it in and saw Ramona's tits, an image he was a fool to try and repress. Bic motioned for them to sit in a pair of worn Appalachian rocking chairs, which rocked spontaneously in the faint breeze. Anwar pictured Abraham Bright and his poisoned wife rocking in those chairs, just as Bic had once described. He shooed away the ghosts to enjoy a smoke with the man he realized was his best friend.

Anwar felt his tongue loosen after a few pulls on the blunt. "I cheated on Hashi, man," he muttered. "I'm a fucking shit."

Bic nearly rocked out of his chair onto his feet. "You did what, motherfucker?"

"Ramona-fucker." Anwar's need for absolution outweighed his shame. Bic had always been one to swap war and love stories. But, as he suspected, Bic did not approve. His stories all predated his marriage to Mauve.

"Damn. I'm not mad about how fine that girl was. She truly was a fine-looking woman. But got-damn, Anwar. Why would you shit where you eat and sleep?"

"This seems to be a common point of consensus."

Bic shook his head. "What the hell happened?"

"I went through the studio door into her apartment one day—"

"Wait—what? You made love to her in your own home?" Bic sucked his teeth. "Poor Hashi. Man." They sat in silence. Even Bic didn't want to hear about his conquest and eventual beatdown at the hands of Hugo. Anwar looked up at a large black cloud in the night sky, hovering until it dissipated into a hundred tiny versions of itself.

"Temptation is real, though." Bic nodded, as if he'd been arguing the point with himself. "But try to see tonight's mess as an—opportunity."

"Thousands of dollars in damages, our garden and Hashi's salon destroyed, a missing mentally ill teenage girl, and arsonists to fend off doesn't seem like much of an opportunity."

"Want to know what you've got to do to get out of a corner like that?

"What?"

"Go back the way you came."

"I'm too high to get you, man."

Anwar tried to spoon Hashi's backside, but she edged herself off to one side of the mattress. "Hashi?"

"You have lost your way, Anwar."

PART II

THE BLACK FOREST

I admit that when the falling hour
begins to husk the sky free of its
saffroning light, I reach for anyone

willing to wrap his good arm tight
around me for as long as the ribboned
darkness allows. Who wants, after all,

to be seen too clearly?

—Tarfia Faizullah, from "Dhaka Nocturne," *Seam*

Note the trees, because the dirt is temporary . . .

—TV on the Radio, "Staring at the Sun,"
Desperate Youth, Blood Thirsty Babes

20

Winter, or *sheet*, was Anwar's favorite of Bangladesh's six seasons. Winter brought marigolds and sunflowers, rice pithas doused in gud. Anwar could practically taste it after twenty-seven long hours, through Berlin, Dubai, and now, finally, Dhaka. The plane ride to Dhaka had been quite odorous, Hashi had complained. Ella was reticent on the flight, while Charu seethed in a foul mood, pissed that they'd bought tickets for a flight on New Year's Eve. Anwar had tried to reason with her, telling her that saving a few hundred dollars was certainly not "ruining her life." She ignored him.

Anwar hadn't noticed.

It was a late January afternoon at Zia International Airport. Nothing seemed particularly festive. Anwar and Hashi pushed through the mass of people to get their three suitcases—filled with mostly candy or sundries made in China—from baggage claim. Ella and Charu held back, trying to get a sense of the decrepit airport, while avoiding vacuous stares from a crowd of hungry-looking men.

Anwar spotted a rather impersonal sign that read in English: MR. AND MRS. ANWAR SALEEM. A very tall man holding the sign wore his shirt unbuttoned to the navel, and quickly buttoned up when he spotted Anwar waving.

"*Arré!*" called Hashi, excitedly. "Rana? Is that you?"

The man waved and strode over to them.

"Ji, Hashi Apa," said Rana, in Bangla. He did not offer his hand to Hashi or the girls, but nodded respectfully. He took Anwar's hand and shook it vigorously. —Anwar Chachu, after all these years. Good to see you. "Happy New Year," he added, in English.

Anwar's face grew serious and he gave Rana a firm handshake. The young man's formality touched him. He was a taller version of the lad he remembered, with high cheekbones and ellipse eyes. Rana had been sixteen when they came back to pick up Ella in 1987. To this day, he remained in his station—driving, cooking, and running any errands necessary. Rezwan had wanted the young boy to become as much a part of their family as anybody else. With Rezwan and Laila's death, the young boy they'd adopted as a son after the war became more of a helping hand.

"You're quite the handsome fellow. How old are you these days?"

"I just turned thirty-two back in December." Rana smiled, revealing a slight gap in his teeth.

"Yes, yes, of course. Thirty-two is a fine age. I haven't heard news of a woman. Or—anyone?"

"I am waiting for her. When she appears one day, you'll hear news."

"Thanks for picking us up," said Charu.

Rana responded in English, "You are welcome." He turned to Ella and patted her shoulder. "Ella, you are the image of Rezwan photos, *ek dom*!"

Ella nodded, but recoiled at his touch. She had been silent the entire period of travel, announcing only a walk or a pee. "Let me help you with the suitcases."

"She can speak!" said Anwar.

"No, no. I can handle," said Rana, deftly lifting the suitcases onto a dolly.

"Sorry to load your car with all of this crap," said Anwar.

"Anwar!" chided Hashi. "They are gifts."

As they drove out of Dhaka's airport, the road transformed into newly built highways. Charu, Ella, and Hashi settled into the backseat, with Hashi sitting in the middle, leaning excitedly toward the front to point at the changes she'd not seen for nearly a decade. Ella and Charu leaned against their respective windows and kept quiet. They'd hardly said more than a few words since the plane took off from JFK thirty hours ago.

"Can we take an alternative route, please? Just to see some things before we get home?" Anwar asked.

"We should get back before Baba goes to bed, no?" Hashi said it halfheartedly, as if her mind could be changed.

Charu groaned. "I really need to piss."

Anwar looked back at her and smiled. "It will only take ten-fifteen minutes maximum."

Baby taxis putt-putted past them, painted with neon-hued, cartoony Indian actresses. Cycle rickshaws were adorned with metallic lotus and rose patterns. All of these modes of transport were beautifully decorated, perhaps to distract from the danger of riding them. For a spell, they were caught in a traffic jam.

"Jams are getting worse by the day," commented Rana.

As they stood still amid the honking cars, scrappy children selling strands of jasmine or cigarettes and candy called out. Countless billboards advertised Bangla versions of soap, soda, and skin-lightening creams. Everything glowed with color here, something Anwar realized he missed. He hoped that this trip would bring him closer to his girls, and to Hashi. So far, the girls seemed more irritated than glad to spend the rest of their winter break in Bangladesh. The plane tickets were courtesy of Aman's credit card, a habit Anwar had not been able to wean himself off of. The overdue bill totaled six thousand dollars, including the boxes of marijuana seed he had purchased.

There was no use worrying about it now. "How's the flat?" he asked.

"Only two families live in our building," replied Rana. "Our tenants live downstairs half the time; the other half they are in London. And of course, there is Stalin Bhai."

"Shameful my little brother's still going by that horrible nickname," said Hashi.

"I think he likes it," said Rana. "Anyway, I should ask you the same thing. How's your house after the fire? Did they ever catch the men who did it?"

"Oh, Stalin never told you?" asked Hashi.

"We never have much time to sit down and talk." Rana smiled.

"The police caught two of the young men," said Anwar. "Their fingerprints were found on the exploded bottles. I spoke on the boys' behalf. I have no ill will toward them."

"I'm not sure it was the right thing to do," said Hashi. "I wonder if they will learn anything unless they pay a price."

"Prison is no place to learn about life, Ma," said Charu, popping her head up from the window for a moment, before closing her eyes again.

Anwar beamed, proud that his daughter's newfound college activism had kicked in. "Very true, Charu. They were charged with what—arson in the fifth degree? They would be in jail for a year. Anyway, Rana, my words on the boys' behalf let them off with time served."

"That's good news, then."

"Sallah S. was convicted of the more serious arson in the third degree. His bail was set at five hundred thousand dollars, which his community was unable to pay. I'm not sure I know what to believe. One minute a man is good, pious. In another overcome with rage and violence. More than anything . . . I feel guilt—"

"There's nothing to feel guilt about," Ella said quietly. "He tried to hurt us. He hurt Maya."

"Any word on the girl?" asked Hashi.

Neither Ella nor Charu answered.

"Well, I do. Feel guilty. For complaining to the police." Anwar sighed. Aman had stopped speaking to Anwar, siding with the cleric. Sallah S. was imprisoned in Rikers Island until October 2005, when his trial was scheduled. Anwar was relieved by Aman's silence, and Sallah's delayed day of reckoning.

Rana obliged Anwar by driving a roundabout route, which took closer to an hour than Anwar's promised ten-minute detour. Rana drove up Fuller Road, passing Dhaka University's grounds, lined with lushly branched koroi trees and groves of eucalyptus and acacia. Anwar inhaled the familiar Dhaka scent of nature, shit, and petrol. He reached his hand back to grab Hashi's. Rana turned onto Kataban Road, where shops sold either exotic fish tanks or wedding garlands of marigold and rose. New Elephant Road had lost much of the green Anwar remembered. New colleges and shopping plazas had sprouted up everywhere.

"Why didn't Baba come?" asked Hashi.

"He wanted to come get you himself, but his health hasn't been so good."

Her face wrinkled in worry. "Is he all right?"

"I'm sure it's nothing a party can't fix," said Rana, smiling in the rearview mirror.

Both Charu and Ella avoided his attention, concentrating on the new world outside the window.

By the time they entered Dhanmondi, dusk had settled. All around Dhanmondi Lake, snack sellers wore boxes strapped to their chests, bearing their goods and tiny kerosene lamps to provide light. The steps of the Robindro Shorobor amphitheater were crowded with young couples milling about, munching on snacks and taking boat rides on the lake.

"Let's grab a handful of the peanuts," said Anwar.

"The girls will get sick if they eat anything washed in tap water. We have to boil the water," said Hashi.

"They are nuts, woman! Who ever heard of washing nuts?"

"Babaaa. You're nasty," Charu muttered.

Anwar shrugged. "They come with their own protective sheath."

As Rana drove over Road No. 8 bridge, Anwar remembered crossing the picturesque lake, an oasis in the middle of the city. They pulled up a dusty road full of brightly painted flats. All of their verandas bore small potted plants. Colorful lungis and salwars were strung on clothing lines. Rana honked at the gate of a modest three-story flat made of whitewashed stucco, with strands of blackened mold running down the sides. Monsoon did a number on buildings each year. Anwar hated the obsession with monsoons—restaurants, weddings, spas, and investment firms all claimed the name. He was happy to take the mangoes and wish the season on its way. But he knew without *barsha*, people and their lands would have no respite from the insufferable heat.

The security guard let them in, mumbling hello. He went back to his desk to watch a drama on a small television.

Rana led them up the stone steps to the second floor.

Hashi lunged toward her father, Azim, who sat at the dining room table. Shards of wood lay strewn about. He wore a white tank top and plaid lungi, and his gold-rimmed spectacles slipped down his nose. "My girl, you've arrived," he said, taking Hashi into his arms. He gripped Anwar by the neck, and the three of them hugged for many minutes. It was the same feeling Anwar had when Rezwan first brought him home to meet his family. He gave the old man a hearty pound on the back.

"What's all this, Baba?" asked Hashi, pointing to the wood.

"Indigenous boats. We will forget what these wooden gems look like unless we know how to make them."

"You're still the same." Hashi's eyes watered.

"Now, girl, you are, too. Please. Don't cry." Azim pinched her cheek.

"Well, keep on with it. I'll help Rana with dinner."

"No, Hashi Apa," said Rana. "I'll be done with dinner in no time. Please, stay with Azim. He's been waiting for you."

"He's right. I'm getting older without all of these beauties around me. Now, let me see my granddaughters. Would you like to make a dinghy?"

"Ummm," said Charu. Her eyes flitted with exhaustion.

"I am joking," said Azim. "Please come closer so that I may look at you." He put his arms around Charu's shoulders and drew her close for a hug. Her eyes welled up, and he said, "My beauty, those are tired tears—this one must go to sleep immediately."

"Yes, yes, she doesn't listen. I told her to sleep on the plane, but she keeps listening to her music," complained Hashi.

"Rana, please take her to Stalin's room." Azim pointed to a hallway leading out of the dining room.

"Yes, sir."

Rana gestured for Charu to follow him.

"I'm sorry," said Charu.

"No sorry," said Azim. He turned to Ella, and said, "Now, let me take a look at you—you are much like your father." He seemed scared to touch her. "Do you remember me?"

Ella nodded. "A little."

"Would you like to make a patam?"

"Sure," said Ella.

Perhaps it's coming back to her, thought Anwar. He admitted that he'd failed to teach her and Charu to read or write Bangla, and because of their constant interactions with customers, he and Hashi spoke English more often than not.

"I would like to make a boat, too," Anwar said.

"I should help Rana with dinner," said Hashi.

Azim's eyes twinkled. "Remember, Rana will prepare this dinner. You rest."

"All right, all right, I'll take a shower then," said Hashi, laughing. Her lightheartedness struck Anwar. Since they'd landed, she seemed all right relinquishing her grasp. "Baba, you haven't aged a bit. We are going to have a huge birthday party for you!" Hashi squeezed her father's cheek.

"No, no party." He held up a hand to reiterate his refusal. It was shriveled and emaciated.

Azim handed Anwar and Ella ten evenly shaped shards of wood and a concoction that looked like rubber cement and smelled like whiskey. "Glue the edges together. They are pre-whittled."

Anwar found that rolling blunts had inadvertently increased his dexterity. There was much he wanted to speak about. He had never had a conversation with the old man about Rezwan's death, face-to-face. They'd not had enough money to attend the funeral back in those days. Anwar carried a certain shame for not having been there to bury his friend.

As they worked on their boats, every so often Anwar caught a glimpse of Ella, then once more he looked at Azim, one eye shut and the tip of his tongue sticking out in concentration. His left hand was atrophied from years of disuse. Remarkably, he constructed the dinghy entirely with his right hand, patting down the glue with the knuckles of his shriveled left hand.

"Ella, you are staring at my hand," said Azim.

"Oh, she doesn't know—" started Anwar.

"I'm sorry," said Ella.

"It is okay. I was doing the same thing." Azim returned to the more complicated task at hand—making a sail—and did not elaborate.

"Do you want to hear about your grandfather, Ella? Anwar, this story may bore you; you've heard it so many times," said Azim.

"I never tire of the story, sir," replied Anwar.

"Still 'Sir' after thirty years?"

"Yes, Si," Anwar corrected himself. "Yes, Baba."

"I would like to hear it, Nana," said Ella, quietly.

As Azim began to speak, he started a new boat, a Chinese-style sampan.

"In the year 1949, I lived in Russia as a medical student at the Moscow Medical Stomatological Institute. I was a romantic man with twenty-twenty vision. This was just after Partition, and just before the 1952 language war between East and West Pakistan. Bangla versus Urdu. I'm not sure if Anwar has taught you or told you any of this. As for me, I wasn't much of a politico. I believed in science. My life was devoted to my studies, in order to become an ophthalmic surgeon. You see, I had great plans of becoming an eye surgeon. I read Sushruta, the Indian father of surgery, and his treatise describing over three hundred surgical procedures and one hundred surgical instruments. This man lived in 800 B.C. but I was determined to become a modern-day incarnate of him.

"Ah, there was vodka—I learned to love that clear, tasteless stuff. And of course, I met a woman. She was a Russian literature student named Tatiana. I met her while we were both searching a notice board of rooms for rent. I would realize later she'd had her eyes set on meeting a doctor. Her eyes fascinated me—they were unlike any I'd ever seen in person. Blue, but not like the sky or ocean. Blue like the lips of a drowned person. A bruise. It was very sexy for me. Until that moment, I'd only known fish-eyed girls who were not allowed to talk to me."

Azim laughed. "Tatiana noticed me struggling with the Russian characters. I worked slowly through the notices, first translating into English, then Russian. It always took me a while. And how lucky for me! Her brother Alexei rented flats near Red Square, and he was happy to rent to foreign exchange students, though most Russians did not want us near.

"Our courtship began over a bowl of ukha fish soup and my first sip of vodka. I became delirious with desire. I let her into the flooded nature of my thoughts. When I professed how much I wanted to marry her, her eyes became warm. Red flags of protest from our families heightened our passions. My telegram to my parents sent a shock wave through our family, though I am certain my father secretly wondered what a blue-eyed child would look like. Tatiana vowed she would convert to Islam. I read Chekhov and Tolstoy, just to have things to talk about with her. Within six months, we were married.

"We had a small wedding. A few of my fellow Bangladeshi nationals, friends from school, and her family. No one noticed my new brother-in-law Alexei glaring at me. He was suspicious of all of the foreign students who'd made their way to Russia, even though they were from homelands sympathetic to the Communist cause.

"One night, in an effort to show Alexei my purest intentions, I asked him over to our flat while Tatiana was in a late evening class. A long-necked vodka bottle emptied between us. We discussed the usual suspects: Trotsky's exile, whether the KGB was the shield or the sword. I made a drunken, passing comment about how Russia's cold put a chill in the people's hearts. In my homeland, people were warm as the land they sprouted from. We had none of this cold, which had made the pogroms possible, which made people drown their misery with a bottle.

"Every word we utter is a matter of life and death, no? Alexei called me a stupid foreigner with a stupid mustache."

—You talk too much, growled Alexei in Russian.

—Nothing well thought-out, brother; I'm still a newcomer, I replied. I'd learned Russian in order to make surviving the hostile environment easier. Besides, it was good for flirting.

—I am not your *braht*.

"He pinned me against a wall by the throat. He ripped my Swiss Army knife chain from my neck and stabbed through my left hand. Blood spurted onto Alexei's face. And me, the roar of a Moscow train rushed over me, and my final thought, *I shall never be anything*, pounded in my ears, before I lost consciousness.

"Irreparable ulnar nerve damage, they said. No one could fix me.

No one could steady my hand. Macula, Retina, Sclera, Fovea, and Iris danced away from me; my naughty quintet of sisters playing a game of hide-and-seek that went terribly awry. Tatiana vowed never to see her brother again and tried nurturing me back. But I nursed my ache with pale spirits and solitude. I ignored her for months, barely speaking a full sentence a day. She left me for a baker, when she was four months pregnant with his child."

"Did she say anything to you before she left?" asked Ella.

"Not a thing. She must have thought it would be easier that way." Azim laughed. "Sometimes I wonder if she is alive. She smoked a lot of cigarettes. And Russian women's noses and ears seem to grow bulbous with age. Maybe she is dead now; I don't know.

"I left Russia, with no degree in hand, and no hand. Things were no quieter when I came back to Bangladesh. Student protests and the inklings of a pending war with West Pakistan welcomed me home. I wanted no part of it. Friends asked what happened, but I offered no details. I met Begum Firoza, a young girl—she was fifteen—innocent and loyal and brilliant though unschooled. We left Dhaka to start a family down south, by the beaches of Chittagong. She bore my three children: Rezwan in 1951, Hashi in 1955, and Stalin, in 1975, after the war had been won. Even if I tried, I wouldn't be able to forget Russia. My own son is called Stalin."

"And the story never grows old," muttered a man who had just entered.

"Speaking of this devil, here is my son, your uncle Stalin," said Azim. "Your uncle is very sensitive."

"Sensitive? I'm not the man obsessed with miniatures," said Stalin. "Anwar, it's been years—how are things, bhai?"

"Arré!" Anwar cried, standing to embrace his young brother-in-law. "Another grown man! Rana and you are both looking good. And you're a university professor and all!"

Stalin gave him a light punch on the shoulder. "Rana's svelte from all of his hard work. Me, I've got the genes, eh? It's good to see you, too." He cleared his throat. "Oh, my. Ella? My big brother's little—girl. Where's Hashi Apa? Where's your daughter? Ey! Rana, get me a glass of water before I die of thirst!"

"Or maybe he is not sensitive at all," said Azim.

21

Stalin cursed himself for coming home for the weekend. He'd spent two hours in a Friday evening traffic jam just to be here, and already there was a bad taste in his mouth. How taxing was it to come home and deal with his father's growing ineptitude. His father, in a word, broke his balls. His entire life existed under the grand shadow of the fallen giant, Rezwan, and his big sister, Hashi, who lived in faraway New York. Not to mention Anwar's suffocating affability, his freakishly mannish niece Ella, and some other idiot niece he hadn't met yet.

He had no time to serve as a native informant to these Americans. Who did he look like—Rana?

Stalin was the former Dhaka University student chairman of the Communist Party of Bangladesh, with a PhD in chemistry. He'd begun an assistant professorship at Jahangirnagar University. At twenty-eight, he was a man of meager means and verdant heart, though he knew that girls preferred cold-hearted industrialists and doctors.

A sleeping beauty lay in his bed. If she was this gratifying with drool crawling down her chin, then he could only picture her awake. Damn. His breath smelled of the roti and dried anchovy shootki he'd had for lunch. But he was looking good, donning his usual kurta and jeans, Kolhapuri sandals, plaid scarf. As always, he'd sprinkled the cologne of all colognes, Brut 33.

After a couple of cat stretches, the girl opened her eyes. "Hello. Who are—oh. You're Stalin, right?" she asked, snapping her fingers. "I'm Charu."

"Yes, yes, how are you?" he said quickly, in English.

"Good. Can you turn on a light?"

"Sure, sure."

Charu winced. "There're only a few things I really hate. Babies. Umbrellas. And fluorescent lights. Maybe you should turn it back off."

She perched herself up on her elbow. Her body was both wide and slender, like a cambering road. "Why is your name Stalin? They actually named you that?"

Stalin wished he had sprayed more of the Brut 33. Charu. A shortened version of Charulata, the starlet immortalized in cinema, a lonely housewife destined to cuckold her man.

"My father has a very ironic sense of humor. He did not like his time in Russia, and perhaps it is a bad metaphor for his feelings for me." Seeing Charu's pitiful look, Stalin continued, "I'm just kidding! My name is Shourov—but my classmates named me Stalin because I sprouted a very big mustache at age ten. That's the truth. But I can't resist giving my old man a jab."

"Wow. And I thought kids in New York were assholes." Charu pointed to a stack of papers spilling out of the sides of his leather briefcase. "What's all that? You a lawyer or something?"

"A professor, actually—and you? What do you do?"

"I'm in college. I work as a party promoter in New York and I'm already over it, I think. Shit, maybe I'm fired, since my fucking family decided to skip town on New Year's Eve. I needed a vacation. I was thinking Mexico, Puerto Rico. Instead, I'm here in fucking Bangladesh. Where I have to keep it all covered up."

Stalin found her sarcasm charming. "Well, if it's anything like over here, pretty girls don't get fired that easy. Besides, I do not have enough money for a new briefcase. I'm not American bourgeoisie, where I can just buy a suitcase every week."

"I think my mom bought you one. You mean you're not going to take it?"

There was a knock on the door.

"Come in," they said at the same time.

"Here he is, everyone gets a hello, except for me!" cried Hashi, hugging him. He embraced his big sister. "I want to hear *everything*. I'm here now, and it's time to find you a wife! Now, come, you two.

Rana's cooked a fantastic fish dinner." Hashi left them in the room to call after Anwar and Ella.

"Gross," whispered Charu.

"What is gross?"

"Fried fish *and* arranged marriages. You won't find me near that shit."

"My sentiments exactly." Stalin laughed. *I'm never marrying some backward-thinking, droll, middle-class slob. Give me a Brit, a German, a Swiss, or—an American*. He glanced sideways at his niece.

Ella was in the guest bedroom next door to Stalin's room. Both rooms connected to the veranda, where she could hear Charu and Stalin chatting into the night. Ella felt imprisoned in the room—she would have preferred to be outside, but didn't want to talk to them. Trails from old ghazals and Benson & Hedges cigarette smoke wafted in through the window.

"Even the Indians banned Taslima Nasrin's latest book. Poor girl can't catch a break," said Stalin.

"Dude. Hasn't she deserved enough respect to be called a woman? She survived some crazy fundamentalist bullshit," said Charu.

"After all those failed marriages—they say she is gay."

"You sound ignorant as fuck. We need to get you *straightened* out!"

Giggles ensued.

"Ella's a burly girl, no?"

"Aw, shut up."

"Why, shut up? Are you close? I barely know my siblings, so I don't understand."

"Right now, we aren't close. We used to be. But things happened."

"What things?"

"Oh, you know. I fell in and out of love. My best friend left and never called or wrote."

"Sounds tragic. You know, on the bright side, Ella looks like you, even if you are not actual sisters."

"Ew! Shut up!"

Ella dumped the contents of her backpack to find her Discman. She didn't want to hear any more. She unfolded three white button-down shirts, two pairs of jeans—one black, one blue—a pair of leather Kolhapuri sandals, and a pair of black Timberland hiking boots. She put on her headphones. She hadn't had time to get her music sorted—all she had time to burn onto CDs: Debussy, Marvin Gaye, Augustus Pablo, and Sam Cooke. Marvin Gaye's voice did the trick—the others made her feel depressed. She let her head sink into the pillow and laid a palm on her crotch. She pictured Maya.

The call of two azans awoke Ella at dawn. She went out to the veranda to peek into Stalin's room through the window. He snored loudly. Charu wasn't there. Ella went upstairs to the roof. Men hammered on development projects with bamboo scaffolding and brick foundations that seemed like they might crumble to dust in the near future. The multicolored buildings resembled ancient movable type. A rickshaw driver rang his bicycle bell to shoo away a stray dog and a group of street children who warmed themselves by a fire. The scent of burning trash comforted her, fitting her mood. The flames swallowed street debris, while providing unwanted children a bit of warmth.

If Maya had made the trip, they could explore Dhaka's streets on their bicycles. She was sure they could figure out how to navigate traffic. She leaned over the edge of the roof, remembering a night in late November. She had sat close to the Cascadilla's edge, fifty feet above a plunge pool, teetering between hallucination and hopelessness. As much as she tried to conjure up the darkness she'd grown used to, she couldn't. Up here, everything was new. Ella realized she felt all right.

A couple of hours later, Ella went downstairs to join Rana and Azim at the dining table for breakfast.

"Come, child. Your Rana Bhai has made us some paratha and roast chicken. Where is Charu? Will she not take breakfast?"

"She stayed up late, I think. So—"

"She will eat later, then. When she wakes up."

"No, actually," said Rana, "Charu is already gone, with Stalin Bhai. I drove them this morning to Aziz Market for a book fair."

"Well, Anwar and Hashi have gone to visit their old university grounds. If you would like, feel free to go in the car with Rana, explore the city."

Shahbag Aziz Market was overrun with men, books, and tea. Charu and Stalin sat at a makeshift café bookstore. He said, "I'll be right back—please do not move. Someone may eat you."

Some were brilliant men; others, simple men, all of them artsy and socialist types. Books and tea suited them all. And Charu suited them all, too, apparently. She'd made the mistake of wearing her tightest pair of jeans. She'd never really given desi brothers love, even though NYU was littered with them. She liked her men brown as coffee, bearded, Black or Latino. These guys mostly fit that description. But they stared at her with their huge brown eyes. She was an oasis in the vast desert of girls who wouldn't give it up without marriage. Sure enough, one man at the next table was drinking her in along with his tea.

Stalin returned with snacks. He scowled at the staring man, who fumbled to the next page in his paper.

"The owner told me there's a citywide hartal," Stalin said.

"Huh?"

"A worker and student strike. All the shops will be closed tomorrow," he huffed. "Hate not being part of the university actions."

"You're a professor now, huh? Not down with us undergrad minions?"

He didn't seem amused.

"What's up with you?" Charu asked.

He shook his head. "You won't understand, American."

"You know, that little catchphrase is like your checkmate. It's annoying." His cocky smile infuriated her, but she sort of liked the old-school flirting. *Stalin is attractive.* "I understand more than you think."

Ella spent the day doing errands with Rana. Besides working for her grandfather, he was a freelance photographer, and had even been in a few art shows in Dhaka. He drove her to the Sadarghat River

Front, so that she could take in her parents' city. The Buriganga River was teeming with the traffic of riverboats, as if Azim's miniature boats had escaped into the river. A passing barge's wave drenched the small dinghies. As Ella took in the new sights, Rana snapped photos.

"How long have you been working—" Ella caught herself. Working for her grandfather was a sad summation of Rana's role. "Living with my grandfather?"

"I was actually brought to their house as a baby. By your father."

"From the village?"

Rana half-smiled. "If you can call it that."

"What do you mean?"

"Your father and Anwar found me in the woods during the war."

"I'm sorry."

"Everyone's always sorry. But I found a good family."

Ella imagined Rana as a feral child, alone and crying, discovered by her father. Seeing no alternative, he must have decided to raise him as his own. "Do you remember him and my mother?" asked Ella. "Did I know you as a child? I remember a boy who told me my parents were killed."

"I remember your mother and father. But I didn't tell you that. I wouldn't have had the heart to. Besides, I was already a teenager. That must have been a houseboy, whoever the houseboy was at the time." Rana's voice cracked. He set down his camera. "Rezwan was like a father to me. We were a family—you were my baby sister. We were going to move down to Rangamati. Then Laila and Rezwan were killed. Begum Nani went mad. She couldn't sleep, couldn't bear to look at photos of her son. Azim Nana withdrew into himself. Stalin and I were young, but getting older, starting to understand things. We could not afford to falter. We had to move on."

"I don't . . . like Stalin," said Ella.

"He is someone who doesn't care if he is liked. We have an uneasy alliance. You know, I am a few years older than him." Rana stood up, and offered Ella his hand. "Let's go to one more place. You'll get to see how another side of the city lives."

As they rode toward Banani, the crowded alleyways of Old Dhaka opened up into wider roads, just as crowded with people. The car zipped past roadside markets displaying enormous bunches of black grapes freshly plucked from the vine. A cycle wagon carrying a hundred watermelons milled past. Ella wondered how the scrawny driver packed enough energy in his calves to move such a load. Men were everywhere. There was hardly a woman on the street. Ella had never been in a place full of brown-skinned people that she felt—kinship with. Some men wore pants; others, lungis paired with funky floral shirts. Everyone was hustling something, selling Nokias or produce, laying bricks or pitching bamboo ladders, or driving baby taxis and rickshaws, trying to evade aggressive drivers.

"This is the most ironic two-minute detour one could take," Rana said, nodding out the window. He pulled over to park his car beside a lake, where tin and bamboo houses stood on stilts.

"Why's that?"

"Korail slum—the largest in Dhaka—is right beside the posh neighborhoods Banani and Gulshan. People in the slum are always being blamed for drugs, organized crime, pollution. But they are the ones without running water or sewage systems." Rana beckoned Ella to follow him as he hopped over the guardrail to walk down a hill into the slum. Garbage and wet marshy grasses squished under their feet as they entered the mouth of the slum. Dust clung to the mangy dogs. They walked past homes of tin, cardboard, and brick, where half-naked children and their mothers cooked lunch. Men stared.

Ella saw a transsexual woman, a hijra, pass by holding a garland of flowers. The woman seemed the least nefarious of all the characters.

"Ey, Tina!" Rana called.

"What do you want?" The woman turned and scowled. As soon as she recognized Rana, she smiled. "Rana Bhai, what's happening? When are we taking the photos?"

"Let's schedule for after my sisters leave. This is Ella. She lives in America."

"Your brother is a good man," said Tina, nodding shyly.

Ella heard the thick bass of Tina's voice, but her lips were painted red, like her fingers. She was flirting with Rana, for sure.

"And you're a good woman," said Rana. He laughed. "Tina is the main subject for my next portrait series, *Korailer Nari*. I'll be taking photos of women and hijras that live here."

"I should go. See you soon." Tina patted Ella's shoulder.

"Nice to meet you," said Ella.

They watched her stride easily down the muddy lane, gracefully hopping over puddles of dirty water.

Ella felt a tug on her arm. A young girl, no older than eight or nine, stared up at her. She held out her little hand and said, "Kola dao." *Give me a banana.*

"Here, child," said Rana.

He pulled out three ten-taka bills. "Buy a bunch of bananas." He turned to Ella. "And that's how it is here. Brilliant characters everywhere you go. But the price you pay is guilt and too much traffic. Come. It's three o'clock. Let's go pick up Charu and Stalin Bhai from the market."

They walked back to the car. A few minutes on the road and they were stuck in traffic. "Are there a lot of people—like Tina here?" Ella asked.

"Hijras?"

"Yeah."

"Yes. There are different shades, of course. Some emasculate their penises; some don't. Many are charming and pretty women; others don't consider themselves men or women. It's complicated. I'm sure you have such women in your country, too."

"We do," said Ella. She'd seen a few trans women the night they went to the party in Bushwick. She wasn't exactly surprised at seeing Tina. But she liked Rana's easy interaction with her.

"Well, everything you've got there exists all over the world." Rana laughed. "I've never understood why people are disgusted by the difference in others. Take me, for example. I'm a Pahari, not your average Bengali."

"Pahari?"

"My people are from the hills. Our features are different. So we've been kept from our share of the world. I've never been rude to another man, woman, or hijra because they aren't like me."

Ella nodded. "Is there a word for the other way around?"

"You mean, a woman who lives as a man?"

"Yeah."

Rana tapped the steering wheel, trying to think. "You know, I've heard of one word—swadhin. An Indian photographer I met—he told me the word meant a woman turned into a man. Over there, they've got a lot of interesting words we haven't found yet. I remember it stayed with me. Maybe because the photographer wanted to take me home after the exhibit. It's a good word. Swadhin."

"Why? What's it mean?"

"'Ultimate liberation.' We use it when we talk about winning the war."

"I've heard Anwar say it."

"But in this case, it means a female finding salvation by becoming a man. Which I'm not sure is possible."

"What's not possible?"

"Finding salvation."

They had arrived at Shahbag Aziz Market. Rana called Stalin on his cell phone. "That's strange. He isn't picking up."

By dusk, they hadn't yet returned. Ella grew anxious. Rana told her that Stalin would take care of Charu; there was nothing to worry about. Ella went up to the roof. They'd been in the city for a day, and already Charu had ditched her. Down below in the alleyway, the street children played a game that resembled hopscotch. Trash piles burned around them, just like in the morning. The fires took on hellish, horned forms. A rock thrown in the air expanded into a Satan-faced balloon.

Suddenly, the roof light came on. "Fuck," she gasped.

"It's only me, child," said Azim. "What's happening up here?"

"Just . . . waiting for Charu."

Azim took Ella's face into his dead hand. This inundated her with déjà vu. "When you were younger, the only thing that would make you relax was pressing into my hand. You claimed you'd seen scary things."

"I did. I do."

Azim zoomed his hands in and out, right up to her face. "I'm going to keep zoom-zooming with my hands. I want you to say what you see, each time I push in, and each time I pull out."

Ella decided to humor him. Nothing he did would do anything to change the jarring array of shapes:

"A hunchback. An army general."

"Good, good; keep on."

"An old man. A coral reef. A pile of bones. A halibut. A severed head. Maya."

Ella watched as the great satanic head down below evaporated into Maya's visage. Her lips looked streaked with tar, or dried blood. Ella shook her head and muttered, "Please, stop."

Azim took out an ophthalmoscope from his pocket and flashed it into her eye. "Look straight into the light, child. Do you see a tree?"

"Yes. Everyone sees the tree."

"I do not believe this is an ophthalmologic problem, I'm afraid. I happen to know a neurologist husband-wife duo, Dr. and Dr. Masud, right here in Dhaka."

Ella looked down at the children playing below. "Nana. I'm not having brain surgery in this country. No offense."

"Of course you're not. I would never assume such a thing, despite how much it pains me to hear it. But why not learn more about your condition, with your Nana beside you? Will you let me make you an appointment? You know it will be painless and illuminating. What's better than that?"

Lightning flashed, and all the rooftops across the horizon lit up for a moment. The steady rumble of thunder followed. The alley children screamed and scattered. The sweet chime of a bicycle bell rang. Below, Ella saw Anwar and Hashi, giggling and paying for their first rickshaw ride in sixteen years.

22

Two days later, Azim, Anwar, and Hashi went with Ella to the Masud Mostishko Center for her afternoon appointment with Dr. Darwin Masud. Azim explained that Darwin and his wife, Sonali, met while completing residencies at Mount Sinai. They wanted to open a private center with sliding-scale options and payment plans, and none of the government hospital red tape. The building's facade had as much character as any old clinic in the States. All services were devoted to the *mostishko*, the brain.

Ella's heart felt as though it might break open her chest. She knew that her few years in Bangladesh were the origin of her hallucinations. But what if there was some tangible cause? With the support of her grandfather, and now Anwar and Hashi, she felt like it was finally the right time to do this. Besides, with Maya gone, she had nothing else to lose.

"Are you nervous, Ella? Don't be," said Anwar. He squeezed her hand. "You know, we could've done this back home. I had no idea the visions were so—strong."

"They're worse when I'm stressed."

"Most things are, my love," said Hashi. Ella could tell that though she was worried, her aunt was holding it together.

"I'm sorry you have to do this."

"Bah! Don't even say it," said Anwar.

Hashi nodded. "We'll be here the entire time."

"But I think the tests will take all day," said Ella.

"We're in the heart of the city that never sleeps," joked Anwar. "Rana can take us away if we get hungry or bored."

"I'm old and like sitting down. So I am just fine," said Azim.

Dr. Masud poked his head out of the doorway. He had a young face and a head full of white hair. "Ella? How are you? Please come. If you'd like anyone else with you, they are welcome."

"Do you want me with you?" asked Hashi.

"I'll go alone," Ella told her.

Dr. Masud walked Ella through the process of getting an MRI. Each time he grew excited, he tapped the cleft on his chin, as if inspired by an idea.

"It will feel strange to be unable to see," said Dr. Masud, as he slipped off Ella's glasses. He pocketed them in his white coat and checked to see if she wore anything else metal. "Do not panic. It's not easy if you're claustrophobic, so try to relax. Just lie completely still inside the hollow tube. We'll administer a contrast dye through an IV in your arm, so we can see clearly what's going on. A magnetic field is generated around your body. Water molecules in your tissues temporarily realign. MRI sends radio waves through you, triggering a resonance signal at different angles. Then, we'll read the 3-D scans to see if there are any cysts or lesions. Got it? Good. Let the tests begin." Dr. Masud grinned.

For the next four hours, Dr. Masud conducted a series of tests on Ella to uncover the cause of her hallucinations.

The MRI was the easiest part, a mere one hour. Afterward, it was time for the electroencephalography, which would measure electrical activity going to her brain. *I should've done the damn thing at home.* She reclined in a hospital bed and ultraefficient female nurses studded her scalp with fine-needled electrodes.

"Now the fun begins," said Dr. Masud.

She felt like a lab experiment, but admitted she was curious to see what Dr. Masud discovered. He introduced an array of stimuli—bright, flashing lights in multiple colors—and asked her to open and close her eyes, breathe heavy, then slow. Ella stared at a black-and-white checkerboard screen that dissolved into stripes and then back to squares. Violet light shifted through the spectrum.

"What are you seeing, Ella?"

"Um . . . the nurses' scrubs are growing big and wide into 1950s-style hoop skirts. Your bald spot is turning into a theater spotlight. And there's—my mother and father. Your head has turned into a stage. My father is lifting my mother over his shoulder. He's riding a horse on a golden carousel. Everything is red, orange, blue, and now violet. Then there's this—girl." Ella paused, blinking. Maya had appeared. Blossoms grew from her eyes, lips, and mouth. She blew smoke from her mouth. Ella materialized as a figure made in this smoke, muscled and naked.

"That's it," she said finally.

"Good work, Ella," whispered Dr. Masud. "We're going to do a polysomnogram to jot down your brain, eye, heart, and muscle movements while you sleep. Now it's time to rest."

Ella woke up around seven a.m. She noticed a massive book on the bedside table, as high as the proverbial stack of Bibles. On the brown leather cover, stamped in gold leaf:

AN ENGLISH TRANSLATION
OF
The Sushruta Samhita
Based on Original Sanskrit Text
VOL. I—SUTRASTHANAM

Ella started to read Kaviraj Kunja Lal Bhishagratna's translation, which Azim had left for her. The book was littered with English, Russian, and Bengali scribbles in the margins. Sushruta, a surgeon-physician from the holy city Varanasi, heralded as the father of modern surgery, documented volumes of his studies on illnesses, remedies, medicinal herbs both anesthetic and antibiotic, even surgeries for the eye. He'd been hailed with many titles, none of them proven—a student of Dhanvantari, physician of the gods and bona fide avatar of Vishnu. Hours passed, as Ella read. Her grandfather had dog-eared several pages, several times. The black ink throughout the volume had faded. Ella found one creased page, stained by brown coffee droplets. There were several passages underlined repeatedly.

A man who sees
The fiery orb of the sun by night,
And the mellow disc of the moon by day,
Or to whom the earth appears
Enshrouded in a sheet of fine linen
Or checkered with cross lines
Or to whose sight
The Pole Star remains invisible
Should be reckoned as already
With the dead.

The droplets grew in diameter near the ophthalmologic treatise *Uttar Tantrum*. More underlined and crossed-out words: Bhu, the muscles; Vayu, the iris; Agni, the blood. Ella had never seen her grandfather drink coffee. She realized the stains were from that fateful night with his brother-in-law.

Why did he leave the book here? What's the point of all this shit?

Should be reckoned as already with the dead.

The words stirred her. Losing his hand meant the dissolution of her grandfather's hope of becoming a surgeon. Losing her parents had rewired her, forced her to survive a primordial loss. She recalled her airplane ride from Bangladesh to New York with Anwar and Hashi. That was the first time she'd ever experienced her hallucinations. She'd watch clouds turn into people's faces. Once they appeared, she had felt much less alone.

At noon, Dr. Masud came by to review Ella's MRI results. He pulled the scans from a folder, and pointed to the film depicting cross sections of her brain.

"It's incredible. Your brain is as clear as the day's sky." Dr. Masud shook his head. "I admit, I am surprised, Ella. The . . . severity of what you've described left no doubt in my mind that there was some sort of lesion or tumor. But every day we are gathering evidence that the brain has unconventional ways of healing our—traumas."

His words disappeared in the air between them.

Dr. Masud cleared his throat and continued. "The elasticity of a child's brain and body is astonishing. We scientists are still trying to understand. Your very young brain has seen a world that many of us can only dream about. Perhaps there is some solace in that. Perhaps, one day, you will no longer see your phantasms." Dr. Masud winced, looked at Ella with pity and wonder. "You've gone through a lot."

He left her to fetch Azim, Anwar, and Hashi.

She had but a few fragmentary memories, wisps of her mother and father, collaged from photographs and others' stories. She no longer had Charu, or Maya, who had almost died trying to see the world the way Ella did. She would be leaving her grandfather and Rana soon, to reenter Ithaca's long winter, alone. Anwar and Hashi would be in Brooklyn, hours away. She didn't have much, if anything, except for these visions. Through them she saw colors, people, and patterns beyond the world she lived in. She saw her parents. She saw Maya. The hallucinations were a residue of what she had lost. She'd come to depend on this predictable magic. In this life where she'd had little power over what had happened to her, they were the wild gift that let her survive.

And no one could take them from her.

Anwar, Hashi, and her grandfather were simultaneously confused and elated by the news that Ella was lesion-free. They returned to the flat, where Anwar and Hashi retired for the afternoon. They'd been unable to sleep the night before. Rana had left to drive Charu and Stalin to a women's studies lecture at Jahangirnagar University.

Ella was happy to lie low with her grandfather. They peeled oranges on the veranda, discussing his birthday plans.

Azim said, "For my seventy-fifth birthday, I want no celebrations, no fanfare, no gifts. We can also do your belated birthday celebrations. I imagine the Christmas holiday is a poor time to ask people to remember you."

"That's true," said Ella. "Maybe we could go out to dinner? Hashi's not going to let you do nothing."

"I want two things: a fried rupchanda fish and a chance to show my granddaughters Cox's Bazar. It is the world's longest sea beach. We can escape Dhaka for a respite in my hometown. Dhaka and her surrounding towns have their share of old ruins, but I prefer the history down south. You'll love Cox's Bazar, I promise. The salt air and beaches were home to Buddhist kingdoms, Magh pirates in cahoots with the Portuguese mavericks, Mughal emperors."

She was starting to think that being in Bangladesh, miles away from Cornell and the familiarity of Brooklyn, was good for her.

"We should also take a day trip to Rangamati. The lake and the hills are lovely. But there is always a dark side, I suppose."

"What do you mean?"

"We've dispossessed people in the hills of their ancestral lands. Abused by the continual sadism of unwanted Bangali settlers planted by the government. Refuge lies in the surrounding forests, just beyond the border of India, Burma. But the land is not ours. It belongs to the Pahari tribes." Azim peeled another orange, and split the slices. "Names sweet and strange on the tongue." As he popped each of the twelve slices into his mouth, he recited the names of the tribes: "Chakma, Manipuri, Marma, Tripura, Tanchangya, Lushai, Pankhua, Garo, Khasi, Kheyang, Khumi, and Mru. There are many more tribes, but I can't remember. Much easier to call them Pahari."

Anwar was excited. In just an hour by airplane, they'd be on the beach. What a perfect way to end the week. Ella was healthy and sound. He and Hashi were getting along well, and Charu seemed in good spirits. Anwar had always loved Cox's Bazar's expanse of unadulterated ocean, the groves of supari, betel, coconut, and pine that grew wild everywhere. The one drawback was the rampant religiosity of the locals. While Azim owned a flat in Chittagong, his father-in-law preferred to stay at his modest beach house in Cox's Bazar, away from the city's congestion and pollution.

"Who should we invite, Baba? What friends of yours should I call?" Hashi asked. She sat next to her father, to figure out details for the party.

Anwar smiled. "Darling. Your father's friends—"

"Are all dead," said Azim.

"I was going to say they'll be there when we arrive, so we can call them later. . . ." Anwar let his sentence trail off.

"I've got my daughter, sons, and granddaughters. I don't need friends," said Azim.

An hour later, they landed in Cox's Bazar's airport. The air was crisp and cool from the ocean breeze. "Nice ride, Rana," said Anwar, as Rana pulled up in a jeep. "Quite renegade of you."

"Thanks, Anwar. I like it, too."

Rana had arrived in Cox's Bazar a few hours earlier, to get the house in order and be able to pick them up from the airport. He drove them past a cluster of ugly high-rise hotels that had popped up on the beachfront, near Inani Beach. *What is this nonsense?* They rode past the city's main roundabout, through a narrow brick-walled alleyway with snack stands along the roadside. Once they got onto Marine Drive, all vestiges of the town disappeared.

For miles, all Anwar could see was the Bay of Bengal's silvery waters. Even Charu and Stalin, who always seemed to be engrossed in conversation, were quietly watching the scenic drive. As with much of the country's most beautiful land, Anwar knew the military had paved this road, which they planned on extending all the way to Teknaf, at the Burmese border.

He loved being at the Indian Ocean, the very end of Bangladesh. Wild grasses and flowers native to the south flourished. Krishnachura trees flashed their crimson flowers and fernlike leaves in the late morning sun. Miniature yellow and pink lantana blossoms and pale morning glories crawled freely over the white sand. He noticed chunks of hillside had been excavated, perhaps to make room for hotels and housing developments. This foolish lack of foresight meant landslides in the years to come.

"There's the house!" said Hashi, pointing excitedly. They pulled up a sandy dirt road, where a two-story adobe house stood. Azim had built the house just after the war. There was an adjacent, equally large house for the cooks and property caretakers. Anwar appreciated the old man's sense of design. Both houses had open floor plans. The kitchen and living room composed the heart of the house. And all of the rooms led to the courtyard bounded by hibiscus, mango, and banana trees. There wasn't much privacy, but it was always airy and sunny inside.

The smell of fried rupchanda fillets, grilled lobster, and roasted chicken and rice wrapped in banana leaves wafted into the car. A sign painted in purple Bangla characters read, HAPPY BIRTHDAY!

"We've been busy," said Rana. "Anyone hungry?"

"Hell yes!" yelled Charu.

"This is great," said Ella, noting Rana's thoughtfulness. He'd prepared blankets for them to celebrate Azim's birthday meal on the beach, which was just a few minutes' walk on a path behind the house. Crescent moon–shaped fisherman's sampans dotted the waters. Young women and their children were shrimping in the adjacent cove's shallow waters.

Rana, Ella, and a buxom young cook named Malika set the baskets of food, plates, and bottles of soda down on the blankets. As Malika began dishing out food, Stalin hungrily grabbed the serving spoon to get more rice and chicken onto his plate.

"Let's give Azim a plate first, yeah?" Rana raised an eyebrow.

Stalin handed his father a plate. "Here you are. Happy birthday."

"Be careful of the tide and the sand," said Azim, taking the plate from Stalin. "It's like quicksand in parts. You can get pulled in."

"Yes, he's right," said Hashi. "Ella can't swim well."

"Girl like you, can't swim?" Stalin smirked. "It's a shame. Every Bangladeshi should know how to swim."

"Shut up," said Charu. "What's a shame is that huge chunk of chicken on your lip."

Ella ignored them. They'd been in their own bubble world and she wanted no part of it. She noticed Malika standing around, as if waiting for someone to ask her for help.

"Malika, please, join us," said Ella.

Rana nodded and spoke to her in a fast southern dialect Ella didn't understand. Malika laughed and nodded. She waved bye to Rana and went back to the cook's house.

"What'd you say to her?" asked Ella.

"That I'd feed her dessert in an hour."

"And that's why she looked so happy." The last time Ella had been on a beach was last summer, and she'd been pretty damn happy, too. She wondered if her parents had been married on a day like this, with the sun glittering like a path of diamonds on the ocean. "I love these wispy Australian pines. They make the beach look even more epic." Pine needles swayed in the wind. These trees looked young, no more than fifteen years old.

"The villagers planted them to guard against the wind. They can't do much to stop monsoons, but they can build a barrier to buy themselves some time," said Rana.

Four young shrimper boys had crowded around Charu, offering her dozens of cowrie and hermit crab shells scored from the beach.

"Oh, thank you!" Charu smiled at the boys. "I love cowrie shells, thank you."

One of the boys waved at Rana. "Hi, sir."

"Hi, Nur Alam."

"Want to play football?"

Rana nodded. "Want to play?" he asked Ella.

"Sure," Ella said.

"Shit, I'll come, too," said Stalin, wiping the last bits of food off on his shorts.

Nur Alam kicked the ball toward Rana, and all the other younger boys howled in delight. They dribbled the ball back and forth, between two makeshift goals the boys had constructed from fishing nets and seashells. Ella had never felt quite *inside* her body. Anwar had never been much for sports, and Ella had always felt gargantuan and shy about trying out for any of the girls' teams in school. She stole the ball easily away from Stalin, who groaned, "Not fair, man, I've just eaten enough to feed the village."

The black-and-white sand under her feet was striated in chevron patterns. She kicked the ball hard, and it snapped into the goal.

"Yaaaaaa!" cheered the boys.

"What's your name, brother?" asked Nur Alam, slapping Ella a five.

"New York Bhaiyya."

Rana laughed. "That's what we'll call you eh, New York Bhaiyya?"

"Sure." Ella recalled last summer, when she and Maya had sat on the beach, watching the shirtless men playing a game of soccer. At the time, she'd watched them, coveting their ease and brotherhood.

Here, at the edge of the world, she felt right at home.

Back at Azim's birthday picnic, everyone was munching on a box of handmade fried jalebis. Ella wasn't a fan of sweets, but took half of the orange twisted pretzel her grandfather offered.

"You know, I think tonight we should go to the koborstan," said Azim.

Hashi frowned. "You're right, Baba. I haven't been in almost twenty years. I can't imagine how I will feel."

"What's that?" asked Ella.

"Your parents' graves," said Anwar.

Since the local mullahs did not allow women to enter graveyards or masjids in these parts, Azim told them it was best to go to the graveyard at night, after evening prayers.

"Are you going to come?" Ella tied her shoelaces slowly, to see if Charu would answer the way she hoped.

"I think I'm going to stay behind," said Charu.

"Yes, me, too. I've been there many times," said Stalin.

"You've been in your own world this whole trip," muttered Ella. "This is important to me."

"El, babe, I know this is huge. But I think you need to do this for yourself. I'll go before I leave. Promise."

"Whatever."

Ella left them to watch whatever stupid television program they planned to watch. Anwar, Hashi, Azim, and Rana were waiting for her outside. They held hurricane lanterns, and Rana handed Ella her own. He led them away from the house and down the dirt path, motioning for them to hurry to cross to the other side of Marine Drive.

"Buses fly past very quickly," Rana said. "So we have to run."

Ella could hear drumming in the distance and passersby took on the outlines of aliens, nearly invisible in the darkness. They walked for several minutes on Marine Drive, and then turned right, down another dirt path.

Row after row of gravestones stood indistinguishable from one another.

"These here are all unmarked graves. Your parents are here," said Azim.

"Allah," Hashi groaned, leaning against Anwar.

Anwar squeezed Ella's hand, and whispered, "It's okay, my love."

"Why are they in an unmarked grave? How can you remember where they are?" Ella asked.

"Each year, the site is flooded. Waters form a temporary lake."

"Do—remains get washed up?"

"They haven't yet. Bodies decompose quickly here. Bones are heavy enough."

"So, we'll never know where they are?"

"No, we won't." Azim sighed. "We tried. When we buried them, I made three scratch lines on their gravestone with a chisel. But each year, floods would render the scratches invisible. When I used to paint three lines, same thing happened—water dissolved the paint. I tried remembering by counting where the grave stood. But after counting twenty graves, I started to feel I was going mad. So I knelt in front of someone's grave in this checkerboard of graves. I wept for whoever this person was. How could I know? Maybe they were Rezwan or Laila."

"We should have buried them on higher ground," said Hashi.

"No use worrying about what we can't change, girl," replied Azim.

They stopped in the center of the cemetery. One of the gravestones shimmered in the moonlight.

"Can we go there?" asked Ella.

"Yes, sure. Why this one?"

"I—I don't know."

"Then, for this trip, these will be their graves. You know, Rezu and Laila would say there's no difference between them or these other men and women buried here."

Anwar bowed his head, and brought his hands to cover his face. He seemed to be murmuring prayers. Hashi cried softly beside him.

Ella and Rana knelt beside the graves, but her grandfather remained standing. She clasped her hands together, as she had the night at the masjid with Maya, and like that night, she had no idea what to say. The grave rose into a statue, until Laila's face crystallized in the stone. Laila began dancing about, sweeping the other graves with the bottom of her sari.

Ella wanted to dance with her. She raised her hand to Laila, and her grandfather raised his. Rana looked uncertain as to what they were doing.

"What was my mother like?"

Azim shook his head. "I can only try to do the girl's memory justice. Laila Ali was the only child of my medical school colleague Dr. Mir Ali, and his wife, Noor. Laila was a brilliant, autodidactic girl. She learned French, Russian, Hindi, Assamese, and Oriya fluently, for the family had a history of working in imperial offices. The only lamentable thing about your mother was that she was very tall. Just as tall as you, but out here, it made her susceptible to teasing."

"Out there, too."

"Ah, well. I suppose nothing is a completely original idea, including teasing. She blossomed, eventually. She wore belled anklets to remind the world—I am *here*. But from what I heard from colleagues in the arts department, Laila was a disastrous student. Impossible to track down. Missing loads of classes and then showing up the day of her examinations. I had my eye on her, not for myself, of course, but for my son, who was also very tall. Rezwan first saw Laila at the Alliance Française—isn't that right, Anwar?"

"Yes, sir." Anwar nodded.

"The Alliance Française had been around in Dhanmondi since the late fifties, still intact after my return from Moscow. We were all there to see a screening of Godard's delightful *À Bout de Souffle*. Laila soaked up all the films, read any articles or books she could get her hands on, before and after the war. She translated an essay—'The Laugh of Medusa,' I believe it's called—for the Bangla feminist journal, *Joya*."

"But Anwar said they met on their wedding day?"

"Ah, yes. Rezwan saw Laila at the screening. But he didn't talk to her. Rezwan had some—strings to tie up."

"He was in love with someone else?"

"Love, or infatuation—I don't know. There had been some girl, a Khasi girl from the north, whom he'd met during the war. I've only seen her by way of photo. She was pretty."

"You saw her picture?" Hashi asked. "I've never seen the girl's picture."

"It was such a long time ago," said Anwar. "Who knows where the picture is?"

"We should've held on to Rezwan Bhai's things." Hashi's voice quivered. "I would have liked to see the woman my brother loved." She steadied herself on Ella's shoulder. "Of course, he loved Laila. . . ."

"I understand," said Ella, her voice cracking.

"Hashi's mother was much more conservative than I," said Azim. "I don't care anything for tribal mentalities. I mean, I married a Russian in 1950. But Begum would become hysterical when she heard Rezwan mention marrying a Hindu or Christian, like this Khasi girl. Anyway, he and Laila got to know each other the night before their wedding. And it seemed as though they really liked one another."

"Doesn't seem like a long enough time to get to know someone."

"To say the least. But the war wasn't exactly a joyous time to wed. To reap the benefits of romance you had to be married. At least back in those days. Dr. Ali and I joked that the match was genetically sound. And we were right." Azim smiled.

"Did they love each other?"

"Very much," whispered Hashi.

"What about the other girl?"

"Her family moved," said Azim.

At the same time Rana said, "She died."

"Oh, my," whispered Anwar. He squinted and peered ahead, as if he'd seen someone.

"What is it, Anwar?" asked Hashi.

"Well," said Azim, patting Ella's hand. He brought her up to stand next to him. "The one thing I do know is that Rezwan never saw her again."

They made their way through the cemetery of unmarked graves, back to the main road. After all of these years, Ella realized that she would never know where her parents were buried, what they looked like, who they had been or whom they'd loved. She looked upward at what seemed like a million stars, blinking and turning colors.

This was enough.

Anwar lasted three days in Cox's Bazar before he and Hashi decided it was time to return to Dhaka. Two weeks in their homeland had flown by. He wanted time to explore his old stomping grounds, and Hashi had lots of shopping to do. They'd grown listless with the carefree beach life—they were New Yorkers, after all. By the end of the week, the girls would take a trip to Rangamati. Afterward, they would all meet again in Dhaka.

23

Charu settled into the backseat on their drive to Rangamati, which cut through gorgeous rural back roads. After a week in Cox's Bazar, going to the Chittagong Hill Tracts would certainly change things up. Stalin had told her the history of the disputed lands—Khagrachari, Bandarban, and Rangamati—home to the Buddhist tribes, with the Chakma as the majority. In the seventies, after the war, scores of Bangladeshis resettled the land, angering the indigenous tribes, who formed the Shanti Bahini in resistance. After decades of violence, they had signed a peace accord with the government six years ago. The Hill Tracts remained tenuous territory, and foreigners weren't allowed to enter without special visas. Charu and Ella would have to speak as little English as possible. Not exactly the easiest thing to do.

Every few minutes, Charu rolled down the window to try and snap a photograph, but the moment had passed.

"Rana, can you please slow down when I'm trying to take a picture?" she asked.

"I'm trying, sister, but you have to give me a warning."

There'd already been so much to absorb. Charu hadn't been keeping up with her journal, something she'd started doing for her Intro to Feminism and Gender Studies class. Everything was so vivid here, colors turned up a thousand percent. In Cox's Bazar, while walking miles of beach with Stalin, she'd met a few Chakma women villagers. They lamented the real estate developments that threatened their fragile fisheries. Happy to meet Charu, one woman, Kalimaya, invited her to her family's hut for tea and biscuits. Kalimaya's hut was composed of woven dried bamboo lattice, dyed indigo blue. She and Charu smoked cigarettes, as the woman recounted her childhood. Her first home had been destroyed by the creation of Kaptai Lake in Rangamati.

"When they built the dam on the Karnaphuli River, they flooded our homes. All of our animals drowned. There used to be tigers there. Now there're only people, no animals. Actually, there are crows. Because the crows will eat anything," said Kalimaya, lighting another cigarette.

"Where did you get that?" Charu asked, pointing to a world map on the walls of the hut.

"In the book market."

"I love it."

"Me, too, didi. Everything is vast. Even if we have no evidence it exists."

They all lauded Rana's impressive driving. Every two minutes a huge bus blasted its horn, driving straight toward them before swerving back into the proper lane. As they drove higher and higher into the hill tracts, jungle green rice paddies turned into dense, untouched swaths of sal forest. Rana pointed out the different trees, some of which they'd never seen before. Shegun trees, or Burma teak, were used for ornate wooden furniture sold by the road. Mile after mile, Sufi mazars appeared. Their archways were painted sidewalk chalk colors not usually associated with mausoleums.

Charu rolled down the window to snap a picture of a young bearded Muslim man, who rode a motorcycle wearing a surgical mask to avoid the dust. He wore a helmet, while his wife rode sidesaddle and helmetless. Charu shook her head at the brazen disregard for his wife's life. The man held eye contact with Charu as she snapped the photo. It was remarkable, the look in his eyes, which treaded desire and disgust.

"The people are quite religious here. At least the Muslims," said Stalin. "So you'll have to cover up those arms."

"Why does it matter? You're here to protect us, aren't you?" said Charu.

"I'm not saying you have to cover everything. Just mind your arms and legs."

"That might as well be everything." Charu didn't mind the performance of piety, though. She'd brought a few of her haute hijabi creations to Bangladesh, just in case she wanted to try them out. Part of her felt it was wrong to appropriate them for experimental purposes. But Maya had always done it because she liked to do it, not because anyone forced her. The Bengali women out and about in the rural hill towns all wore hijabs, it seemed. Charu much preferred the striped Chakma skirts. But in this man's world, where a bare arm would welcome the evil eye, who wouldn't want to be covered up? Hijabs were like a protective and beautiful room, built just for one.

Once they arrived in Rangamati, Azim Nana told them he felt dizzy from the winding roads, and would need to rest. They were staying at the Parjatan Hostel, the town's only decent accommodations provided by the government. Tired from the drive, Rana wanted to hang around the hostel, get a bite to eat and drink. Ella told Charu she'd rather just stay with them.

"All right. I guess we drove out here to be the only ones down for an adventure?"

"Never mind these boring people," Stalin said. "We'll do what everyone else does here—a boat ride on Kaptai Lake. We'll even explore a local Chakma village. It should take up the entire day."

Charu had been looking forward to this. Her uncle had talked about the tensions between Bengalis and Chakmas. The religious and landholding customs were incompatible, to say the least, Stalin had told her.

They walked down the sandstone steps behind the Parjatan, to the red suspension footbridge that stood over the tranquil lake. Huge rain trees spread their thick branches, perfectly open for a swing or tree house. They made their way across the bridge and walked down the hillside, where boatsmen sold rides. They saw a signboard that read: BABLU'S CHITTAGONG—COX'S BAZAR—CHITTAGONG HILL TRACTS TAXI AND BOAT SERVICES.

"Bablu's smart enough for all this business," muttered Stalin. "Let's try him."

Charu watched Stalin haggle with an elderly boatman with paan-stained teeth. After going back and forth on the day's rate, the man spat at their feet.

Stalin nodded for her to climb onto the boat. "There's a hood for us to sit under." A tin hood was secured with bamboo stalks at the nouka's center.

"Spitting is his way of saying he's down to take us around?"

Charu climbed in and sat in the sunny side of the boat. Stalin followed her, but retreated to the hooded portion himself. As they set out, Charu caught sight of a family of four—a mother, father, and two daughters—trying to score a boat. The elder girl watched a Chakma woman weaving a bag with repurposed lanyard. The old woman smiled at the child, with her cigarette dangling from her mouth, and skin like crumpled brown paper. The toddler rode high on her father's shoulders, while their mother meditated toward the lake.

Charu wondered if the woman wished she were alone.

Kaptai Lake was stunning, but she kept seeing Kalimaya's descriptions of displacement everywhere. Tens of thousands of people forced to move because of a damned dam. The Chakma king's palace was submerged, probably somewhere under the continents of tiny purple flowers that floated on the water's surface. They drifted past an enormous snag, a skeleton of a great rain tree clawing the air. They rode up to the Shubhalong waterfall, a so-called tourist's gem.

Stalin muttered, "It looks like a dusty trickle of piss. Winter's not the season to see this. Are you certain you want to get out?"

"Good point. Let's stay on the boat."

Charu turned her attention to the boatman's son.

"What's your name?"

"Raahil, ma'am." The young man flashed Charu a bright, white smile.

"No. Please. Don't call me ma'am. How old are you?"

"Twenty."

"That makes you older than me!" Charu laughed. Raahil smiled at her, but made no comment.

While the boatman was sinewy and sun-dried from years of arduous labor, his son was a strong, barrel-chested youth. He and his father massaged ripples into the water. She wondered how on earth the guy kept his teeth so white, when most of the villagers had teeth yellowed from the hard water and chewing paan.

"Attracted, eh?" Stalin smirked.

"Shut up. I'm trying to take this all in."

"He doesn't understand a word you say," said Stalin, lighting a Benson. He handed it to her and lit himself another.

Charu pulled the cigarette to get it going. "How do you know that? We seemed to be communicating just fine."

"He doesn't need to hear anything you're saying, the way you're looking at him."

"What is wrong with you? Can we just enjoy this?"

"I'm terrible. Forgive me. Didn't mean to offend with my comments, American."

"It feels like I just got here. And I'm leaving in a week."

"We'll see each other soon, if I ever decide to come to your awful country—"

"Would you shut up about how awful it is? I'm the one that has to go back!"

"You will have a beautiful life. Ahead of you." He brought her close and pressed his nose to her forehead, his signal that the sparring had ended during their daily repartee. "Come under the hood," he said, taking her by the elbow.

They let themselves hug each other. He was hot, he was twenty-eight, and he was her goddamn uncle. Long-lost uncle, but still, Hashi's brother. His pulse raced against her throbbing chest. She felt him flex his arms as she slowly pulled out of his embrace. *This is a case of misdirected love.* She realized she loved him in this complex, inexplicable, and completely taboo way. There was no real way this shit could happen. But she did get that she'd never come close to this level of learning and connection with her roots, however tangled a mess they were. Nothing close to this with any of the guys she'd slept with since last summer. Not even Malik. But this shit was too crazy. *Even for me.*

"I'm going to go sit back in the sun," Charu whispered. "You stay here."

But Stalin had already moved away from her, distracted by the man waving his arms wildly in the distance. It was Rana, shouting from the bridge.

24

In Dhaka, Anwar and Hashi rediscovered their city. They carved out a simple routine: morning toast, biscuits, and tea (a shame how there was no decent coffee to be found), afternoons spent wandering their old haunts. Dhaka was a developing city. But they had no interest in discovering what was modern, sleek, shiny, or huge. They wanted the tarnished and hidden, everything they'd left behind. It was a week to forget their responsibilities. They avoided the guest room that Ella had stayed in. It was an eerie simulation of Rezwan Bhai's old room, with the same too-short bed, armoire, and full-length mirror. Though he wasn't trying to snoop, Anwar discovered a photograph of seven-year-old Rezwan at the beach. Hashi the toddler was perched on his shoulders, covering her brother's eyes with her tiny hands.

"I'd almost forgotten what he looked like," she whispered.

Hashi had been too young when Anwar lived in Dhaka to enjoy any of the romantic trails common for young lovers. On Monday, they visited Lalbagh Fort, the poor man's Red Fort, Anwar joked. The joke was lost on Hashi, as she'd never visited India. Manicured hedges and water fountains surrounded the massive unfinished Mughal palace. Prince Muhammad Azam ditched his fort when summoned back to Delhi by the Emperor Aurangzeb. Shaista Khan, his successor, failed to finish, too distraught by the deaths of his son and daughter. Anwar and Hashi walked the muddy pathway around Bibi Pari's tomb, hand in hand.

"It's strange to see ancient things in the city," said Hashi.

"It's strange to see so many people interested in ancient things." Anwar gestured at the crowded pockets of people scattered around the monument. A young couple took photographs of one another by the water fountain. The girl posed with an impish sweetness by the fountain, while her husband snapped a photo.

"Lovely sari, no?" said Hashi. "A jamdani. Rare you see girls wearing them on the street."

"Mughals loved jamdani," said Anwar. "Their weavers drew and dyed the designs with insects and flowers. Even good ol' Queen Vic loved it, until the East India Company drove down the price."

"So much in just one garment, *na*?"

"Value is arbitrary. Once it became available to us, Englishwomen didn't want it. But this young girl is looking quite lovely."

Hashi narrowed her eyes. "Oh you. And your appreciation for all the girls." She pulled her hand out of his.

"Now, come here, let's snap some photos."

"I'm not in the mood."

"Well, then, let's sit down. My feet are hurting," said Anwar.

They sat at the edge of the fountain. Anwar looked at Hashi, but she kept her gaze lowered. A horde of elementary school girls rushed around them, to drop coins for wishes. Hashi gasped in delight. The girls wore the standard salwar kameez and a shawl draped in a neat V across the front, hair plaited with ribbons. With closed eyes, the children muttered their wishes. Anwar wondered what their tiny wishes could be. (A copy of the latest Harry Potter? A vacation? A new father?) Dozens of small hands let go of the coins.

"Caught in a crossfire of wishes," said Anwar.

"Ha," said Hashi. "I wonder sometimes, about the places we sit."

"What do you mean?"

"What happened here once, long ago? Where we sit, perhaps in this very spot is where Shaista Khan's daughter Bibi Pari died."

"And tell me, history prof, who the hell *is* Shaista Khan?"

"Governor of Bengal, m'dear. Sixteen hundreds. Mystery how his girl died. No record from what I have read. He believed this place to be full of bad luck and never finished it before he went back to

Delhi. In this very spot, it could have happened," muttered Hashi. She shook her head and gestured to the tiny red flowers on the ground. "Did she eat raktakarabi, unaware of its deathly effects?

"Oleander flowers are never a good idea, for sure. But it would take a lot to kill a girl." Here they were, so far from Brooklyn, but Anwar remembered Maya eating his flowers to escape. Was this what had set everything in motion? Now he was forced to rebuild his damaged home, a project that required more time and money than he wanted to sacrifice. *No fault of the girl. But the foolish father who drove her to it in the first place.*

"And in this very spot, Shaista Khan grew consumed with building Bibi Pari's tomb, leaving the fort almost-finished forever," said Anwar.

The next day, they ventured to Shakhari Bazaar, in Old Dhaka. Along the narrow lane of centuries-old colonial redbrick buildings and twenty Hindu temples, people sold conch shell shakhas to newlyweds, sipped tea, and read the paper.

"Third world or Third Avenue, hustlers rule the sidewalks. Why did we come here again?" Anwar stood behind Hashi as she haggled for a pack of the bazaar's namesake bracelets.

"I'm not paying four hundred taka for shakhas!"

"Dear, it's five dollars, let me—"

"That's not the point. I will not pay—"

"Inflation, Apa," said the shopkeeper, his teeth stained from the trifecta of tea, cigarettes, paan. "You're not from here. I can hear it in your voice."

"*Arré*, take fifty; give her the bangles, man," said Anwar, pulling Hashi aside and handing the shopkeeper a bunch of coins, which he accepted in disgust. "Let's go somewhere a bit less crowded."

Hashi pointed across the street. "I remember going to this temple with Rezwan Bhai and Amma as a child for Durga Puja."

"You want to go in?" Anwar asked, incredulous at her sudden syncretism.

They held hands and crossed the narrow lane. It was three o'clock in the afternoon. A dreadlocked sadhu welcomed them and offered them a look at his bangles and Kali statuettes. Apparently, everyone sold bangles. Anwar rang the bronze bell at the temple's entrance. Hashi followed suit, placing twenty taka into the man's hand.

The sadhu nodded for them to enter.

Orange and pink bougainvillea grew wild around the temple courtyard. Anwar marveled at how symbology shifted from East to West—a repeating pattern of satkonas and swastikas were carved into the temple's walls. He realized he'd been away too long; seeing the Star of David beside the Nazis' hate mark rattled him. In the center of the courtyard, a havan of Burma teak logs burned. The incense pit where devotees lit their alms cloaked worshippers in a perfumed smoke.

"My god. There're three weddings going on in this place!" All around the courtyard, wedding ceremonies commenced. Pujaris performed the rites to seated couples, while their friends, families, and strangers stood around them in a circle. Anwar and Hashi walked to a porcelain statue of Kali, which stood at the back of the temple. They took a seat on the jute-matted floor in front of the statue.

"Do you feel anything?" asked Hashi.

"My knees hurt. I have not sat in this so-called Indian style in years."

"No, I mean, do you feel . . . Allah here?"

"I—I don't think so," said Anwar.

"Hm."

"Do you feel—anything?"

"I don't think so either."

"I'm not sure I ever do."

"But there is something . . ." Hashi let the sentence trail off, and arose from the floor to kneel closer to the Kali figure. There was a small basket of flowers and sweets, and she offered another coin and grabbed a piece of sandesh. She nibbled on it, grabbed a larger piece, and went back to sit next to Anwar.

"Eat this. It tastes exactly the same as it did in the sixties."

Anwar popped the tiny sweet into his mouth. "It does. Incredible."

"My brother and I came here for Durga Puja. I was little, must have been three or four. I remember there were shakharis selling their wares in the very spot where that sadhu welcomed us. They laid out their conch shell bracelets for new brides. But I didn't care about that. I wanted a conch trumpet. Rezwan bought me one. Once we got inside the temple, I started blowing it. Everyone's heads turned, hearing the sounds of mangal dhoni, all the omens of the new, the forgotten, breaking through the chatter of the crowd like a ferry horn cutting through the fog. When they saw me, a toddler perched on Rezwan's head, the crowd laughed at the culprit. Scared out of my mind, I pissed on Rezwan's head! And the crowd laughed even more. We never showed our face here again. And now I'm back."

"In this very spot," said Anwar. He stood up on his feet, feeling nimbler than he had in ages. He offered Hashi his hand to help her up. They lit two sticks of incense and circled the smoke around each other. He closed his eyes for a moment. When he reopened them, he saw Hashi smiling.

On Wednesday, Anwar and Hashi went to see the sunset by the Sadarghat River Front. They sat on the concrete harbor, legs hanging over the edge. Anwar curled his toes, scared to lose his sandals. Hawkers sold lozenges and cigarettes. Anwar suddenly wanted to smoke ganja badly. He'd held out during these day trips, not wanting to hear it from Hashi. He'd even scored some low-grade hashish from Rana. Hash was the only thing of quality out here. Anwar had forgotten the shitty highs of his youth. But in Dhaka it was either hash or weed that smelled like a skunk sprayed your face. He supposed he had become spoiled.

"In this very spot, an old widower prepared himself a fujka every afternoon, watching the boats dock ashore," said Hashi. She did the same, preparing a small dried puri pocket with tamarind chickpeas. "Open wide." Hashi stuffed the whole thing into Anwar's mouth.

The snack was cold but as delicious as Anwar remembered. He hoped he wouldn't get *Dhaka kaka* because of these few bites. *Well, that's what the weed is for, right?* "You know, in this very spot," said Anwar, "a nawab jumped into the early morning high tide to fetch the court singer's slipper, after he made love to her by the banks. But two riverbed pebbles became lodged in his ears, and he could no longer hear her sing."

"In this very spot—" Hashi stopped to swallow. "Agh, I'm no good with our little stories today. You're too good at it. I can't think of anything."

"It's quite all right," said Anwar, wiping a drop of tamarind sauce off her chin. "In this very spot, I realize we've only been hanging out in Old Dhaka. We need to change it up, *na*?"

The next day, they went to the Liberation War Museum. At first, Anwar felt it was sterile and generated the same detachment as any museum. He supposed distance and time allowed him to behold the artful mound of human bones and skulls. After a half hour, the scenes started churning his stomach. Faded black-and-white photographs of raped girls, bald-headed, stripped, some younger than Charu or older than Hashi. His heart clutched with memory.

"Rezwan and I—we had saved a few girls from a farmhouse where they were being raped."

Hashi winced, aghast. "You never told me that story."

"It's not easy to talk about, my love. Not easy to remember it either." Anwar traced his finger along the photograph of two women whose eyes looked hollow and defiant at the same time. *Birangona*, the nation decided to call them. *War heroines.* As a people, their capacity to euphemize astonished him. There was no recourse. Even the children they bore after being raped by the Pakistanis were abandoned. Shunned by their families, with nowhere to shout how they'd been broken.

His mind drifted to the second time he and Rezwan went back to the farmhouse, to try and capture the Rajakar twins. Their enemy was not at the house, once again. But they found a pair of sisters and their two buas, locked in the kitchen. Anwar and Rezwan had busted the door open, to find all four women huddled, crying.

One of the young girls shrieked when she saw them in the shadows, but was immediately shushed by one of the elderly women.

—Don't worry, sisters. We're Muktis. We won't hurt you, said Rezwan gently. —We're here to kill the men who have been hurting you.

—They're going to kill us, whispered the youngest-looking girl.

She pointed at the elderly woman moaning into her hands. —They beat Bua nearly to death.

Anwar's throat tightened. He averted his eyes from their torture, feeling ashamed that they hadn't come sooner. Cigarette burns festered on their arms, broken bottle neck tributaries carved into their emaciated legs. Eyes blackened, wounds split open. They smelled like infected animals, Anwar remembered thinking, ashamed. Shit and piss and sex. *How on earth did men summon enough evil to treat a woman this way?*

In the darkness, Anwar and Rezwan led the four women through the fields of watermelon and spinach, until they reached their motorcycle. Rezwan plucked a watermelon and hacked it open with his machete. The women ate the fruit hungrily.

—You won't be able to take all of us, whispered one of the buas.

—We will make as many trips as we need, insisted Anwar. —We'll take you to our friends' village so a doctor can help you.

—Take the girls first, murmured the bua. —I don't care if I live.

—Go, Anwar, said Rezwan. —I will stay with the buas.

Anwar hopped on the motorcycle, and Rezwan helped the two sisters onto the bike. The girl directly behind Anwar clawed her fingers into his ribs. As they rode, the stagnant air picked up a breeze. One of the girls started laughing witlessly, and in the rearview mirror he saw her sway her head from side to side. He rode his bike as fast as he could to the riverfront, where he paid a young boatman to take them across to the Khasi village where Hawa's family lived.

—Take them to Our Lady of Grace, the church, do you know it?

The boatman nodded.

—Tell the caretaker you must get a doctor for the girls. Tell him that Rezwan sent you.

—I will do as you say, bhai. Just make sure you give me a little more. The boatman held his hand out for a few extra rupees.

Anwar grabbed the man by his shirt collar. —I have given you enough, he growled. —If you molest these girls, I will find you and I will kill you.

The girls looked at Anwar, then at the boatman. It broke Anwar's heart to see the look in their eyes: They didn't believe either of them.

He watched the three of them cross the moonlit river. When they disappeared, he headed back to Rezwan and the buas. By the time he arrived, the bua who had insisted they take the girls first had died.

Anwar tried to focus on the captions.

"It's a good thing this place exists," whispered Hashi.

"It's good. But very strange to be inside a museum about a time we lived through," said Anwar. These grave artifacts were the same age as Rana. He hadn't had a chance to properly sit with the young man, to tell him things he ought to know. Anwar thought about the things he not yet been able to tell Ella. He wouldn't be able to write her about the girls they'd found in the farmhouse. He couldn't bring himself to say *the girls we saved,* because he had no way of knowing if they had survived.

The night in Cox's Bazar when they'd visited Rezwan and Laila's unmarked graves, Anwar had felt a chill in his bones. In the distance, he saw a swirl in the sky, a deep pink cloud that lingered after sunset. It had reminded him of the same pink fire of tracer bullets that marred wartime nights. Ella knew only a little about Rezwan and Laila. *We've only let her scratch the surface.*

Anwar hoped his letter would explain the story of him and Rezwan during the war and their descent into the Black Forest, a place they were safe, and the fateful night they encountered the Rajakar twins.

Once Ella read his letter, she would learn the whole truth. And he hoped that she would not think ill of her old man Anwar.

"Where did you go?" asked Hashi, concerned.

"Inside, my dear."

"I think it's time we went outside."

They hailed a baby taxi back to Dhanmondi. In the guest room furnished with some of Rezwan's old belongings, Anwar found Hashi curled up in bed, clutching a pillow between her legs.

Anwar whispered, "In this very spot . . ."

"My brother slept."

He wrested the pillow from her legs, and slipped into bed with her. They stayed in the room for the rest of the evening, then all of the next morning into the night. They only left for the shower and toilet. Anwar made tea and assembled a hodgepodge of snacks from the kitchen. He'd missed the opportunity to dote on her in this way. Sure, he made her products for her beauty salon. But the way she cooked, dressed, and kept their home—he had never shown her this love back.

The past week opened him up to her. He untied her hair from its familiar bun and let the black knot unravel. The parts of her that fell easily into his hands, her loose breasts and belly, delighted him. It was as though gravity was working in his favor. Anwar lit a pipe with some hashish, and Hashi had her first high.

"You're smoking me, Hashiiii-shh," she joked.

Anwar grabbed a fistful of her hair and pulled her close. It was the wonder of spending most of your life with someone; you could still experience firsts. "Hashi."

"Anwar."

He felt a swell of regret flood him, and for once he wished he'd shared more of himself over the years. It only now occurred to him that her reserved nature was not static, but a reaction to his tendency toward hiding his own nature. Ramona had been beyond thrilling. He'd needed to be awoken from his quotidian slumber, and Ramona had needed a distraction from her heartache. But Anwar wondered if he'd feel this rush of longing if he hadn't squandered the trust of the woman he'd always had. *Turn it to shit to turn it on. I'm a terrible man.*

"My love," he said, voice cracking, "I am so damned sorry."

"Apology accept kori. Shob kichu bhule jai."

Let us forget everything else, indeed.

"Last year might have been the hardest year in my life. I cursed you for breaking my heart. After the girls left, when we finally had some space . . . I realized just how much I must have loved you. I was that *broken*. I see that there are ways we both just take each other as a right, as a duty. But where is the life in that? Where is the laughter in that?" Hashi gently plucked the last nub of their joint, and took a sensual inhale. "You have always been real, for better or for worse, Anwar. I remember the evening that we got that awful call. Rezwan

Bhai and Laila Bhabi were—gone. You immediately said we would take Ella as our own. But I had a moment of hesitation. Shit, days of hesitation. Uprooting a child and raising an orphan seemed like a lifetime of difficulty ahead. But you were generous. You saw no division between my bloodline and yours. We were, and will always be—"

"One." Anwar traced blades of gray on Hashi's hairline, something she'd never let show before. "No dyeing," he whispered.

"No."

"I cannot tell you what you've said any better. I must show you." Anwar flipped himself over Hashi and tickled her bosom with his nose, making her laugh and laugh.

Rezwan's head visited him once, while Hashi slept and Anwar smoked a blunt, imagining his friend happy. They were both back home, after all. *I need some privacy, friend.* Rezwan raised a brow. In the trail of smoke, he floated out through the window. Each time he slipped into her, all he heard was the muffled concrete wilderness of Dhaka. *Let us forget our children, forget the dead, and the hurt we carry.*

After a couple of days, they decided to leave the house. Anwar relented and went with Hashi to brave the madhouse known as New Market, her favorite destination in Dhaka, as a child and now. She'd asked him right after they finished making love, so he couldn't say no. She loved buying un-necessities: bangles, pillow covers, bindis, sandals that would fall apart in six months. Her excitement stirred his newfound desire. She was much more accepting out here than back in Brooklyn. Dhaka's half-finished buildings, traffic jams, air pollution, six-year-old beggars, hijras—she didn't criticize any of it. She deferred to the wild city.

New Market was jam-packed for Eid-ul-Adha, which would be on the first of February. Everyone was shopping for new jewelry, saris, and groceries. Sacrificial cows were being herded in the alley.

Headed for the slaughterhouse, poor beasts. "You know, I never really liked Qurbani Eid," said Anwar.

"You shouldn't say such things!"

"Come on, I'm just saying the actual city becomes something of a horror show, no? Decapitated cows, hides left to dry in the sun—

takes the joy out of eating. At least in America you don't know where your meat comes from."

Hashi pulled out a handwritten list of gifts. "A sari for Charu, kurta pyjama for Ella, Baba, Shourov. My brother wears the same pants every day!"

"Don't forget Rana."

"Of course I wouldn't forget him," sniffed Hashi. "Oh yes, and of course, we need to buy a new one for you. As for me—you find me something!"

"Please don't make me fail before we've even started." Anwar followed her from store to store. He tried to take her hand into his, but she refused, making him carry bags instead. He didn't mind. Hashi settled for cotton kurtas, suitable for everyday use. Anwar nodded his approval. While she paid for the shirts, he had an idea. He would take a little trip to Narayanganj, a riverside town outside of Dhaka. He wanted to buy her a sari from the renowned Jamdani Market in time for her birthday in late February.

"All this shopping has made me want to lie down with you." Anwar pulled her ear to his mouth.

"You've lost your mind!" Hashi laughed. "But so have I. Watch." Hashi finger-whistled at a nearby rickshaw. Anwar nodded, proud of this latent skill he'd forgotten. As the driver pedaled them away from New Market, Anwar held Hashi's hand tight. She pressed her fingertips into his palm. Their accelerated heartbeats echoed in each other's ears. Anwar started to tell her, *You are a damned good woman*—she was staring upward at the darkening sky—

A pair of runaway cows, fleeing their fate, leather strap hanging loosely at their necks, charged into their rickshaw headfirst. They were flung onto the windshield of an oncoming baby taxi. The onslaught of bamboo sticks, shattered glass, and the tremendous scent of motor oil took Hashi first. Anwar tried to reach for her, but was trampled a minute later.

25

Ella sat on the porch of the Cox's Bazar house, waiting for Azim and Rana to arrive. This sense of dread in her throat was suffocating. Charu had locked herself in a bedroom. Because of the open nature of the house, everyone heard her alternate between howling and total silence. She had avoided Ella since hearing the news, and spoke only to Stalin. But Stalin had disappeared into town. With Charu out of commission, Ella said she would prepare Hashi's body for burial. Azim would ready Anwar. Three nights ago, on the car ride back from Rangamati, Ella found herself waiting for her hallucinations to begin. Perhaps Maya would appear, to comfort her.

Somehow to test them, and see if they would come when she needed—

My parents. Ella dropped her head onto her knees, letting tears wet her jeans. She wondered if they'd known that she loved them like real parents, not mere substitutes. She heard Charu wail from inside the house. Just as her cousin had promised, they would go to the graveyard together.

Around four o'clock in the afternoon, a minivan festooned with neon-painted lotuses and peacocks pulled up the dirt path. It was the young man named Raahil. Apparently Stalin had met him in Rangamati during their boat ride. They'd rented his van to pick up the bodies from the airport.

Azim limped out of the van, leaning heavily on a bamboo cane. "Ella. How are you, beta? Where is your sister?"

"In bed," said Ella.

"I see." Azim turned to Rana. "Please, my boy, wait here. You and Ella must walk over Anwar and Hashi together, to the preparation room. Unfortunately, I am too old to be of much use, but I will keep you company."

"Yes, sir."

Together, Ella and Rana lifted Hashi's wooden casket out of the back of the van. They needed to walk it over to the local masjid, a ten-minute walk from the house. No cars were allowed on that dusty strip of land. The casket was heavy, and Ella felt the black strap handles boring into her palms.

"The body is heavy as lead when a person dies," Azim whispered.

On the dirt path, they passed a woman who carried a giant water drum on her head. She lowered her eyes as they passed.

Masjid al-Hajj was a spare limestone building with a lone minaret. Ghats led to a bathing pond beside the masjid. Only a few men lingered for night prayer. The imam nodded, acknowledging Azim's loss. While there were separate entrances for men and women, Ella, Rana, and Azim went through the men's entrance in order to get to the bathing chamber. The men seemed not to notice any breach as Ella passed by. A dried-up fountain stood in front of the bathing chamber for the dead. It was a small redbrick house shaded by a large koroi tree, which kept the building and corpses cool in the ungodly heat.

Ella and Rana looked at one another as if to ask, *Ready?*

They unlatched the pine box and hoisted Hashi out of the plastic shroud. Ella felt the furious clenching in her throat. Her mouth was dry and she needed a glass of water, but there was no water to drink besides the basin's unfiltered tap. They rested Hashi on the platform in the center of the room. Early evening light shone through the thatched ceiling and cast shadows across Hashi's embalmed face. Azim gasped, "Allah re!" Rana held the old man in his arms, steadying him to keep him on his feet. "My poor girl."

Rana had explained yesterday that last rites—burial within twenty-four hours—was in accordance with nature's way and made logical sense. But embalming, forbidden by faith but deemed necessary in modern times, allowed Hashi to look intact. The mortician who'd reconstructed Hashi impressed Ella. Whoever he was, he'd spared them the sight of her aunt's injuries—a crushed windpipe had killed her. Hashi's lips were painted the same shade of rose she'd worn in life. Azim Nana cupped her chin in his withered hand, then pointed toward the easterly wall of the room. "See that, child?"

"Yes," said Ella.

"These are the instructions you must follow."

The wall was made of tiles and bricks from the villagers' leftover construction projects. Nailed to it was a sign, with hand-painted instructions from the Hadith, Sahih al-Bukhari, صـــحيح البخـــاري. Azim recited the words first in Arabic, then in English, for Ella and Rana to understand.

> *Said the Apostle:*
> *"Bathe my daughter.*
> *Wash her three times with water and Sidr.*
> *Sprinkle camphor and shroud her in simplicity.*
> *Comb her hair and divide it in three braids . . ."*

"Wear these, child," said Azim, his voice suddenly taking on a no-nonsense tone. He pulled a pair of latex gloves from his pocket and handed them to Ella. "Rana and I will prepare Anwar. We will see you quite soon." He started to leave, but stopped and said, "After the fiasco with Rezwan's grave, I thought I should want a proper burial ground for myself one day. A place for my family to visit me after death."

Rana led Azim out the wooden door. It banged closed; a drumming echo trembled through the chamber. Hashi lay still in the dissipating light.

Ella peeled off the linen shroud.

Hashi's face seemed browner with postmortem cosmetics—something she would disapprove of—but her body was so pale she seemed translucent. Ella dipped a washcloth in the basin and dabbed Hashi's face. The lightest trace of makeup smeared the towel. She did this again, harder. Unnamed alarm rose in her—the guilt of one healthy and alive. Ella felt like a mother desperate to cool her feverish child's temperature. She recalled last summer, when Hashi bathed her in the ice-cold water. Now she washed her aunt's body, her most private parts, her flattened breasts pinched into red brown nipples ringed with the finest hair, her trimmed pubis—the hair of the dead does grow, Ella realized, noticing the faintest stubble on her legs. It had only been four days since she had died.

Ella filled a small bucket with water, and poured it over Hashi's entire body. She did it three times, remembering Hashi once told her that Muslims liked to wash in threes. She pressed her fingertips into a jar of camphor basil, collected the pungent wax. Gently, she rubbed the stuff into Hashi's skin. Limb by limb, Ella covered her aunt in a linen shroud.

She did not realize she'd been crying until Hashi was completely covered. She clutched Hashi's hand, which was cold in a way that Ella had never touched. She took several deep breaths. *Something great will happen to you,* Hashi had told her last summer. Something great had happened. And just as soon as Ella had realized it, Maya disappeared. She wondered if they would meet again, and if she would find the words to say things, do things differently.

She pulled a comb from a tin can of combs and divided Hashi's hair into three parts. Even when Ella'd had long hair, she'd never combed it. Ella braided the wet, dyed-black strands into thick plaits. Hashi would be proud.

Charu opened her eyes to total darkness. There was a sensation of drifting through a lucid nightmare, one in which she was being shaken awake for school by her mother. As soon as her brain formed the thought *Ma and Baba,* Charu felt a howl spread from her belly across her entire body. But still, she could not let the howl out. She tried to sit up in bed, but swooned every time. She took in a deep breath, picturing herself a hot air balloon, willing herself upright.

Why didn't I convince them to stay here? Her parents often required the slightest show of concern to tilt them toward a decision. She realized she hadn't wanted them to come to the coast. The thought of being isolated with Stalin had thrilled her. It would have been impossible to move under Hashi's watchful eye. She'd ignored their calls for months and had a semester's worth of voice mails she hadn't listened to. And now, using calling cards Stalin bought her, she listened to their voice mails. They were the only line she had into her parents' love, concern, and quotidian ramblings.

Finally, she rose from bed, but did not bother to turn on the lamp. She wanted to revel in the darkness, a purgatory she deserved. She wanted to cut apologies into her skin with a razor. Instead, during the days of exile in her room, Charu had shaved her head with Stalin's shaving kit. When she went to open the door, the knob turned, but the door wouldn't budge. Something was blocking her exit.

"LET ME OUT!" she roared, panicked, finally letting the howl out. "LETMEOUTLETMEOUTLETMEOUT—"

Ella opened the door and Charu spilled into her sister's arms, still banging her fists.

"I'm here, I'm here," said Ella. She gestured to a jute mat on the floor. "I've been sitting here, worried about you. What did you do to your hair?"

Charu wailed loud, in unison with crows that had flown into the courtyard to feed on a pile of trash. Charu followed Ella to the back of the house. It would be good to catch some fresh air.

Ella gestured for her to lie down on Azim's hammock, and sat on a jute stool next to her. The scent of rajanigandha flowers filled the night air. Charu could hear the cooks bustling pots of food in the kitchen next door. As sweet as Malika the cook tried to be, checking in on her with food and water, Charu had no appetite.

"I'm an orphan, El," whispered Charu. "New member of the melancholy orphans club, largest chapter located right here in Bangladesh." She rested her buzzed head against Ella's shoulder. Her soft, virgin scalp was sweaty. Her temples throbbed.

"Animals here look so crazy to me," said Ella.

"What do you mean?" Charu pulled her head off Ella. *Leave it to Ella to zone out when emotions are on the table.* But her predictable shit was comforting now.

The next day, at twilight, they returned to the cemetery of unmarked graves. Ella and all of her male relatives wore panjabis. Charu wore a white sari that Malika gave to her. From twenty feet below, where the sea gleamed in the setting sun, boatmen and swimming children saw their silhouette as a portentous falcon. The shrill call of hill mynahs filled their ears. They breathed in the earth and salt water. Azim Nana leaned on a shovel as though it were a cane. He recited Janazah from a parchment scrawled with his loopy script. His voice cracked on each word that began with *A*.

Ella faded in and out of the prayer, hiding behind sunglasses. Trees cast camouflage-like shadows on the gravestones. Ella tried to focus on her grandfather's words. Azim pulled back the shrouds. Anwar's mouth had settled into a hint of a smile. Azim motioned to Ella and Rana and Stalin. The four of them lifted Hashi's body first, then Anwar's, setting them into the plot that Azim had purchased for his own death. Rana stabbed the soil next to the graves, lifted a mound of black earth, and threw it into the pit. Water ran down his cheeks.

A shudder from Charu, who cried, "Baba." She reached out for his body. But Stalin held her back, whispered something to her. Ella was certain that only she could see their affair—Charu wept into Stalin's neck, and he held her close, playing all the roles: protective uncle, substitute father, brother she never had, lover.

"Ella," said Rana. "Did you hear me?"

"No, sorry—I was—what did you say?"

Rana frowned with pity. "You and I can handle this." He handed her a shovel.

Ella, Rana, and Stalin began filling the graves. Her grandfather's final word, *Amin,* struck her, as the last mound of earth swallowed up the only parents she'd known, buried beside the father she barely remembered.

Azim's voice, taut with heartbreak, snapped like an old guitar string.

Night fell. Rana and Azim snored in the courtyard hammocks. In the parlor room, Charu and Stalin watched an ancient television playing *Lawrence of Arabia* with useless Urdu subtitles. A knob had broken off when Stalin tried to raise the volume, rendering the movie inaudible.

What in hell are we watching? Stalin wondered. Somehow Charu had convinced him to let her borrow his clippers. And now she was bald like some goddamned temple devotee.

Oh, his siblings had this way about them. Ruining things. Dying. Stalin rubbed his temples. *He* was dying for a drink, a late-night fuck. He had not fucked anyone in the past month, since before Charu had arrived in Dhaka.

He was an idiot. His niece was an idiot.

"I'm going into town. I need a drink." He stood up abruptly.

"Can I—come with you?" Charu asked quietly. "I don't want to be alone."

"You know the rules around here. Girls are *not* allowed."

The door clicked shut behind him.

Charu rocked on the porch swing, waiting. Mosquitoes bit her ankles and arms, but she felt as though she could barely move enough to scratch the bites. She had no idea what time it was. Stalin still had not returned from town. She'd felt his chest heaving under her cheek—he felt all the same shit she'd been feeling, right? But there was no way to name what they had. It was already over, anyway.

Rana snored steadily on the hammock in the front yard. With this driver-boatman extraordinaire Raahil around, Stalin hadn't been able to convince Rana to give him rides. Azim had retired for the evening, and Ella was nowhere to be found.

"Where the fuck are you?" whispered Charu.

As she uttered these words, a figure became clear on the path to the house. For a moment she thought it was Stalin, but this person had the whimsical gait of a boy, much lankier than Stalin. Charu recognized him—it was Raahil.

"Where's Stalin?" called Charu.

"Stalin Sir sohor-e."

Still in town, huh? Maybe he decided to walk.

Raahil came up to Charu on the porch, and he handed her a single sprig of some daisy-like flower. "Charu . . . ami—sorry. Bakul phool," he said, pressing a flower into her hand.

"Thank you. What's your name again?"

"Raahil," he said.

"Sit with me," she said, gesturing to the swing.

"Accha," he said. He sat down, careful not to touch her.

Charu didn't want to speak in Bangla; for some reason she worried if she did, she'd start to cry. She rested her head on his shoulder instead.

"Sorry," Raahil whispered again, stroking her buzzed head. "Cholo, amar shaate asho." *Come with me.*

Raahil led her to a small stretch of beach where all the huts belonged to Raahil's extended family, but they weren't for living in, he explained. At least that's what Charu understood of his warbling coastal Bangla. The huts were for fisherman to sleep in, for those days they expected a big catch after a storm.

Raahil brought her into one of the huts and lit a hurricane lamp on the floor. Only a bare fishing net lay in the sand. The whole place had a rank, fishy smell to it. Charu tried to hold her breath, but couldn't for very long. He waved his hand across his nose, as if to ask—*Too stinky?*

"Yeah, it fucking stinks in here, dude," said Charu.

He unknotted a mosquito net from the ceiling, and gestured for her to sit in the middle of the fishing net. He draped the mosquito net around them.

"I'm a catch," muttered Charu.

Raahil didn't get the joke. His face had grown serious and sweaty from the effort to create a vibe. He grabbed Charu's hand and rested it on his erection. He pushed her onto her back, and untied the knot of his lungi, letting the fabric unravel on her. He stretched the lungi flat on the ground and bade her to roll onto it. Naked, he seemed less gaunt, Charu noticed. Raahil untied the knot of her baggy salwar pants and pulled them down to her ankles. She'd stopped wearing underwear in this heat, and he let out a delighted gasp, deftly pressing his callused palm against her pussy. He grinned and brought his mouth down to her. His steady slurping reminded Charu of shucking oysters on Montauk with her father and Ella. It felt as though there was no room in this place for the memory. She wanted him to stop, so that she could remember.

"Babaaa," she cried, pressing herself harder against Raahil's palm. "Babaa."

Raahil looked up, alarmed. After a moment, inevitably he said, "Sorry?"

Charu heaved. She tasted nothing but the ocean, feeling as though she were being brined and breaded in sand.

"I. Want. To. Fuck you," he said.

"Please, stop talking in English. Jesus. You sound terrible."

This time, he didn't apologize. He turned Charu onto her back, then up on all fours. She stopped thinking about the oysters. She stared at the shadows they cast on the woven bamboo walls, the bristly hairs along his abdomen. She pressed her bottom against him, pushing back as he thrust inside her faster and faster. She gave one hard push, so hard that he lost his balance. He chuckled and let her ride him. Raahil scratched her back, then tugged her tits. Here she was, with this lean, brown-skinned man from the country her parents had grown up in. Where her parents had died.

She wasn't sure she'd ever return.

Raahil sat up and twisted her around to face him. He fell on top of her and fucked her steadily until she came. She pressed her fingers into the small of his back and started kissing his mouth, tasting his sweat and her own tears.

When he came on her belly, he did so loudly, as if to warn anyone who might try and enter.

Ella had been watching the black sky and ocean forge into a single abyss. Bioluminescence in the ocean rotated in a zodiacal wheel upward, spinning constellations out of the waters. The tide started to rise higher. She heard a loud, raucous wail from the beach huts. It sounded like Charu. Ella ran toward the lamp's glow from one of the huts. She stooped in the doorway. "Hello? Is everything okay?"

Charu was lying on her back, legs wrapped around a strange, naked boy.

Charu gasped. "What are you doing here, El? Shit!"

The boy pulled himself off Charu. "Ki chao? Ki?" As he oriented himself, he noticed Ella and jumped to his feet. "Sorry—"

"Stop with the fucking sorry already—stay here," snapped Charu, getting to her feet. "Ella—"

Ella left without a word. She ran across the beach toward the rocky cliff path up to their grandfather's house. Charu panted behind her.

"I thought I heard something. But it was the two of you fucking," said Ella, between clenched teeth. She quickened her pace to leave Charu behind.

"Stop!" called Charu, racing after her.

Ella ran away from the huts toward the ocean. The tide had started to come in even higher, and the claylike sands pulled her feet into the water. Charu caught up and spun Ella around to face her.

"El. Sometimes fucking is a good—I just needed to feel something."

"Maybe you need to try crying."

"You've fucking heard me crying. I can't cry anymore."

"Well, I was too busy washing your mother's dead body." The words felt ugly, but Ella wanted to hurt her. "You think fucking a random kid would make them proud of you?"

"It's not like that," whispered Charu.

"And your stupid haircut," Ella continued. "You're crazy."

"You're the one acting crazy. Don't take your pent-up bullshit out on me—"

"Fuck you—"

The wet sand loosened under her heel, pulling Ella into the night tide.

Salt water filled her nose. Ella sputtered, trying to blow bubbles, thrashing instead of floating as Maya had tried to show her. A maniacal pendulum throbbed in her head. *Had I been raised here, I would swim.* Ella sank and surrendered to the blackness of the water. Here, her body shed its awkwardness. She let go, floating and letting the waves bring her up to the surface. She slammed into one of the sampans anchored in the ocean. The boat's sharp side sliced open her flesh. Strong arms pulled her head out of water. "Put your arms around my neck," said Rana, heaving. He sounded as far away as the screaming above. "Oho!" he shouted, as he made the grueling swim back to shore.

After nearly drowning, Ella had two gashes from hitting the sampan's edge. One scar was on her left thigh, sickle shaped like the boat that had given it to her. The other was a long serpentine scar on her side, which healed quickly. She wrapped gauze around her chest to heal the wound. Binding her breasts became a ritual long after the scar had healed. Her breasts had always felt unnecessary. She'd taken to wearing the plaid lungis her grandfather and Rana wore, paired with tank tops. Most of the villagers assumed she was a boy. She never bothered to correct them. It didn't feel like a mistake. She liked that they saw what she wanted them to see. She navigated the town with ease, which she recognized as a privilege that her cousin didn't have. By the same token, she knew that Charu didn't mind being stared at.

Ella and Charu took leaves of absence from school to spend the rest of February until the end of March in Cox's Bazar. Stalin bade them all good-bye to return to his teaching gig in Dhaka. He made it no secret that he was relieved to rid himself of them.

They spent time with Rana and Azim, Ella learned to swim, and Malika's home cooking seemed to help Charu process her loss. Ella apologized for the way she'd acted on the night of the funeral, but Charu assured her that she was simply glad that Ella was alive.

The evening before they were leaving for the States, Ella and Rana sat in the courtyard, drinking a bottle of Johnnie Walker Black that Stalin had left behind.

"I want to bring you back to Brooklyn with me," Ella said.

"I've been thinking about this." Rana grinned. "My only two shitty ideas are for us to get married or to win the DV lottery."

"Both impossible," said Ella. They both laughed.

"I'll see you soon, New York Bhaiyya," said Rana. "Sooner than we'll both realize."

Ella would make a point to visit them, Rana and her grandfather, at least once a year. Maybe she'd do her senior year at Dhaka University. She would find her way back.

Rana left to go flirt with Malika while she finished preparing dinner. Ella heard Charu and Azim enter the house, back from their stroll on the beach. Charu still had to pack her massive bags. Ella knew her cousin would rather leave her stuff to Malika than schlep a heavy bag.

Ella took a swig of whiskey and settled into the hammock. *Little details like this hammock and whiskey are evidence these people are family.* It was stifling hot these days and nights. The air was no longer tinged with brown delta dust. Instead all they felt was a rainless heat, with no succor until monsoon. This was the perfect time to go home.

Her ruminations roused motley images. Maya held out a pinecone in her hand, and rested it on Ella's head. From her back pocket, she pulled out a bow and arrow, and released her first arrow. She missed. Ella looked above to see the pinecone take on new shapes—an apple, a crow, and a candle—until the entire room turned into her garden. Maya had started to disintegrate into a pixelated sand in brilliant hues of blue. Each tiny block swirled around, dancing, until they spelled out a word, but Ella couldn't make it out. She blinked several times, and reached out to touch the letters.

They were gone.

Swadhin, thought Ella. Ultimate liberation. She repeated the word. She traced the scar on her side, grazing the gauze with her fingertips. The word filled her up the way her visions did. She felt more complete, somehow. Ella decided she would be called what Charu had always called her—

El.

26

Traffic obeyed lights, lanes, and signs, as they stepped off the C train at Clinton-Washington. The air was unusually cold for April. El wasn't the tallest person on the street; no one paid El any mind. They hadn't been gone long, but Charu swore there were more white women with strollers and tattooed brown queers with oversize glasses. A natural hair salon had opened, and would draw the clients who could no longer get a fix at Hashi's. As they turned onto Cambridge Place, a brick wall with black spray paint read: *Everything is Everything. After winter must cum spring.*

They were home.

Dried-out vines crawled up the side of 111 Cambridge Place. Specks of rust corroded the wrought iron gate. Flaking brownstone paint reminded El of a Butterfinger bar. The limestone pots on the stoop held no flowers. Of course, after winter, the garden was in shambles. Every broken twig seemed an accusation, for being away so long. "It's like no one ever lived here," whispered Charu.

El's throat swelled. Maintaining the grandeur of this old house had never been effortless. Now it was their responsibility. They wheeled their suitcases into the living room.

"What is that suitcase doing there?" gasped Charu. "What is that smell?"

Had someone broken in? No—

"Aman. Bastard. He must be squatting here."

"Is he going to be living here?" Charu groaned. "I'm going to go back to school. I can't deal with that motherfucker."

"We'll figure it out. He won't be here much longer. Now, let's air this place out." El opened the curtains and windows. Millions of dust particles floated in the afternoon sunlight. Piles of paper and Anwar's leather-bound diaries covered the sofa.

"I'm going upstairs," said Charu, sneezing. "I can't deal."

El went to check on the garden. The remaining hibiscus trees had flowered into two colors, half the buds pale purple, the other half white. Open. Roses sprouted out of the demolished flower clock. Flowers grew out of concrete in this city, just as lotuses sprouted from shit, Anwar would tell her. The cucumber trellis was a crisscross of rotting beams. Soil and leaves were grayed, thirsty for water and seed. Unkempt morning glory had turned into a vicious weed.

Inside the seed vault, permanent winter reigned. El flipped through the card catalog of thousands of varieties of heirloom seeds that Anwar had amassed in his lifetime: rice, wheat, barley, soy, cannabis (thirty-six varieties), carrot, tomato, potato, cilantro, lavender, peony, gardenia, magnolia, myrtle, and pine. Missing were poisonous varieties of datura, of course. *Maya's recklessness forced Anwar to throw the seeds away.* El shivered and went back into the house.

El went upstairs to check on Charu. Anwar's side of the bed looked mussed; the other side was as neat as it had always been. The ceiling door to his studio was open. Without the help of Anwar's chair, El climbed up to his studio, immediately greeted by the smell of herb burning.

Besides some dust and cobwebs, Anwar's studio was pretty neat. Books arranged by color, papers collected into piles. There was a Rorschach-like stain on his rug. On his desk, El recognized the brown parchment paper Anwar had been writing on with such concentration. Taken as a whole, the parchment seemed to be broken into a map. It was divided into two sections, by a thick black line, like a river from which civilization sprung. El pocketed the parchment, and remembered the task at hand.

"Charu?"

"I'm back here."

She spoke from behind a white curtain that quartered the studio kitchen from the rest of the space. El peeled it back, discovering an annex wallpapered in silver Mylar.

Charu was sitting there, crying and smoking a joint. "This shit is so good. I fucking love Baba. The will thing pisses me off, though. Leave it to Baba to cut Aman a piece of the action, outta guilt. But at least we have a stash of weed to last us the rest of our lives." She started giggling. "Have some."

El took a puff. They'd never smoked together before. At their feet, a border of nineteen pint-size mason jars—each with nuggets of pungent dark green bud laced with purple—lined the floor. So, this was Anwar's clandestine adventure. Surrounding them were dozens of small cardboard boxes, filled with enough cannabis seed to start a proper harvest. The recipient address read: Mr. Aman Saleem.

"Charu, look," said El. "Aman's name is on all of these boxes." Lying on the floor next to them, a folder with credit card bills. All in Aman's name.

They went outside to the veranda to watch the sunset and get high.

"I see them every day," said Charu, inhaling the joint. She passed it to El.

"I do, too."

They stayed on the veranda all evening, smoking Anwar's stash and searching for their parents, suspended somewhere in the unreadable city sky.

El had always loved Anwar's easy take on morality, but the man's secret had given them the perfect solution. Anwar had used two different credit cards for his purchases. El found one of the cards in his wallet, cut it up, along with the corresponding receipts, and threw everything away. El would keep the seeds bought with this card and harvest them as Anwar had intended. However, the other card had been used *after* Anwar's death, according to the latest credit card statement. Anwar must have left the credit card in the living room. Aman had found it, mistaking it for his own.

Though Anwar had named Aman the conservator of the estate, if he was unfit, then Bic Gnarls would take over.

The next day, El paid Aman a visit at the pharmacy, armed with the incriminating receipts. Furious, Aman threatened to get his lawyers involved. El reminded him that he'd still inherited the deeds to Anwar's Apothecary. If he wanted to hold on to that, he'd better keep quiet and get the hell out of their house.

Aman's suitcases were gone by the next morning.

27

In between fixing up the house and garden, El read Anwar's handwritten parchment, but it was hard on the eyes. Then, a missed note in the corner: *And the story continues on the computer. . . .* Sure enough, on Anwar's laptop, El discovered the transcribed parchment. And so, El started to read Anwar's story, which he had titled *The Black Forest.*

> In November 1970, half a million people and even more cattle drowned in the deadliest cyclone that the Ganga delta had ever known. Your grandfather Azim's family home in Cox's Bazar was destroyed, along with all the fishermen's boats and the harvest. After the storm came a landslide. Sheikh Mujibur Rahman won a majority in the National Assembly. Groucho Marx's evil twin, Yahya Khan, and future hanged man Zulfikar Ali Bhutto, president and prime minister, conspired to put us—those dark-skinned, backward kafir runts—in place.
>
> Of course, Kissinger and Nixon had their back. So did the Chinese.
>
> In the last hours of the 25th of March 1971, the Pakistani army's bloodbath in Dhaka commenced. They swarmed Dhaka University, massacred Hindu students in Jagannath Hall, security, cooks, and the beloved botanist Mr. Zahar Lal. Most of our Hindu friends were native to Dhaka and its surrounding districts, so they stayed in the dorms. We'd known things were amiss—Westerners had been forced out of the country in the week leading up to it. Those of us fortunate

to have family homes outside the city had evacuated. I went with Rezwan to his mother's hometown in Sylhet, where her family owned a large tea garden. We'd been there for a week already, when we heard word of the siege on Dhaka.

(My brother Aman was in Manikganj with his girlfriend Nidi's family—they had been at her parents' flat; Nidi lived in Rokeya Hall. I think surviving the sack of the city brought them closer together; if they had met under ordinary circumstances, Nidi probably would not have kept him around as long as she did.)

Your grandmother Begum's home in Sylhet was a gem of a house, a golden meteor made of brick and mica that overlooked the orderly rows of tea plants. Rezwan loved this house; he preferred the hills to the beach. Though he was a spectacular swimmer and boatman, the vastness of the southern ocean made him feel at the edge of the earth, small and insignificant.

Everywhere in Sylhet is a green that tackles the sky, head-on. In the contours of those verdant hills, we saw breasts, bottoms. All the local girls seemed more nubile, fertile for the environs. Sorry. I hear myself, and I sound like a middle-aged pervert. But then, we were young. I had a half-witted hope of running into Hawa, a long burning wish, long ago spent like a matchstick. She could be anywhere, and I prayed she had returned to her home district of Sylhet. This was the land of Shah Jalal, a Sufi saint in the mountains, and I don't know—maybe it was the caliphate green, fantasy, guilt, the war—but I prayed a lot.

While I prayed and stayed a virgin, Rezwan (also a virgin) met girls. Most of our peers held off until marriage. Some dishonored a housemaid. And some lucky bastards had sex with their girlfriends.

Your stud father met a girl his first week in town. He was a flirtatious man when he remembered to be. He met his girlfriend Nayana Das in Jaflong, a border town forty miles from the tea estate. Bored in the tea gardens, Rezwan and I would hitch rides to try and scope out any action on the border. Mostly we saw refugees crossing over to India. Rezwan ached to cross the border to join a training camp. But I thought we had it pretty good at his parents' house.

Besides, I'd developed a slight crush on his little sister.

Rezwan's girlfriend Nayana Das hailed from a family of Hindu stone collectors on the Piyain and Goyain rivers. On these hotbeds of grueling labor, families sifted for stones tumbled down from the Himalayas. In Meghalaya, the same river was called the Dawki, named for the Indian border town across from Tamabil. Nayana and her brother and sister, Mukul and Putul, worked from morning until sunset, crushing stones. Not exactly glamorous. But for us city guys, this valley between two not-yet-formed states was beautiful. It always felt like sunset there, because of the amber-colored rocks in the water. We could watch the women all day. It sounds creepy, I know. But their silhouettes against the mountains of collected boulders felt unearthly. These rock-river women would find nooks along the river to bathe or wash clothes. It amazed me how strong their bodies were, how they'd spent their entire lives bathing with their clothes on, because they'd never had, and would never have, the privacy to be naked.

We helped Nayana wheelbarrow those massive stones. We liked doing it. It showed us a different way of life. And that was interesting enough.

* * *

In late June, the Pakistani army's jeeps and tanks rolled through Sylhet city. Rezwan wasn't home. Probably with Nayana, I figured. I flirted with teenaged Hashi, laughing about parabolas or some other silliness. Begum was in the shower, Azim fixing himself a snack.

A terrifying pounding on the door.

Two beige-suited SSG officers brushed past Azim. They stepped into the living room, where Hashi and I sat.

—Yaha kisko ghar hai? demanded one of the officers, a mustachioed fellow with a serpentine head tic. He looked from Azim, to me, to Hashi.

—Mera ghar, hai, sir, said Azim, gesturing with his crippled hand for them to look around.

The second officer, a man in his forties, wiped his forehead with a handkerchief. He was sweating profusely in the June heat.

—Pani do.

Hashi fetched two glasses of water, which they drank in one gulp. The mustachioed one gripped her wrist and asked her to show him what she was reading. I almost explained quadratic functions, when the older officer tilted his head—daring me to interrupt. It was a warning: His buddy was a loose cannon.

—Rani meri favorite actress, hai, said Hashi shyly, opening her notebook plastered with images of the Pakistani film heroine, Rani.

The officers started laughing, then grew serious. They motioned for me to stand up, and patted me down.

—Vaha kuch bhi nahi hain. I was unarmed.

Perhaps it was our limited faculty in Urdu, or Hashi's star-studded notebook—they left us be. Nothing amiss in the golden house on the hills.

When Rezwan heard he'd missed the action, he was incensed Pakis would dare invade his home without him being there. Azim reminded him that another strapping young man would not have helped their cause. Rezwan stayed at home the next day. We prepared Coke bottle bombs, for nothing.

I wondered where Rezwan had been, and finally mustered up the courage to ask—was he having sex with Nayana Das?

—I've been seeing another girl, actually.

—What, man? Two girls? Who is she?

—Her name is Hawa. Hawa Lyngdoh.

* * *

I'd never told Rezwan about my Hawa. I pushed away the thought that this was the same girl, my first love returned, in the flesh. After she'd left my family in Jessore, she'd returned to her family's village in Narayanpunji. At least that's what I'd heard from our neighbor's servant girl.

* * *

—Anwar, you're a man now. Hawa clapped her hands in delight.

—I have tried to be one, I said, making a silly joke. Rezwan slung his arm protectively around her. She pressed herself into his arms. There was none of the cowering I'd seen with her and Aman.

—This man here is the one person I trust with my life, said Rezwan.

—When did you come back? I asked. I regretted this as soon as I said it. Hawa's memories of her time with our family could not be pleasant.

—I came here . . . just after I left your family. Hawa stared at me, then looked at Rezwan and smiled.

Here we are, five years later. Hawa was Khasi, a classic Pahari beauty—lips full, black, lunate eyes, black as the hilly tea we drank. Her father, Marx Lyngdoh, was owner of several betel leaf gardens on the northern Bangladesh–India border. He acted as syiem, the spiritual leader of his village. They were better off than other Khasis, who were very poor jhum cultivators, never in one place longer than a slash-and-burn.

I learned that Hawa's family lived in Meghalaya, a-state-not-yet-a-state, like ours. Their home was in Mawphlang, a forest just beyond the reaches of Shillong, the capital city. She was as well versed as ever in local medicinal herbs, and I was still fascinated by her knowledge. I respected their law of the forest (the word for which is "law" in Khasi). Their faith was a mix of Hindu, Christian, and tribal ritual. Not a drop of Islamic din in the mix. Hawa knew the dawai kynbat of each and every plant, flower, seed, or vine. Rezwan learned a broken Khasi, and I learned a lot, from her. His favorite phrase: shit-dang, or feel very hot. She gave him a name that sounded close to his name in Khasi—Reit-shan, which was a durable, hardwood post.

How befitting.

—Name me, name me, I begged.

I became Ang Ang, or in the open sun.

I learned that Hawa wasn't named for the first woman on earth.

Hawei-ha-ar, or to be elsewhere. The lilt of her real name reminded me of distant valleys.

They had been seeing each other while I was praying, picking my nose, and flirting with Hashi. I suppose I was happy for him. But I felt a despair, too, that somehow fate had given me a true brother, and taken away my true love at the same time.

* * *

Rezwan admitted feeling bad for having disappeared on Nayana, since he no longer spent time at the riverbeds. Rezwan and I searched for her, just to say hello. She wasn't working. We looked for her along the dusty roads, in the market. When we went back to the riverbeds, we noticed a pile. Fibers of coir and jute, dried leaves of palm were arranged on a raft of sticks. Funeral pyres. Two purohits brought out a young child's bayoneted body, her eyes closed as if she were amid a dream, her body split in half at the guts. The child's burning body turned to ash upon the river, and our resolve hardened.

We never found Nayana Das.

***

July. Rezwan turned twenty-one.

Rezwan was in love with Hawa. And no longer a virgin.

Barsa's monsoons have been the bane of conquerors' existence since the days of the Delhi sultanate, and by August, the rivers' waters turned into oceans. Word was that Paki morale was plummeting.

Azim and Begum gave their reticent blessing for us to leave for the Dawki training camp. Besides finally being able to join the war effort, Rezwan would live closer to Hawa.

***

Exodus to Meghalaya brought millions of people—exhausted, on foot—to Sela, Mailam, Balat, and Dawki refugee camps. Cholera outbreaks rampant. Fires set by local Khasi, angered by the presence of outsiders. We heard rumors. Motor oil instead of cooking oil poisoned some refugees, while a family was killed stealing fruit from an orchard. Murder seemed gratuitous for a crime committed out of hunger. Black market prices for rice, dal, and saline skyrocketed to Rs. 500, when it should be no more than Rs. 50. No matter how much they doused the camps with bleach, cholera persisted. Even for Bangalis who stayed with relatives in Shillong, locals demanded that refugees be turned away if they did not properly register.

In those days, rail, road, and maritime routes were vital arteries between our nations.

People swam across the Surma, Someshwari, and Goyain rivers to get between India and East Pakistan. With only a canvas backpack rolled with some clothes, toothpaste, toothbrushes, flashlights, and a pistol Rezwan inherited from his grandfather, we headed for the Tamabil-Dawki border in a rowboat. Our boatman was one of the purohits who performed rites for the dead at the camps. He bade us luck, and rowed back to Jaflong.

Once we were in Dawki, an Indian BSF jawan, a pockmarked boy in his early twenties, made an unenthused inquiry about our arrival.

—Training, sir. Mukti Bahini, said Rezwan.

—Welcome to India, said the jawan, stamping our registration papers.

* * *

Our trainers were proper military men. Former members of the Pakistan Army gone rogue. While Indira Gandhi would not officially declare war until December, heeding General Sam Manekshaw's directive to wait for the rivers to recede, Mukti Bahini would be trained.

Mud, leaves, and twigs became our camouflage. We learned the physical art of guerrilla war. We shot bayoneted rifles—practicing first with bamboo, then the real thing—and simulated hit-and-run sabotage. Treaded through swamp. Blasted sacks of rice with Molotovs, hand grenades. Stabbed the sacks with the bayonets and kukris, right where the entrails should spill out. By mid-September, Rezwan and I were selected to join the Mukti Bahini. With three other young men—villagers from Tura—we were given our first order: to attack Tamabil's police thana, where Pakistani officers had created a temporary headquarters. A pair of Rajakar twins would be there, said the most talkative boy on our team, Khaled. The twins had raped and killed women in Tura village, and had moved throughout Sylhet. Reddish-haired, faces angular enough to sharpen knives. Easy enough to recognize.

* * *

The damned thing about guerrilla warfare is that it's a quick business. You have a minute to make your move, retract, make another move, escape. My nerves and spoiled stomach made me a very bad guerrilla.

On that darkest of nights, we bided our time in a ditch, waiting for the light to go off in the police thana. We were twenty feet away, hidden in swamp grass. In the window, I saw two Pakis listening to radio news, laughing. A shiny black Royal Enfield Classic 500 motorcycle gleamed in the moonlight. A man—he did have reddish hair—rode up the dirt road and parked his motorcycle in front of the station. He left the ignition key hanging off the bike. I noticed that he was not fitted in a beige uniform, just a regular pant-shirt, and a fez on his head. Khaled nodded. This man was one of the twins.

Our band of guys was pumped on adrenaline, trigger fingers on their rifles. Rezwan put a finger to his lips and motioned for us to follow his lead. He pointed to the basket I carried, grenades covered in water hyacinth.

Lights off.

Each of us grabbed a grenade, as pranksters grab rotten eggs—in denial of the potential consequences. We yanked the grenade pins and flung them with all of our might. Some landed in front of the police station, and one exploded through an open window. Men cursed and shouted. Grenades would not take down the bastion, and just as soon as we saw flames, machine guns fired. We threw more grenades.

Suddenly, Khaled ran toward the Royal Enfield, and miraculously fumbled the motorcycle on. He looped away from the station, toward us, gesturing for his two Tura village men to hop on.

—What are you doing, sister fucker! I shouted.

Our Rajakar target, owner of the stolen motorcycle, stumbled out of the station. He pointed a gun at Khaled and one of the Tura villagers. Two shots, two men down.

Rezwan shot the Rajakar in the kneecap. The man groaned and collapsed in pain.

We hopped onto the Royal Enfield. Me first, and Rezwan behind me, his gun held ready to fire. The last of our Bahini men had fallen, bleeding out from his stomach. I turned away at the sight of his viscera.

—Make it stop, bhaiyya, the boy begged.

I sped away, just as Rezwan delivered the coup de grace to our comrade.

* * *

On our way back to Sylhet, to visit Rezwan's parents, we passed the Dawki border post again. This time, however, our new mode of transport piqued the jawan's interest.

He narrowed his eyes at the Enfield. —Kaha se? Where's it from?

—Courtesy of Pakistan, I replied. Bang. I shot a fake gun with my thumb and pointer finger.

The jawan nodded with approval.

I felt his coveting eyes as we rode away. When we arrived at the house, Begum was beyond herself with happiness at our survival, despite yelling at us for being filthy. I took Hashi on a spin on our new ride. Azim just shook his head, as if to say, I don't even want to know.

* * *

We realized we couldn't keep going back and forth between the training camp and the comforts of the golden house in the tea gardens. There were rations for petrol, and the forty-kilometer ride to Sylhet was not sustainable. A week after we had won our prized Enfield, we went to meet Hawa at their usual spot—behind an abandoned Christian missionary school in a Khasi village, just across the Piyain River. Hawa often came here to spend time with her aunts, uncles, and cousins. She would sell woven shawls and pinafores that her mother made. This cluster of villages was still on the Bangladesh side, but they had more in common with their cousins in the north.

The Khasi tribe survived callous neglect. Their borders were redrawn and erased every couple of decades. Bengali Muslims grabbed their land after marrying Khasi girls, because the youngest daughter was the one who inherited property. We had never shown respect for their matrilineal, religious, or social customs. So they didn't trust us Bengalis. For good reason. We'd all but pushed them out of their lands into the river.

This particular village, called Mahapunji, had a Christian church—Our Lady of Grace, I believe it was called. We literally bought the trust of villagers by giving donations to the church. I loved the building. It was painted red with a long white cross as tall as the supari trees in its yard. We left a tip with the minister to watch over our motorcycle while we went to find Hawa.

Hawa fell into Rezwan's arms. She seemed quite—emotional.

—My mother wants to meet you, Hawa told Rezwan.

—I—I can't do that, not yet, replied Rezwan. He buried his face in his hands.

—Man, Amma wants to meet you; maybe your parents can meet hers. Her father is a distinguished man, I told him.

—No! My mother will never go for this.

Hawa played with a loose string on her pinafore. —What are you saying?

—Yes, man. What are you saying? I asked.

Rezwan wouldn't answer.

—Besides, you both can stay at my parents' house. It's only 15 kilometers from the camp, said Hawa. You will be safe, fed. Hawa patted her belly, which showed as she unraveled her sarong. Modest dress is a great concealer. But I'd noticed slight appetite and skin changes. But I attributed that to sex.

—Hai, Allah, I muttered.

—How can this be? Rezwan asked.

—You know exactly how it happened. Hawa narrowed her eyes. —Are you happy?

—This is great news, man, I said. Rezwan Lyngdoh has a nice ring to it, na?

Hawa laughed.

Rezwan said nothing. I wondered if he felt shame for having sex, or for being with a Pahari girl. I didn't see the problem. She had good roots and good genes, and as far as I was concerned, I would marry a girl like that in an instant.

—We will have a roof over our heads, I told him, as Hawa left us to finish selling her shawls. —Focus on that if you don't realize how lucky you are.

A few hours later, we drove back to the border post, to cross over to Hawa's forest village. Different BSF jawan this time, an older, bearded man in a turban, who didn't let us pass as easily as his younger colleague. Suspicious of two Bongs toting around a young Khasi girl, he raised a hand. For all they knew, we were taking the girl back to the training camp to do terrible things to her.

Hawa was quick to answer in broken Hindi:

—My father owns betel leaf gardens in Shillong. We're going there for a business matter. This one's our driver, and this is my business partner.

Great. I was happy to play the role of driver, if it meant we could pass.

After a moment's scrutiny, the BSF jawan let us pass.

—Fantastic bike, he muttered.

* * *

We traced the mossy broadleaf and evergreen lip of the Pamshutia Canyon; by charting this lesser-known route toward Shillong, we saved an hour. As we journeyed north, a dank fog settled, muting the jungle with its misty outline. Rezwan, Hawa, and I wove past trucks loaded with boys and mules and freight, zooming up and down the deadly, cambering ten-kilometer stretch. Again, I drove, while Rezwan straddled me, and Hawa sat sidesaddle, behind him. From my side-view mirror, I could see that Rezwan held her tight, perhaps protectively, around her belly. The closer we rode to Shillong, the less we had to worry about Pakis, but the more Khasi and other tribesmen posed trouble, as they were pissed about the Bangali refugees.

It was around noon. We had only about a half-hour drive left, until we were stopped in a traffic jam. Flares marked the road. Members of the Tribal Youth Welfare Association had stationed themselves at the helm of the route. Police hovered lamely at the scene. The students, armed with the fearlessness of youth, carried signs protesting the entrance of Bangladeshis to Shillong. Hidden from sight: rifles, unlit barrels of gasoline. The danger was not lost upon the policemen. Or us. There would be no rest until the sun rose and the students scattered homeward, more afraid of their parents than of the police.

—Where are you headed? asked a policeman.

—Shillong, sir, said Rezwan.

—No, you're not. Not safe for refugees. The policeman shooed us back toward the border.

* * *

Hawa directed me to turn northwestward, away from Shillong and Dawki. Signs read Mawphlang, and she ordered me to keep driving, until we reached a closed chai and momo stall. We got off the motorcycle, and wheeled it toward a clearing. Multiply the green in Sylhet by a hundred—this was very ethereal stuff.

We came upon a wondrous bridge composed entirely of gnarled rubber tree roots, which ran over a stream. Villagers trained the roots to grow through hollowed-out betel tree trunks. Roots grew across rivers, finally settling in the soil on the other side. Trees grew older and the bridges formed, connecting villagers long separated by waters. After one hundred years, the bridges would grow to unearthly proportions.

Borders erased in twenty years' time.

The road tapered into a barren moor. A single stone obelisk stood on a hill, erected by ancient Khasis. This would be our landmark. Hawa motioned for us to leave the motorcycle here. Someone would take it, Rezwan protested. She shook her head, and took off her shoes. We removed ours. We were to touch nothing, take nothing. Not even a fallen branch (or widow-maker, as the locals called it) could be molested. Even a dead man should not be moved unless the syiem allowed it. No one was permitted to come in at night. Some ancient code and sense of honor kept intruders at bay. Dewy grass crunched under our heels. Barefoot, and worried about large spiders and thorny trees, we trudged deeper inside the forest; the wind ceased. I remember thinking, I am a plains person, not a mountain man. Chirping, croaking, hooting, trilling—all manner of fauna bursting alive. A mountain bear, lion, or tribesman could kill us.

We walked past a bamboo grove.

—This means a famine is near, for bamboo brings rats, said Hawa.

Above, dim spots of sunlight filtered through the lush canopy of trees.

Hawa lead us to a circular house. Sitting on the porch were a wizened woman and a man, burning a smudge stick of some sort.

—Hawei! exclaimed the woman, delighted.

—Kpa, Kmie, said Hawa, calling to her parents in Khasi. She nodded at Rezwan, rubbing her belly. —Sengkhún. I'm pregnant. And this is the reason I am here.

Her father simply nodded, chewing away at his betel. He smiled, revealing teeth degraded by betel juice and tobacco. For a syiem, he seemed like a simple man, not the angry chief I had imagined.

—Welcome to the Black Forest, sons, said Hawa's mother. She was a replica of Hawa, but a foot shorter. She fiddled in her shirt for something. She handed Rezwan a small jute bag. It was full of cowries for protection, for her daughter's care. And so, we had whisked Hawa on our newfound Enfield, to the Black Forest in the Scotland of the East, Meghalaya.

* * *

For the next two months, we went back and forth, your father and I, between Jaflong and Mawphlang, regrouping at the training camp and instigating hit-and-run attacks.

Each time, we survived.

More important than any of those guerrilla moves, I came to learn much about the land, the sacred Black Forest, or law kyntang, as the Khasi called it. Hawa and I would walk together, in the stillness of that jungle. At our feet, ferns ancient as time, orchids in hues of pink I'd never seen. Rezwan slept a lot when he was back in the forest, resting from his pursuit of Rajakars. You see, I didn't have a stomach for killing. Bayonets, never. I threw grenades, ran as fast as I could, sped away on our motorcycle.

—I am a pussy, I once told Rezwan.

—There are worse things to be. Besides, you're not the one letting your child take its mother's last name.

* * *

One morning, when Rezwan slept, Hawa and I walked to that old root bridge, to sit by the stream. She taught me the names of trees, the ones used to make guitars, utensils. A hearth could not be made of twigs from different trees. Tender ficus leaves meant that fish would multiply in our rivers. Pungent herbs, ginger, pepper, turmeric, cinnamon—all at our fingertips.

—Tit, said Hawa. Tyng-shain.

—Pardon?

—Stop looking up, Ang Ang. Look down.

At our feet, a circle of bioluminescent mushrooms, aglow. I looked down. Up again.

I looked at Hawa. Without thinking, I kissed her neck. The taste of salt reminded me of a double entendre—Mawmlah: To lick the salt off someone's back, in Khasi, signified an oath, a promise.

In Bangla, to lick the salt off someone's back was an indictment.

Hawa gave me a look, somewhere between pity and amusement.

—Don't do that, Anwar. You know better.

I nodded, feeling weak for what I had done. Did she think of me as some sort of violator—the way she might think of my brother, Aman?

—I'm sorry. I would never hurt you. Not like Aman.

—Then don't, she cut me off. Hawa's expression hardened into agitation. She didn't want to talk about the past.

Hawa, or Hawei-ha-ar, had retreated elsewhere. She lived in the recesses of my mind. I remembered the old traces of her face, but she was long gone.

What did I have now? Love I could not have.

***

When the Indians joined the effort on December 3, it became clear that Sam Manekshaw's tactics would fracture General Niazi's slippery hold on the eastern front. Halfhearted Pakistani troops stood landlocked, encircled by Indians on land, water, and air. Days later, the BBC announced that India's fearsome Nepali Gurkha battalions rained down from helicopters to capture Sylhet. Their placid descent by parachute had the Paki brigadiers shaking in their boots. Fewer than five hundred Gurkha mercenaries—skilled at living off the land, wielding kukris with a butcher's skill, no fear of death—glided easy as skydivers.

We knew then, the end was coming.

***

We weren't flying out of planes. We were a terrestrial force of wily coyotes preying on Rajakars, our own men who had turned traitor. Desperate, they intensified their killing. The Rajakars in Jaflong had already been abandoned by Pakistani troops, who were en route to Ashuganj, in a miscalculated move.

The day of the Nepali Gurkha heliborne takeover of Sylhet, Rezwan and I drove back to Mawphlang, to the Black Forest. Hawa had not been feeling well, and her aunt warned that the baby might come earlier than it should.

A few miles from the Tamabil-Dawki border, we noticed a blockade had been set up. Circling the blockade were a pair of jeeps, and a black Royal Enfield Classic 500, same as ours.

—What do these animals want? Rezwan said, revving the engine.

A man cried, Ay, Shaitan! He jumped out of a jeep, and hobbled toward us.

—I think he is the man you crippled. And he wants his motorcycle back.

Rezwan rocketed around the blockade as fast as possible toward the border post. Our regular BSF jawan nodded—go, pass, pass—the young man had gotten much friendlier in the past couple of months.

We heard the Rajakars, stuck at the post, arguing with the jawan.

* * *

That evening, in the center room of the circular house, Hawa's mother delivered Rezwan and Hawa's son. (I'd started calling her mother Kmie and her father Mr. Lyngdoh, and they didn't seem to mind.) A few weeks shy of perfect timing, the child was small, perhaps only five or six pounds. Kmie cut the umbilical cord with a sharpened splinter of bamboo—metal was forbidden. I'm not sure why, but perhaps the element was considered too strong at such a young age. She washed the boy's body in an earthen bath. She placed Hawa's placenta and a brown hen's egg in another clay pot.

Mr. Lyngdoh placed a bow and three arrows beside the boy.

—My boy is an Indian, said Rezwan, sadly.

—Your boy was born in a jungle and he is alive, so be quiet, said Hawa.

They ruminated on names, Khasi, Arabic, Sanskrit. In Khasi: Rain, which meant honor; or Ranain, plenty of foliage.

Definitely not Ran, which meant to shrivel or shrink. Ramia, which meant dreams or hallucinations, suggested Mr. Lyngdoh. He could learn the syiem's traditions with plant medicine, perhaps.

Rezwan shook his head. —Too feminine.

They settled on Ranap, the slope of a hill, commemorating where they first met.

Ranap Anwar Lyngdoh.

* * *

We returned to Jaflong a few days later. Hawa wanted her whole family in Mahapunji to be involved in a proper naming ceremony. I would make two trips—the first with Rezwan and his brand-new family; the second with Kmie and Mr. Lyngdoh.

Our motorcycle resembled a poor man's version of a clown car. Again, I drove, Rezwan straddled, and Hawa and swaddled baby rode in precarious sidesaddle. Now that I think of it, I never would've risked that with you or Charu. America, in all of her sanitized glory, makes a man realize his mortality. You'd think with a war and all, we'd be more aware. Nope.

At the border checkpoint, the young BSF jawan nodded at Hawa.

—Your business is done, madam? Back to the betel gardens?

—Yes, sir.

Something in his tone, I don't know; perhaps in hindsight I am remembering malice.

In my rearview mirror, back at the border post's gate—

A twin to our black Royal Enfield Classic 500.

* * *

We started the naming ceremony in the afternoon. Unless a ceremony involves some sort of inebriating substance, they're boring. And this naming ceremony did not bore me. In a lush clearing behind the Our Lady of Grace church, Hawa's clansmen came by with roasted chickens, rice wine, hashish, and eggs. Eggs were very important if someone was born, married, or dead. Hawa and Rezwan were dressed in Khasi regalia, so to me, the whole affair felt like a wedding. Having the child's naming ceremony before a wedding was no problem. I loved these godly, unwound people.

Hawa wore a silver crown threaded with marigolds, a red blouse, and a tied yellow sarong. Rezwan had converted into a legit tribesman, in a turban, dhoti, and cotton jacket. He held his baby, swaddled in the same fabric as his father for the ceremony.

The clan and I collectively mumbled names we thought the child should have, until finally, we agreed on Ranap, the slope of a hill.

—I just won't say the P, Rezwan whispered. —Then at least part of his name will be in Bangla.

Hawa's father spoke a prayer in Khasi, and grabbed the bowl with Hawa's placenta, rice, water, and an egg and suspended it from a tree.

The bow and arrows were handed to Rezwan, who placed them beside Rana. Warrior father, warrior son.

I became drunk on rice wine, tinged with melancholy, wanting my own family.

* * *

We all decided it was best to stay in Mahapunji overnight, rather than risk being on the roads after dark. Hawa's mother would have preferred to go back to the Black Forest. She wanted Rezwan and me to be comfortable and not sleep in the small cave at the perimeter of their homes.

We assured her that we would be fine. The cave wasn't as bad as I'd feared. (Or as it sounds!) Besides, the Sufis' abodes of choice were caves, no? Jute mat, a pillow, a kantha—it was like sleeping on a very hard floor.

—Your parents cannot help but love her, I said. If not your old lady, then your old man will take to her. She's beautiful, smart, loving—

—You're right, of course. Maybe we can hide here, forever. Rezwan laughed.

—When will you tell them?

—Once the war is over.

—Elation is a good time to reveal secrets.

As Rezwan slept, I stayed awake. It was our habit. By flashlight, I read the only printed thing I had, a copy of the Quran. My mind wandered to Hawa. In one stroke my brother, Aman, had snatched her innocence. And now, my best friend did not realize his fucking luck.

I heard a scream, like a bird caught in a trap.

She screamed again, and again.

Rezwan was awake, on his feet. He grabbed his pistol.

—Get up, Anwar. Bring your rifle.

We ran toward the screaming woman, until we reached the pathway to the outhouse.

Two red-haired shadows hovered over Hawa. She was on the ground, clutching her belly. I fell beside her. In the dark, her wounds were invisible, but her blood was warm, resinous as sap on my fingers.

—Riet-shang!

Rezwan fired his pistol. He did not stop to calm Hawa. His shot cleared the air, cleared my mind—and I realized. The Rajakar twins had bribed the BSF jawan with a motherfucking motorcycle. One of the twins reclaimed the stolen motorcycle and drove off, yelling at his limping brother to hop on. Already maimed by Rezwan before, the leftover twin could not prop himself up.

—Stop him, Anwar! Go! Rezwan yelled, as he beat the man to the ground.

I did not hear him. Running was futile. Instead, I whispered, Hawa, as she whispered, Rana. We repeated our rhyming mantra, until she said one last word, which I could not quite make out.

—Pongka, she moaned, shaking her head no.

Don't let my son be a bastard.

* * *

Hawa's mother and father, her aunties and uncles bolted over to their child. I didn't hear the shrieking cries I expected. Instead, they murmured names for god and spirit, and dragged her away from the scene. Murder in the presence of the dead was an unnecessary sin.

—I stole your leg; now I'm going to steal your face.

Rezwan said the words, calm. He slathered the Rajakar's face with a salve, as tender as a barber.

—W-w-what are you p-putting on my face, devil! screamed the Rajakar.

Rezwan slipped on a pair of leather gloves.

—We've got enough people in this country to worry about. Don't need any more ugly, crippled bastards, right? Step back, Anwar.

Rezwan held the man down and struck a lighter to his face. He kicked the man over and over again, as his face burned in the flames.

—Who's the devil now? shouted Rezwan.

* * *

The next morning, I presume, the Lyngdoh family burned their daughter's body. They would collect her remaining bones for the family ossuary. We were banned from the ritual, from ever returning to their gardens or forest. Dare we enter, we would be killed, I imagine, the old-fashioned way, by bow and arrow. As a parting gift, Rezwan kept his son. We brought baby Rana to the golden house in Jaflong. The Anwars believed we'd found the adorable crying babe in the woods, next to his murdered mother.

Once more, Azim shook his head—he still did not want to know.

So this fiction was told, and retold, until we believed it was true.

* * *

No matter of searching for that cursed Enfield turned up the other twin. We walked to the border post—a much more strenuous journey by foot—to see if the BSF jawan had sold us out. He wasn't there. Neither was the motorcycle.

He'd ridden off into the sunset. And I had missed my chance to kill the man who would eventually kill Rezwan and Laila.

* * *

In the years after the war, famine and chaos knocked us out. The assassination of Sheikh Mujib simultaneously stunned me and confirmed what I expected. An empire would not rise out of ashes, with so much to reckon with.

Aman was among the first ones to leap to America. Others went to Britain. You might call these men useless during the war, brave enough to enter a new world without second thought. But others of us, we feared the depression that comes with failure and fear. I spent years lost. I farmed in a few villages, trying to regain that feeling I'd had in the Black Forest. I finished up a degree in pharmacy, the boring guarantee out of the country, instead of phytogeography. Rezwan married another beauty, your mother, Laila, whom he'd met once at a film screening. And they learned to love each other deeply for many years until they died.

We learned how to divide past from present, desire from duty.

When I told Rezwan I was leaving for New York, he laughed.

—You and your brother are more alike than you and I, after all.

Rezwan and Aman, they were more alike than they would ever know. Strong, controlled men with a wild side they held close to the vest. Yet, I admired Rezwan, and despised my brother. I wonder now if Rezwan was telling me that he despised me.

—You are my brother. My real brother, I told him.

—That's what you say, now. You'll forget me in no time.

He was wrong, as usual.

* * *

Ella, this is my confession. I am sorry for telling you, for not telling. I hope that you find this when you are an old woman, and tell Rana when he is an old man. When I am long dead, lovingly remembered, and easily forgiven. With Love, Always, Anwar

El printed the document and put it in an envelope addressed to Azim's Dhaka flat. What could one say to Rana? Although El had a feeling that Rana would understand, maybe this would be confirmation of something he'd always believed to be true. What if Rezwan had sought the protection of his parents' golden house in Sylhet? Then Rana would never have been born. Anwar, the hapless, lovelorn romantic, unfit for war, left behind more damned questions than answers. Had Laila ever known about Hawa? Had Laila loved this baby who wasn't hers? The photo of Rezwan and Laila, the teenager between them, it looked as though they were all—happy. Both El and Rana had grown up in exile, entombed by desertions few could comprehend. El scribbled a note, but could not yet send the letter: *We have two mothers, one father. You and I, Rana and El, brothers.*

28

There's nothing like springtime in Brooklyn, thought El. The neighborhood burst alive in May, winter's residue a memory until next year. Leaves everywhere. Crocuses sprouted their ephemeral purple flowers, then gave way to magnolia and myrtle trees. El planted azalea, lilac, and peony, proper spring blooms, and where the moon garden had once been, El built a circular fire pit of sand and old bricks. Wildflowers erupted from the concrete. Climbing aster, wild bergamot, licorice-scented anise hyssop, and the monarch butterfly's chosen home, milkweed—El had never paid much mind to these weeds, yet now discovered an appreciation. They required no nurture or attention. Weaving in and out of the bustle were teenagers on their BMX bikes. The longer the days, the more people out and about. The season of stoop sales had begun.

It was time for El and Charu to sell Anwar's wares.

One Saturday morning, Bic drove them to Anwar's Apothecary in his van. This was the last time these keys would open the storefront before it became Kings Pharmacy. They parked in front of the apothecary. Closed gates for both Anwar's Apothecary and A Holy Bookstore seemed to be a show of mourning: an owner dead, the other imprisoned. Ye Olde Liquor Shoppe buzzed with a new neon sign, the victor over the kooky shampoo spot and judgmental bookshop.

El and Charu stared at the apartment above the apothecary.

"Wouldn't it be crazy if she was home?" muttered Charu.

"It would be."

They could hear the tinny sound of a television, and nothing more. *Mema has the house to herself,* thought El. The boys would be in school, her husband in jail, and her daughter, Maya, run away.

The arresting scent of tinctures filled their nostrils as they entered. The little brown glass apothecary bottles climbed the shelves all the way to the ceiling, a kaleidoscope of jeweled shadows on the walls. They divvied their tasks by genre—tinctures (Charu), beauty (Bic), miscellany (El)—and set to work. Charu wrapped each tiny brown bottle in Anwar's enormous stack of *New York Post*s. Bic stacked the shampoos, scrubs, and soaps, while El arranged the superfluity Anwar had acquired over the years—a second bicycle, boom box, cleaning supplies, a score of DVDs and vinyl records from Rashaud Persaud, and extra pairs of shirts and shoes. They worked in silence for a couple of hours, ordered a pizza, worked some more.

"I thought we might do well with an extra pair of hands. All this stuff is heavier than it looks," said Bic. He lifted a box of tinctures. El attempted the same, but dropped the box for its surprising weight.

"Shit, you're right."

"Charu, you mind calling Malik? I'm gonna take this over to the car." Bic hefted the first of many tincture boxes on his shoulder and went out to the van.

El laughed. "You haven't talked to him since we came back, have you?"

"Nope. Sigh," said Charu. She picked up the landline to call Malik.

"Hello?" he answered, sounding a bit freaked out—Charu realized ANWAR SALEEM must have shown up on his caller ID.

"Relax, it's not my dad's ghost."

"You're terrible," muttered El.

"Charu?" said Malik. "I've been wanting to see you—see how you're doing—I'm sorry—"

"Could you come over to the store? Bic said you might be able to help us move Baba's stuff back to our house."

"Of course; I'll be there in fifteen."

Charu and Malik rode with the boxes and Bic, while El gave the place a thorough cleaning and locked up. Charu preferred heavy lifting to housework any day. After every last box was brought into the living room, Bic bade them adieu—it was date night. Charu wondered if this had been his and Mauve's elaborate ploy to get Malik back in the fold. Not that she minded. Malik had traded his adolescent scruff for a dapper beard, shorter dreadlocks, and a fresh-inked sleeve of the Tale of Genji on his arms. He would be heading off on a Southwest tour with Yesterday's Future in a few days.

They sat in the living room, feet propped up, drinking beers, courtesy of El.

"This is a lot to take care of," said Malik, looking around the living room.

"It is," said Charu. "I'm not sure what's going to happen when we go back to school. We need to rent this place out."

"Just don't ever sell it. Unless you sell it to me. You know, I've never gotten the grand tour."

"Follow me," she said.

They went upstairs to her parents' bedroom, where she'd been sleeping.

Malik pointed at the photographs mounted on the walls. "Wow. Look at this—your family's beautiful. I love these old-school photographs. They say a lot." He pointed to a photo of Anwar and Hashi. "Anwar rocking killer white bellbottoms *and* a velour shirt? I dig it." Another photo of Charu showed teeth charmingly missing, wearing a hot pink jumper. "What are you, like, six in this photo?"

"I think so. Kindergarten—were we six or seven?"

"Only if you're stupid," he said.

She jabbed him in the ribs.

"Ow! Just kidding, babe—relax."

"We're so ridiculous in this," she said, picking up a professional photo of a homecoming dance: Charu in a silver gown, Malik in his skinny tie and tapered suit pants, fingers laced with hers.

"At least we weren't stupid enough to go to prom."

"I don't think I had permission to go, remember? Now I can do whatever I want." She sat on the bed's edge, and Malik stood beside her, and brought her face into his side.

"I'm so sorry," he said. Charu looked up at him, surprised by this gesture. Just below her chin, Malik's pants bulged at the inseam. "Shit. Don't take this the wrong way, but looking at all these photos of you, your family, it got me—wanting you." He tugged at his jeans as if it would make his hard-on disappear, and then he sat beside her. "I like this new look. Pixie. Earthy pixie. You always just smelled like body," he said, inhaling her underarm.

Charu leaned over to grab her pipe and a nugget of Baba's stash. "Smell this." She lit the herb and took a toke before passing it to Malik.

"Rest in peace, Anwar," he said, kissing his fingers and putting them up toward the ceiling. He took a ceremonious breath in, and then blew the smoke into Charu's face. "You know, your pops gave me this excellent book, *Divan-e Shams-e Tabrizi*. Rumi spent years inseparable from Shams, a homeless wanderer-mystic-weaver guy. Super skeptical of him, at first. Shams walks past Rumi, who was reading a book. He doesn't give a shit about Shams, so Shams asks him, 'What are you doing?'"

"Wasn't he just reading?"

"Right. But Rumi, being Rumi, tells the homeless guy, 'Something you wouldn't understand.' Suddenly, the book catches fire, Rumi freaks out, drops it on the ground, and shouts, 'What the fuck is happening?'"

"What the fuck is happening? Rumi said that, right?"

"Fine. He said, 'What is happening?'" Malik agreed. "He thought he knew; then some random-ass mystic destroys it."

They passed the pipe, back and forth. Charu blew the smoke back into Malik's mouth. He started kissing her, hard.

It occurred to her that they should move to her room; screwing in her parents' room felt wrong. But she pushed the thought away, not wanting to ruin the moment. She sat on him, and simply pulled up her skirt. He slipped off her underwear and she unbuttoned his jeans.

"Button fly, really?"

"You gonna clown me every step of the way?"

After wrestling to get naked, Malik flipped Charu onto her back. He broke into her, fluid strokes that made her think he'd picked up (or someone had taught him) new tricks. He smacked her hard across her bottom. She cried and he froze for a moment, worried that he'd hurt her.

"Don't stop," whispered Charu. "Sorry."

As they came together, they cursed loudly. The garlic-jasmine scent that hung stale in her parents' room mingled with their juice. Charu felt indescribably sad. She traced nonsensical words onto Malik's brown and hairless back. Her mother had told her once, when Charu had ripped one of Hashi's old saris into a dress pattern, that she destroyed everything she touched. She had been angry and apologized after saying it, of course. But Charu knew she'd mostly meant it. She did destroy things, because the process of fixing it, making it better, was more thrilling that way.

One last look, and El brought down the gate of Anwar's Apothecary.

She looked up to Maya's apartment. The television had been turned off. It was about time for evening prayer. El debated for a moment but then figured there was nothing to lose.

El rang buzzer 2F once, then twice more.

"Hello?" said a woman's voice, crinkled and tired.

"This is your—neighbor. From downstairs."

"Oh. I will come in a minute."

Maya's mother has lupus. Getting up and down the stairs can't be easy. From the doorway window, El could see her, taking one cautious step at a time, leaning heavily against the banister with one arm, cane in another.

"Hello. Can I help you?" she asked, opening the door.

"My uncle owned the store downstairs. I was friends with Maya. My name is El. Ella."

Upon mention of Maya's name, she took El into her bosom. "Oh my goodness, come, come. I am sorry about your father. Come. Upstairs."

"Thank you, Mrs. Sharif."

"Oh, no. Call me Mariam or Mema."

Mema leaned on El as she had leaned on the bannister. They entered the apartment, met by two young boys at the dining table. El remembered Maya referring to them as the twins, but they were quite fraternal. The thin, straight-haired one scowled—he was losing the game. The chubby one flashed El a naughty smile. Open notebooks and pencils lay on the table, but they were occupied playing on bootleg Game Boys.

"I didn't mean to interrupt."

"No, please. As you see—the boys were just going to do homework," said Mema. "Ahmed, get El a glass of water."

Now the cherubic one scowled, but Mema gave him a stern look. She gestured for El to sit in the living room, which was a few steps farther into the apartment. Three bedrooms connected to the living room from different sides. To share this space among five would drive El crazy. But it was immaculate. Between Mema's health and the age of the kids, El wondered how she kept it so tidy. The sheeny rugs from Morocco and mother-of-pearl-inlaid coffee table stood in stark contrast to the faux flower arrangement and faux suede modular furniture set. They sat down.

The scowling son presented a glass of water.

"Oh, thank you." El drank the glass empty. A headache behind the eyes stirred, a newly discovered signal that an episode was near. *Shake it off.*

"Homework time," said Mema, unaware that anything was wrong with El. She pointed at the backpacks on the floor. Her two sons groaned, but started writing in their notebooks. "So, Maya. She left after the . . . accident. Maya is in Mexico, working at a hostel. She got a job through a woman, Ramona. She promised that she is coming home in June. At least that's what she last wrote. I have only spoken to her a few times on the phone. Things are so—you know, with her father, gone," said Mema. She wiped her face with her hands. When she brought them down, her face was covered in tiny insects, the same scarab pattern as on the table.

El blinked several times. Headache worsened. "I would—love to see her. It's been a very long time. I'm around this summer. Please tell her I stopped by." El stood up to leave, but swooned back down to the couch.

"Are you all right?" cried Mema. "Please, take rest in the bedroom. Boys, help her!"

The boys set down their recommenced video games, again, and rolled their eyes at this high-maintenance houseguest. El let Mema, the boys, and a million creepers lead the way to the bedroom.

Midnight came, and still Malik slept. Baba's weed had done him in. Charu left him on the bed, and walked over to her own bedroom. It was neater than it had ever been while she had lived there. Her mother had hidden all photos, candles, idols, fabrics, and sewing gear—basically anything indicating Charu's existence.

She pillaged the closet. Stacks of her unsold hijabs, a fashion project that had never taken off, were folded neatly. She pulled them out, and then added a huge pile of flannel shirts, denim jeans, some of El's unfortunate cargo pants. She found her sewing machine and supplies. She started cutting the clothes into long strips with the rotary cutter, and laid the patches on the ground. She had a lot of blacks, whites, reds, but could use more blues. Charu ran back to her parents' room, where Malik still slept. She swiped his button-fly jeans—a classic shade of denim—and went back to her project. She settled on a simple patchwork quilt, the only kind she could figure out how to sew. Black strips zigzagged into blue ones, with hand-cut arrowheads in white and red scattered throughout. She worked, uninterrupted, until sunrise.

An orange rhombus of streetlight shone on El's face through the blinds. How did anyone sleep in this room? Mema had checked in a few times, but El feigned sleep, letting the hallucinations run their course, realizing that this time they had been particularly jarring, in front of Maya's mother. Insects had taken on the form of jinn in the Black Forest, wicked beings who held Rezwan's severed head as an offering to a crowned Hawa. Disturbed stories from Anwar's letter pranced around in El's head.

El sat up and drew the blinds open, illuminating the room like a stranded car on a highway. Maya kept her room Spartan. Maybe her father hadn't let her decorate the place. Or he'd torn it up when she ran away. There was a small photo of a sacred black cube, and lots of books piled on the desk. That copy of Ernst Haeckel's *Kunstformen der Natur* lay at the bottom of a stack. El thumbed through the pages, reciting Latin names—*Thalamophora, Diatomea, Nepenthaceae*—and for the first time missed being in school. In between the symmetric biological plates were perfect renderings drawn by Maya, captioned with musings, notes. On a black-and-white sketch of *Aspidonia,* or trilobites, was a note:

ELLA.

I came to your house for many reasons. To save up money for college. To leave the suffocating hold of my mother's illness. I remember a long time ago, when my parents were happy, the three of us living out by Coney Island. After the twins were born, my mother became very sick, and we moved here. My father couldn't bear the loss of his vital, beautiful wife. Maryam Sallah, the girl who had once taken his breath away, couldn't breathe. Her rashes, especially, sickened him. I took care of her, the boys, and my father. You know, cooked, cleaned, and picked clothes for them to wear.

I listened to my father practice his Friday khutbah. We grew close. So when I got into UC Berkeley, I thought he would be over the moon for me. Turned out, the last thing he felt was happy. I got the silent treatment first. Then some flowers, a gold necklace as an apology. He said that without me, they would all be lost. He would be lost. He cried in my arms. When I refused to back down, he got angry. Not the way a parent gets angry with their child, but a man with his mistress. No daughter wants to bear the burden of her parents' depression, illness. Not even the burden of their joy. So I left. I'm never going back.

Thank you for letting me read your books and sleep in your bed. I want to see the wild and twisted and beautiful shit you see. I've taken this book for a lot longer than I should have. I guess we'll just say it's my birthday present.

I love you.
Maya

P.S. The hour has come near / the moon is split in two / we see a miracle / we turn away and say / this is passing magic/ Surah al-Qamar

Atlantic Avenue seemed smaller from this unfamiliar height. El looked out the window to see if anyone lingered on the street. Nobody. Maybe the upstairs tenant was staring out the window right now wondering the same thing. *There's no way to know.* El pulled Maya's sheet tightly around the shoulders. Being in her room, reading the letter, inhaling this freshly laundered scent was crazy—and arousing.

Both Anwar and Maya's letters were intimate discoveries. Her father's fixation on her had driven Maya as far away as possible. El couldn't really fathom what that sort of love felt like. Rezwan, Laila, Anwar, and Hashi—gone. Even Maya had chosen to go live in Mexico, alive and well and MIA.

Dr. Masud hadn't found anything wrong. But there had been too much unsteadying revelation and ruin these past few months. Just as Anwar's and Maya's letters undid confusions, they created new ones. There was no release from seeing this crazy shit. *That's what I fucking need. A release.*

A garbage truck stopped in front of the building. El watched one of the workers hoist Anwar's unwanted leftovers into the truck. Tied stacks of newspapers and half-empty bottles of cleaning supplies had been the only unsellable things in the shop. Tearing off the bedsheet, El climbed down the fire escape, just as Maya had probably done many times before. The truck that held vestiges of Anwar's Apothecary drove off, and El chased it down the street.

It felt good to run.

By ten o'clock in the morning, Charu heard a knock on the door.

"Come in."

Malik popped his head into her room. "Why you always stealing my pants?"

"Go on and take these." Charu threw a pair of orange side-button track pants; Malik jumped to catch them.

"These shits are ugly, girl. C'mon."

"You're too cute to look ugly in anything. Anyway, I don't have the right needle to run this through the machine."

"Come back and lie down with me."

"*This* is my room. We shouldn't have been fucking in there."

"Aw, Charu. I knew we should've stopped."

"Stopped what?"

"You know."

"Stop *what*?"

"This. Stop this. Y-you're ruining—"

"I'm sorry you feel that way. This is what I'm doing. Want your pants? They're right here." Charu pointed to a long strip, cut from his jeans. She returned to the machine and pressed her foot on the pedal, to avoid hearing what he was saying. Malik lifted her foot off the pedal, and brought her hands to his chest. She felt his heart pounding, strong and healthy.

He knelt beside her. "I'm here with you. I'm not going anywhere."

"You're not?"

"No, I'm not. Not right now."

"I—I just need to get rid of this stuff. I can't look at it anymore."

"I understand. Come on, let's enjoy Sunday morning." He pressed his fingertips on the nape of her neck, raking down to her tailbone.

"Fuck," moaned Charu.

"You say it like it's sacred."

A couple of hours later, Charu and Malik ordered two coffees, scrambled eggs and bacon on rye at Mike's Diner, the neighborhood greasy spoon. Sundays were packed with churchgoers, regulars, art students, and unemployed graduates.

"What are you going to do with the quilt?" asked Malik.

"Send it to my grandfather."

They walked hand in hand to the stoop of 111 Cambridge Place. They kissed, in open air, something Charu thought she would never do.

"I'll call you when I'm back from tour at the end of the summer."

"Sounds good," whispered Charu.

Malik enveloped her in a hug. They kissed for a while, until he whispered, "Soon."

He skated off on his long board. She listened for the scraping asphalt until he had disappeared down Greene Avenue. Her first lover. Not her best, nor her last. It didn't matter. He was the only man who would know who her parents had been.

Charu found El sitting on a lawn chair, rolling strange soil balls in front of the resurrected garden. She sat down next to El.

"Whatcha doing?"

"Making bombs."

"They look terrifying," said Charu, rolling her eyes. "Where were you? I didn't hear you come back last night."

"I was at Maya's house."

"What? After we packed up? Did you *see* her?"

"No, apparently she's in Mexico."

"This whole time?"

"Yeah. Ramona Espinal helped her out. She'll be back in June. Maybe."

"Wait—this is crazy."

"I know. I hallucinated at her fucking house."

"You're still upset she left," said Charu. "I would freak out, too."

"She didn't say anything to us. After everything we did for her."

"Exactly. We gave her what she needed: a fucking escape. That's why I let her stay in the first place. So she could figure her shit out. If she told us, wouldn't you have tried to convince her to come back? I know I would have, if I was in love with her." Charu waited for a response that she knew El would not give. "It is what it is. You think she's an enigma? Look in the mirror, E." Charu left El in the garden, to keep on packing the weird little bombs.

That evening, El asked Charu to read Anwar's story of the Black Forest, before it went in the mail to Rana. She took one look at the long letter and begged El to summarize.

"So you have a real brother, not just a fake sister!" Charu cried.

"No," El protested. "I love the dude, but he definitely feels like a fake brother."

"I wonder if Baba would ever have told us if he'd lived. Did Ma know?"

"I don't think anyone knew. Definitely not Hashi. She was just a teenager back then, in love with Anwar. Maybe Rana has always known, though. I remember when I went to visit my parents' graves he said that Rezwan's first love had died. I'm not sure how he would know that. But maybe he always suspected it."

"I can't believe they're missing out on everything. I mean, Malik and I finally just—connected. I spent the last few years hiding; now I'm wishing they could see everything, you know?"

"Yeah."

"You don't have to hide, either," Charu took a toke of a one-hitter shaped like a tube of lipstick. "Have some."

El laughed. "How do I look?"

"Beautiful."

"I look stupid."

Charu fumbled while threading the bobbin, and El marveled at how handy she was, in a completely complicated and different way. Charu held up the finished section of her quilt. "How do you think it looks?"

"Great, as far as I can tell. Who is it for?"

"Azim Nana. He'll need it because he's old and cold all the time.

"Not Stalin?"

"Oh, that. You know, I was all sorts of confused. On some horny undergrad-type shit. I mean, sure, he's our cool long-lost uncle or whatever, but I just felt excited by a world I'd never seen. Drinking tea or riding in a boat was a fucking adventure. I needed to feel that. Another case of misdirected love." Charu ran the quilt through the machine. The steady whirring comforted them, although it reminded El of the terrible fight they'd had after Maya ran away. Charu shook her head. "How stupid is that? I needed to feel something. Fuck me. And now, I've never been *this* fucking sad, ever. I can't stop feeling, everything." She gasped for air, sobbing into a corner of the quilt. "Fuck. I'm not sure I'll ever be anything but half-happy," she whispered.

"I think I've spent my entire life a third happy."

"I love you, El." She stepped on the pedal again, letting the machine fill the quiet.

"You were right."

"About?"

"Maya. I guess I learned how to stop hiding when I was with her. Even if only for a few months. She's the first person I ever . . ."

"Loved?"

El said nothing. "I love you, too."

It didn't sound crazy. *It was just a case of misdirected love.* Leave it to Charu to pinpoint the truth, no matter how shameful it might have been. Once confessed, it was gone.

EPILOGUE

On the second Saturday morning of June, El and Charu held their first stoop sale of Anwar's Apothecary products. They'd plastered the neighborhood with signs, the sidewalks with chalk arrows: !!!TINCTURES ($2), BEAUTY ($4), AND THE BIKE AND BOOM BOX (NEGOTIABLE)!!!

They lined the stoop stairs with Anwar's goods, and a few dresses Charu had sewn in her new atelier—Hashi's. Charu joked that Baba was somewhere pissed at them for the slashed prices, but, like anyone, he appreciated a bargain. People they had seen throughout their lives—at the apothecary, the salon, neighborhood block parties—former patrons commented on their friends' untimely departure, reminding Charu that despite not having held a ceremony, this was becoming one.

Bic came by for a whole box of Sandalwood Barber Salve, which had become something of a trade secret for him.

"When we leave for school next semester, will it be a drag to keep checking up on this place?" asked Charu.

"This old house always has a way of coming back to life," said Bic. "And I've never grown tired of seeing that happen." He balanced the cardboard box on his head, and walked Anwar's last batch back to his barbershop.

By late afternoon, their stoop sale had turned into a block party. Neighbors fired up their grills, the hydrant that had once saved 111

Cambridge Place was broken open, and Maze & Frankie Beverly thumped out of a Caprice Classic. They had sold almost all their beauty products, except for the Magic Mustard Face Oil, too strange-colored and pungent for most. After making about a thousand dollars, Charu and El decided to pack up for the day. Charu went into the house to put away the money they'd earned and to change out of her clothes.

El wheeled Anwar's spare bicycle to the backyard.

"How much are you selling the bike for, Ella?"

Maya.

Her hair, uncovered, chin length, and curly. She wore a plain white tank top—a marcel—and fitted jeans. Her skin was tanned. She seemed at ease, waiting for El to answer her question.

"These days I'm called El." El continued wheeling the bike to the backyard. Maya followed.

"El," she said. "It suits you."

"Thanks."

"You've changed things up here. Everything looks like it blooms in the day."

"I'm not out here much at night."

"El. I'm so sorry about your—Anwar and Hashi. Mema told me. I wanted to write to you, but you were still in Bangladesh."

You could've written anyway, thought El, surprised at how bitter this reunion felt. "It doesn't matter. You'd already been gone for a while."

"I left so that I could come back. I had no idea that my dad would get himself locked up. As much as I know he deserves it, I didn't want that for him."

"You don't?"

"He's a loveless man. Prison won't change him. Although I hear he's popular among the inmates. For his faith, that is." Maya shook her head, as if it were better to abandon the thought. "I heard you slept over."

"I had to get my book back," said El.

"Mema liked you."

"I read your letter. And—I liked her, too."

"Somehow I knew you would. I wanted you to, anyway. Mema's

doing much better, I think. Now that I'm back, she doesn't want me to go to Cali."

"But you have to."

"I do."

"You can have it."

"What?"

"The bike."

Maya took a step closer to El. "Do you want to hold each other?" She didn't wait for a response, and took El into her arms.

Sunset turned the white walls in El's room golden, while the verdigris wall shimmered like the imminent gloaming. El fumbled to lock the door. Maya pulled El onto her, and they both fell into the bed, kissing. El felt like devouring her mouth, which tasted like salt and cinnamon gum. El swept up Maya's tank top, and unhooked her simple white bra, with ease.

"Have you been practicing?"

"I've been hallucinating, if that counts."

Maya took El's glasses off and put them aside on the table. She brought El's lips toward her nipple. "Anything. Do anything." Her husky voice sounded the same. Her breasts were sloped and heavy. El obliged and sucked Maya's nipple, feeling it harden. Teeth and tongue back and forth between her breasts made El dizzy.

Without a word, El stripped each leg of Maya's jeans and brought fingers down to Maya's pussy, swirling her wetness around. El kissed her down the trail of hair on her belly, until Maya's thighs rocked El's head in a pulsating grip. As her thighs tightened around El's ears, everything became soundless, like falling into the ocean. Maya quaked and released herself on El's fingertips.

"Can I take yours off?" asked Maya, unlocking her thighs from El's shoulders. El took Maya's hand, guiding it around to feel the binding. Maya unpeeled the gauze, one layer at a time, undoing the pants afterward. Cupping El's breasts in her hands, she rubbed her hands across the sternum, as if trying to draw out El's heart. She pressed her index and middle finger together, rubbing El slow, then fast and faster—

As he came, he understood. Everything in this past year, maybe everything his entire life, seemed to have brought him to this moment, this moment of swadhin. He hadn't been ready for her, not until now.

The scar on El's thigh will become the port of entry. Over the months, and eventually years, El will see more of Rezwan, Rana, and Anwar in himself. *Swadhin*, or salvation, comes from changing course altogether. He will speak in the tenor of a pubescent boy, until a resonant bass settles. He will sprout a mustache and beard that would have made Anwar proud. Each time, there will be a rubbing alcohol stream, a prick of the syringe, fluid in his vein. He will become a cartographer, inking a border town beside a river on a map. Each time, closer to completing his atlas.

They held each other until the amber light faded into silver. Maya's head rested on El's chest. "Did you ever feel scared?"

"Of what?"

"This?"

"Only because I thought I should feel scared of it. But I don't anymore."

"When I took the datura—I suggest sticking to mushrooms, by the way—I knew I wanted to escape. But I didn't want to die. I just didn't want to feel contained by anyone ever again. The thought of having to carry someone's happiness or bear someone else's pain scared me, like I did with my father and Mema. With you, I thought I'd have to do both."

"You were wrong about that."

"I know."

No stranger to the sounds of pleasure, Charu noticed El's door was locked. Was she by herself? Why was the bike parked right in front of her door?

Charu busied herself with making a tray of watermelon, potato chips, root beers, and weed. She'd just sit in the garden, and if El wanted to join her after she finished, she could.

It was cool for a June night—it looked as if it might rain—so Charu started a small fire in the pit.

"We've traded hair," said a voice.

"Fuck!" Charu jolted up. "*You're* the one I heard moaning!"

"Oh, god," muttered El.

Maya tussled Charu's pixie. "This is you. You look perfect."

"So do you! When did you stop covering?"

"I still wear it. Even wore it in Mexico sometimes. Depends on what I'm feeling, I guess."

"You look amazing. How was Mexico—was it amazing?" Charu looked at El. "Sorry, I say 'amazing' when I'm at a loss for words, except this time I really mean it. Tell me about Mexico!"

"We haven't talked about that yet," said El, throwing a few twigs into the fire.

Charu studied her sister's face staring at Maya. Maybe everyone looked sensual and alive beside a fire pit, but El radiated. Charu heard the slight tenor of pain in her voice. Though El had not planted any moon blossoms, the regular summer flowers seemed aglow in the fire.

Maya stared into the fire pit while she spoke. "The trip, right. Incredible. Amazing, as you'd say, Charu. And I thought I'd be lucky enough if I could do a semester at Brooklyn College. I guess getting away never seemed like an option. My family never traveled, not even back to their own countries. It was just too hard with Mema's health. While I was recovering, Ramona Espinal had been the night nurse. We started bonding when I came to—you know, just shooting the shit. She'd seen us from time to time from her window, gardening, kicking it. When my folks arrived, Sallah lost his shit on the staff, pissed that they hadn't contacted them immediately. I wasn't underage, so they didn't have to tell him anything. The way he carried on made everyone uncomfortable. They felt sorry as hell for me. Here I was, coming down from delirium, and yes, you were right, El—I couldn't take a piss for the life of me—and I'm being yelled at; the nurses are being yelled at. He just made a total scene. That's my father.

"At some point, Ramona came in to check my vitals, and pump me with more of the activated carbon. She asked my father to leave so that I could undress, while Mema stayed in the room. Ramona tells us she's going to Mexico; her cousin had opened up a hostel in Mexico City and needed some help getting it off the ground. And then, Mema says, 'Maya can help you in the hostel. She's very organized.' She told Ramona that being mistaken for Dominican my whole life had made for good Spanish lessons. Mema had brought five hundred bucks in cash. First she tried to pass it off to Ramona, but Ramona nipped that in the bud, saying taking Mema's money would make her feel like a coyote or some shit. So, Mema gave it to me for my plane ticket. I saved a few thousand from working all summer. I had the blessing of the one person who might die if I left her."

"So have you traveled a lot?" asked Charu. "Or you're always at the hostel?"

"Most of the time, I'm just helping folks get their linens and Internet password," said Maya, laughing. "But I've made time to see things. All the D.F. touristic hotspots were incredible—I lost myself at Frida Kahlo's Blue House, the Xochimilco boat rides, the *museos*, Teotihuacán. As I started to get more situated, meet folks, travelers and *chilangos* alike, I met other queers in Zona Rosa. Nothing romantic. But to know that there's this parallel universe, people scattered and searching, like our city; it was a relief. I didn't have to have this grand experience. I didn't have to be riveted. This is happening, while that is happening. Mexico City has the elite, the impoverished, the fashion boys, the intellectuals, the markets, the subways, the parties, the food, the expats, the dirty, the mountains, the drugs, the youth, the dust and the ancient and divine. All the time."

As the fire dwindled, they threw water onto the embers. Smoke shrouded them, the same color as the clouds above. They heard sounds of celebration on the block, the party they had started and abandoned. A pair of dogs barked at one another.

"Will you stay in Brooklyn?" asked Charu.

"I'm leaving for Berkeley at the end of the summer."

"It's a good night for a ride," said Charu.

"Where do you want to go?" asked Maya.

"I don't know."

Maya looked at El, waiting for the next move. El nodded. Maya hopped onto her new ride, and lapped around the garden. Charu followed her for a few loops, until they both knocked a trellis on El's vegetable beds.

"Oh shit," Maya and Charu said at the same time, shooting guilty expressions at El.

El walked over to Anwar's seed bank. He placed the dirt spheres he'd made of Hashi's beloved wildflower seeds, compost, dirt, and clay in the girls' bicycle baskets. "Throw these wherever you want." He unlocked his bike, and hopped on. "Now, let's go where we first met."

"Doesn't that mean something different for all of us?" Charu rang her bicycle bell, and led the way out of 111 Cambridge Place. They rode in a triangle, as a migrating flock obeying unspoken directions. Past the masjid's worshippers and the humdrum of the subway. Past the crowded park and a thunderous applause in the distance. They scattered seeds across familiar terrain, throwing dormant blossoms into decayed buildings, neglected lots, barren yards, and cracks in the sidewalk. Dispersed in front of barbershops and beauty salons, churches and schools and housing projects. They spanned different neighborhoods, riding silently in the dark, in an agora of sound. As night fell, they crossed a narrow bridge to the ocean. One by one, they flung the last of their bombs into the water. Millions of years from now, all that was written in them would reemerge, forever altered.

Everything behind them, and everything ahead, vanished.

ACKNOWLEDGMENTS

In the last decade of working on this novel, I am forever grateful to so many wondrous people in my life:

My parents, Neelu and Ashraf, encouraged me to follow the creative path, no matter how much meandering and uncertainty it has required. My sister, Promiti, is the smartest, warmest, and most kindred spirit I have in this world. Ours is a family where art, love, and laughter happen in step with mistakes and life's travails, but still we keep on.

Rebecca Friedman, my agent, for her vivacity, passion, and friendship. Sending you the basket of herbs on your birthday, the same day we sent *Bright Lines* on its way, was auspicious, to say the least. To my editor, Allison Lorentzen, for her vision and trust in this book, even when we didn't know what this would be. Thanks to the entire team at Penguin, for all of their efforts in making this whole.

To my family in Bangladesh and beyond, for their love, generosity, support, and knowledge: Subarno, Boshudha, Shilu Ma, Shaheen, Nanu, Putu Bhaiyya, Ferdous Mama.

While working as an organizer and teaching artist, I met bright and talented young women writers, actors, and playwrights in high schools around New York City. Adilka, Santy, Sarah, Oona, for the magic that is Make the Road, my first gig where I learned that all teaching is learning. To all of my teachers: Kiese Laymon, for those early lessons in how we must have an abiding love for the truth that fiction unwittingly leads us toward. At Brooklyn College, I learned from glorious writers, masters of craft whose lessons have stayed with me: Francisco Goldman, Fiona Maazel, Ernesto Mestre-Reed, Josh Henkin.

To all the random hustles and heartbreaks I've worked through, the Brooklyn cafés I worked out of, the music of Mulatu Astatke, Johnny Osborne, OutKast, Erykah Badu, and Juana Molina for being easy to listen to on repeat. So much love to the writers and editors at the Asian American Writers' Workshop, VONA Workshop, *Hyphen* magazine, *The Feminist Wire*. Being a part of these communities has nurtured an electric, vital connectivity.

I'm grateful for friends and teachers whose artistry, love, and openness is my muse. Ngozi, for our endlessly blossoming soul-sisterhood. Alex, Shilu, Sunita, for being first readers and lifelong friends. Alicia, Fran, Carina, Amita, Max: Our early creative collaborations at Vassar were numinous experiences, full of possibility, and here we are, years later, still experimenting. Victor, all this, from a random hello. Isabel Saez, for your guidance in unfurling the past to make way for the future.

Mojo Talantikite, my love, for his profound support during this homestretch, as a keen reader and loving partner. I stay tripping over you.

To my inspiring crew of artists, activists, and creative entrepreneurs, for being bright and beautiful spirits who reiterate that we must make art to live.